D0906700

FICTION

By the same author

The Dixie Association

THE HANGMAN'S CHILDREN

DONALD HAYS

A MORGAN ENTREKIN BOOK
THE ATLANTIC MONTHLY PRESS
NEW YORK

Published simultaneously in Canada
Printed in the United States of America

Library of Congress Cataloging-in-Publication Data

Hays, Donald.
The hangman's children / by Donald Hays.
ISBN 0-87113-309-1
I. Title.
PS3558.A865H3 1989 89-30184 813'.54—dc19

Design by Laura Hough

The Atlantic Monthly Press
19 Union Square West
New York, NY 10003

FIRST PRINTING

For Eddie Lynch,
Who survived these times,
And in memory of Mark Whittington,
Who did not.

In here, it's us madmen against you idiots.

George Konrád, *The Loser*

PART I

1 MALEDON

Lord, I remember. For me it started on the eighth of April, 1968, at about three thirty in the afternoon. God was in the process of delivering his punch line to America. Martin Luther King had been dead four days. The big-city ghettos were flaming up like kerosened kindling. Slumlords and insurance agents argued over the fine print in the nigger clause. In Atlanta, Ralph Abernathy, Hosea Williams, and Jesse Jackson inspected the mules that, come tomorrow, would be drawing the good doctor's coffin—they didn't want them looking too sleek. Neil Armstrong was in Houston sipping Tang. William Westmoreland, still squinting at the light at the end of the tunnel, would be replaced in two days by Creighton Abrams, who loved the same damned light. Spiro Agnew sat in a padded chair in a paneled office in Annapolis, accepting bribes. Richard Nixon, his upper lip sweating, his paranoid eyes jerking from aide to aide, was being taught, by the kind of men who'd beaten him twice, how to become a television commercial. The cool career minor-leaguer Eugene McCarthy was suddenly in the pennant race, upsetting everyone but the fans. Lyndon Johnson, barricaded deep in the White House bunker, rubbed his scar, kicked his hounds, plopped his feet on Hubert Humphrey's lap, and devised a grudging retreat. Robert Kennedy and the once-blooded remnants of the knights of the Round Table had drunk a toast and drawn their swords. In a darkened LA back-street room, Sirhan Sirhan lifted his pistol from its resting place atop the Koran.

And me? Well, ol' Samuel Langhorne Maledon, aka Job Samples, aka Uncle Hugh Harp, aka Tasker H. Bliss, aka Isaac C. Parker, aka George Maledon, was backing the Hangman's van into a parking lot seven stories below the moon ward, where my once and future son, on the morning of the day of the Memphis marksman, had been committed by his mother and stepfather for having, two days before that, at a hearing before the Blue Mountain, Arkansas, branch of the Selective

Service System, set fire to his 1-A draft card with a twenty-six-year-old U.S. Navy Zippo lighter.

"Good time," I said to the long-legged apprentice revolutionary who'd had an easy job talking me into this. Her name was Gloria Alice Wilder O'Leary, but she called herself Gloria Alice Dawn, which was fine by me. "They'll be changing shifts."

I got out of the van and looked over once more the fatigue-green paint job, the door's black legend: U.S. ARMY—OFFICIAL VEHICLE. It looked properly grim, so I put on my hat, tilted it a notch to starboard, shifted my briefcase to my left hand, clicked my shining heels, and saluted. "How do I look, Sarge?"

"Like a proper soldier," Gloria Alice Dawn answered. "The kind who never soils his uniform." She slid her consummate haunches across the seat, framed her face in the open window. "A kiss for luck."

She had twenty years less of life than me and believed she and my boy, Jesse, could ride point for the New American Revolution, the Revolution, she called it, of Ecstasy. I took the kiss, regretting the years and her fanaticism.

The hospital hemmed in a mortuary gloom. A pant-suited receptionist watched the riots on a portable RCA. White nurses and doctors, crepe-soled, slipped down hallways toward exits and automobiles, highways and home. Black aides and orderlies clustered in corners. Grieving? Plotting? Was Little Rock worth burning?

I had the up elevator to myself, the hired help all either gone or going down, their relief in place. It was a straight shot to the seventh floor, where I got out, read a sign, and followed green arrows taped to the tile. At arrows' end a door stood open. I walked right in.

"Where you think you headed, Napoleon?"

Turning around, I saw a huge black woman—Mandingo and Masai I'd say if I had her in the show—thoroughly occupying a pea-green vinyl chair.

"Would the nurses' station be this way?" I motioned up the hall behind me with my left thumb, warped a good decade ago back of the Shoot the Moon Lounge in Harmony Grove by a Hot Springs jujitsu instructor, cockeyed, cuckolded, whose wife, at the very moment he snapped my thumb for her honor, was probably rutting in a rented room with her other man, the speaker of the Arkansas House, a misogynist possessed of prominent wattles and oil money.

"The recruiting office is out to the Park Plaza," the black woman told me. "I don't expect you better be doing none of your business here."

Walking toward her, I took out and opened my wallet. I showed her an ID card my old West Memphis friend and cousin Alvy Wolfe had made me.

Her name tag, pinned to polyester above a breast that could've nursed a nation, said VIOLA PUNT—AIDE.

"Colonel Albert Pike Sturdivant III," Viola Punt said, handing back the card. "Might do you fine in the War Room; don't carry no water here."

"I need to see the chief resident."

"Seem like that's the way with most everybody."

"So it does." Recalling myself to my role, I stiffened, glared at her like Patton on a bed wetter, turned, and clipped smartly up the forbidden hall, passing on my way two shuffling, parched-mouthed patients who were discussing *Cat's Cradle.*

"It changed my life," said the first. "I never could hold down a job after I read it."

"Literature," the other one sneered.

There weren't any other patients in sight. I figured they were either turning out ceramic ashtrays in occupational therapy or bullying the weakling in group therapy. Besides, due to the King killing and the riots, most of them were probably forced to take double doses of Thorazine or Stelazine, the religion here being based on the therapeutic equilibrium.

Thick, wire-reinforced glass enclosed the top two thirds of the nurses' station. A young woman in blue jeans and a Dave Clark Five T-shirt who looked like she might've just given herself over to the seductions of anorexia nervosa sat behind the counter, some poor bastard's chart open in front of her.

Through the half-moon hole in the glass just above the counter, I heard her talking into the intercom. "Yes, Mrs. Punt?"

"Soldier broke in."

The skinny woman looked up at me. "I see him," she said.

She got up, ventured the two or three steps to the half-moon opening, and bent over so that her mouth was nearly level with it. "Can I help you?"

I bent over too, reminding myself as I did that this place had been built for lunatics. "I've been ordered to perform a preliminary examination on Jesse Lee Cantwell. I believe he's a patient here?" I slid the ID card through the slot. She read it, pushed it back.

"Do you have hospital authorization for this?"

"We contacted a Mr. Dalton Hofenstahl, who, I believe, is your hospital administrator. He gave his authorization. I had assumed he would notify you." I lifted my briefcase to glass level. "I believe I have all the necessary forms here."

Still stooped, we spent silent seconds studying one another through the glass.

Then I said, "As I'm sure you're aware, young Mr. Cantwell is in serious legal difficulty. There may, indeed, be reason to suspect him of using this ward as a sanctuary from conscription. If such is the case and you resist the legal process, we will use the courts to damage your reputation. If I were you"—I made a show of squinting to read the name tag above an absence of breast—"Jean Partain, R.N., I'd let one of my superiors handle this."

I straightened up. She stayed stooped a couple of beats longer, then raised herself, turned away, turned back, bent again, and said into the slot, "They're still in staff meeting. Would you wait in the visitors' lounge?"

I shot my sleeve and checked my watch. "I'm pressed for time. I'll wait here."

I watched her walk to the intercom box, heard her ask Dr. Bowders to report to the nurses' station.

Ten minutes later, after some introductions and hand-shaking, I opened my briefcase, intending to show a court order to Bowders, a short, dapper, mustachioed analyst who was trying to impress me with his recent conversion to behaviorism. Like most late converts, he was filled with the faith. "I think I've made something of a breakthrough," he said. "Last year I read a paper to the American Psychiatric Association which demonstrates that one can, if one scrupulously defines one's terms, believe in both Skinner and freedom."

I stood there holding the court order, which required that one Albert Pike Sturdivant III, Colonel, U.S. Army, be allowed to examine one Jesse Lee Cantwell. Alvy Wolfe had printed it up all proper looking and I'd forged the flamboyant, illegible signature of Judge Rufus T. Maze.

"It's easier, of course," I told Bowders, "to believe in neither."

"Nihilism," Bowders said, as if that were that. "We need a middle ground. A synthesis of Laing and Skinner."

"Chaos with positive reinforcement," I said, handing the order to Bowders.

He took his reading glasses out of his shirt pocket, put them on, and carefully read the order, twice raising his gaze to look at me. Then he sat the document on the counter, slowly folded his glasses, returned them to his pocket, looked up at me, jutted a frail chin, and said, very matter-of-fact, "Scum."

It caught me by surprise, but I managed to raise my eyebrows and show him a supercilious smile.

"You're no psychiatrist," he said.

"My credentials are as valid as yours."

"You're a government hack."

"You're free to state your opinion of my character, Dr. Bowders. You're even free, in this blessed nation, to castigate your government. It's entirely irrelevant to me. But you are not free to obstruct the order of a federal court. The Constitution has its limits. Your little ward is not sacrosanct."

"We'll see." He turned to the starving nurse. "Jean, would you bring Jesse Cantwell in here?" She left. Bowders told me, "If he refuses to see you, I'm throwing you out."

"We'll see," I said, thinking how pleasant it'd be to just let go and pull this job off with brute force, me against the moon-ward master.

I went to the rack that held the patients' charts, reached to lift Jesse's from among them.

"No."

"It would merely save time."

"No."

"Fine. I'm sure it's immaterial."

A moment later the anorectic nurse led Jesse into the station. He looked vacant and a little sickly. I figured that was less the result of four days' psychiatric treatment than of a year's meditation and vegetarianism.

"Jesse," Bowders said. "This is a Colonel Sturdivant. He has a court order demanding that he be allowed to examine you so he can make a report to your local draft board. This is irregular and, I suspect, unconstitutional. I feel certain I can persuade the hospital to appeal the order. But it's your life involved here, and I cannot, in good conscience, make the decision alone. If you don't want him to examine you, I'll show him the door."

I give the kid credit. Looking at me, he showed no sign of seeing anything but another government functionary. "I don't mind talking to him," he said. "I just won't wear his uniform. The insanity is theirs."

His little stand on the sanctity of psychiatric institutions spoiled by his patient, Bowders, like any good behaviorist, damned the patient. "He's not capable of making this decision," he said, his voice a combination of piety and pique.

"If that's true," I said, "he'll have no further problems with us."

"There's nothing a man like this can do to harm me," Jesse told Bowders.

I allowed myself a half-grin. If Jesse was capable of this kind of deceit, there was hope for him yet.

"I hope you're right, Jesse," Bowders said. "I sincerely hope you're right." Then, turning abruptly to me—"Your war stinks."

I nodded. "As do they all. However necessary."

He motioned toward a door at the rear of the station. "You can use the examining room."

I walked to the door, opened it, looked into the room, shut the door, turned back to Bowders. "I don't intend to administer electroshock treatment. A simple office will do."

A moment of tense waiting. I stood there wondering why anybody would turn anybody they cared about over to these bastards, these solemn inventors of electroshock, insulin shock, lobotomy.

Bowders said, "I refuse to endanger my relationship with a patient by consenting to have this done in my office."

"The room doesn't matter," Jesse said. "This is a mausoleum."

Another shorter silence. I grinned again, careful to color the grin with the right hue of psychiatric arrogance. Bowders sighed, shrugged, showed us his palms. "Let them use the roof," he told the anemic nurse. "When this is over, bring Jesse to my office." He walked to the door, grasped the knob, then looked back at me. "Notice the view while you're up there, Colonel. Try to imagine what napalm would do to it."

I couldn't resist. I said, "It would eradicate Dutch elm disease."

Bowders glared and was gone.

"What's on the roof?" I asked the bulimic nurse.

"It's real nice. We got patio furniture and shuffleboard and a Ping-Pong table. The Jaycees paid for it. The patients love it."

"Would be a long fall," I said, smiling.

"Oh, no. It's got a chain link fence around it. Even over the top."

"I'm sure."

"If the wind's bad, you can sit in the gazebo."

"The gazebo? Sounds ideal."

"It's down that way," she said, returning to her desk.

When she turned away, I lifted the chart from its slot. The less they got on you, the better off you are.

"I'll buzz you out," she said.

Jesse and I left the station, followed the hall leading to the northeast end of the ward, knocked on the heavy, windowless door, heard the buzz, opened the door, and passed into the stairwell.

The way to the roof was clear, but there was another thick, locked door barring the way down.

That seemed to please Jesse. "Cleverness," he said, "only goes so far."

" 'O ye of little faith.' " I took a lock pick out of my uniform's pant pocket. It looked like a button hook made of stiff wire. I slipped it into the keyhole and began turning tumblers. This was a good lock; I had to turn three tumblers. It might have taken me as much as a minute. But it came open—they'll all come open.

When all three tumblers had fallen, I turned the knob with my left hand, shoved the door toward the way out.

"Freedom, Jess," I said, sweeping a grand arm toward the descending stairs. "From here on, Son, it's all fresh air and open road."

2 JESSE

Somewhere the sun beams gently on charred cities. The world has tilted. Sunday will be Easter.

And here?

Here where the fire has not yet been I am riding again with my father, sharing with him what he thinks of as freedom.

My father has given his life to this kind of freedom, rolling from town to town, fair to fair, assembly to assembly, day to day, dollar to dollar, mark to mark, identity to identity. His faith is in his wits, in trapdoors, back alleys, forged papers. He believes his enemies are always in power and that if he weakens they will have him in a factory, an army, a jail. So now he drives the Hangman's van, camouflaged in enemy green, north and east up 67, past the Jacksonville Air Force Base, where my bright-faced peers vie to become death's ushers, and through Cabot and Beebe and Searcy, and then north for twenty miles on a county dirt road, and finally down a lane that leads across a pasture and a wet-weather branch to a rock house on the wooded crest of a bluff above the Little Red River.

"A couple of days," I say, as we are crossing that pasture, after I have said nothing for miles. "Then I'm going home."

"Back to the moon ward?" he asks. And Gloria laughs. Gloria, who admires his relentless energy, his infinite practicality.

"Home," I say again. Three months ago, six hours short of a perfectly irrelevant degree in philosophy, I dropped out of the University of Arkansas. Since then home has been a tepee on forty acres of Blue Mountain forest I rescued from my stepfather.

"Sainthood's the idiot's dodge," he says. "All you got to do is give up."

"I did not ask to be rescued," I say.

"He's right, Jesse," Gloria tells me, her fingers brushing softly on the back of my hand. "Letting them take you to court and then pleading *nolo contendere* would be no more than a symbolic gesture. It's too late for that. There are half a million men in Vietnam."

"I've done nothing wrong," I remind them. "I'll make my stand on my own ground."

"Stupidity's wrong," my father says. "Ain't no point in keeping on drawing from a rigged deck."

Gloria likes the absurd metaphor. "We need a new deck," she says brightly.

"No," I say, turning my face to her. "We need to stop thinking life's like a game of cards."

The van bounces us over flint rock and stump root to the door of the stone building. A man is rocking on the porch, waiting for the sun to sink into the river.

"I'm glad you took me from the ward," I tell my father as he kills the engine. "But from now on I have to do it my way."

"Might be hard getting you out of Leavenworth while you still got a one-way asshole."

"My asshole is the least of my worries."

"There's your mistake."

The man leaves his porch and comes across the yard to offer welcome. My father makes the introductions. The man is Conrad Villines, professor of history and assistant to a dean at Harrold Smith College in Searcy. It is a small, grim Church of Christ institution, an indoctrination center for the John Birch Society.

"Fine looking pair," Dr. Villines says of Gloria Alice and me. "And, by God, Sam, you do look good in uniform. Should've gone to West Point."

"Scored too high on the entrance test." He slaps Villines's back. "How you been, Doc?"

"Looks like they're going to make me a dean," he says. "No work at all, big jump in pay."

"At Harrold Smith?" I ask, curious about his motivation.

"Good cover," my father explains, as if to a fool.

We take a few steps toward the plank porch. I believe in asking directly the questions that come. "How do you reconcile the one life with the other?"

My father laughs.

"I don't," Villines tells me. "I just find it amusing to work among people who think that any time they look up at the sky there's an even chance they'll see either the Russians or the Messiah."

This scorn for the common run of humankind: He is my father's friend.

We follow him up three stone steps and are on the porch.

"A day or two and we'll be moving," my father says.

"Keep the janitor's job till you can testify at the Good Friday Chapel, and I can probably get you some road money," Villines says. "Safe here as anywhere, probably."

"Maybe," my father says. "Need another paint job, too. Can't figure far ahead, though. Boy of mine's set on turning himself in."

The inside of the house is one large room with plank floors, a sleeping loft, no electricity, no running water. Three thick white candles sit on the long pine table at the room's center, and a kerosene lamp rests on protruding rocks in each of the two longer walls. Army cots line those same two walls. At the end of the room, below the loft, is a wood-burning cookstove, and at the other end is a stone fireplace, which (my father tells us) had been, five years earlier, when Villines bought the place, all that remained of the original settlers' cabin.

So he is not of a piece, this man Villines, this prospective dean of arts and sciences at Harrold Smith College. His soul is not of a piece.

He walks to the northwest corner of the room and removes a gallon jar of sweet milk from an icebox, white, chest-high, which stands beside a faucetless stainless steel sink and below raw-wood shelves of plates, jars, bowls. He carries the milk and three pint mason jars to the table. Pouring the milk into the jars, he says, "That icebox is our primary concession to a bad century. Two or three times a week I buy a block of ice at Frank's Bait Shop."

"We have taken to the catacombs," my father, half grinning in the quarter-light, tells me.

I decide I like Villines. I will drink his milk. I look toward the rectangle of window opposite the door and make a small joke for my father: "But there is a light at the end of the tunnel."

"Almost always is." He nods. "If you dig your tunnels in the right place."

"The real thing," Villines says, pushing a pint of milk to Gloria. "Unspoiled by Pasteur or homogeneity. The genuine article, pure and ungraded, pulled straight from Ol' Shirley into a wooden bucket setting on dried manure. Ideal for refugees."

I smile. "It's all we have any right to want."

My father drinks. "Damn," he says. "The pastoral life."

3 GLORIA

It was the fig leaf that fucked us up. Costumes and disguises. A flash of thigh, a glimpse of cleavage. Seduction and sin, adultery and betrayal. Clothing is the first hypocrisy.

When we heard the semi turn into the lane, I was in the middle of the yard, lying on my back, nude on a patchwork quilt. I had my head propped against a pillow, and I was reading *The Wretched of the Earth*.

After a day at Harrold Smith College, Maledon and Villines were on the porch, Maledon drinking a Lone Star, Villines having his pint of milk.

I could feel their eyes. There was no menace, no threat, just confusion. And probably disapproval.

Maybe I misinterpreted their attitudes. Maledon confused? I'd heard Jesse say that his father was often wrong, but never confused. But I sensed that he was a little confused there on the porch.

Earlier—right after getting out of Villines's car—he had tried to joke with me. He told me I was risking whatever was left of my innocence by exposing myself to two desperate mid-life males. I told him I wasn't in the habit of tempting men and leaving them unsatisfied. "Just ask Jesse."

He showed me that back-roads grin of his. "Not a saint yet, is he?"

I gave my head a coquettish toss, knowing my red hair would catch the sun. "Rumor says even Martin Luther King played around some."

"Maybe it was a cuckold that nailed him."

"Where's Jesse now?" he had asked.

"Went for a walk."

"Doing penance in the wilderness?"

"Recuperating," I said. And I gave him a vixen's smile. "Gathering his strength for the night."

He'd looked me up and down then with an assayer's eye. "Well, if this don't keep him on the road with us, ain't nothing will."

So there was no blushing or shrinking from either of us then. That came later, when he was on the porch with Villines and the beer. And I merely sensed confusion. I may have been wrong. Maledon was not ordinary.

Anyway, they were silent, there on the porch. And it amused me to think that Maledon, the raw man, the pilgrim without destination, was mulling over, like some suburban shoe salesman, the possible complications of sharing a woman with his son and maybe his host. Then the semi stopped, backed, stopped, backed, and finally twisted its way into the lane and came groaning across the pasture toward us. Another complication.

"It's Jimmy," I said, standing on the quilt. "He's found us."

"Won't be near as hard for the next fellow," Maledon remarked.

I wrapped myself in the quilt and left Fanon in the grass—he could use the sun. The truck pulled into the yard and stopped alongside the porch steps. Jimmy, wispily bearded, scraggly haired, and dressed in patched jeans, tire-tread sandals, and a Drop Acid Not Bombs T-shirt, climbed out of the passenger's side, then lifted my five-year-old daughter, Aura, to the ground.

She ran to me, and I knelt and enclosed her in the quilt. Jimmy took his army-surplus duffel bag out of the cab, set it beside the steps, looked at Villines, and asked, "You Job Samples?"

Villines tilted his head toward Maledon.

"Sometimes," Maledon said.

"Jimmy Song," Jimmy told him, "delivered to your doorstep by Ouachita Best Freight." He extended his right hand, cocked up.

After hesitating an instant, Maledon shook it, traditionally. "Don't get many semis here," he said. "Bad sign."

"Aw, you can trust Troy," Jimmy said, jerking his thumb toward the driver. "Me and him seen all of North America in Gloria's old man's trucks."

Maledon looked at the driver, then at Jimmy again. "Can't come in something that big and loud without leaving a trail."

"You're safe," Jimmy said in that tone he used to talk you down from a paranoid high. "I had directions, and we still went up three lanes before we found the right one."

"Don't reckon you called any attention to yourself, then, did you?"

The driver leaned toward the passenger window and asked, "Everything all right, Mrs. O'Leary?"

"Just fine, Troy. Thank you."

"Your daddy told me to ask. Wanted me to get it straight from you." He leaned back behind the wheel, started the truck, circled the yard, and left.

Jimmy was hungry, so we went inside and I served the potato soup and cornbread I'd made that afternoon. As the men ate, I dressed—in jeans, boots, a Che Lives T-shirt.

Villines asked about my father. I told him that his name was Jonathan Wilder, that he owned Ouachita Best Freight, and that whenever Jimmy wanted or needed to go somewhere he could ride with Troy, who made regular trips to the Mexican border towns.

"Delivering defective merchandise to the Mexican bourgeoisie," Jimmy said. "Bringing home fruit picked by starving peasants."

"Jimmy grew up on a farm," I said. "Daddy thinks he's better than most I've been with."

"I am," Jimmy said, wiping some soup off of his beard.

"Little girl yours?" Maledon asked Jimmy. Aura was in the fireplace smearing herself with ashes.

"I had her by my husband," I said. "John O'Leary. He's in India. In the Peace Corps. He's a lot like Jesse."

Maledon finished his soup and went to the icebox for another beer.

"I loved John," I went on. For some reason I wanted Maledon's approval. "But he believed in reform, and I think reform only delays the necessary revolution."

"Might even make it unnecessary," Villines said. He stood. "I have to milk."

We followed him to the shed and then went on to the bluff above the river. We sat there with our faces to the dying sun. I told Aura to walk back up the path and pick me a bouquet of wildflowers. "But stay where I can see you."

"She needs this," I told Maledon when she was gone. "She was already being spoiled by Daddy's money. And the last time I was home, Mother had her sing "My Country 'Tis of Thee" just to spite me."

"Well," Maledon said, "in no time you can have her reciting *Howl.*"

I laughed. "Jesse warned me about you."

"It's just that I don't believe in believing near as strong as y'all do." He seemed relaxed again.

"Why not?" I asked him. "You have to believe in something."

"I believe in doubt," he said. "I believe in keeping clear of believers."

"You're selfish," I said, trying to make it sound friendly.

"By and large," he agreed. "But here I am, trying to save my son from principle."

Aura returned, carrying a bouquet of bluebells, wild iris, and hogweed. I thanked her and sent her after more.

Jimmy rolled a joint and started telling Maledon about the Eureka Springs commune we'd belonged to until the pigs busted us for eating peyote buttons as part of a ritual.

"It was like a real church, man," Jimmy said. "Without the hype and hypocrisy. We even had a stained-glass window and advertised in the religious section of the *Arkansas Gazette*. They did a feature on us once."

"That happened right before you got busted, be my guess," Maledon said. He glanced to his right, and Jesse stepped out of the woods, walked over to Aura, and leaned down to show her the arrowheads he had found.

"I'm like you," Jimmy told Maledon. "I thought it was stupid to call attention to ourselves." He took a hit off the joint.

"A cop's main job is to keep misfits from warping the works," Maledon said. "A man's different and knows it; he's a fool to wear a bull's-eye on his chest."

"We have to change the works," I said. It's the simple truth.

Maledon shrugged. "There'll still be misfits. I'll settle for a six-pack and a head start."

Aura had come to me and was holding out the arrowheads Jesse had given her. "Were there real Indians here?" she wanted to know.

Eighty years ago," I told her. "Then the government killed them all."

"President Johnson?" she asked.

"No, but someone like him."

"Why?"

"Because the men in the government weren't as nice as you are," I told her. "Why don't you go find some more flowers."

"I'm tired of flowers. Can I go play in the water?"

"It's too cold." Jimmy passed me the joint. I took a hit and offered it to Maledon. He shook his head, stood, and told me he would take Aura with him to check his limb lines.

I leaned forward and touched the back of his left hand. "I wanted you to stay so I could change your mind about politics." Then I smiled up at him to let him know I was only half-serious.

"Waste of time," Jesse said. "Trotlines are about all he believes in."

"Limb lines," Maledon corrected. "And you can't ever tell about them."

4 MALEDON

Two days and three nights went by. The fires kept burning. The war kept going. The protesters kept protesting. The cops kept clubbing. Johnson kept whining. Humphrey kept waiting. Nixon kept lying. Agnew kept stealing. And Harrold Smith College kept praising the Lord.

Posing as Job Samples, janitor and reformed drunk, I was concluding my testimony to the Good Friday faithful, gleaming faces, pious eyes—the future. I was wearing a khaki shirt and khaki pants and a black tie—just the right touch of working-class humility and middle-class ambition.

"I have risen twice and fallen twice. And now I have risen a third and final time. Twice I have yielded to the devil's bottle and the gutter's women. But now"—I raised, brandished, the mop whose handle I'd held throughout the testimony—"I have scrubbed my heart clean of Satan's stain. I yield now only to the pure bottled water of life, surrender myself only to the seductions of angels." I paused, lowered the mop, dried an old scavenger's eye. "I thank you all for your faith, for your inspiration, for giving me a home here, where I could once again and once and for all reclaim salvation. And I pray that you, young Christian men and women, will never falter as I have done, never yield to lust, never succumb to despair, never fall, never tarry in the service of the risen Lord, but I pray too that you will always remember that there is no one, anywhere, any time, however depraved, who is, while he yet breathes, beyond redemption."

I stopped again, waited for the water to fill my eyes, went on. "I must leave you now, must abandon this sanctuary of the righteous, must venture forth again into the world where I have too often been too weak. God has called me to carry his message to our nation's capital. It is a frightful commission, but I have his blessed assurance. I am in God and fear nothing. So I leave you now, offering you my gratitude and my prayers. Pray for me, dear children of the Lamb."

I retreated to the high-backed, velvet-padded oak deacon's seat behind the pulpit, held the mop at my side like a scepter, and listened with bowed head and closed eyes as the Reverend Dr. Buddy Rounds, president of the college and a summertime evangelist, delivered a ten-minute benediction, during which he asked God to deliver us another day from the Kremlin and to be with our boys in the National Guard in Washington, New York, Baltimore, Chicago, Detroit, Los Angeles, Kansas City, Saint Louis, Memphis, Atlanta, etcetera.

After the students had filed off to choir practice and stake-building class and the Reverend Rounds had whooshed away in his white Continental, I rolled the Hoover institutional vacuum cleaner out of the closet behind the baptistery and started putting a new bag in it.

"Well, Sam, ol' buddy, looks like you still got it."

I recognized the voice, so I didn't look up. "A man goes on," I said.

"Hard to figure you fucking around with that vacuum sweeper when you could be running the place."

"Work my way up from the ground." The bag inserted and secured, I stood and faced my one-time crony and longtime foe, the six-term sheriff and collector of Crawford County, Spoof Lyons, now, after a court-ordered audit of the jail funds, semiretired. "Better move on, Spoof. You're soiling the rug."

I tried to roll the cleaner around him, but he blocked the way. "Man comes across three quarters of a great state like Arkansas, Sam, just to see you, have a few words, check on your health, maybe pass on some news about the home folks, chew over the ol' days and such. And what does he get? First thing, he hears testifying that makes him think, why, the Lord's sure enough done wonders for pore ol' Sam. Course the testifying was done under an alias, but I don't reckon the Lord gives a shit. Then he hangs around to offer his congratulations and welcome you back in the fold and, Christ, all his ol' running buddy can think about is sucking up the spots off some crooked preacher's carpet." He gave his head a sad shake, stared up at the cruciform fluorescent light fixture. "It worries me, Sam. I tell you it worries me something fierce."

"I found the Lord, Spoof, and he won't cater to me if I take to hanging around with crooked sheriffs."

"Ain't a sheriff no more." He took a twist of Cotton Boll from a shirt pocket, a folding knife from a pant pocket, cut off a chew, and positioned it in his jaw.

Staring hard into his small, carnivorous eyes, I said, "Yonder," and pointed to a door at the end of the hallway. Then I just stood there calm, holding the vacuum-cleaner handle, waiting for him to move, knowing he wouldn't.

"Mr. Cantwell has a deal for you, Sam. Wants to help you run Jesse to freedom." He chewed a couple of times, then showed off his huge, brown-toothed, avaricious smile. "Now why don't we go stand by the shitter where I won't have to spit on this rug."

"Don't get this done, lightning strikes," I said.

"Aw, hell, now, Sam, you just come on back there with me. I ain't much of one to just stand and watch some pore ol' whiskeyed-out bastard Hoover up a church. I'm all growed up now. Been that way for some time. I seen white men do nigger work before."

"Tell Cantwell he can't think of a deal that'd interest me. I don't owe him anything, owe you less. I see Jesse, I'll tell him money's calling. You go on back there and spit all you want. I got to get this done so the Lord won't get shit on his sandals."

But he just stood there, like I knew he would, and starting a fight would complicate my leaving. He said, "I ain't drove all this way to collect duns. I come offering opportunity. Little investigative work. You'll make money like a whore at a hootenanny. And it'll do you good." He worked his jaw a second, adjusting the plug. "Think of your boy, Sam. You'll be needing cash getting him clear. Cantwell's willing to just hand it to you. I got to spit."

He stepped around me, ambled a few feet down the hall, opened the toilet door, lifted the commode lid, spat.

"See to it you hit the hole, Spoof." I was rolling the Hoover toward the sanctuary.

"Aw, you know me, Sam," he said. "I can hit a spittoon from a moving train."

"Yeah," I said. "It was always what you was best at." I lowered the Hoover down a pair of steps, turned the corner, unrolled the cord, and plugged it into an outlet hidden by the communion table.

A moment later, Spoof squelched the Hoover's roar. I turned, and he was standing there with the plug in his hand. He said, "Ain't got the time or the humor for this, Sam. I want five minutes, and I like it quiet when I talk. So why don't we just let's you and me sidle on back down that hallway to the shitter, where I can spit and we can have our talk without having to worry about anybody breaking in on us to pray or count the take?"

I heaved a disgusted sigh.

"Five minutes ain't much out of a lifetime," he said. "You make me I can cost you a damn sight more."

"Five minutes," I said, then made a show of looking at the gold pocket watch the warden of the Oklahoma State slam had given me for putting on the Hangman act at the prison rodeo.

"Head Christer here give you that for rededicating your life?"

"That, seventy-five a week, a place to sleep, my daily bread, and a pure heart."

"Ain't much life, is it?"

"You must be born again," I said.

He looked around the sanctuary, then back at me. "Lord, I hope not," he replied.

We walked back down the hall, stopped at the open shitter door. Spoof spat. "There was a time you amounted to something, Sam. Not much, but something. And you never was the kind that'd turn down good currency. I can't figure what's become of you."

"Preaching's something I get plenty of here."

"I expect you do."

"A minute's gone."

From the same pocket that held the Buck knife, Spoof took a roll of bills the diameter of a jailor's key ring. "Three thousand dollars, Sam. You want the simple life, want to keep running this Saint Francis scam, you buy yourself thirty acres of Ozark hill ground. Clear you off a little homesite, throw up a cabin, couple of hundred foot of garden, chickens, hogs, maybe a milk goat, go fishing in the morning, go fishing in the evening. Meadowlarks and turtledoves be eating cornmeal out of the palm of your hand." He removed a rubber band from the roll, watched the hundreds uncurl in his left hand, spat again. "Course, you'll do what I figure you will: You'll buy yourself a new van and a bucketful of fried chicken and haul ol' Jesse to Canada. Or, hell, you could just drive him to the Little Rock airport and mail him to Sweden. They say the women there got no morals at all. Might try it yourself. Hell, you might even take up painting again, Sam, like you done all them times on the sides of your van. Drop Jesse off in Montreal and drive yourself on up a day or two due north and paint a picture of the aurora boris. Ain't never been done right as far as I know. Somebody could find your pictures after you was gone, and you could wind up being a famous dead man, like Grandma Moses."

"My hands shake."

Spoof glanced at my mildly begrimed hands, fingernails terminating in little arcs of dirt. Then he stuffed the bills, unbanded, in his shirt pocket. "They been pushing too many brooms, them hands, shining too many shitters. I was pleased to hear you tell your congregation you was getting out. This ain't a dodge a man like you can run long."

"I don't know," I said. "You played sheriff twelve years."

"Shit, that's easy. That's just being a uniformed outlaw. But this here, now, Christ, it's pure stupidity. Preacher's going to claim most of the cut and leave you to suck the muck up out of the rug."

"And you figure a big roll of Cantwell dollars'd be just the thing to steady my hands?"

"Be my guess. If you're still the man I always knew." He yawned, propped his body against the doorjamb, stared into the sanctuary at a shaft of light altered by stained glass. "Never thought that kind of glass was what it was cracked up to be," he said, and I couldn't tell if he meant the joke or not. "Man ought to either let the light in or shut it plumb out. Ain't no call to color it."

"Dirt's piling up, Spoof. Time's passing. Finish your say and be gone."

"Sometimes what counts is what gets said getting there. It ain't so much the last depot as the rail in between."

"Trip's about over." I took out the pocket watch and tapped its face with an index finger.

"We'd played this out straight, we'd be done. Wasn't me insisted on you playing the Christian janitor. Takes a man a spell to settle into the role you want to give him." He spat again.

"Deal is, I take Jesse to Canada, Cantwell gives me three thousand dollars?"

"No sir. Won't work that way. Cantwell thought it was worth a try, but I knew you wouldn't ever own up to having Jesse, and I knew too that three thousand dollars don't mean no more to him than a roll of nickels does to you or me. So what I done was I talked him into just giving you the money. You and that Gloria Alice Dawn sprung Jesse out of the bin, and now you got him hid out at Villines's place, and, well, you know, Sam, I figure you'll spend at least part of that money in Jesse's behalf." He spat again, then closed the lid of the commode and laid the money on it. "This ain't but the start, either. This here's April's money. You need more in May, give me a holler. I'll be around."

I picked up the money, counted it, folded it into my right front pant pocket. "I'll use it to further the Lord's work."

"You do that, Sam. Donate it to Lottie Moon if you want to. But let me tell you this: This ain't one of them times you got room to fuck up. Last thing Cantwell wants is Jesse coming to trial and shaming him before the home folks. Bad for business. And then Mary, you know how she is, she'd be on his pore ol' rich ass to take her precious boy's case all the way to the White House, and, who knows, high strung as she is, might hire somebody to shoot Johnson—or whatever asshole takes his place. Anyway, ain't no way that trial can go that'll let Cantwell come out clean."

"Fuck him," I said.

"More power to you. But many a man's tried, and he's still cherry." He raised the lid again, spat the whole wad into the water. "But he may not even turn out to be your main worry. Up beside Gloria Dawn's daddy, Cantwell's a five-and-dimer." He clapped his right hand down on my shoulder. "You fucking with power, Sam. Jack around too much, you'll get fried. But then you're God's own hand at keeping clear, ain't you? And that's all you got to do. So maybe this is right up your line." He removed the hand, nodded twice, and said, "Happy Easter."

I watched him shamble away from me, turn right at the end of the hall, and disappear. After hearing, a few seconds later, the heavy opening and solid closing of the chapel door, I patted my freshly moneyed pocket and, smiling, returned through beveled hallway light to the vacuum cleaner. I replugged it, laughed out loud at the prospect of the road before me, and, accompanied by the Hoover's high, relentless inhalation, began to make my way up the center aisle, humming "Just As I Am."

5 JESSE

"I have to go back," I tell him. "Monday, probably."

The cork goes under, and my father gives the pole a short, upward jerk. then he stands and pulls in a crappie.

"Damn near a pound, that one," he says. "Skillet-sized. Bastards are crazy this time of year. Bite at anything." He unhooks the fish, drops it into the cooler, replaces the minnow, and swings the line back out over the darkening river.

I say, "In rut there is no wisdom."

Almost as soon as the cork is on the water, it is tugged under again. Pulling in another crappie, my father says, "All the wisdom they need is not to eat and breed in the same pool. They keep moving, they keep clear. They hold still, they're prime prey."

"Is this allegory hour?"

"The seven o'clock sermonette," he says. "Brought to you this evening by *Brother* S. L. Maledon and the Church of the Open Road."

"We can't be free until we learn to be still," I say.

"That's sleep you're talking about, Son." He lays the fish in the cooler, wraps the line around the pole, props the pole against the willow, and sits back down in the sand. "I'll fillet them. You build a fire."

I'm not ready to let it go. I don't want him to end all our discussions with a joke. I rise, look down at him, and say, "Sometimes you just have to stand and risk the hook."

"Yeah. Don't want the man with the skillet going hungry."

So. There is always a joke. I am too serious, an unwitting straight man. My father dances around me, quipping.

I gather deadfall, chop it into campfire sections with Villines's double-bit ax, pile it in the clearing of sand. I scoop a depression in the sand with my sneakered foot, place a flat rock about half the size of a skillet at one end of the depression, then build a steeple of dry twigs against it. That done, I take my dead uncle's U.S. Navy Zippo from my jeans' pocket, hold it open beneath the apex of the steeple, and light the fire.

My father, using the cooler top as a butcher block, is still filleting crappie. But when I look up, I catch him studying me. Then he says, "The man that gave me that lighter is coming tomorrow."

"Alvy Wolfe?"

He nods.

"Trying everything, aren't you?"

"Sure," he says. "Hard for me to see any reason to let blood of mine go to jail."

I lay a slim length of oak branch across the new fire. "Your boy's grown."

"Yes," he agrees. "In his prime and dead set on throwing it away."

The branch catches, and I lay another beside it. "I could argue that you've thrown your life away." I speak without malice. My father has lived with courage, if not always with grace.

"You could, but then you didn't live it."

"And you're not living mine."

He finishes the last crappie, wraps all the fillets in a sheet of waxed paper, and places them inside the cooler. Then he walks to the edge of the river and says something I can't hear. I move to his side, and he speaks again. "I'm real simple, Jesse. There's a lot I don't understand. I can't see why people spend forty hours a week doing somebody else's work. I can't understand why grown men sign up for a uniform as soon as they hear the parade."

"Most of them aren't grown."

"You are."

I am tired of this, but I want him to understand. "I'm not going to wear their uniform."

"And I never have understood why some people—some of the best people—will go to jail to spite an outfit that'd rather have them in jail than anyplace else."

"It isn't spite," I say. "Some of us believe that what we do can make a difference."

"Oh, I believe that," he says. "I just don't believe it makes any difference to Lyndon Johnson. Or General Hershey. Or the Blue Mountain draft board. If I didn't think going to jail made any difference

I wouldn't be trying to stop you. Chopping off your foot makes a difference. That don't make it right."

High above us, against the darkening sky, a formation of wild geese, guided only by biological necessity, ride the wind northward.

My father, looking up at them, says, "When you feel the heat, you go where it's cool. When you feel the chill, you go where it's warm."

"I want life to mean more than that."

"What's to keep it from meaning more in Canada?"

"Memory."

He turns back, goes to the woodpile, sets a heavy piece of driftwood against the back of the fire, lays two forearm-thick sections of hickory limb in front of it, and watches a moment while the fire catches and crackles.

I remain at the river's edge, turn to watch him and the fire, turn back to the river, and tilt my face upward again to the geese. So my father speaks to my back. "Your stepdaddy had Spoof Lyons carry me a bribe today."

"Wants me to go home and get in line," I say without turning around.

"Probably. But he's pretty much give up on that, looks like. He gave me three thousand dollars to get you to Canada."

I watch the geese another moment before turning and walking to a spot across the fire from him. "You take the money?"

"Yeah. What the fuck? He'd've just hurt somebody with it."

"I'm not going to Canada."

"Oh, I know. I just thought I'd give it one more try." With a booted foot he shoves the hickory branches down into the young coals. "And from my side the money didn't have anything to do with you."

"Of course not. They offered it; you took it. Might help you migrate." I do not intend malice, even now, but it is there. I do not like the way he can justify anything.

"Yeah, and this ain't but just seed money. I need more in a month, he's got it for me." He stacks several more lengths of wood on the fire. "We'll let this burn down; then the others ought to be here."

"If you can be had with money," I say, "Homer can have you."

His face shows me that he catches the double meaning. "That's something you ought to keep in mind, Son."

"And you?"

"If Homer wants to buy me weapons to fight him, that's all right with me."

"There are things money can't buy." As soon as I say it, I know I have set him up again.

One side of his mouth slides upward. A slanted grin. "Not in court there ain't."

"Let it go," I say. Across the fire from me his face still wears its irony. I pick up a thin length of wood and poke at the coal. "Whatever you think about it, it's a condition of life to me. If this doesn't matter, nothing does."

My father moves around the fire, sits in the sand a few feet behind me. I step back and sit beside him. "I'm not saying don't take your stand," he tells me. "I'm saying take it right."

"In this case, right is just straight up."

He leans back on his hands. "Homer's what passes for big time in Blue Mountain, and you have to figure he can keep right from being that simple there. He's apt to have you taking your stand in the moon ward. Drug-addled sociopath suffering from Messiah delusions. Hell, he's already proved he'd rather the boy he partly raised be judged a lunatic than a traitor. The flag's a cash-and-carry item to Homer. He's going to do what he can to keep you from ripping it apart. My guess'd be he's already had new papers drawn up on you. For some place with several dozen more locks to get through."

There is truth there. But—"I have to take my chances with that. There are people who'll know better."

"No, you don't, and no, there ain't. At least not any that make any difference. Won't be nothing for your buddies to say but, 'Yeah, Jesse took his stand, and now they got him taking the lunatic tour.' No sir, Son, you stay with me till August, we'll see to it you get to stand up right—on your own terms. We'll go back to Fort Smith and put on a show for Old Fort Days. I'll stand up on the scaffold with a noose, and you can stand over the trapdoor and have your final say. That show always draws around a thousand people, and we can make sure this one does a whole lot better than that. The local TV always covers it. I can get a reporter there from the *Gazette*. You got from now till then to write your say. Shit, Son, you do it right, you could damn near muzzle the motherfuckers. You play it solid, ain't a goddamn thing Homer or anybody else can do about it. When it's over, I'll retire the Hangman, and you can fly to France or march to Montreal or get you a deferment for knocking up Gloria Alice. Or if there ain't nothing else for it, you can walk off to jail with your head high. If that's how it goes, I'll stand outside the pen every day you're there, waving a little sign that says, FREE THE BLUE MOUNTAIN ONE."

He can do all this, I know. No one does what he does as well as he does it. The question is whether I can prevent what he does from consuming what I wish to do. "What would we do between now and then?"

"Practice, boy. Sharpen our skills on the road. Get the play right before showing it to the home folks. George Wallace rally next weekend in Little Rock. Mark Twain Days after that in Hannibal. The Poor People's Campaign. The Democratic Convention. Whatever the hell we want to do wherever the hell we want to do it. There's a world out there a-dying, Son. We can spend the next three months dancing to the throes—or grieving, if that's how you feel about it. But don't just rear up out of pride and let it drag you down with it. Take your stand on your own terms."

"*Your* own terms, you mean."

"All right. I'll grant you that. And you can make them yours. I'm just offering you a stage."

I stand, step once toward the fire, then turn to face him. "I don't know," I say. "I'll think about it tonight."

"There's a start."

6 GLORIA

"It'll be fun that matters," I said. "Farce, parody, and truth. The People's Theater."

"You can't beat this," Maledon said. "Crappie and coleslaw. Buttermilk. A fire and a river. The moon rising over the Little Red. They ought to have shot the first man that built a house."

"Coleslaw, buttermilk, and skillets imply a settled existence," Villines said. "Ergo, houses." Like so many reformed drunks, Villines prided himself on his realism. Romanticism is intoxicating.

Maledon looked at him with a cocked eye. "Ah, the fucking schoolmaster. Ergo T. Villines."

"And Sam the Wanderer, the Brigand, the Highwayman, the Knight of the Road. Quixote and Huckleberry Finn. The truth is a moving thing. Fleet and fleeting, vagrant and American, available only to the footloose. You must be willing to accept everything but home and logic."

Maledon laughed, easy, confident, and looked at Villines's face, which flashed red and hard in firelight. "Hell, Conrad, you can go with us. You make a good Judge Parker."

Villines set his plate on the sand, laid his palms on his knees. He is uptight, I thought, and weary of his double life.

"Come on, Conrad," I said. "Let's all go. See America, man, in the year of her death."

"She's not dying," Villines said, glancing at me. "Just shedding skin."

My daughter, in her bag, was sleeping by my side. Jimmy sat at the edge of the darkness, his back against a tree, his face illumined only by the occasionally brightening coals of his second after-dinner joint. I had shared the first one with him. And Jesse, who had eaten nothing, sat with his back to the fire and his face to the moon. The spirituality that originally drew me to him now separated us. It was his father to whom I was now drawn.

Maledon leaned over, opened the cooler, and got himself a beer. I wished Villines would drink one. There are times even a drunk needs a drink. Villines needed to let go. He was gripping his life too tightly.

Maledon said, "You know you're welcome, Conrad, if you want to come."

"Even if she is dying," Villines, ignoring Maledon, said to me, "it isn't cause for celebration. Jefferson's vision was sound, and we haven't entirely failed it yet."

"We've gone from Jefferson to Johnson to maybe even Nixon," I said. "After two hundred years our economy is still based on racism. I'd call that a failure."

"We can vote them out," Villines argued. "It's still possible for one election to change everything."

I feigned astonishment, tried to look at him as if he'd said he believed in the accuracy of Joe McCarthy's lists. "You don't really believe we have a choice, do you? I mean, you have to be a member of the club to run, man. You have to be rich, white, male, and stupid."

Nodding, Villines said, "Yes. But it doesn't have to be that way. And you have to remember that the rich, white, male stupid rulers have given most people what they want: higher wages and softer chairs."

"And in exchange they've taken their souls," I argued.

"Don't be too quick to condemn higher wages," Villines said, peeved and paternalistic. "And don't judge other people's souls."

"Let's talk about the damn river," Maledon said. "The metaphysics of crappie."

Jimmy Song snuffed the roach and then walked to the campfire. You could look into his eyes and see to Tierra del Fuego. "Saw a piece in the paper the other day, man. There was this poll. Said fifteen percent of the electorate had never heard of Richard Nixon." He sat down. "Never fucking heard of fucking Richard Nixon, man."

"Could be they just didn't want to own up to it," Maledon said.

Now Jesse spoke, as if addressing the moon. "We should try to live so that men like Humphrey and Nixon and Johnson are essentially irrelevant to our lives."

"Sure," Maledon said. "That's what you aim for. But you got to take care to cover your ass. You don't, they take a pretty young fellow like you and stick him in a cell with some damn three-hundred-pound killer queer."

I disliked Jesse when he became oracular. "When the storm troopers come," I said. "There won't be room for spiritual detachment."

Villines laughed at me. "There won't be any storm troopers. Sooner or later the government'll see that if it ignores you, you'll do yourselves in. Hedonism is no basis for revolution. You're just unconventional consumers. As American as Mickey Mantle and not nearly as important."

"America has become a country of anal retentives," I replied, aiming the sentence at him with narrowed eyes.

"Storm troopers, man," Jimmy said. "Wow, wouldn't that be a gas? Hide out in the hills and pick them off one by one like birds off a wire." His face had on a stoned, idiot's grin.

Maledon stood, walked to the bank, and pissed in the river. When he came back to the broken circle around the fire, he said, "I figure we ought to leave Easter morning. We got posters to print up, arrangements to make, rehearsing to do. Ain't much to it, but you got to know who you are in the play."

I moved over besides Jesse, placed my hand softly on his forearm. "You'll come with us, won't you?"

"I don't know," he said. "Maybe."

"Jess believes God takes care of believers," Maledon said. "We just got to leave him believe."

Jesse looked hard at his father. "I believe the believer must take care of God," he said. "When He has gone from our lives, not even the storm troopers will matter."

7 MALEDON

After we finished eating and arguing politics, Jesse went off by himself, looking, I guess, for a hill high enough to provide a view of the mystery. Jimmy Song carried Aura back to the house. Gloria walked beside him, and Villines followed along, lugging a cardboard box filled with knives, forks, plates, and bowls. I scrubbed out the skillet with sand and river water, figuring on frying more crappie come morning. "I'll sleep here," I'd told the others. "Time to get close to the ground again."

I sat there content without thought for a spell, watching the firelight and listening to the bat squeaks in the blackness high above the water. Then the deft, blind hunters took their radar on upriver, leaving the sandbar night to frogs and crickets and me. I nestled there, comforted by a beer and a blanket, by the light at the bottom of the circle. I drifted off once, but then the night chilled me and I got up, wishing I'd brought my sleeping bag, and stacked more wood on the fire.

As the fire flickered up between the new logs, I remembered a night me and my brother, John, and Alvy Wolfe, our cousin from Blue Eye, had spent at the mouth of Webber Creek almost twenty-seven years earlier. After a day of fishing and swimming, we'd built a fire like this on a sandbar like this and had fried ourselves a catfish supper. And after that, Alvy, quick Alvy, the hustler, the talker, the dreamer, had surprised us by producing a quart of cheap whiskey he said he'd bought the day before in Blue Mountain out of the back of the Full Moon Recreation Parlor. The sixth of June, 1941, it was. John's eighteenth birthday. John the Perfect. Quiet, kind, smart, and strong. The good friend. The good brother. The kind of boy scout the Boy Scouts don't have. Nice to old ladies, hell on bullies. Alvy opened the bottle, took a drink, handed it to John, and said to me, "We've signed up, Sammy."

"Signed up?"

John took his drink and passed the whiskey to me. I swallowed a throatful and gagged.

"The Navy," Alvy explained.

I asked them the very question then I'd ask them now. "Why?"

"There's nothing for a young man here," Alvy told me. "I want to get the hell out of Arkansas, see some things, do some things, fuck some women I don't know."

I stared down at the bottle. Alvy told me to pass it back. I did, then looked a question at my brother, who said, "It's Hitler, Sammy. He's evil, and sooner or later we'll have to do something about him. I want to be there when we do. This is a duty I don't want to shirk."

"Ain't nothing draws pussy like a uniform with combat medals on it," Alvy added.

John accepted the bottle again from Alvy. "There's that too," he said. "And I'm afraid if I hang around here much longer I'll get hitched to Mary. And I don't want that yet. I'll come back here and live my life with her, but I want to be able to say I been somewhere first."

Hitler was a name I might have heard once or twice before, but it didn't mean much to me. Marrying was a thing a man could do or not do, according to his lights. I'd been to country dances where pussy could be had for the asking. The weather was clear. The fish were biting. And if you didn't like it here, there were roads leading off in every direction. None of what they were saying made any sense to me.

I said, "You'll just be floating on a hole of water you can't see across. They probably won't even let you fish."

They laughed at me.

In July, on the buddy system, John and Alvy went to boot camp in San Diego. They came home after that, wore their uniforms everywhere they could, told the Tijuana tales of strippers and whores and their acrobatic cunts—the things they could do with Coke bottles and donkeys.

During that leave, John got engaged to Mary Travis, who, having just graduated from Blue Mountain High, was planning to take advantage of the two years of college and the public-school teacher's certificate offered by Arkansas Tech at Russellville, seventy miles of graveled state highway distant. They agreed to delay the wedding until after John had finished his uniformed service to the nation. He'd see the world, sow his oats, do in the Hun, then come home to a farm, a woman, a life.

I fished, brooded, and asked myself questions. Why would a smart man plan a wedding he couldn't carry off until after he finished fighting the big war he thought was sure to come? Was it just a way out? Was it just a way of making sure Mary stayed faithful while he was shooting his seed into the bellies of dusky whores? And, Christ, if he was sure war was certain, why wasn't he trying to find a way out? Hell, I'd read the history book. And I knew that over the centuries millions of men had died on the battlefield of Europe, died in war after war, fought over such things as who ought to be pope, where some line ought to be drawn separating two countries nobody I knew knew the name of. Men had charged into spears and arrows, bullets and bombs, so that So-and-So II could be king instead of So-and-So VI. Men had died in piles over the price of wheat, the doctrine of transubstantiation, the beauty of a woman. It was all a game that let the rich folks watch the poor folks bleed. Even the few wars that were supposed to have been fought to better the life of the common lot had been botched. The French Revolution led to Napoléon. The Russian to Stalin. No sir, as I saw it, history didn't yield up but one clear lesson: When them motherfuckers call, be scarce.

In October, a little after John and Alvy left home again, this time for Norfolk, Virginia, and sailing orders, I quit school and went on the road with Dr. Jacob Ladders's Marvelous Modern Medicine Show. Dr. Ladders, born Jefferson Davis Jones, was not marvelous, modern, or a doctor. But he sold whiskey in bottles of various sizes and labels, sang Stephen Foster songs, and harangued Depression audiences about arthritis and eschatology. I drove the old parti-color ramshackle Chevrolet ton-and-a-half truck between towns and, during the shows, would, whenever necessary, guzzle down some of the elixir, shout for joy, toss a pair of crutches aside, and rush, forever healed, toward the good doctor, who calmly observed this miracle from the tailgate of the truck.

He was little more than a colorful thief, a carnival barker set off on his own, but, in spite of his drunkeness and his almost absolute pessimism, he provided me with a vision of a way of life, of a way of moving through the world on your own terms, of a kind of freedom rooted in deception.

And, during my year and four months with Ladders, I fell in love for the first, and maybe only, time. Magdalen Abbey (Was the name real? They swore it was.), orphaned at fourteen, rescued at fifteen from the Baptist Home for Girls in Blytheville, Arkansas, by her putative uncle, Jefferson Davis Jones, and, by him, broken to the road, the spiel, the barker's dollar. She played a piano and softly sang a hymn as background harmony to Dr. Ladders's medicinal evangelism. And there were nights, after days of incessant prairie or backwoods roads had rendered the world a weight to Ladders, when the evangelist resorted to the flesh. Then, with Ladders playing a raunchy piano, Magdalen would dance a garish, firelit hootchy-kootchy before a crowd of Saturday-night farmers, Main Street merchants, and letter-sweatered delinquents.

I couldn't keep my eyes off her.

Ladders, made impotent by years of immoderate doses of his own tonic, told me, "A fine pair you be. Young Sam and my Meg. My approval. Love is all there is."

And it was, for a while. In the months just before and after Pearl Harbor, during dust-laden nights in Okie campgrounds along highways between dying Depression towns, Magdalen and I gave ourselves, without stint or calculation, to each other. I gathered her bouquets of highway right-of-way wildflowers. She played for me, with some fair skill, Mozart and Chopin on the rinky-dink piano. She made, every time, at the moment of climax, a series of low throaty sounds. I always wanted to hear them again.

In our honor, Dr. Jacob Ladders composed a sonnet sequence.

"You young'uns may cure me," he said one day on the road between Sand Springs and Muskogee. "The years come down on a man, and he turns to the tonic. Ain't nothing here but the pain, he thinks. Ain't nothing for it but something to ease it. Ah, but then somehow or other he gets a glimpse of love blushing full." He shook his head. "Can't tell at this age whether the glimpse is good or bad. Just makes it clear the tonic's no substitute. I will say this, I ever get another hard on, I'm going to shellac it."

Sure enough, two nights later, in Fort Smith, he hired himself a whore for the night. And, come morning, he had her in the truck with him. " 'Who ever loved that loved not at first sight,' " he explained.

A week after that, in West Memphis, she left him for a black drummer in a roadhouse band.

"Closer to her own age," Ladders said between sips of the tonic. "And hung like a fire truck, I reckon."

I started the truck and pointed it east. Ladders had planned a working tour of the Great Smokies.

"No," he said. "Let's head back west. I'll be needing the bleak spaces again."

He went on with his life, but without energy or care. The enthusiasm with which Magdalen and I went about our love seemed now merely to depress him further. He was subject to fits of rage, rage against his own inert body, rage against young love, rage against a life wasted. Suddenly, coming up out of what had seemed to be a stupor, he would sling a bottle of the tonic into a campfire or, more dangerously, at a passing car, take a violent vow of sobriety, and condemn all of the ignorant yokels, type by type, awaiting us in the next town. Once, well after midnight, he lurched into the back of the truck, where Magdalen and I had made our nest, and wondered, in a shout, whether it were too much to ask the glandular young to take the clamor of their coupling outside earshot.

"Not to mention the smell," he said. Magdalen sat up, holding a sheet to her neck, and tried, through tears, to apologize, to explain something. He wouldn't have it. "I'm a goddamn eunuch," he said. "Have mercy."

But then, gradually, he settled into his depression, assuming the aspect of a saint. He might even have left the road, gone into seclusion, if habit hadn't been habit. If he had lived a sedentary life, he'd've been apt to settle himself into a bedroom chair and wait quiet for the end. But, having nothing but the road, he became a white-line shut-in.

The medicine-show oratory disappeared. Warmed by a lap robe, he sat in a padded rocking chair at the edge of the tailgate and, in a low, resigned voice, delivered apparently extemporaneous meditations on the nature of despair.

"When physical lust abandons you, you are conscious not that the impediment to wisdom has been removed. You are conscious only of the memory of lust.

"You may awaken one morning and ask yourself why. If you do not suppress the question, it will destroy you. There is no answer. You can survive only by kidding yourself.

"When your sons return from the war and the seductions of death, they will never again be satisfied with the peace and monotony of life. They will rush to the tumult of the cities, and the concatenations of the assembly line will be their dirge.

"Give me a bestial ignorance. I would trade all my learning and whatever future I have for one happy night with a woman."

Nothing he had ever done had worked so well. Magdalen, behind him, would softly play "Just As I Am" while he spoke. Hangdog, I worked the crowds, letting them talk me into telling them that Dr. Ladders's oldest son, Theodore Roosevelt Ladders, had gone down with the *Missouri* at Pearl Harbor.

When Ladders had finished speaking and closed his eyes, a big part of the crowd would form a polite line and wait for the chance to whisper a word of encouragement to the despairing saint and to drop a coin or a greenback into the crock beside the old man's feet.

Young women, inspired by Ladders's stated willingness to swap all he had and all he might become for a night's roll, came to him. Some stayed through the night, but every one of them left by, at the latest, the following dawn. And the ones I saw leaving seemed chastened, themselves now aggrieved.

I began to suspect that this new incarnation of Ladders was just another hustle, a hustle pulled off by spreading sorrow, by appealing to pity, by posing as one of the elect now deprived of faith. I figured that in the beginning Ladders had suffered from a mild dose of actual despair but that the success of that despair as a carnival item had probably cured him of it. It was all too calculated. The show always started on time, an audience always arrived, and Ladders always delivered his despairing aphorisms with a professional virtuosity. The role didn't call for much range, but he played it right down to the ground.

I was wrong.

On the evening of the Fourth of July, 1942, in the firecracker air of Sedan, Kansas, Ladders concluded his oral meditations by saying, "There is no reason for anything. All motives are both ulterior and irrelevant. Nothing matters." Then he removed his old Colt .45 from the crock, raised it to his temple, and left us.

Even then, for an instant, I suspicioned another con—a blank shell and monkey blood. It wouldn't be till later, years later, that I'd come to suspect that Ladders's suicide had been the ultimate revenge of the despairing—a way of making of his own death a wedge between the lovers who survived him.

If that had been his target, his aim was true. The medicine show ended. And the energy that had for nearly a year pulled me and Magdalen together now started pushing us apart.

Twenty-six years later, sitting by that sandbar campfire along the Little Red, I could remember precisely the day and hour it ended: Saint Petersburg, Florida, Sunday, September 6, 1942. We had rejected the possibility of the forced conviviality of the Baptist charity Sabbath meal and were eating the suckling pig I'd stolen, gutted, wrapped in burlap, and roasted in hobo coals. We hadn't made a cent since Ladders's suicide, had spent most of what his final weeks of meditations had accumulated for us, and had come to Florida hoping, with little enthusiasm, to hook up with a wintering circus.

I sliced another strip of loin from the pig, laid it on my plate, and sat back down. "They might hire us," I said, "just for the truck."

We'd been through it all before. Magdalen said nothing, picked at her pork.

I said what I didn't believe. "It's what he'd want. As long as he had his strength, he believed in going on."

"As long as he had his mind, you mean," she shot at me. "You think he was crazy."

"No. Just tired."

She set her plate on the ground and studied it. "He wanted more," she said. "He wanted it all to mean something." With her fingertips she pulled long strands of hair away from her face. Then she looked up at me with lost button eyes. "There's got to be more to it than this. He knew it, but he couldn't find it."

"He just lost faith," I told her again. "There ain't but two choices. Live or die. He made the right one for a long time, then he fucked up."

She shook her head. Not, I thought, at what I was saying, but at everything. "Maybe you have to do it a certain way. Maybe we always kept moving away from an answer."

"Jesus." I set my plate down, walked a few steps toward the truck, turned back, and said, "Life ain't a goddamn question, Meg. It's just here, and it's all there is."

"When we get tired of making love to each other, what do we have left?"

"I ain't tired yet." But I saw that she was waiting for more. "Just because something won't last forever don't mean it's not worth doing."

"I want permanence."

"Lord," I said. "If anything's permanent, it's just because it don't have enough energy in it to wear itself out."

She stood. "I want to go home."

"Home?" I asked. I honestly didn't know where the hell she meant.

"Blytheville," she said, sounding as if that were an old and obvious answer.

Two afternoons later we were in Blytheville. I spent three more days living in the truck and trying to talk her out of returning to the orphanage that'd been her home before Ladders'd come along. She was wanting to work there as a housekeeper, as a cook, as whatever the directors would consent to her being. You want to do shit work cheap, somebody'll let you. All she asked for her work was bed and board. They gave it to her.

We said good-bye to each other that time over weak coffee in a booth in the A.W. West Café. She laid her right arm on my left one, leaned forward. "I don't expect you to understand. I don't even understand it myself. I just know I have to go back to where I started. I have this feeling I might find something there. A way of starting over, maybe."

I didn't say anything.

"I love you," she said. "This doesn't mean I don't."

"It'd be easier if I could believe it did. Then I could just drive off and tell myself, Well, she was pretty, and she made the time good, but then she went out of her fucking head."

I did drive away that night—to Memphis, where I spent a week drinking cheap whiskey and throwing the bottles in the river. Then I drove back to Blytheville and tried to see her again. But, stubble-faced and whiskey-stained, I was denied entrance to the home, my way blocked by a two-hundred-seventy-five-pound preacher and two dyke handmaidens.

So I drove to New Orleans and devoted another week to throwing more bottles in the same river. After returning to Blytheville again, I shaved, got a fifty-cent haircut, gave my breath a day to clear, and showed up at suppertime on the orphanage steps in a pin-striped, double-breasted Hart Schaffner & Marx suit. I showed the preacher a card that read T. ROLLEY WILSON—ATTORNEY-AT-LAW, told him I was on private retainer by Nathan B. Grove, the planter, and that Mr. Grove had charged me with the responsibility of determining whether the Blytheville Baptist Home for Girls was worthy of becoming a beneficiary of Grove Charities. The preacher led me to the dining room and commenced introducing me to little girls.

I ate a bowl of thin stew, humored the orphans, and asked the preacher if he knew the whereabouts of any of the home's former tenants who might consent to an interview.

"Why, we have one on our staff. A perfect saint."

I let my tone become lawyerly. "I'd like to speak to her privately for a few moments in your office. Send her there. Please don't accompany her. I must be certain she is under no duress."

She had apparently been practicing severity. She wore a stiff black dress. Her face was pale, her hair in a tight bun. The apprentice priestess of grief, I thought.

She sat in the chair across the desk from me, her calm white hands folded in her starched black lap. "I knew it would be you," she said.

I replied, "There ain't nothing they can do to keep you from being beautiful, is there?"

"I'm glad you came. I wanted to talk to you one more time."

"*One* more time?" I stood, walked around the desk, and laid my head on her hands, still folded in her lap.

"Please don't," she said. "I need to say something."

Slowly, gently, my right hand moved under her dress and onto her thigh. She stiffened. "No, Sam. Not here."

Without moving the hand, I looked up at her. "Where, then?"

"I didn't mean that."

I moved the hem of her dress upward, laid my cheek on bare thigh. She pressed her legs together, then stood. "I'm going to Utah next week," she told me.

Coldly, from my knees, I stared up at her and said, "Just because the old man couldn't get it up don't mean the world ought to go sterile."

"We're starting a mission in Ogden."

I stood, took a step toward her. She backed away. "Christ," I said, "the Baptist ministry to the Mormons."

"Give me a year. Then I'll know for sure."

I stepped toward her; she backed away.

"I love you," she said. "I'd want you to come with us, but you wouldn't come in the right spirit."

"So it's you and Brother Broadass?"

"He has a thyroid condition. Reverend Boatright is a good man."

"It's him or me," I told her.

"It's not that simple."

"The truck or the church, then."

"The truck left Jacob without anything but his pistol. That road doesn't lead anywhere."

"And this one dead-ends in Utah."

"You might be right, Sam. But I have to find out."

We stared at each other for what seemed like a long time.

"Say good-bye to me, Sam," she said.

"Fuck it," I answered.

She closed her eyes, nodded once, and hurried out of the room.

I drove the truck then to Blue Mountain, to wait out the year in Conrad Villines's cabin just above Peeveehouse Ford, on the western edge of property that had once been called The Hangman's Hundred, creek-bottom land purchased in 1898 by the Reverend Frank James, the outlaw turned prophet, as a gift to the widows and children of the victims of George Maledon's rope. But the idea had been a failure. Conrad's father, Elbert, had bought up the deed after returning from the Great War, and it had been nearly thirty years since any of the gallows' orphans had lived there. Villines himself, after two years of surviving on sweet milk and bourbon, was living in a boxcar in Columbia, Missouri, and studying for his master's degree in nineteenth-century American literature. So I had the hundred acres and the one-room, book-lined cabin to myself.

I used the last of Ladders's money to buy a milk cow, a dozen laying hens, and a rooster. I got up before dawn, milked the cow, gathered the eggs, and then, usually, spent the rest of the day fishing or hunting. Saturday afternoons I'd walk the three miles to Delzell's

General Store, trade eggs for canned goods, sit on one of the old rockers on the porch, and listen to the radio talk about the war. The tales of Allied valor, the descriptions of German, Italian, and Japanese atrocities, and the highfalutin salesmanship of Roosevelt and Churchill didn't do a damn thing to help me see why men like my brother would sail to the other side of the world to wear a uniform and risk death. There weren't any Germans or Japanese in Blue Mountain, and if they did come here, they wouldn't know how to live.

Other than Rubin Delzell, with whom I exchanged only the language of barter, I didn't talk to anybody but Uncle Hugh Harp, who lived in a tin room nailed to the side of Delzell's store. Uncle Hugh, arthritic and ninety, had for twenty-two years, from 1875 to 1896, ridden Oklahoma as one of Isaac C. Parker's marshals. He had no good to say of the famous judge. "The pompous bastard was worse than the men he hung. And they were scum."

I told him that, yes, it was possible I'd descended illegitimately from the Hangman's daughter, Annie, and her outlaw drunkard lover, who later murdered her. But there wasn't any record of her having a child. So it was more probable that my father had just rode into Blue Mountain and appropriated the name.

"Where'd he ride in from?"

"Colorado is what they told me."

"Annie and that drunk of hers went to Colorado for a year. Rumor was she bore a child out there. Male."

"Yeah. They used to say Daddy was raised in the ass end of a Denver saloon."

Uncle Hugh nodded, rocked. After a while he said, "George Maledon, now, he was a man. Closemouthed, dead shot, knew all there was to know about ropes and weights. Killed a man clean and kept his own counsel. Parker, though, he mistook himself for Moses."

"Why'd you ride for him?"

"I liked riding." He spat. "I liked the way you could do damn near anything in Oklahoma then. I liked the way it'd be a town here and a tribe there. Varied like, it was. Each little clump of folks going by their own rules, living by their own lights. Parker thought everybody ought to live by his."

"Why bring men in for him to hang?"

"Ones I brung in needed hanging. They was preying on their own. It wasn't the hanging I objected to, it was the way he dressed it up. He was trying to stitch a borrowed order over Oklahoma." He shook his weathered head. "And he did it, of course." He rocked forward, spat again out of his toothless mouth. "Used to be you could ride across the Oklahoma line and start all over again. Ought to be a place like that yet."

Over the course of these Saturdays, Uncle Hugh told me the stories—of Smoker Mankiller, of Cherokee Bill, of Rufus Buck, of Belle Starr and her Pearl and her Sam, of Cole Younger, of Bill Doolin and the Daltons, of the Hangman, George Maledon, and his beautiful renegade daughter—that I would, within two years, begin to fashion into my livelihood.

And it was on that porch, while listening to the story of the capture of the Rufus Buck Gang, children all, that I next saw Alvy Wolfe and learned the fate of my brother. Alvy was home on a sixty-day survivor's leave. He and John had been aboard the *Joseph Hughes*, a transport ship, when on November 11 a German torpedo struck her bow. The survivors, John and Alvy among them, treaded the Mediterranean, an ocean none of them had call to be in, until they were rescued by the *Tasker H. Bliss*. Twenty-two hours later, at four in the morning, another torpedo found the *Bliss*.

"It got us dead center that time," Alvy said. "Me and John was laying side by side on hammocks on the aft deck. Couldn't neither one of us sleep after what happened the day before. Right when it hit, I was lighting a Camel with a new lighter John bought at the ship store that afternoon. Fucking ship went up like it had been doused with coal oil. Shit was blowing everywhere, shooting through the sky. We was running for the side, and a line come down and caught John. I stood over him, pulling at him and yelling, but he was gone, and then the ship started rolling over, and then somebody grabbed me and pulled me to the side and we went in. I swam around awhile, looking for him, but there were bodies and pieces of bodies everywhere, and he was dead on deck anyway. And then a PT boat picked me up and took me to the beach."

I stared at him, not knowing yet what to make of this story out of another world. I'd be needing a couple of days before I could understand it even well enough to feel grief.

"Navy Department's been trying to get word to you," Alvy went on. "But I didn't figure they'd have a proper address."

Uncle Hugh Harp said, "Ol' George Maledon, now, he fought for the Union. Once refused to hang a Yankee veteran." He spat again.

"Me, I missed all the wars. That's one thing. Never shot a man I didn't know."

Alvy Wolfe handed me the lighter. "I saved this for you. I didn't know what else to do."

"Oklahoma," Uncle Hugh said, as if he were answering a question.

I went back to cabin, cow, and laying hens and stayed there, seeing no one, until two days before Christmas, when Conrad Villines returned from Columbia. We spent nine days together, quietly drinking bourbon until we passed out, then getting up and starting in again. Then, on the morning of the first day of 1943, I sold the cow, the hens, and the rooster to Conrad for twenty-five dollars, went out and got in Jacob Ladders's truck, and started driving to Ogden, Utah.

Another chill there at the river's edge brought me up out of memory. I got the ax and cut some more wood, laid four narrow lengths of deadfall across the dying coal, waited for a flame, then set the butt of a hickory limb across that.

"Fuck it," I said as I sat back down. And "Fuck it," I said again, letting the hard words linger. She hadn't been in Ogden. The mission had never opened. When I found that out, I turned around and drove straight back to Blytheville. She wasn't there, either. She and the Reverend Boatright had gone to Sedan, Kansas, to establish the Jacob Ladders Memorial Baptist Church. I'd lost her to a dead man and the bright promise of resurrection.

So I took to the road again, drifting from town to town, taking odd jobs, trading yard work or field work for a meal and a tank of gas, and reading whatever I could find about Judge Isaac C. Parker and George Maledon, the Hangman. On V-J Day 1945 I started repainting the truck, covering Ladders's slogans and jingles with portraits of Parker and Maledon, Cherokee Bill and Rufus Buck, Belle and Sam Starr. When I had that done, I drove toward Fort Smith, looking for an audience and a beginning.

I found them both and kept on going. The road, in the years sincc, has paused but briefly, a week here, a month there. In 1946, Mary Travis came to me, conscious of time, even at twenty-three, and desperate for a child with Maledon blood. I took the woman my brother widowed without marrying, but on my terms—and the road's. And we rode together nine years, each serving the other as surrogate. Stopgap love. It worked well enough until Mary, worried that we were excluding our child from any but a renegade's future, went back to her family in

Blue Mountain, taking Jesse with her. She renewed her teaching certificate, got a job teaching English at Blue Mountain High, and, to broaden her son's prospects, married Homer T. Cantwell of Cantwell Enterprises.

I walked to the edge of the river, stared up into the darkness and the pinpricks of light. Mary had been good to me, and good for me. She'd seen me to the end of my youth, shared my black laughter each autumn as, on our way to the Chautauqua County Fairgrounds in Sedan, Kansas, we drove past the Jacob Ladders Memorial Baptist Church, which seemed each year to have sprouted a new wing. There had been times, I thought, when Mary's presence had been all that had kept me from relinquishing pride, entering that church, and rededicating my life. And when the fair ended, when I'd packed gibbet, ropes, and child into the truck, when Magdalen had again failed to appear, when I was standing by the truck and looking back at the little town, Mary would come to me, touch my arm, and say, "We'd best be going. It's a long night before us."

And what, I wondered now, had I given her? Well, a taste of the horizon and the son she wanted. And, yes, practicing so often the role of Judge Parker's wife had aptly prepared her to become Mrs. Homer T. Cantwell.

So we were even, more or less. And Magdalen? Well, she was twenty-six years gone. I'd chosen my life, and I'd led it. Fuck it, I thought again. No debts and no regrets.

All that remained was to bequeath the inheritance, like the lighter, to my son.

8 JESSE

At the center is silence and perfect bliss. My father believes only in the phenomena on the surface of the circle.

Without faith we move from darkness to darkness. Faith is not that which allows us to see the light. It is the light.

Gloria is the advocate of change, the champion of progress, the believer not in the goodness but in the possible goodness of life on earth. Life will be good when man makes it good. In this she differs from Lyndon Johnson only as to definition. Lyndon Johnson uses force to make a Little America, an Andrews Air Force Base, of Vietnam. Gloria would use force to make a socialist paradise of America. The will to force society to conform to one's own convictions is the basic ingredient of tyranny. Given that will, the tyrant requires only the apparatus of power: a Selective Service System, a KGB, a CIA, an SS, a cadre, a rifle, a Molotov cocktail.

My hope for Gloria is that her passion for life, her simple pleasure in the things of this world, will prevent her from assembling any of that apparatus. Once assembled, on however small a scale, the machinery is not easily repudiated.

We must always remind tyrant and would-be tyrant that there is a mystery greater than any or all of us, that a single, living cell is beyond our comprehension and that, therefore, whatever rules, codes, laws a society must devise must be devised out of reverence and awe for that mystery. The foundation of just government, like the foundation of wisdom, is the recognition of our own ignorance, our own fallibility. We must be willing to acknowledge the terrifying truth that, ultimately, each of us is beyond the law.

* * *

When I do not go, they will send another in my place. Poor white or poor black. I am responsible for more than my own soul. I must make my stand accordingly.

9 GLORIA

"How did you manage to stay out of the wars?" I asked the question as I entered the circle of firelight. I carried a sleeping bag and a flashlight. I had been thinking about him.

He said, "Jesse's still up on his hilltop."

"I wasn't looking for him." I laid the sleeping bag beside him, unrolled it, sat down.

"Christ," he said.

"You don't like me?" I said it with a teasing kind of mockery in my voice.

"I don't know you well enough not to like you."

I laughed. Even a man like him, who had lived most of his life outside many of the old customs, was made a little nervous by a young, aggressive woman. They can rarely quite accept our freedom. "Ask me some questions?" I said. "Or do you have a form I can fill out?"

"Left it in the van," he replied. "Don't carry them around with me like I used to. And women nowadays, lots of them, well, they'll lie on a form like that."

"We're just learning to be more like men."

"It's a shame." He got up and stacked more wood on the fire.

When he returned, I said, "Women have been fucked over forever because we always worried about our manners."

"Maybe so," he agreed. "But then most of you had the advantage of not being expected to take steady work."

"Bullshit," I said. "We've always done the dirty work."

"Okay," he conceded. "Have it however you want it."

I lay back on the sleeping bag, my hands folded behind my head. He stared into the fire, thinking, as if I weren't there. I said, "Something happens to most people by the time they reach your age. Their dreams die, they give up, they start worrying about retirement plans and their kids' education." I waited for him to respond. When he didn't, I asked, "Why not you?"

"Got started moving and couldn't stop."

"Don't feel like talking?"

"Don't feel like talking about me."

I sat up. "You want some pot?" I took a joint from my shirt pocket. "Colombian. Jimmy brought it in from Mexico."

He shook his head. I asked for a light. He pointed to the fire. I went to it, lit the joint with the glowing end of a stick, returned to the down bag, and assumed the lotus position.

"Did I ever tell you how I met Jesse?"

"SDS," he said.

"No. Before that. We didn't even have SDS in Fayetteville until last year. And Jesse never even really belonged." I gazed into the fire and took another hit of the joint. "Damn that's good."

There was a silence. Night sounds.

"You know what it does?" I asked.

"It's better than being drunk, and you don't get the hangover. It mellows you out. It makes you hear the music in everything. And it makes sex great. You just can't believe it." He showed me that wizened, cocked grin of his.

I smiled at him. "It forces you to feel whatever's going down right now. It makes you live the moment."

"*Carpe* fucking *diem*," he said.

I laughed, took another hit, laughed again. "You are old," I said, still smiling.

"Mine is the voice of the concerned father. The voice of the Silent Majority that has made this country what it is."

"A voice crying in the night," I said, through laughter. I held an index finger to my lips. "Listen. You can hear it."

Fire snaps. Wind songs.

"Did you hear it?"

"Yes," he replied. "But it's so familiar I can't make sense out of it."

"It's saying, 'Yes, sir. Yes, sir,' over and over again."

"Ah," he said. "Yes, ma'am."

For a while the fire held us hypnotized. Then I remembered—"I was going to tell you about meeting Jesse." I straightened my legs, stretched them, brought them up to my chest, wrapped my arms around them, and gently rocked.

"Probably a night like this, wasn't it? A fire, a river, the stars above. Some Colombian."

"It was about this time of year. Three years ago, '65. Phil Ochs came to Fayetteville. Jesus, Johnson had just been elected, and most of us were still thinking how lucky we were to have been spared Goldwater. Ochs sang from a platform they'd built in front of Old Main. It was a Saturday afternoon. A pretty day. Spring and all. The people there were the radicals at Fayetteville, but he must've thought he'd wandered into a Young Republicans picnic. God, we were clean-cut."

"Always a mistake," Maledon remarked.

"Most of us had never done anything more daring than argue with our parents about Martin Luther King. The boys had just begun to let their flattops grow. The girls had ventured out in ironed Levi's."

"Tight pants," he said, giving me that nod. "That *would* be where it started." He leaned back on his hands. "Probably be where it ends, too."

I had one more drag off the pot, then, with moistened thumb and index finger, snuffed the roach. "That night," I went on, "we went to somebody's apartment, and everybody got drunk and stoned, and most of us crashed. When Ochs woke the next morning, he wanted to see Oklahoma. Pretty Boy Floyd country, he called it. I had a car, and Jesse knew the territory, and so we took him. Went down through the Cookson Hills and on into Sallisaw. Jesse took us to the Floyd home-place and showed us some of the banks he robbed. We even met Pretty Boy's brother, the sheriff. Jesse took us right to his office."

"The old fart," Maledon said. "Folks there liked having Pretty Boy dead. Then they could pin a badge on his shadow."

"After that we drove on to Okemah, Woody Guthrie's town." I watched the fire a minute. "It was fucking great, man. Jesse had this way of getting people to trust him. People in the café told us stories—and the people on the streets, and the sheriff. It was like Jesse knew something about how people lived and what they thought and how to get them to open up that I didn't know. And I wanted to learn, so after we took Phil Ochs to the Tulsa airport, I just went home with Jesse and stayed there."

"Lord God," Maledon said. "A man sends his son off to college to learn logarithms, and look what happens to him."

"It was good for a few months," I went on. "But Jesse was looking for God. You know, seriously. We tripped together some, but he didn't like it much. He thought acid was too easy. Thought it was all bright colors and quick chemistry. He wouldn't have a God that required nothing more of him than swallowing window pane. He was different. The rest of us thought we knew something, and all he knew then was that we didn't. He quit smoking and drinking, and he'd fast for days at a time. He was reading the Bible and the Bhagavad-Gita and Thoreau and Nietzsche and Suzuki, and he used to just pore over parts of *Arabia Deserta*. And when he wasn't reading, he was thinking—just sitting there in the middle of the floor with a stiff spine, staring out the front window at, like, the cosmos or something." I looked at Maledon. He had his face tilted back parallel to the sky, and he was wearing that knowing half-grin. "I got tired of all that. I wanted to *do* something. So I left. I never quit seeing him. Or sleeping with him some. He's a good lover. But I moved out."

I turned around, then lay back on my sleeping bag, propping my head so that I could look up at his face. I guessed he thought both of us—Jesse and I, I mean—were fools. But maybe not. I don't know. Maybe he just made me a little nervous. "I knew America needed to be changed," I said. "And I wanted to start helping to change it. Jesse was into something a lot more private."

"He was just looking for something to take the place of his football coach," Maledon said. "Wanted God to make him run red lines."

"No," I said. "He was serious. He has a spiritual nature." I closed my eyes and, for that few seconds, thought I could feel Maledon staring at me. But when I opened them, he was looking toward the river. "We're different, you and me," I said. "We have to be doing. We have to find meaning in action."

"I don't have to be doing much," Maledon answered. "The sun comes up on you every day but one. There's the meaning you got to make do with."

I sat up and touched his knee. "I need to learn what you know," I told him. "How to live off the road, how to vanish between the white lines, how to emerge under a new name, and how to disappear again."

"There's already too many kids on the road," he said. "Running away from home because their momma and daddy don't like the Jefferson Airplane."

"That should make it easier for a smart woman to get by."

"No. Just gets the cops to swarming."

"You won't let me come with you, then?"

"Oh, yeah," he said. "I'm needing somebody to play the Hangman's daughter."

"So why the warning?"

"I want you to be clear on one thing. This ain't the revolution. It's just a road show."

"Sure," I said, and I showed him my good smile. "But it'll be like boot camp for me."

"After it's over with, you can make of it whatever you want."

Separated by several feet of sand, we slept the night through beside the fire. Maledon rose at dawn, splashed river water on his face, arranged more wood over the morning's few coals, and untied the canoe.

"Where you going?" I asked him. I could feel the puffiness around my eyes. I had dreamed that night of making love to him and watching his face change into mask after mask after mask.

Knee-deep in the Little Red's shallows, he turned to me. "Checking limb lines," he said. "Catfish breakfast."

I stood, tossed my hair back, brushed it twice with my hand. "I'll go with you."

"No. I like doing this by myself." But he didn't move, didn't quit looking at me. "Morning looks good on red hair," he said.

I walked to the river, cupped its water in my hands, and washed the night out of my eyes. Still kneeling, I looked at him again. "I came here last night to make love to you. It's still not too late."

"I know," he said. "And there'll be lawyers in heaven before I get something so fine offered to me again." I watched him slip into the canoe, lift the paddle, and begin to backwater to hold his place. "It's fatherhood weighing on me. I got Jesse to consider."

I almost laughed at him, but managed to restrict my mouth to a smile. "Oh," I said, "he won't mind."

"Probably not," he replied, and he shook his head as if we were discussing someone whose values were completely outlandish. Then he paddled toward the current, stopped, turned the canoe around, and said, "You still willing when the boot camp's over, I'd be right honored."

And this time I did laugh, but easy and warm, I think. "Oh, it's a standing offer," I said, "for Gentleman Sam Maledon."

When Maledon returned, five catfish further away from poverty, but seeming still a little depressed, maybe by his hours of fatherly rectitude, Conrad Villines was on the sandbar with me, waiting. "Van's gone," he said, as Maledon dragged the canoe ashore.

Maledon stopped dead, stared at Villines, then, hard and for a long time, at me. "Another verse from Jimmy Song," he said finally.

Villines nodded. "He's gone anyway."

"Shit." Maledon kicked the canoe. "Hippies," he added. And then in a high, mocking voice—"The van belongs to him who drives it." He gave me the hard look again. I know he thought I'd played the whore that night just to divert his attention from Jimmy. "Another deal going down in Mexico?"

"I don't know. I didn't know he'd do this."

"Little two-bit thief."

"Getting moral in your middle age, aren't you?" Villines asked.

Maledon shook his head, then, for Villines, showed a slanting grin. "Always been moral," he said. "That's why I'm poor."

A few minutes later, in the cabin, I tried to assure them that it would be all right, that Jimmy had probably only driven into Little Rock to tie up some loose ends before we left.

"A doper in an army truck," Maledon worried. "It ain't going to take Sam Spade to spot him."

I tried to reassure him—"Jimmy has his own moves."

"I was afraid of that." Then he turned to Jesse, who was at the table eating a bowl of Villines's homemade cottage cheese. He looked better rested than any of us. "How about you, Son? Get proper guidance last night?"

"I'll be with you as far as Hannibal," he answered. "I need to see the show again before I decide about the rest of the summer."

"Fair enough. Now let's hope we don't have to get up there by poling barge."

10 MALEDON

We sat around then, letting the day drag by, wasting it with waiting. Aura chased Conrad's chickens back and forth across the yard, stopping now and then to demand that somebody take her to the store for candy and Cokes. Nobody did. Villines sat on the porch reading *The Confessions of Nat Turner*. Gloria sunbathed with *The Wretched*. Jesse returned to the mountain. I brooded till about noon, thought about just going on and getting good and drunk, but then I got up, borrowed Villines's car, and drove it the five miles to the nearest gas station. I changed a couple of dollars into dimes and started making phone calls: Jacob Stein at Mo's Pawn; Bobby Don Pence at the Riverside Warehouse; Troy Purifoy in El Dorado; George Pickett at the Cotton Belt Hotel down in Camden; Colonel John Norman Bannock, who was running the Wallace campaign in Arkansas; and Brazos O'Flaherty, the man in charge of setting up most of the Mark Twain celebration in Hannibal.

It all gave me a sense of being back in control of things again. I didn't doubt that Jimmy Song had fouled things some, but I figured I could plan around him, could hope even that he'd gone far enough or got locked up tight enough that tomorrow we could roll off without him. Whatever he meant to Gloria, I didn't think it was enough to keep her from skipping with us. And I wanted her in my troupe, thought that'd help keep Jesse riding.

When I'd done what I could, plotting and calling, I drove into Searcy, picked up a waitress I knew that worked in a café that closed at two o'clock, took her home, and laid with her till suppertime. She wasn't Gloria, but she wasn't bad.

By the time I got back to Conrad's they were all sitting around the table talking to Alvy Wolfe, who for the last twenty years had been running a photography and print shop in West Memphis. He'd arrived in a gunmetal-blue 1966 Dodge van that was towing a Volkswagen beetle.

Alvy, in middle age, was a dark, ball-bellied man who drank Old Crow straight from the quart. If you wanted pictures of a wedding, he was a right fair hand. And if you wanted some papers done up quick and right and on the sly, he was the best there was. He'd learned what there was to learn from the Big War.

When I walked in, he gave me a nod, knocked back a swallow of the bourbon, and offered the bottle to Villines, who shook his head.

"He's trying to become a reformed drunk," I told Alvy.

"Pardon my generosity," Alvy said. "Me, I just drink on the holy days."

"Wouldn't work for me," Villines told him. "I'd be drinking on Pontius Pilate's birthday."

"Why, hell," Alvy said. "There's one I been leaving out."

Me and Alvy spent the next hour or so telling stories, each having less connection to truth than the one before. Alvy wound up the session by saying he'd been the very man who'd found Hitler's body in the bunker. "He was laying there with Eva, wearing all the medals he gave himself and looking like any other damned overdressed German fool. I took some snapshots of him and then ripped off the medals and stuck them in my pocket and commenced to hum 'The Ride of the Valkyries.' I was going through his pockets—not a reichsmark one—when a pair of English intelligence assholes came up behind me and wanted to know what I was doing. 'Little Dolph, his very self,' I told them. 'Stinking broke.' They bent over him and had themselves a good look. Then one of them straightened up and, in his Cambridge voice, said, 'Now he belongs to history.' I saw what was coming, so I got my pliers out quick. 'History ain't got no use for these two gold molars,' I explained, and set to work. 'Yanks,' said one of the Englishmen, his voice full of imperial scorn.

"Never went anywhere without those pliers back then, did you?" I said.

"Paid off handsome. Sold the pictures to *Life* and the gold teeth to Joe Stalin and the medals to the Grand High Imperial Wizard of the Tennessee Klan and used the proceeds to set up shop there in West Memphis."

"Sold out awful cheap," I said.

"Not a bit of it. All I ever wanted was my own darkroom and a quart of Crow on the holy days."

Gloria Alice Dawn lit a joint and offered it to Jesse, who declined, stood, and said, "I'll go check on Aura."

"I imagine she's fine," I told him. "Probably out back rocking the chickens."

Jesse went out the back door.

Alvy watched him until he was gone, then turned to me. "Boy's not like you much, is he?"

"Got principles."

"A shame," he said. "Nice looking kid." He handed me the bottle. "So you're fixing to take the Hangman on the road again?"

"Spring's here. Blood's running high." I took a drink, wiped my mouth. "Folks'll be hankering for moral uplift."

"I've decided to play Belle Starr," Gloria announced.

"Belle Starr was ugly," I told her. "And she never got hung."

"Who then?" she asked. "The Hangman's daughter? Why her? Belle Starr may've been the first truly liberated American woman."

"Liberation ain't what the crowds want," I said.

Villines added, "And Belle Starr was just a whore with saddle sores."

"Well, what do the crowds want?" Gloria asked me.

"The good girl gone wrong. The lawman's daughter laying down with layabouts. They want to see the best-raised, best-looking girl in Fort Smith turn into a sneak thief's, swill drunk's, night rustler's moll. They want to see her change from the Hangman's proud beauty to the Friday-night special at Rosetta Hegel's Riverfront whorehouse." I took another drink. "It makes them feel better about their own spawn."

"Ol' Sam Maledon," Alvy said. "Always giving them a little wedge out of the American heart."

Gloria laughed then, easy and confident. "I can play her." She stood up and swept her arms out. "Welcome, ladies and gentlemen, to the Saturday-afternoon Western at the People's Revolutionary Theater."

"A losing proposition," I said. "Revolutionaries don't pay their way in."

The back door swung open. Jesse came in with Aura.

"That big rooster's mean," Aura said.

"It won't play without somebody to hang," Alvy remarked.

"He bit me," Aura told us.

"Pecked," Gloria corrected.

"Hell, there's always a line at the gallows," I reminded Alvy.

"You shouldn't throw rocks at them," Jesse, kneeling, told Aura.

"Can you play a killer?" Gloria asked Jesse.

I looked at Jesse kneeling there, gently rubbing the red peck mark on Aura's right thigh. I said, "He's going to play Saint Francis of Wetumka."

Then Gloria went on for a few minutes, telling us how she would play Annie Maledon—what she would wear, what she would say to her father, the meticulous Hangman, in a confrontation after her rebellion, how she could make a statement about the condition of women in the 1890s and how she could make that statement relevant to the 1960s.

"She was just another whore," I said when she was winding down.

"A special whore."

"Yeah," I said. "That costs a man a little extra."

Alvy took the quart from me, awarded himself another drink, set the bottle on the floor, then stood and said, "Have to use my batteries, I reckon. No problem whatsoever. I'll get the rig."

I walked with him out to the van, and we came back carrying batteries, lights, and tripod camera. While Alvy set things up, I argued mildly with Jesse, who couldn't see any good reason to have his picture taken by a drunk.

"Humor your ol' derelict daddy," I said. "Alvy takes a nice picture. I want one for my wallet. And you don't want to insult the man that sent us Uncle John's lighter."

"I know what you're doing, and I don't need it. I'll go with you as far as Hannibal. But I'll go under my own name."

I gave him a shrug and a pair of upturned palms. "Well, when we get the cards, you can throw yours away. You keep making these little stands, you'll be too tuckered to buck up for the big show."

"The little stands are preparation," he said. "Bravery is an acquired trait." But then he offered the beginning of a smile, mimicked my shrug, walked across the room, and stood, facing the light, back against the wall, to be the first of us Alvy photographed that night.

Gloria went next, then me, then Conrad.

"Might as well get Aura too," I said to Gloria. "You never know."

When he had finished with the child, Alvy took his paraphernalia apart, and I helped him carry it all back outside, put it in the Dodge van, and release the tow bar.

A new Buick was parked about halfway up the lane. Spoof Lyons was sitting in it. I went inside and told the others it'd be smart to slip on down to the river.

"Spoof Lyons?" Jesse asked.

"Sure," I said. "Just reminding us he's around."

"I'll talk to him."

"This one's mine, Son. You show your face now, you make me out a liar. Anyway, I been playing jump tag with Spoof since before you was born. It was Cantwell himself, it'd be different."

He let me have the point. I left the house, got in the van with Alvy, and rode down the lane. "Mail the stuff to the address in El Dorado," I said.

"Done." And then, "All this ain't much like you, Sam."

"He's my son," I said. "The government's already took my brother."

He guided us around a stretch of high center. "Still," he said.

"Fuck it," I told him through a grin. "I been bored."

We were drawing up close to Spoof. I turned on the radio. Hank Snow was singing "I'm Movin' On." I said, "Take a left at the road and keep bearing left. I'll meet you under the bridge first chance I get."

"This bad trouble."

"Not yet. But it's a sign."

I got out of the van, watched Alvy drive on, then walked across the lane to Spoof's burgundy Riviera.

Slumped in his seat, head on his chest, Stetson over his eyes, Spoof was taking in the radio news. George Wallace was coming to Little Rock. Richard Nixon had a secret plan.

"Well now, Sam," he said, lifting his head and pushing his hat back. "Imagine running into you way out here."

"Couldn't help noticing you, propped up so proud and all in a big ol' purple Buick. Out for a drive?"

"Oh yeah. Spring and such. Thought I'd pull over and sit a spell, listen to the little birdies sing and watch the rest of the trees bud out. Don't do enough of that sort of thing this day and age, most of us." He raised a pint of Four Roses. "Care for a swaller?"

"Gave it up."

"Now there's some news. I'll pass it on to the home folks. They liable to hold a parade." He unscrewed the cap, stood himself to a drink.

"Birds've closed up the melody shop for the evening," I said. "And the light's commenced dimming on the trees, ain't it?"

On the radio, Orval Faubus threatened a comeback.

Spoof nodded at the dial. "All news, that station. Can't stand the music nowadays. Jack too much juice into it. Even in Nashville." He took another drink, screwed the cap back on the bottle. "I've commenced thinking you been right all along, Sam. The bastards is going to fuck things up thorough."

"Don't mean you have to help them."

"Man might as well be drinking whiskey in a Buick when they blow it away."

"You're going down awful cheap."

"I satisfy easy."

"Give up the whiskey and the car, and you're a free man."

"Who wants that."

The radio said a tornado had laid waste to a strip of Kansas. Spoof reached over and turned it off. "Hand of God," he said. Then he leaned back, stretched, took a Marlboro out of his shirt pocket, and lit it. "Got another question for you, Sam."

"Figured you'd be getting there. Wasn't right sure it'd be a question, though."

"Ever meet up with a fellow called himself Jimmy Song? Long-haired, spindly fuck given to the unauthorized use of drugs?"

"Jimmy Song." I said the name slow, letting it linger in the air. "Odd name. Seems like a man'd remember it."

"Gone now. Little Rock PD found him in Room 412 of the Hotel Marion. Caught it from a .38 special right behind the left ear."

I looked straight at him, deadpanning it. "Drug deal?"

"Be my guess. Could be some scraggly headed politics tied up in it too. Cops'd been after poor ol' Jimmy awhile. Think he might've knew something about a branch bank blowing up out in Palo Alto. Marijuana revolutionary."

"Better off dead, sounds like."

"Can't say about him, but it was likely a favor to the rest of us."

"Got a suspect?"

"They're looking for a woman might could tell them something. Tall, young, reddish-blond hair. Nigger stool out at Granite Mountain claims he bought himself a pocketful of black beauties couple of days ago from a pair looking a lot like Jimmy Song and this reddish-blond piece. Nigger says they sold it out the side of a flowered-up truck. They's cruising around the projects doing business like a ice-cream vendor." He gave his head a slow, what-the-hell-are-we-coming-to shake, reopened the Four Roses, took another drink. "Sure you won't have none?"

"Worried about my liver."

He held the bottle up, stared at it a second, clicked his tongue, and jerked his head approvingly. "I figure this here's what they drink in heaven," he said. "That'd account for the tornadoes."

He turned the radio back on. Richard Nixon promised to reestablish law and order.

"Well, Sam," jutting his jaw and scratching his chin, "you and me both know ain't none of them Little Rock shoes ever going to be mistook for Dick Tracy, but sooner or later they apt to connect all this up to Jesse."

"Be just like them," I said. "Though they'd have to make up the connections."

"They ain't much used to seeing past what's right in front of them." He tipped his hat back, leaned forward, started the Riviera, then looked back up, his eyes hard on mine. "I'm more than a little tempted to just go into that building yonder and fetch Jesse. But I figure you got him holed up scarce. And I'd just as soon it don't come to a showdown between you and me any sooner than it has to." He puffed on the Marlboro, grimaced, threw it out the window. "I bet I had seventy-five of them sonsabitches today. Only time I ain't smoking, I'm chewing, and now my gums is going on me."

"Ought to quit it all."

"Can't. It's how I tell time."

He pulled the automatic gearshift down a notch, into reverse. "You need more money, holler. I'm around. But you better not fuck up."

He backed the car a few feet, stopped it, poked his head out the window, hat and all. I took a couple of short steps toward him. "I was you, Sam, and knew where that reddish blond was—might be that Gloria Alice Dawn I mentioned to you the other day, you reckon?—I'd hang her out on somebody else's line."

"I run into her, I will."

"And you might be figuring a quick way for Jesse to come in clear. Weather's getting way too foul out here for your ordinary pacifist."

Then he grinned, started rolling backward, and flashed me the peace sign.

11 JESSE

I will go because I am yet American, because I cannot yet resist curiosity, because I have not yet divorced myself from ephemera. Movement lures me, and the urge to bear witness to a death and a resurrection, an historical swerve, a political upheaval. Though I know nothing will die, nothing will be reborn, nothing will change except fashion. People will continue to work too hard for too little, will continue to die without having learned to see or to care. But I cannot resist the spectacle. I am still the creature of an age of journalism—image, voice-over, conclusion, next image—an age without depth. This will be the revolution designed for journalism. Dinnertime, news-hour diversion. Movement without change. Fire without heat. Answers without questions. The quick cut, the glib quip. The revolution of the bored. "Revolution for the hell of it." Revolution as an excuse for a parade. Revolution as sexual foreplay. And it will end, finally, as a psychedelic cartoon, interrupted periodically for commercials.

But I must see it. The urge to witness: strength or frailty?

When it is over, I will be done. I will give myself to the discipline. I will become the discipline.

Saint Augustine: "Make me chaste and continent, but not just yet."

I pray: Give me the courage to stand still, but not just yet.

I can say, "My will has failed me." But it has not. Perhaps I have failed my will. Perhaps there is no failure. Perhaps this is but part of the process of the will's development. Perhaps I have been too conscious of will, too analytical. Perhaps will and world must become one—interwoven, inseparable, unconscious, one and eternal.

Who knows?

To look at the world, say "who knows," and smile. There it is. There, in the smile that has become part of the mystery.

I must find a way, my father, to that smile. For the moment, I will allow you to choose the road. Two weeks? A month? A summer? And then I will begin to become myself.

But now it is the road. Your road. I follow.

12 GLORIA

They have murdered Jimmy. And they will pay. The motherfuckers will pay.

PART II

1 MALEDON

It was Easter.

Israel and Jordan, honoring their respective Gods, shelled each other across a truce line. Berlin students, radical and having a hell of a time, spent their fourth day throwing rocks and setting fires in remembrance of Rudi Dutschke, shot by an assassin. Hubert Humphrey waited in Florida for ol' Lyndon to call and offer him the party machinery. Dean Rusk, secretary of state, turned down Hanoi's proposal that Warsaw be chosen as the place to hold the peace conference. Them Commie bastards was apt to bug the joint, and he damn sure didn't want word getting out. Ol' Lyndon, the man with the word to give, ate barbecue at his ranch, listened to records of Franklin D. Roosevelt's World War II speeches, and, come evening, got drunk with Sam Houston while a valet packed the presidential bags for Hawaii, where, next day, Lyndon would confer with the Korean populist Park Chung Hee. Bob Goalby won the Masters in Augusta because Roberto de Vincenzo marked his scorecard wrong. Timothy Leary, the former Harvard psychology professor facing a marijuana rap, was ordered by a Houston federal judge to take some psychiatric tests. In Pella, Iowa, Lorin Oxley, school-bus driver, was fired for refusing to drive his bus with the flag at half-mast in honor of Martin Luther King. O.D. Wilson, forty, father of six, black, who earned a dollar sixty-five an hour collecting Memphis garbage and had been on strike sixty-two days, looked down at the sidewalk, found a negotiable cashier's check for eight thousand four hundred and twenty-one dollars, and returned it to its owner, Howell Mallory, a white man, who gave him a fourteen-dollar reward. But in spite of everything, the news from the war was good. Our marines had captured Hill 881 North.

And in Montgomery, Alabama, Governor Lurleen Wallace, after six weeks' recuperating from a futile cancer operation, left Saint Margaret's Hospital and returned to her husband, who had more important things on his mind than a dying wife. Hell, he was headed for Little Rock.

So was I.

But first I had a false trail to leave.

At midnight, as the Western Hemisphere began to turn to face the day of its savior, I had driven Alvy Wolfe's Volkswagen and three passengers across fifteen acres of Conrad's pasture, guided it and them down a washed-out logging road through a mile of steep hillside woods, come out on a gravel bar at river's edge, switched off the lights, followed the narrow bar south two hundred yards until I was under the plank-and-beam bridge over Baptist Ford, where I found Alvy sleeping in the van. I left the Volkswagen, went to the van, tapped on the driver's window.

"Took your time," Alvy said, waking.

"Got to make it look good."

"Think Lyons's still on the stake?"

"Will be till he gets a better offer."

He opened his door, stepped out onto the gravel.

He was shaded by the bridge from even the moon, so I couldn't see his face clear, but I sensed something there wanting out, a question, a warning, and I wanted him to ease his mind by finding the words for it.

"You get tired of the dog races and the river bums," I said, "come join us. You know where we'll be."

"I'll have a man drive the papers down," he said. "Buddy Rounds, Route 3, El Dorado."

"I'll be there waiting for them."

He laid a friendly hand on my right shoulder. "Watch your ass, ol' Sam. Civilization's buckling up."

Nodding, I gave him a short laugh. "Hell, Alvy, ain't nobody likes a good joke better than me."

Nobody liked the road better, either. I wasn't sure about my company this trip, though. As we headed toward Little Rock, I asked myself again if it wouldn't be better, easier, cleaner for all of us if I'd just cut Jesse and Gloria loose. Jesse had his damned principles, and if he rode long with me he'd get to watch me violate every one of them. Gloria, sitting on a pad in the back of the van, a child's head on her thigh, was brooding over police brutality, official murder, and trying to line out some kind of revolutionary revenge. I'd told her what Spoof'd told me about Jimmy's killing because, first of all, she had a right to know, but, more especially, because I'd hoped it might prompt her to break free of us, set her off on her own. I'd told her too that she ought to take a lesson from it: Jimmy hadn't died because he was selling dope; he'd died because he'd been stupid—and when you're living on the free side of the line and you're dumber than the boys they send out to get you, you're doomed. But the only response I got from her was outrage, that fearful combination of innocence and social zeal.

In the seat beside me, Jesse, the reason I was traveling with a crew less than hale, the reason I'd finally put up with Gloria and her barricade dreams, sat ramrod straight, silent, stoic, seeming neither bored nor interested, a passenger absorbed in something other than the passage, a mystic meditating movement away, a man-child adrift in the realm of the impossible. So I sang railroad songs and hobo ditties and filled the spaces between songs with stories.

"That was one ol' Jacob Ladders particularly liked. Before he lost his mind," I told Jesse after singing "Didn't He Ramble?" "I ever tell you about Dr. Ladders?"

"Yes," Jesse answered, moving nothing but his lips.

And, ignoring that absolute lack of interest, I proceeded to tell about the time—Valentine's Day 1942, Palestine, Texas—Dr. Ladders passed himself off as Henry Wallace, vice-president of the United States, arranged to make a patriotic speech in Palestine's largest hall, the First Baptist Church, where his oratory inspired the good citizens to put one thousand four hundred twenty-six dollars and eighty-nine cents in the galvanized Remember Pearl Harbor bucket me and Magdalen Abbey passed along the pews as the church organist played "God Bless America."

"When he was right," I said, "there wasn't a soul on earth could match him."

Silence. I started looking for my next song.

Then—"A thief," Jesse said. Matter of fact.

"Yeah, Lord," I agreed, laughing. "But you can't forget style, Son. That's what made him what he was. That's where character is. Hell, when he straightened up and got serious, he had to kill himself."

"A thief," said Jesse, judgment unmoved.

I glanced over at him. Youth and idealism. The rejection of all that moves and changes. The yearning for simplicity and order. Peace.

Death. I said, "They hadn't dropped that money in our bucket, come Sunday they'd've put it in the preacher's plate."

He looked at me that time, then said, "They did both. They were robbed twice."

"Comes from believing," I told him.

He turned back to the road ahead, his face set and solemn. He wouldn't've been surprised, I think, to see the Buddha beside the road. Their eyes might've met briefly in acknowledgment, one pilgrim to another on the changeless way, then they might've gone on, each a part of his own order, serene and separate, missing everything.

I started singing "Jay Gould's Daughter"—

Jay Gould's daughter said before she died,
"Papa, fix the blinds so the bums can't ride.
If ride they must, they got to ride the rod.
Let 'em put their trust in the hands of God.
In the hands of God,
In the hands of God."

We rode 167 into North Little Rock, cut east over to Main Street, and followed it until, a block short of the old Arkansas River Bridge, I turned down a narrow, dimly lit street, Barge Road, a mile-long boundary between begrimed brick minimum-wage mills and the moonlit mephitic river.

Near the end of Barge, I turned onto a parking lot, drove across it, and stopped the van beneath a sign that read PERSINGER'S WAREHOUSE—VEHICLE ENTRY.

"I'll get the door. You drive her in," I said to Jesse.

Jesse showed me a censor's face.

"It's on the up-and-up, Son. These folks're getting the best end of it." I left the van, slipped my lock pick into the garage door, pressed a button, and watched the door rise. Jesse drove into the opening.

Cars and trucks were parked along both the long inside walls. I guided Jesse toward a space at the far end, on the right. "We'll be taking that hearse yonder," I said when he'd parked the van.

Jesse and Gloria managed to carry Aura from the van to the hearse without waking her, and we left the warehouse through the door opposite the one we'd entered. After locking the door behind us, I drove across railroad tracks, down a gravel lane, up an alley, and onto a back street, which I followed back to Main and the bridge to Little Rock.

All of it had brought Gloria Alice Dawn down out of her retributive schemes—for the moment, anyway. "A hearse," she said, excitement in her voice. "Man, we're rolling now."

"Needs a valve job," I said. "But it ought to get us where we're going."

"Who does it belong to?" Jesse asked.

"Papers say Hugh Harp. An ol' dead friend of mine."

"How'd you work that?" Gloria wondered.

"Papers're easy. Ain't much more to it than typing them up." I glanced back and gave her a grin. "You tell me who you want to be, woman. I'll get you certified."

2 JESSE

My father guides us through the night, his element. In Little Rock he finds an alley off Capitol, parks the hearse at the rear of Mo's Pawn Shop, fits his pick into a series of locks, and enters. Less than a minute passes, and he is in the alley again, clicking the locks to, a battered, roped-together suitcase on either side of him.

Careful not to awaken Aura, he sets the suitcases in the back of the hearse, returns to the driver's seat, starts the engine.

"Damned ol' Jew," he says as we back away. "Believes in locks the way a Communist believes in torture. Was all I could do to keep him from bolting it from the inside."

Gloria leans forward, rests her forearms and chin on the back of our seat. "You could've gotten in anyway," she says. She is infatuated with my father, his burglar's skills, his hobo's habits. He is a man who might steal from her own father and get away with it. She admires him for that. The daughter of wealth.

"Yeah. That's how I convinced him to make it easy on me. That and the off chance I might've had to do some damage to his door."

My father doesn't like Gloria—idealism is anathema to him, and hers, in his eyes, is more dangerous than mine, if not as foolish—but she is young, beautiful, exudes sex, and wants him. Though he would not admit it, he is flattered: He strikes poses, brags. Soon I think she will have him. Temporarily. But that is all she wants. And all he will allow. But perhaps, at his age, he will be left with a wound that will cause him to limp farther away from the rest of us.

Limp? Does my father limp? And is his way of living merely the method by which he deals with a handicap? Or is he simply stronger and smarter than we are? Is this the ultimate strength, this rejection of any order transcending one's own horizon?

"Wasn't there a burglar alarm?" Gloria asks.

"Yeah, but it don't go off. He rigs it so it just shoots a little beep up to his apartment. Bad as he hates thieves, he'd rather deal with them straight on than have the cops messing around in his work. I shut it off for him." He turns right on Main. There is no traffic. Ahead of us blinking yellow caution lights mark intersection after intersection.

"The luggage full of counterfeit bills?" I am unable to keep an edge of disgust out of my voice. Am I disgusted with him or with Gloria's attraction to him?

"Why, you remember Mo, do you, Son?" He cocks his head and grins. The buccaneer. "Helluva printer. But this time we just needed posters. Bastard overcharges. But he does it right and quick."

"And you can always find a way to do business with him in the dead of the night," I say.

"Hell, sometimes the darkness serves justice, boy."

Gloria laughs.

I say, "How would you know?"

"Hearsay."

We ride on, leave Little Rock, give ourselves to the highway. You cannot argue with a man who will abandon any principle for a laugh.

3 GLORIA

My father, Jonathan Wilder, who had everything that could be bought and wanted more of it.

My father, Jonathan Wilder, the last male in the line that transformed these thousand acres, this stretch of pine forest, salt flats, and gas deposits, step by step, tree by tree, square foot by square foot, life by life, from wilderness to plantation to corporate headquarters.

My father, Jonathan Wilder, who supported the war because the U.S. government was a client of his.

My father, Jonathan Wilder: the silvered temples, the steel-blue eyes, the gray tailored pin-striped suits, the tasseled Gucci loafers, the silk handkerchief.

My father, Jonathan Wilder: *Esquire* handsome, highway tough, boardroom smart.

My father, Jonathan Wilder: power as style.

My father, Jonathan Wilder: elegant greed.

My father, Jonathan Wilder: the enemy.

Once upon a time, in the land of honeysuckle and hummingbird, when I was young and his, I loved him. Loved him like the prince he seemed to be. Loved his laughter. Loved his dreams.

But I am no longer the homecoming queen, Ouachita River royalty, the beautiful blond bait for the prospective heir. I am the person he warned me against.

Hallie, some member of whose family has kept house and raised children for some member of mine for nearly a century and a half, opened the door of my home to me and my daughter.

"Land, child," she said, "a hearse. What on earth gon' come of this baby?"

I embraced her, kissed her bronze cheek. She returned the embrace, her heavy arms holding hard, and I could feel her affection overcoming her disapproval. They have had so much to forgive that mercy has become habit to them. But your sons and grandsons, Hallie, your daughters and granddaughters, are weary of mercy without reciprocity, weary of being forced to accept the shit end and being called stupid for doing it. There is blood in the streets, Hallie, and fire in the air. And I must go. I must pay my dues. I must make a down payment on three hundred forty-eight years of guilt. The hour has come.

She withdrew her arms, stepped back, examined me. "Even in them rags, child, you a wonder to look at."

Aura pulled at her skirts, saying, "Hallie, Hallie, sing me a song."

"Hallie be singin' here fo' you know it. Be singin' all day. This be the day that save us all." Then she looked back at me. "You breakin' you daddy's heart, girl."

"I may be hurting his pride," I said. "But not his heart. He carries that in his wallet."

"You wouldn't know," a voice said, smooth, clear, condescending—my father. "You're incapable of recognizing anything that isn't tie-dyed."

He was already dressed, sharp-creased, wrinkle-free. Sanforized. Customized. Pasteurized. Mr. Fucking America.

My daughter ran to him.

"She'll be here awhile," I said.

"Leave her until she's grown," he replied. "Might be your first act of real motherhood."

I started to say something, but Hallie shushed me. "You all one blood, now. Quit that quarreling." She turned to my father. "You keep fussing at her, Mr. Jonathan, she be gone just like that. I go fix Miss Gloria a bite of something, and y'all set down around the table and talk like Christian kin. Scripture's all the time warning about this kind of carrying on. And this *is* Easter."

We did what she said, followed her to the dining room and sat on hundred-year-old walnut chairs at a hundred-year-old walnut table. Built by a former slave named Nazareth Wilder in honor of his freedom. Traded to my father's great-grandfather for a buckboard to ride north in. Three years later, 1871, he came back with nothing and sharecropped his life away. A bad history, ours. I know the stories.

Hallie brought us coffee, juice, said she was making us omelets. Aura took a piece of Hallie's chocolate cake onto the back patio and started playing with Springer—Archibald Yell Springer, the family golden retriever. My father turned the lights on for her.

When he returned to the table, I was sipping my coffee. He sat down and said, "The police were here."

I set my cup in its saucer, looked through the glass doors at my daughter and the champion dog, looked back. "They murdered Jimmy."

"He was pushing dope. They caught him at it. He started shooting." He took a pack of Viceroys from his inside jacket pocket, pulled a cigarette from the pack, and lit it. "I thought he was better than the other little small-time cheese-heads you've so consistently humiliated us with, but I was wrong. It was wishful thinking. He was using me. And he was using you so he could use me." He held the cigarette, between thumb and forefinger, a foot in front of his face and seemed briefly absorbed by the burning tip. Then his eyes followed the smoke as it rose and drifted to his right. "A two-bit street hustler. A punk." The eyes jerked back to me, vehement, but the voice remained boardroom calm. "A loser, an idiot. Died over a hundred-dollar deal."

"They murdered him." I used the same cold tone he had chosen. "He was different, so they murdered him."

He sipped his coffee and arched one confident eyebrow. "Have it your way." A shrug. "He's dead. His life meant nothing."

I leaned forward, jutted my face toward him. "It meant something to me," I said. "And I'm going to make his death matter."

"It'll be a battle cry, right? 'Remember Jimmy Song.' " Sarcasm and disdain. The corporate sneer.

He took another hit of the Viceroy, then stubbed it out in a crystal ashtray.

Hallie brought us Spanish omelets, English muffins, bacon, orange juice. "You know," she said, serving from the tray, "standin' over that stove, it come to me how it was twelve years ago this mornin' Miss Gloria been baptized. Brother Bayshore done it."

"It didn't take," my father said, buttering a muffin. "Just another of her ways of getting attention." He took a bite of the muffin, set it down, pushed the plate away from him, sipped his coffee, lit another cigarette.

I ate a bite of my omelet, told Hallie it was perfect—it was.

"Ain't nobody here eats right no more," she said. "Mr. Jonathan, he grab whatever's handy, take a bite, put it down. Your momma, she'd turn her nose up at ambrosia."

"Dawn," my father said. "New sun on red-gold hair. A white sheet. A spring river. The hand of God on her forehead. The beautiful girl at the center of the ceremony. That's all it was, Hallie. There's never been more to her than surface beauty, superficial laughter, ingenue charm. Put her at the center of something, give her an audience, and she could smile and toss her head and let the tears roll down, and, oh, it'd make you proud and high and, finally, just break your heart." He shook his head once, took another hit of Viceroy. "Sunrise service salvation, homecoming queen, sorority sweetheart, and none of it anything but a way of getting on stage."

"You hush, now, Mr. Jonathan. You be sorry when she gone."

"I'm sorry now. She's gone already. We've lost her. We spoiled her, and now we've lost her."

"Folks come back," she said. "Young folks always be growin' up and comin' back. You got to leave her room to keep some pride when she do."

"Pride?" A haughty laugh. "We raised a debutante and wound up with an ersatz Emma Goldman. We gave her too much, made it too easy. We got what we deserved."

I continued to eat my omelet, pausing once or twice to smile, amused at his little game: homecoming humiliation.

"These are idiot times, Hallie. She's not going off to the city to make her fortune. Because—you see, don't you?—making a fortune's work. These kids now, they already have their fortunes. Momma and Daddy did that for them. This will be the first revolution ever financed by the rebel's parents. The Revolution of Ecstasy, an interlude paid for by Mr. and Mrs. Bourgeois Levittown."

The Viceroy again.

"They's things need changin', Mr. Jonathan. The young folks, they be hurryin'. She just like you 'bout wantin' what she wantin'. But you already give her what you was after. She got to find her own. You got to let her."

He pushed his chair back, crossed his legs, folded his hands in his lap. "No, Hallie," he said, "there are things a father can't abide. Gloria doesn't want merely to find her own way; she wants to force the rest of us to reject ours. The things that matter to us—family, home, community, responsibility, career—she doesn't want any of that and doesn't want us to have it, either. No, that's a waste—it's tight-assed WASP shit as far as she's concerned. Gloria, you see, she wants to live; she wants to take drugs and blow things up, to be the lead whore in an SDS charade. She's seen God, you know, Hallie, met him at a rock concert. He was playing lead guitar and pushing acid. Didn't need it himself, of course. He'd gone beyond that. But taking it is the first step toward discipleship."

He brought the Viceroy to his mouth again, inhaled. "You see, don't you, Hallie?" Smoke came out with the words.

"You all crazy. I see that. I see you ain't gon' give one another room to be one another in. Mule-headed, both of you." She untied her apron, took it off, folded it. "You lose yo' family, Mr. Jonathan, bad times is all they is." She glared at him. The eyes of judgment. In an odd way, she was free: Lear's fool.

I forked up the last of my omelet.

"Eats like a field hand," my father said. "Table manners are bourgeois."

"Ain't nothin' here she can spoil by dribblin' egg," Hallie said. She turned to me. "But you have got awful high and mighty." Her eyes narrowed. "You ought to stay, till you finds something useful to be doin' anyhow. That girl needs a momma." She turned, started away, said, "Put them plates in the washer. I got my own service to go to." And left us.

My father carried his plate to the glass doors, opened them, whistled, fed the omelet to Springer.

A moment later, putting his plate in the washer rack, he said, "I told them you were here Friday night and Saturday morning. That you knew Jimmy, but nothing about his activities Friday night." He slid the washer door to. "That's the last favor you get from me. You'll have to earn the next one."

"I didn't need that one."

"Old habit," he said. "Looking out for my damn-fool daughter."

"Well, break it."

"I plan to. I have."

We stared at each other. Silence. History. Resentment. Change.

"You've eaten," he said. "I guess you'll be on your way. I'd wish you luck, but that'd be bad for the country. And you, for that matter."

I stood, stacked knife, fork, spoon, cup, and saucer on my empty plate, looked at him again. "I'd like to see Mother."

"She doesn't need that. It upsets her."

"You've made an invalid of her." My mother was the kind of southern lady who frequently retreated to bed, sometimes under prescribed sedation, sometimes simply drunk. Beautiful and empty. The magnolias are dying.

My father cocked his head and one eyebrow. Sardonic. "She heard you drive up. If she wants to see you, she knows she just has to walk down the stairs."

"It's her choice. I won't force myself. But would you tell her I'd like to see her. I don't know when I'll be back."

With a head and hand gesture he indicated an indifferent willingness, then walked from the room. I went out the glass doors and onto the patio, called Aura to me. She was just beyond the light, chasing Springer with a badminton racket. When she came, I hugged her. "I have to go," I said. "I'll come back for you."

"Why can't you stay, too?"

"I have to do things," I explained. "I have to try to help make the world better for you when you grow up."

The truth. But an excuse to her. I know. A dodge. A way out of her life. Like—"Mommy has to work so you can have nice things. I do it because I love you." I cannot expect her to understand now. The cause is more important than she or I. What could motherhood mean in a dead world?

"It's nice here," Aura said.

"Yes," I said. "You'll be fine here for a while. Be good." I hugged her again, stood, sent her back to the dog. Springer had the badminton bird in his mouth, teasing. She retrieved her racket and resumed chasing him. I watched, tears in my eyes. We must rid ourselves of sentimentality.

My father was waiting in the dining room. "No," he said. "She says she can't bear to see you leave us again. Not like this. Go or stay. But don't linger."

"All right." I nodded. Memory welded our gazes for a last long second. Then I turned, breaking the tie, and walked quickly from the room and toward the front door.

To my back he said, "Remember Jimmy Song."

4 MALEDON

I spent the next couple of days rambling here and there in the hearse—Magnolia, El Dorado, Texarkana, Prescott, Delight, Fordyce, Arkadelphia, Stamps, and Hope—pasting up posters and taking out ads, making it look like I was setting up a series of rodeo-arena and fairground shows in southeast Arkansas. I figured any little local hullabaloo I could stir up would be sure to get Spoof Lyons's attention. As to whether that would divert him long, I had my doubts. Spoof was a drunk, a glutton, and a bigot, but he had a keen nose for the main scent—one of those cops that had spent his working life neck-deep in bullshit and knew it, never letting it confuse him. He saw himself as a bit player in a big joke, but he took the joke serious. That way the laughing was real.

Anyway, I had him sized as the kind that could've done Jesse in in about five minutes, could've had Jesse doing out of spite just what he wanted him to. So I did my work, work that would drop a final curtain on my shows in south Arkansas—you advertise that many shows and skip out on all of them, ain't many folks going to trust you again. But I had a son to set free, and if you have to cross a piece of the map out of the rest of your life, south Arkansas isn't a bad place to start.

Late Tuesday afternoon, I drove south on 7 down past Wilder Junction, named for and by one of Gloria's ancestors, and just north of Louann I went right on a county road and, half a mile later, pulled up beside Colonel John Norman Bannock's rusting TravelAire trailer. The back end of the trailer rested on two bald, flat tires. Cinder blocks held up the front. By the front door an old, faded American flag hung limp from a cane pole. The flag didn't have but forty-eight stars on it. I knew that because I'd known John Norman—and that flag—for a long time—oh, twelve, fifteen years, I guess. He didn't think Alaska and Hawaii should've been admitted to the Union.

I knocked, and an old black man came to the door. "Leavin'," he said. I stepped aside, let him pass, and watched him hobble across the hardscrabble yard.

"Well, Sam," came a voice from the trailer. I was still watching the old black man, who turned down the dirt road and started, patient on ancient legs, toward what I guess he'd have to call home. I could use him in the show.

I turned back, and John Norman was in the door. "Ought to give that man a ride," I said.

"George?" The idea of it started to curl up the right corner of his mouth. "Hell, he's eighty-five, Sam. Walked everywhere he's ever been. Going to walk up to Saint Peter at the Judgment, and Peter be saying, 'You get out of line much, George?' And George'll shuffle once and answer, 'Naw suh, Massa Peter, I been a good nigger. Knowed my place.' And then Peter, he'll say, 'Well, you just come on in, then, George. We needing us a hand in the harp factory.' "

John Norman was dressed like he had been every time I'd ever seen him: baggy, wrinkled, stain-spotted white pants and jacket, cornflower-blue shirt, white bow tie, and white suspenders. "Like the South," I'd heard him say. "Faded elegance. We get us a proper government, I'll get me a new suit of clothes."

He leaned over, spit a dip of snuff into the yard, straightened, ran the tip of an index finger across his lower incisors, and invited me in.

It wasn't much of a home—or office, either. Especially considering that he came from slaveholding stock, plantation blood. No more than a couple of hundred yards up the road stood the old Bannock mansion. Pillars and porticoes. Magnolia and mint julep. But about the time John Norman graduated from the Harvard Law, his family had run through all their money and most of their land, and his father sold the home to some kind of historical preservation outfit. State or county—I can't remember which. Doesn't matter much. House is no good to nobody no more. Got these old blue-haired ladies wandering around in it dreaming about the pickaninny days.

So John Norman just had the trailer. A narrow bed, a hot plate, a half-sized refrigerator, three straight chairs, a folding card table, a file cabinet, and cheap gray walls covered with snapshots of him posing with various eminent segregationists, Theodore Bilbo to George Wallace.

I reached over to the card table and picked up a framed picture of

Wallace shaking hands with a sharecropper, John Norman in the background.

"Voting for him?"

"Might vote for the sharecropper," I said. "Give the poor bastard a shot at getting even. Otherwise, I'll abstain."

"These're bad times, Sam," he told me. "Country's going to the hopheads. But giving up's not the answer."

"Ain't give up," I said. "Folks giving up are the ones thinking they're solving problems by voting for some damn fool."

"Representative government," he reminded me.

"Never cared to be represented."

"How about a drink?"

"That I'll take."

He opened a file-cabinet drawer, took out a pair of Dixie cups and a fifth of Old Grandad, and poured the cups full. "No ice," he said. "Bad for the system, anyway."

"Here's to the American Independent party," he said, raising his cup. "And to ol' George Corley Wallace, hope of the working man."

I touched my cup to his. "Here's to the working man," I said. "May he see the way out."

We drank a swallow apiece, then sat in straight chairs at opposite sides of the card table. He gave me a curious look and said, "Odd toast, yours, Sam. I'd be interested in knowing what you think is the working man's way out."

"Different for each of them, I reckon."

"Give me an example. I never got over being literal-minded."

"Well, you take the man in the picture yonder"—I jerked a thumb toward the framed sharecropper—"man like that ought to just go burgle the landowner's house, steal his car, and drive off."

"He'd get caught within twenty-four hours."

"Not if he planned it right."

"And you never got over being simpleminded, did you, Sam?"

"No, and hope I never do. Might wind up working the fields for some fat rich fuck."

He shook his head, grinned. "Thank God there ain't many like you."

I shrugged. "Fewer there are, easier it is."

He had another swallow. "So? Been lining up some shows."

"Been looking to."

"Whereabouts in particular? Might send out some campaign volunteers to work the crowd."

"Oh, here and there. Maybe yonder."

"I see," he said.

I sipped at my whiskey. "Came here on the other business," I said. "Thought any more about it?"

" A little. Boys in the national office couldn't see much point in it. Thought it was a little risky too."

"Ain't no risk at all. I can get you a half-dozen hippies and a couple of niggers to come heckle Wallace Sunday at the coliseum. Simple as that."

"Hell, they'll already be picketing, Sam. Be there on their own. We don't need any more."

"Sure you do. Those'll be outside. Be two separate stories in the paper. And remember, them'll be Arkansas hippies and niggers. Way too tame. Not near enough commotion. And even at that you won't be able to afford to let any of them inside. One of them might just be an outsider with a gun. Now me, I can get you a pair of blue-black bucks, about six foot eight, two seventy-five, sneak them in your hall there, have them rear up right on cue, yell something fierce and foul, put the jungle fear in the white folks, and then your man, knowing right when it's coming, can put them down just as quick and smart as you please. I'll rush in then, in cop garb, and drag them out." I showed him my palms. "I got hippies. I got niggers. I got both. Whatever y'all want, however y'all want it. Hundred bucks for each of them. Five hundred for me. Dirt cheap."

He got up, walked a few steps past me and toward the door, stopped, and stared at a photograph of Orval Faubus. "If they got caught and yelled fix, it'd look bad for us."

"They won't know it's rigged. That'll just be me. Won't nobody get shit out of me, John Norman. You know that."

"I don't know," he told the picture. "I'll have to see about it."

I finished my whiskey, walked to the door. "You tell them it'll put your man on the evening news. All three networks. The nation'll get to watch ol' fist face put the niggers down. Priceless publicity."

5 JESSE

Most men spend their lives either in search of or in the grip of a comfortable anesthetic. Sheer routine works a majority of the time for a majority of people. The work done by all but a few Americans is absolutely meaningless except as a tactic for self-diversion, a hedge against chaos. Such work is ritual devoid of any metaphysic, and the attachment to it (hourly, daily, weekly, monthly, yearly, until all else is gone) is an addiction yielding no high. The addiction becomes its own end, the socially acceptable method of whiling the time away. Because we so deeply fear death, we avoid life.

It is Thursday, my fifth full day with this room as my centering place, this fourth-floor room in the Cotton Belt Hotel, Camden, Arkansas. For three days I fasted. Yesterday I broke the fast with raw peanuts and black raisins. Tonight I will eat again. And Friday. Saturday we go to Little Rock, and the ordeal begins. We will disrupt the Wallace rally. I am prepared.

I write this record sometimes when I have finished my exercises and my wanderings. My need for record keeping, for this journal, signifies, I know, imperfection, indicates a lack of faith. To completely be is sufficient, is all. A record of such a state would be absurd, incomprehensible. Pure being is beyond language. Language signifies; life is.

We are too often but arrogant cowards. Compelled by circumstance to face political reality. A man will blame the state, the times, excusing his own lack of commitment, ignoring his own decadent heart. When confronted by dread, by the fear and the trembling, by the apparent emptiness of forever, he will turn to the hollow reassurance of the established church, to the comforting cant of psychotherapy, to the false warmth of the bottle, to the quick rush of a drug, anything to keep from having to begin the fearful task of nourishing his own scurvy soul.

We are the times. Our hope and our dread as a people lie at the center of each man's soul. We must reach inward.

I do these exercises twice daily:

1. Sitting calmly on the floor, spine straight, legs relaxed before me, eyes open but unfocused, I become aware of my body. The awareness moves from feet through legs, through groin, through torso, through arms, hands, and fingers, through neck and into head. When I have properly centered myself, when I have perfectly negated what we call consciousness, I will be aware of my brain as organ. Not as mind, but as organ. Mind and body perfectly one: no dichotomy.
2. I fold my legs beneath me, regulate once again my breathing, and stare, seeing nothing, out the window. I keep open to the fathomless forever.
3. When, hours or moments later, my meditation has ended, I allow my eyes to focus, and I recite some lines from Blake or the *Tao*.

Having concluded these exercises, I will then sit for a time in the chair beside the lamp and read from Ecclesiastes or the Gospel of Saint Mark. Then, often, in apparent contradiction of the *Tao*, I leave my room, walk the streets, and observe the others, the many of whom I am one, as they go about their busyness, as they navigate the maze that fear has superimposed on nature, as they hurry, the narcotized and the frenetic, past everything, as they throw another day at death.

I do not know whether I love them. I do not know whether I should. I do not know.

Christ's example is this: We should live our lives with constant courage, with a joyous soul, with a love both general and particular, excluding no one or no thing, knowing all the while that we face his death.

But I am an apprentice.

6 GLORIA

So Jesse went into one of his monk phases. Fasting, meditating, sitting around in humble silence. Now, don't get me wrong. I admired Jesse, sometimes even thought I loved him. He was strong willed, honest, brave. He faced the hard truths, about himself, about our government, about life in general. He lived in constant recognition of mortality. He gave Caesar nothing, no taxes, no cooperation, would not wear the centurion's cloak. But he underestimated Caesar's power, I think, or maybe overestimated the power of individual purity. Well, both probably. I mean, how much good did the Talmud or the kosher diet do the Jews when Hitler came after them? Orthodox or Reform, devout or lapsed, it didn't matter. It was jackboot time. And it was jackboot time again. No matter how thoroughly Jesse purged himself, no matter how pure a spirit he became, no matter how rigorously he exercised, chanted, and prayed, Caesar would continue to occupy American cities, would continue to napalm Asian babies. So, given the times, Jesse's stance was essentially irrelevant, and (no matter what he said or thought) it was a manifestation of the most extravagant kind of ego.

And, after leaving my family, I needed him. Needed his reassurance, his tenderness. Needed him, yes, to make love to me. No, I won't hide coy and ladylike behind euphemism: I needed him to fuck me. Pity-fuck, mercy-fuck, I didn't care what it would've been for him. I needed his cock. That's all. In my mouth, my cunt, my ass. An hour or two of jungle lust to rid myself of middle-class guilt, to clear the air I breathed of the cloying stench of my father's self-righteous hypocrisy, to make the break complete again. And when he had done that to me, or with me, or for me, when we had ridden our very flesh beyond bourgeois hang-ups, then I would've wanted his tenderness, the gentle, spiritual reassurances, the caresses. Then I would've wanted him to make love to me. I needed to fuck my way back to instinct, then love my way back to reason.

But he gave me nothing.

"They're gone," I said when I entered his room that morning. "I've left them."

He sat full lotus at the center of the room. He said nothing. I walked around to where I could see his face. He was gone, oblivious, flying the astral plane. Anybody else I would've thought was calmly tripping. But not him. He wouldn't touch acid anymore. No, he was just off in this self-willed trance.

I sat on the edge of the bed and waited. A minute? Five? Ten? I don't know. I had no patience. I needed him.

I waited some more, lay back on the bed, stared at the ceiling, sat up again, started talking. "I left her, Jesse. My own daughter. Left her with my father, the war profiteer, and my mother, the closet drunk, the barbiturate junky. Left her in money's nest."

Nothing. The blank eyes.

I sat directly in front of him. "Talk to me, goddamn it. You're my friend. I need you. Say something."

Nothing.

I slapped him. The eyes focused. Brief anger, quickly concealed by the superimposition of stoic tolerance. The ultimate condescension.

"What is it?" he said, hiding irritation, I think. But I'm not sure. He had become an adept at the invisible struggle.

I started to tell him about my father, my daughter, but stopped. Then said, "Why, Jesse? Why this? People need you, and you're retreating. Come back to us."

He stared, nodded once. The mouth wore the smile of blessed assurance, but the eyes were sharply focused, narrowed, analytical. They held only me. The cosmos was on its own.

He said, "Each of us must find his own way. This is mine."

I leaned forward, touched his cheek with my fingertips. "The madness will just go on and on. What you're doing changes nothing."

"And everything."

I brought my fingers back, laid them in my lap. "Paradox," I said. "Fuck that shit, Jesse. They've got the monopoly on that. War is peace. Freedom is salvery. The Phoenix Program. Pacification. The Department of Justice." I looked hard into his eyes, which now seemed amused. "Paradox is propaganda," I said. "The only effective resistance is militant. It's too late for anything else. This spiritualistic pacificism is horseshit. They're napalming nirvana."

He smiled again, gentle, assured, calm. *Fatherly*. "I refuse simply to substitute one political ideology for another," he said. "Our only hope is to begin again. An absolute resurrection of the spirit."

"The new Jerusalem," I said. "Sacred texts and holy wars." I stood, turned, walked toward the window, turned back, leaned against the sill, looked down at him. "Jesus is dead, Jesse. Has been for two thousand years. And Constantine co-opted the faith. It became the dogma of empire. The Buddha's a fat man who says, 'Be still,' while all around him millions starve. The Hindus are absolute fascists. The caste system as religious doctrine. Islam is a mad warrior's dream. No, Jesse, there's nothing beyond what's right out there—a corrupt political order imposed on human mortality—and what's out there needs to be changed so that the few can no longer feed on the many. That's all. Politics. Mortality is a given. Politics can be changed. That's all. Wake up, goddamn it."

Unmoved, he said, "I have nothing to do with your leaving your daughter. Or your father. Face your guilt honestly. Don't attack me."

I stood there before the window and began removing my blouse. "Fuck me, then, Jesse. Can you still do that?"

"I can," he said. "But I won't."

I dropped my blouse to the floor, a slow, teasing, burlesque gesture, then stepped toward him, cupping a tit in each palm. "You always liked them," I said. "Afraid of them now?"

"They're beautiful," he said. "Right now you don't deserve them."

"Look at your crotch, Gandhi. The column hardens. The old agnostic cock, rising only for what's there." With my right hand, I unbuttoned my Levi's, slid the hand beneath them, began fingering. "Come on, Jesse. You like this slutting as much as I do. Fuck me, man. Forget the rest of it. Just fuck me."

He unfolded his legs, stood, came to me, held my face between his palms, kissed me. "No," he said. "Not like this."

And left the room.

So I found someone else.

Maledon was already gone—he must've taken the hearse as soon as I returned it; I didn't see him again until that Friday morning, when we left for Little Rock—or I would've gone to him. Hell, I would've laid a traveling salesman had there been any in the lobby. But there was only the desk clerk, and he was watching Oral Roberts's Easter service on TV. I went to a pay phone and called Bebo Hummel.

I'd gone to high school with him. He was an all-state halfback the year I was homecoming queen, and I'd dated him during football season. We'd petted to climax but had never, as the phrase went, gone all the way. He had this huge, thick cock. Some of the other football players used to call him Horsecock Hummel.

His wife answered the phone. I forget her name—if I ever knew it. I said I was Mary Ann Walker from the office—he'd worked for my father ever since he flunked out of Henderson State—and asked to speak to Mr. Hummel. She put Bebo on, and I started right in, telling him I'd been fantasizing about him through all the years since we'd broken up, saying I'd always regretted refusing him when I'd had the chance to have him and that I wanted to rectify that this morning.

A hesitation. Then—"It's Easter."

"Tell her it's an emergency at the office. Truck wreck in Texarkana or something."

"I don't know," he said. "Why now?"

"It's Easter."

Nothing.

I said, "Just this morning. No strings. Then I'll be gone. Nobody knows. Nobody gets hurt. It's free, Bebo. Absolutely free. And I'm good. Real good."

"All right," he said. Then for the wife—"If I have to, I have to."

"I don't have a car," I told him. "I'll be sitting on the bench on the west side of the courthouse. Then we can drive out to the cabin at Poison Springs. You remember?" He would. We had once been fully naked together there, had almost fucked. But I'd made him settle for fingers and tongues, the way good girls did.

"Yes," he said. Then the aspiring young executive—"How long will this take?"

"Until you've had all you want. And, Bebo, I do everything." I hung up.

There was no one on the streets. Nothing going on. A little Bible Belt town on Easter Sunday, during the morning hours between sunrise service and regular church. A town with nothing to offer except a stage for people trained to be the pawns of preachers and politicians. Even on an empty street, even in the empty square, I could feel the accumulated resentment of a doomed citizenry. These small southern towns are neither pastoral nor picturesque. There is too much barely concealed, indeterminate anger. There have been too many generations of repression. Nobody matures. From out of the darkness, from down the magnolia-lined, verbena-scented path, worn smooth by forefathers and forefathers, gallop the hooded boys, brandishing fire, howling "Nigger! Nigger!"

An entire culture—if you can call it that—founded and maintained by blaming its victims.

Apocalypse looms, motherfuckers. Up against the wall.

I sat on the appointed bench and let my hatred rise and focus. This town, this history, this people. Then I rose and walked away. I no longer needed sublimation. Bebo could masturbate.

7 MALEDON

By the time George Wallace strutted up to the podium that Saturday night in Little Rock, we were ready for him. So I just stood there.

The choir of the Calvary Baptist Church in Pine Bluff was singing the last line of the chorus of "We're Marching to Zion." Wallace joined in for the last phrase, and when it was finished the eighty-six hundred people filling Barton Coliseum rose and roared for him.

And he basked in it, laughing and shaking his head and waving now and then at somebody he recognized, or pretended to. After several minutes of that, he extended his arms, palms down, and motioned for quiet. The roar subsided some, but the crowd kept standing. Leaning into the microphone, Wallace said, "Lordy, ain't that fine? Ain't that just mighty fine?"

And so they gave him another great holler. He let the tide of noise rise and crest and begin to ebb again before he turned to the crowd behind him and said, "One more time, brothers and sisters, one more time." And then, back to the crowd, "Evuhbody this time. Evuhbody sings."

And as they joined in, I let my eyes and mind move from face to face over the crowd. They're passing strange, these crowds, if you stand back and look at them. The way it all becomes one thing. Their need for a banner and a band. Their need for a bully to lead them. Their need to give everything over for a while to a barker's dream of another day. So they're always prime to be fleeced, and sometimes subject to being marched off to the murders, by some son of a bitch with a tune to dance to and a mouthful of promises can't nobody keep.

Oh, it didn't surprise me any. I knew it was there, knew just about how it would be. Hell, I'd made a good part of the cash I'd spent on a living by skimming off the edges of it. And I figured to make a pretty good haul off it that day. But I'm goddamned if I really understand it. The why of it, I mean. And sometimes, like right then, when there were enough of them in one place, when there were thousands of them all letting themselves get caught up in some slickered-down shyster's shined-up shill, well, Lord, it came close to amazing me.

We're marching to Zion,
Beautiful, beautiful Zion . . .

I don't know. It's boredom, I guess, with lives that go slowly round and round, over and over, like a circle getting smaller till it's gone. And fear too, of course, of the question that has no answer. But why? What's at the root of that? You're here and you're alive, and, yeah, the world has its limits, but you have to go some to get to them, and even then you can just take a left and start again. Aw, I know, you get to the edge of it all, the big boys say, and, lo, there's the great darkness—and what's a man to do then? Well, I agree you can't make sense of it, that darkness, but you can shine whatever little light you got down into it, or you can shrug and turn and face the sun, or you can just stand up there on the edge of the bluff and piss down into it and wait to see if you can hear a splash at the bottom. It's not sense that matters finally, anyway, it's laughter. So why turn it all, hope and anger, love and fear and laughter, over to some carpet-game con artist who's never done anything but make up enemies for you?

We're marching onward to Zion,
That beautiful city of God.

Sometimes I suffer a little seizure of compassion and have to beat down the urge to rise up and yell, "Come to, you poor, stupid fucks.

You give this man his way, he'll line you up, pick your pockets, and ship you off to the slaughter."

But I never do. I know better than that. That's treason.

After he'd dragged out the last syllable of the chorus, Wallace threw back his head and laughed. His hard fist of a face glistened in the coliseum light. The mouth gaped, and the teeth shined. The crowd again roared its approval of him, and of themselves. He wasn't just another politician. He was the messiah of the Confederacy. And they longed to be his cavalry.

I looked around to see how my own temporary troops were holding up. Conrad Villines, wearing bib overalls and holding a farmer's straw hat in his hand, stood at the end of the first row of folding chairs, that bemused smile on his face. Jesse and Gloria, dressed in jeans, sandals, and T-shirts asking WHERE HAVE ALL THE FLOWERS GONE? were further back, in aisle seats near the center of the coliseum floor. The Memphis blacks, two men and two women, two old and two young, I'd had Alvy Wolfe hire for me stood on one of the exit ramps. They wore black berets, black turtlenecks, black slacks, black socks, black shoes. The nightmare. Spook revolutionaries.

Grinning and gesturing, Wallace began to quiet the crowd. As they were beginning to take their seats, he spoke again. "Mighty glad all you good folks could make it out here today. They's tornado warnings, I'm told. But let me tell you this, we gon' be making our own tornado in this country. Me and you, and all the decent, honest, hardworking folks like ourselves, we gon' band together and sweep across this once-great nation like a cleansing wind."

And they're to their feet again, egging him on. All the decent, honest, hardworking folk.

"We gon' sweep down on Washington, D.C., and we gon' lift up all the trash, gon' jerk up all the bureaucrats and all their bicycles and briefcases, gon' roar through the Congress and the cabinet rooms, gon' rip through the Supreme Court, gon' raise 'em all—atheists and agnostics, anarchists and appeasers—we gon' raise 'em all up into that filthy air over that dying city, and we gon' carry 'em out over the Potomac and on out the Chesapeake Bay past Newport News and Norfolk and Virginia Beach, and we gon' head 'em east then, out over the great Atlantic, on out to where the Russians are stealing our fish, and when we come to one of them big ol' Communist trawlers, well, we gon' drop 'em then—all them bureaucrats, bicycles, and briefcases, all them atheists and agnostics, anarchists and appeasers—yes sir, we gon' swoop down low over the water and drop 'em all, and we gon' hang there in the sky just a minute and watch which way they swim, back towards shore or on out to the trawler and into Mother Russia's net, and then we'll head back the way we come, back up the bay and the river, all the way back to our capitol, and we'll come down again on that mall in front of the Washington Monument, and we'll stand there awhile, looking out over the city we made pure again, the city we made whole again, the city we claimed again, this time forever, for God-fearing, family-loving Americans everywhere. We the ones that built it, and, by God, we gon' take it back."

The next day's *Arkansas Gazette* said Wallace spoke forty-two minutes and was interrupted for applause forty times. They were probably right, probably had a reporter there with a stop watch and some counting beads, but the speech seemed longer than that to me, and the cheering was damn near constant.

"If I have to keep thirty thousand troops there, thirty feet apart, with a ten-foot bayonet and loaded guns, folks gon' be able to walk the streets of Washington safe. And I'm not talking about race."

No sir. Not that.

He talked a spell then about getting on the ballot in Arkansas, which, he said, is one of the tougher states to do that in. But Justice Jim Johnson, who's in charge of seeing to just that for him, had told him he already had more than the eighty-six thousand required signatures on the petitions. "And we may just go ahead and get another hundred thousand or so. Just to be sure there ain't nothing no Rockefeller can do about it. We gon' be on that ballot in Arkansas, friends and neighbors, and we gon' best all of 'em, national Democrat and national Republican too. I know you folks, known folks like you all my life, and just as sure as my name's George Corley Wallace, we gon' carry this great state. We gon' carry lots of states, 'cause there's folks all over feel like we do.. Then we gon' go to Washington, D.C., and we gon' set things right. We gon' set 'em right and nail 'em down good so them limp-wristed pointy-heads can't meddle with 'em no more."

And what would he do for Arkansas in particular? he asked. And commenced answering.

"Well, first thing, 'fore I got set down good in the Oval Office, I'd take the HEW out of every school, every hospital, every domestic institution in America."

HEW was the cue. I looked up toward the ramp, and the blacks I'd hired emerged from the runway and started down the grandstand aisle toward the coliseum floor.

"We getting mighty tired down here of gubmint agencies telling us what we can do and when we can do it. They telling us we too damn stupid to know where we want our kids to go to school or who we want to sell our house to or who we want to hire to do a certain job. They think we ought to leave such choices to bureaucrats who've been to Harvard College and live in big townhouses in Alexandria, Virginia, or Bethesda, Maryland, and send their kids to some high-tone private school and ain't none of 'em ever done a honest day's work in their life. Well sir, I don't know, but I kind of figure I'd as soon make up my own mind about such things as leave it to them boys."

My quartet reached the floor and started, two by two, toward the far end of the arena.

"Naw," Wallace said. "Here's what I figure on doing. You see, these HEW bureaucrats, they always so down in the mouth about the lot of the poor colored folks and always coming up with ideas about how gubmint can help 'em, why, I figure I'll give 'em the chance they been looking for. I'll just shut down the HEW main office there in Washington and open up a series of branch offices—one smack in the middle of Harlem, one in Watts, one in Roxbury, one in south Chicago, one in East Saint Louis, one in Detroit and so on. Put 'em right out there amongst the folks they say their heart's bleeding over. Then I'd do 'em the favor of cutting their salaries so far they'd have to live above the office there, have to make their home right there where their heart is, back to where they couldn't afford to send their sons and daughters off to Phillips or Exeter or Miss Vanderbilt's Elite Academy for the Spawn of Privilege. Why, no sir, I'd see to it their kids got the benefit of a *public* education right there in Harlem or Watts, see to it them fine, compassionate white children who've had all the breaks got to set a high and cultured example for all them poor, underprivileged Harlem nigra chillun."

The crowd laughed and yelled. The band did a few bars of "Hail to the Chief." When the noise had begun to die down, Wallace motioned for quiet. And from the rear of the coliseum, the four blacks (old man and old woman first, young man and young woman immediately behind them—lined patient dignity followed by fresh hot rage) started walking toward Wallace, down the long aisle that split the floor.

They were silent for the first second or two, and then they began the song—they were singers, I'd told Villines to get singers.

We shall overcome,
We shall overcome,
We shall overcome someday.
Oh, deep in my heart
I do believe,
We shall overcome someday.

Their voices filled the place. I'd have to remember to compliment Villines on his selection.

Thousands of white faces turned toward them. Then there were a few seconds of surprise, confusion, and hesitation, but pretty quick you could hear the word *nigger* echoing around, mouth to mouth.

We shall end Jim Crow,
We shall end Jim Crow . . .

A pair of uniformed cops and a man in a dark suit made a move toward them, but Wallace, grinning, said, "Leave 'em go on with it. They always been good singers. We glad to have 'em here."

So the law let them walk, but stayed with them, the plainclothes fuck backing down the aisle in front of them, the two city cops doing tail duty, palms on the butts of their pistols.

The four blacks joined hands then and held them up in the air, according to plan. It made their progress more awkward, the older, lead pair having to twist an outside arm and reach back for the hand behind. But it kept things safe. And it was part of the deal.

We are not afraid,
We are not afraid,
We are not afraid today . . .

"Ain't no *reason* to be afraid," Wallace said. "If you do right."

The singers stopped at the mouth of the aisle. There was a beat or two of silence. Then the old black woman said, her voice confident and strong enough to be heard from where I was, a good hundred feet away, "You a bad man, Mr. Wallace. Goin' roun' feedin' on fear and handin' out hatred."

The cops started trying to head them to the exit.

Wallace said, "When you get 'em out, give 'em a ride home. They harmless, just been confused by outsiders. They ain't been paid yet, help 'em find the man that owes 'em and make him pay up. Tell him they done good."

The crowd laughed. The blacks sang.

We shall all be free . . .

When they were out that side door, Wallace, his voice stage-sweet, said, "Gooood-bye."

And, with that, he had completely won the crowd's confidence in him and in themselves. Actually, now that it was over, the whole thing seemed to have a calming effect on them. Four niggers? What were they? Ol' George could handle them with a grin and a couple of quips. The world, today, had ordered itself. They could hear the old harmonies. Oh, the darkies had cut up some, but that was in the darky nature—that was part of the harmony.

Wallace, making a transition of the interruption, started telling *them* what *they* had to overcome, what he'd see to it they *did* overcome, once they put him in the White House—big government, big business, the bleeding-heart liberal press, welfare chiselers, crime in the streets, the coddling of criminals, a government that sent young men to war but wouldn't let them win it, the absence of God in the public schools, drug-addled demonstrators, draft-card burning, desecrations of the flag, the threat of general anarchy. "These hippies raising hell in the streets, they just pampered rich kids. They ought to all been jerked up some time ago and spanked. Getting late for that now, though. Man might have to turn to harsher measures. Six, eight months, maybe a year, of breathing penitentiary air probably straighten most of 'em out. It don't, they can breathe some more of it."

Applause. The chant of "Wallace. Wallace. Wallace." General jubilation.

"And I tell you this for sure," he announced, referring to a tactic demonstrators had used a few times to halt official cars, "Ain't none of them anarchists better lay down in front of any car carrying George

Corley Wallace. They do, it'll be the last damn car they stretch out before."

And so on.

After a while he focused on Vietnam. The most powerful country in the history of the world ought not let itself get pushed around by a nation the size of New Jersey. "Hell, if we'd just let 'em go, no strings, the Alabama National Guard could whip North Vietnam.

"But we don't have to fool with that, no point in risking our boys' lives. I'm president, I'll call Ho Chi Minh on the phone, person to person, and I'll tell him straight out, 'Ho, this here's George Corley Wallace, and this here's my peace plan. You get all your soldiers and military paraphernalia out of South Vietnam by this time next week, you set free all the American boys you starving in your concentration camps, you tell your Russian and Chinese friends to go on back home and go back to persecuting their own kind and to quit sending you planes and tanks and bombs and the like, 'cause we through fooling with you. You see, you don't do like I say, why, we'll bomb you right off the map.' "

He threw back his head, laughed, took in the cheers.

"He don't think we will, I'll tell him, 'Just ask the Japanese.' Might even airmail him one of them Hiroshima films the goateed professors is always showing on the college campuses. That'd get his attention, I reckon. That one phone call'd be all the peace conference George Wallace'd need. Won't be no months of trying to decide where we going to meet and what shape table we going to sit around. No sir, just the one phone call. Then it'd be up to them. They'd have their choice—peace or doom. 'Cause I tell you what, there's too much needs doing right here at home for the president of the United States to be wasting much time or worry over a little ol' bitty country like Vietnam."

Then Gloria, who had a seat—last one, third row—within just a few steps of me, stood and commenced chanting:

Sexist! Racist! Fascist pig!
Sexist! Racist! Fascist pig!

Wallace looked at her, cocked an eye, gave us a grin. "Somebody mind hepin' the little lady to the powder room?"

She kept chanting. The three other white student revolutionaries

I'd hired, males, sprang to their feet and joined her, fists jabbing the air.

Sexist! Racist! Fascist pig!
Sexist! Racist! Fascist pig!

"Ain't many words to that song, is there?" Wallace asked them.

They kept it up. I let it go on maybe another fifteen or twenty seconds more, long enough to keep them from complaining later, then walked up to them. "Time to go now," I told Gloria.

She spun around and slapped me, a move not included in the plan.

"Spirited wench, ain't she?" Wallace said.

She tried the slap again, but I blocked it with a forearm.

"Now cross with the right," Wallace, the former boxer, advised.

I jerked her out into the aisle. "Move, bitch."

A good half-dozen other cops, all makes and models, converged on us, nightsticks brandished.

"It's all right," I said. "They gonna go. Just having theirselves a little lark."

A big lantern-jawed, wall-eyed Little Rock bull used his sap to motion the other three chanters out into the aisle.

They chanted on, but moved.

In the aisle they all went limp, Gloria included. I grabbed her under the arms and commenced pulling her toward the exit. Three other cops did the same with the three other hippies. Even as we dragged them, they kept up their song.

"Lord, now, I ask you," Wallace said to the crowd, "ain't this a show?"

When we had them off the floor, under the grandstand, and out of sight of the crowd, Wall-Eye let go of his man and said, "Now get up off your ass, punk."

"Get fucked, pig," the kid said. He was big. He showed no fear.

Wall-Eye drew his sap and took aim.

"None of that shit," I told him. "Fucking press is here. We don't need a filmed clubbing."

And the press *had* surrounded us—microphones, notepads, cameras, and questions. "No comment," I said. "We just gonna give 'em a ride home. These kids got schoolwork to do."

We could hear the crowd roaring at something Wallace had said.

"They're unarmed and stupid," I said. "No problem."

A TV man stuck a microphone in Gloria's face. She told it America was governed by imperialist pigs.

"They're obstructing justice," I told Wall-Eye. "Back 'em off."

He started shoving reporters and photographers. A couple more cops hopped in to help him. Scum on scum, I thought. I ordered two other cops to grab onto Wall-Eye's hippie, and we started dragging longhairs on down the way. When we came to the elevator, I let go of Gloria and pushed the down button.

When we got down to the underground garage, I took a cop aside and told him to take the two more pacific hippies to the Greyhound station. They were working for us, I explained, undercover. We just needed to see that they got a bus out of town before anybody took any more pictures of them. We might need them again. He nodded and a minute later drove away with his back seat full of hired hippies.

The big hippie was still cussing and struggling. I had the boys throw him in the back of the paddy wagon that was down there. On her own, Gloria climbed in after him. I gave her a look that she answered with a wink and a grin. We locked them in. I went around and told the driver to take them almost to Poplar Bluff, Missouri, turn off on a quiet dirt road somewhere, then push them out and leave them. "Don't want them giving no goddam interviews," I said.

"Got no jurisdiction in Missouri," he told me.

"Fuck jurisdiction," I explained. "We fighting for the highest office in the land."

He looked at me and shook his head, confused, uncertain. A young guy worried about his job. Police procedure. Right and wrong. What the hell was he doing here?

I sent one of the Little Rock cops back up after Wall-Eye. He came down a few minutes later, and I told him to take the driver's place. He saw the wisdom in my plan. "Might have to bruise 'em up some while I'm getting 'em out."

"No," I said. Don't need no bruises backing up their stories. Just leave 'em stranded. That'll do real nice."

He got in, started up the engine, and I finished my instructions. "We was putting these fucks in the wagon when somebody from outside opened up the garage door. The hippies seen their chance and made a run for it. We had to either let them go or fire into the crowd. They didn't have no identification. They got away. Clean. Ain't worth looking for. We hope they keep running. North."

I looked at them one by one. "Got it?" I asked the rookie I'd removed from the wagon.

He nodded, but doubt spelled itself on his face.

"He fucks it up," Wall-Eye said from the truck, "we'll make him a hall monitor at Central High." He backed toward the door, which began to open.

I told the cops there with me to stay in the garage until the rally ended. "No need in giving the press a clean shot at you. Don't tell nobody nothing until you have to. Then feed 'em the story."

Then, saying I had to go check on the governor, I left them there.

Wallace still owned the crowd. He was in the process of wondering about something that had been bothering him. "If the Rockefeller, Carnegie, and Ford foundations are so interested in a guaranteed annual wage, why don't they just contribute their own tax-free billions? To a ol' country boy like me, the stuff that comes so steady out the doors and windows of them fancy foundations smells a whole lot like what I used to shovel up out of our ol' barnyard."

I looked around for Jesse, couldn't spot him.

Ol' George commenced winding down, pounding hard on a few sure keys one more time—HEW, Supreme Court, rioters, anarchists, welfare cheats, old men in the war room hobbling young men in the field. And then the payoff: "We doin' what we can. We already put the dread in them national Democrats and them national Republicans. And I got a feeling, a clear feeling, we gon' take it all. But it won't be easy; they stacked the deck against us, stacked the deck against *you*. It'll cost tens of millions to run their race the way it deserves to be run. No foundation gon' give George Wallace money. No corporation. And I wouldn't take it if they did. No sir, our campaign depends on the openhandedness of common folks, folks like you, folks that don't have much to spare, but folks that know their country's goin' down a dark road at a bad hour but suspect maybe George Wallace, with their help, can get us back to the main road and put on the high beams and drive us back to the sunrise.

"I'll sure appreciate your vote come November. But I'm here asking you for more. I know some of you can't really afford it, I know how hard you work for what little you get, and I wouldn't be asking you for a penny if I didn't think the world depended on it. We're gon' have the choir sing again now for you, and while they're doin' that some friends of ours will be moving among you with donation buckets, and we're asking you to let us have whatever you feel you can afford. Now don't you be takin' no food out of your young-uns' mouths, but give what you can spare. That's all we're askin'. You got my word we'll put it to proper use."

He stepped back.

They stood, cheering and cheering. Listening to that, day in and day out, a man could get the big eye on himself.

His band played the first few bars of "The Old Rugged Cross," and then the choir rose and began singing it.

Where the hell was Jesse? He'd promised to be here for the last act, the collection, to say his piece, to do what he could to keep these people from giving their money to evil. I'd told him that was fine with me, figuring whatever he said would just cause folks to give more. But I didn't see him. I worried that maybe Spoof Lyons had decided to quit jacking around with us and just haul him on back home.

There was a job of work to do, though. Conrad and I were in the bucket brigade, two of a dozen or more men working the floor. At least twice that many were in the stands on either side. Confederate-gray plastic buckets brightened with red DIXIE and red-white-and-blue WALLACE stickers moved back and forth through the crowd, row to row, hand to hand, filling with pocket change and wallet money. Here and there, I saw people making out checks, but this was mostly a cash business—these were country people, and they did their business on a barrelhead. It was money there wouldn't be any accounting for. And the man at the head of the hall had known that from the start, of course. Just like I had.

After the choir had finished hacking another notch into its cross, there were a few seconds of relative silence that let me hear, from above and behind me, a low, human hum. I turned, glanced up, and there he was, Jesse, the damned fool, in his white hospital linens, sitting cross-legged, medicine-man style, on a steel camera platform up near the roof, high above where the basketball goal would've been at the far end of the arena. Just up there, doing nothing in particular, his palms-up hands in his lap, his eyes open but seeming to see nothing, staring straight out, way above the crowd, and the little, barely audible, tuneless hum. He was risking his ass for that little hum.

I tried to size the place up quick, looking from cop to cop and to the Wallace bodyguards. A couple of the guards were looking at him, or seemed to be, through their dark glasses. They were still, poised, not yet ready to make their move. I hoped they thought this was another part of the act I was being paid to put on. For a minute, I didn't know whether to go get him down or leave him be and hope nobody thought he was worth paying any mind to. Going after him would draw attention, and I might not be able to get him down anyway—he seemed set on the act. But leaving him there might get him blown away. Some Alabama sharpshooter might mistake him for a vegetarian John Wilkes Booth.

Then a man at the end of the aisle nudged me with a bucket, and I handed it to the woman ending the next row up. There was no way I could get to Jesse without jacking up the risk. I'd have to go all the way to the back of the place, climb to the top of the stands, then cross the metal walkway to the platform. And there could be no rush, no hurry. I'd have to do it all with a measured calm. And even if I had the time to do all that, I might just be making it worse, making them suspect this wasn't part of my act. No, I'd have to go on about my work and hope the fool didn't make any sudden moves.

The lights went down, and it was "America the Beautiful" time. The buckets, steadily filling, had wound nearly halfway home. Devoted, uplifted, enchanted, the folk reached into the pockets of bib overalls and K-mart khakis, drew forth and opened wallets (many of them made from Tandy kits, Christmas presents from sons to fathers), and dropped worn, green bills into a bad hope's gray bucket. The hope himself stood by the choir director, singing fierce and pious.

I passed another bucket to another row and glanced back up to where Jesse had made a target of himself. In the half-darkness he was visible only in silhouette. And the hum, if it was still there, couldn't be heard at all. He had cover now. I hoped he'd use it. Even a fool has to be given leave to find his own way.

A money bucket came to me again. I held this one, moved up a couple of rows, and waited for the next one. When it came, I took it too, turned right, and left the hall. There were a few people, reporters and campaign staff mostly, in the wide, bright-lit hallway I went into, but I walked right past them, calm, official looking, and they didn't say a word. I walked past the elevator, took the stairs down. There was an ashtray built into the wall a half-floor below. I stuffed it with three big handfuls of cash from one of the buckets, went back upstairs, caught the elevator, stuffed more money into the ashtray in there, moved money from the full bucket to the nearly empty one, and rode on down to the garage.

When the doors opened, Colonel John Norman Bannock said, "Well, lookee here. Ol' Sam. I bet you were wondering what to do with that money, weren't you, Sam?"

"Oh, I don't know," I said. "I thought I had it pretty well figured."

"Bet you did." He had three huge, young, no-neck good ol' boys behind him, looked like Crimson Tide tackles. I said, "Ain't you boys got spring practice?"

No answer. Bad knees, maybe. Had to turn to the bouncer's life.

"Well, John," I said to Bannock. "I'm mighty glad you're here. Otherwise, I might've been tempted to make off with some of what ain't mine."

"Pleased to be of assistance," he said. "Let's ride back up." He punched the elevator button, told the interior lineman to hold their ground. "Sam's not prone to violence," he explained. "Just the common swindle."

When we got in the elevator, he went to the ashtray, lifted the cover, and said, "Aw, Sam, Sam, Sam."

"Well," I said, "some days it's a living." I shook my head. "Guess I should've known you'd be shadowing me."

He took one of the buckets from me and put the ashtray money back into it. "Oh, I knew better than to trust a man like you when the money started floating around the room in milk pails."

The door opened on us. I handed him the other bucket.

"I thought you did fairly well up to then, though," he said. "Served your purpose."

He walked past me, headed down the hall toward the arena. I caught up with him. "What about my wages? I earned that. I got people to pay."

"What's in that stairwell ashtray ought to about cover it."

I got around in front of him, looked in his face, blinked. "Nowhere near," I said.

He made a mock commiserating sucking sound. "You take your chances, you pay your dues. Go to the cops, you want to. See who they believe, the back-roads hustler or the governor of Alabama."

"You're fucking me, John."

"Caught you red-handed, is all I did. And even aside from that, you damn near caused more trouble than you could ever possibly be worth. Something bad could've come of that draft-dodger boy of yours playing Buddha up there in the sky. Could've nodded off and tumbled ass-over-karma onto the working class."

"I didn't have anything to do with that."

He cocked his head, gave me a hard look. The governor's man, all knowing, the law. "Who's to say?" he said. "We kept an eye on him for you. Ought to be grateful."

I said, "Well, the boy does need looking after."

We could hear "Dixie" being sung in the hall.

"Here's what I want you to do now, Sam," he told me. "Go on back in the hall and stand at attention up there to the left of the podium. You can hold your hand over your heart while they finish "Dixie" if you want to. Do you good. Then bow your head real nice while Rev. Cutler brings the benediction. Soon as it's over, be gone. I see you messing with the money again, it's your ass."

"You awful high and mighty, ain't you, John? Man that don't stand for nothing but not giving the niggers theirs."

It pissed him off. "Let me tell you something, Sam. You won't understand it, but I'm going to tell you anyway. This cause is bigger than we are, bigger even than the governor. Some of us have dedicated our lives to it. We're in it for the duration. We don't win now, we'll win in '72 or '76 or '80. We got right on our side, and history, and most of the people, though a lot of them don't know it yet. They've been had by Harvard boys and fancy dancers who don't know the first thing about what most folks have to do to get through the day. And we got nothing against Negroes, either. We use them, we play up the case against them, because right now we have to. It's how we get everybody else to pay attention. But when we come to power, they'll be better off too." He studied me then to see if I was catching on. I gave him the wiseacre grin, one con man to another. He shook his head. "But you, now, Sam, not much anybody can do for you. You've been playing kids' games all your life, the carnival hustle, the shell game, hawking bits of nothing and skipping town. You're getting old now, and you're ridiculous. Sad. Pitiful. Small time. And today, maybe for the first time in your life, you were playing with the big boys, and nothing you knew worked. We predicted every move you'd make, Sam. We used you. It's time you grew up."

"Man'd want to take a lot of time off for thinking before doing something that drastic. Didn't watch himself, he might wind up working for George Wallace."

He nodded, as if he had predicted that too. "Have it however it suits you. Keep on drifting till you fade away."

"Maybe come a week or two I'll find me a fit cause to live for. Seems to pay good. Right now, though, I believe I'll go on down and get my little bit of money out of the well."

They were finishing "Dixie."

"When this is over and most everybody's cleared out, one of our boys'll be down there with your son. And you might take time out to thank whatever it is you believe in we didn't have him arrested. That money'll be safe too. You get it then. But now you better get your ass inside."

I did.

The good Reverend Cutler was filled with the spirit. He called the buckets of money a love offering and finished his prayer like this: "Our Father, we thank you for not only this occasion but for this privilege of having a part in this great campaign—this great crusade that is perhaps the greatest movement in the history of our people. May God keep us united until this victory is won for Jesus' sake. Amen."

Folks stood around for a minute or two, congratulating one another for being part of a crusade, for loving ol' George together, for seeing the light and following it to Barton Coliseum. Then they started leaving, heading out onto streets where the niggers lurked. I served as an usher.

The Wallace workers were out in the halls, shaking hands, slapping backs, passing out stickers and banners and pins, yayhoo-ing and amen-ing, accepting further contributions. A couple of people thanked me for being a cop in a bad time. I gave them the official nod, the grunted thanks. After fifteen or twenty minutes all but a few stragglers had left the main hall, and the janitors had come in to start folding chairs and sweeping hardwood. Conrad, in gray custodial garb, was with them, pushing a rolling trash bin, picking freedom's droppings off the floor.

I went after my son.

Still in hospital whites, he was there, guarded by another of the Tide's finest, who gave me a superior, all-American half-grin, handed me an empty Church's Fried Chicken bag, and went up the stairs, taking them two at a time.

While I was getting the money out of the ashtray and putting it in the chicken sack, Jesse said, "They beat you."

I said, "Son, don't ever trust a goddamn politician."

We went on down, walked through the garage, out the door, and into the parking area. We got into the hearse, and I started it up. "Your sutra, or whatever it is you call it, didn't seem to have much effect, either."

He smiled easy. "You can't be sure about something like that."

"You done said a mouthful there, boy."

We rode Roosevelt until I turned in toward the veterans hospital.

"What do you plan to do here?"

"Wait for Conrad."

We parked in the rear lot.

Then he turned to me again, giving me the leery eye, beginning, I think, to suspect the answer. "Why?" he asked.

"He's got the money." I showed him a beaming smile.

He shook his head.

And when, a good half hour later, Villines pulled up in a Harrold Smith College Maintenance Department van, he did have the money, six of them gray buckets full, down at the bottom of that big, gray rolling trash bin, all covered with newspapers and gum wrappers and pop cans, Northern Tissue and Dixie cups and campaign flyers.

I stuck the whole shebang in the ass end of the hearse. "I thank you, Conrad," I said. "I'll be mailing you some of it."

"My pleasure," he answered. "Never had a better day in my life."

We were out of Little Rock headed north before Jesse said anything. "How?" he wondered.

"My part was just to be sure they were watching me. The rest of it I leave to Conrad. Lights go down low the way they did, and a choir starts singing holy for a cause he don't like, well, a case like that, he's the best hand on earth. No, I just leave it to him. Everybody knows I'm a thief; everybody thinks Conrad's one of them." I looked at him. "Course, you helped too, in your way. Had 'em looking up in the air."

We were quiet awhile. I felt like singing, but I wanted to leave Jesse the space to ask the questions he finally came around to.

"So you beat them," he conceded. "In your small way you beat them. How does it matter?"

"It just does."

"Because of the money?"

"No," I told him. "The money just means we won. It's the game that counts. Playing it right. Taking on the favorites before a packed house on their home ground. Playing a game they made up. And making off at the end with a nice piece of the gate and leaving them there smiling, convinced they've won again, convinced there ain't no way but theirs, ain't nothing that matters but their ball and their scoreboard and their gaggle of half-wit cheerleaders. Day I get outsmarted by a bunch of political fuck heads, I quit."

He had what seemed to be an amused look on his face. "But nothing changed. They go right on, making the world worse. They didn't even know they were playing you."

"Well, first of all, Son, short of trying a new road to see what comes of it, I never aim to change things. And, then, yes, by God, they did know they were playing me. Fact, when it was over, Colonel John Norman Bannock thought he had my balls in his hand. There's the fun in it. Picking them proud, shyster pockets and them not even knowing it. There's whatever meaning there is. Beating them and laughing, knowing they won't ever even know you did it, much less how." So I laughed. "It's all illusion, boy. The Zen of swindle."

I pulled a pint of Jack Black out from under the seat, opened the cap. "Here's to the road, Son, and the glory of the night."

PART III

1 JESSE

The Zen of swindle, he says, joking. There is truth in his words. But they were not uttered for their truth. His intent was to remind me that my own way had failed. The implication was that before such a crowd at such a time, the way of the spirit is futile. Only the rational, practical mind can prevail. And I feel the failure, feel it as a wound to pride, feel it as unfulfilled desire, feel it, especially, in contrast to my father's success. I have not achieved detachment.

What did I expect? A miracle?

Yes. I wanted my mantra to make hall and people and cosmos one. I wanted each of us to be both whole and part. I wanted to bring the Way to the multitudes. And on the simplest plane, and, as my father says, perhaps the purest, I wanted to beat George Wallace.

Desire. Desire. Desire.

I want to win. But I have not mastered loss.

I want to be both Jefferson and Buddha, to be the perfect democrat and the pure spirit.

I want to help develop a political system that will eliminate the need for a political system.

I want the workplace to be such that the worker can achieve satori during lunch break at the box factory.

I want an American mind and an Oriental soul.

I want infinite patience, and I want change now.

I want to accept the world as it is, and I want it to be filled with palpable miracles.

I am an arrogant dreamer. I am a fool.

And yet . . .

In a kind of foolishness lies whatever hope we have. The logical, reasonable, Western way has led to the compartmentalization (ugly

Western word) of the world. We are the culture of category and classification. And whatever we cannot categorize—which for those without the dogmatic scientific bent is much, is the whole of the essence—we personify. We remake the world in the image of our image of the surface of ourselves. This thing or being becomes a symbol for that idea or this human trait. The lion becomes courage, the dove peace, the rock faith. And on and on. Piece by piece, object by object, being by being. Until each and all is something other, something false, something artificial. Until we cannot see the thing itself. Until we have lost the ability to see that the miraculous abides in the particular.

Until only a fool can see such a thing.

As we navigate the Missouri night, I listen to my father's raucous singing, watch as he sips from his pint of good whiskey. And it comes to me that perhaps he has accommodated himself to this life as well as anyone I know. He has found a way, not the Way, but a way that suits him, a way as eccentric and as essentially predictable as his own personality. He needs but the day and the night that follows. Laughter and movement are his dogma. He is the existential clown.

So I say to him, "You are at peace, aren't you?"

"Fuck peace," he says. "I'm happy. I like this road and this night and the memory of my day with Wallace. But I know it won't be long till I'll have to start doing me some finagling to get me back to someplace like this again. Peace, now, Son—Lord, that's dangerous. Makes you stand still. They got you then."

To him, then, time is linear, life a series of confrontations that produce victory, defeat, escape.

Silence. The night is filled with insects.

Then I ask him the question—"And what do you do when you come to the darkness, when the road ends, and there is only the abyss, without sound, without light, without end?"

He turns his face to me, and I can see in his half-drunken eyes that he understands, that he has been there. Then the eyes widen and shine, reflecting oncoming light. He laughs and says, "Turn left."

2 GLORIA

Gunner Grant could talk.

He was tall and strong, and everything about him seemed to be moving all the time.

He started raving through the grate at the paddy wagon pig as soon as we left the garage.

"You want to use that sap on me, Jack, just come on, just pull this motherfucker over, and come on back here, Bubba. Anytime. Any fucking time you feel up to it, Brother Law. Use the sap, Jap, use the gun, Hun. Call some help in, Captain. You know, get your goddamn buddies in on it. Saturday-night pig party, Paul. Whup up on the hippie, Harold. Gang-bang the broad, Buck. Shee-it, what a night it'd be for the ol' law-and-order boys. Write it all up, Willie Lee, and send it into the *FBI Journal*. Make a name for yourself, man, be Pig of the Month."

The pig said, "Keep it up, punk. It's a long ride. Gonna be a dark night."

"Yes sir, Mr. Sarge, all kind of prospects loom up ahead. Why, fuck, man, maybe you can shoot a nigger on the way home and be Pig of the Year. Aw, but sure, you're right. One wouldn't be anywhere near enough, now would it? Competition being what it is. But then maybe you could catch 'em in a herd, man, grieving over Dr. King or something, you know, or just wait till the first of the month, Coach, catch 'em lined up in front of the welfare office, snuff, Christ, two, three dozen, one go around, save the fed all that bread, Ned, send it to the boys overseas. Blue hat and black sap, man, blue hat and black sap. There's the fucking ticket. Wins the prize every time."

"Can it, hophead."

"Got to get on the local news, Cap'n Jack, and say, 'It was sultry in Little Rock. A dank mist rose from the ghetto sewers. I was working the night beat. My name is Billy Bob Badass.' Yeah, shit, Jack, shit yeah, make a name for yourself, put the sky in your momma's eye, get on the goddamn TV. Think about your fucking career, man. How you gonna make chief, you keep your sap in its sheath. Got to take action, Jackson. Can't be shy. Damn freak back here taunting you, pig, you can't take that. Got to put the fear of God in the odd. Got to jump, Stump. Got to quell the fucking disturbance. Else ol' chaos takes the land, Bland. No sir, smart punk like me, you got to rub the club to the nub, Bub. You just sit there and drive, man, keeping your own dumb-ass counsel, you never gonna rise. They don't give you desk and a secretary and a plainclothes suit, Newt, till you get you some blood on them blues."

When we had turned onto University and were headed out of town, the pig, his bad eye seeming to go all white, glanced back at Gunner and said, "Time to snuff it now, punk. You smelling up the wagon. And sooner or later you gonna get more beating than you can handle."

But he didn't slide the door to, the little metal door that would've blocked the grated opening. No, he needs this, I thought, needs the abuse. He'll let his masochism drive him into a sadistic fury.

"Beating's something I can take, Jake. Been trained to it. Take all the incoming you got, man. Been to 'Nam, Sam. Winter, spring, summer, fall. Seen it all. Seen it fall, seen it fall. Nam Can to Quang Tri. Was home to me. Everybody I knew been killed. And I just stayed on and kept firing, Mr. and Mrs. America, trying to work back up to even, and falling farther and farther behind all the time. Wanted to make the world safe for piss-eyed politicians and paddy-wagon pigs. Yes sir, God love me, I done it all. Done it in the name of God and country and General Nguyen Van Thieu. Hacked the heads off little baby slants and mailed 'em to Robert McNamara, special delivery, so he wouldn't fuck up the count. I'm a fucking marine, Gene, ever time I take a piss, it kills a half-acre of grass."

"You been to Vietnam," the pig said, "it's no wonder we ain't won."

Gunner's voice changed tone, became ingratiating. "Hey, listen, man, what say you pull off up here 'fore we get out of town. I get us some black beauties. Keep the road jumping. Long night, you know. Bad time to be straight in."

"You've had a lifetime share, Herky."

"Come on, man, do it for a veteran."

"I'll let you go turkey in jail. Be the best thing I could do for you. Christian charity."

Two men playing cowboy games.

"Listen up, Jack. *Listen up*. You talking to a champeen soldier. Show me a half-inch of head a half-mile off, and I'll blow the motherfucker across the Great Divide. I come home, I's carrying so many medals on my chest I couldn't stand up straight. Give me back trouble, man. Had so damn many of them, Jim, I set up shop. Sell you a silver star for a buck and a quarter, Mr. Reporter, purple hearts're a dime a dozen." He sucked in a breath. "And look at you, Copper Blue, Mr. God Almighty Patriot, won't even do me the favor of making a little pit stop."

Then, for two or three minutes, he sang "The Marine Hymn," his voice harsh and loud and sarcastic. I listened and laughed, my eyes going from Gunner's long, twisted face to the pig's cocked eye. I liked Gunner right off, his energy and his irreverence. He was crazy, and he was dangerous, and I liked him.

The hymn ended. Silence. The rattling of the wagon. Little traffic. The edge of the city.

"Nice song," the pig said, as if offering a cue. Masochism again? Or just the simple desire for amusement?

"Did you know Andy Harper?" Gunner asked him, sounding straight. "Grew up right here in Little Rock. Went to Sylvan Hills High. Nice kid."

"No," the pig answered. "I'm from Benton."

"Dead. Sniper Charlie. He was passing me a joint when he got it. We was sucking the dew, Lew. Seeking the crease, Mr. Police. Coming for the calm, balm, the quiet at the end of that goddamn tunnel."

"Should've kept his eyes open. Shouldn't've been taking dope."

"Shouldn't've been there. Should've been home walking a mail route or something. Should've married the girl from the home ec class and had kids named Mike and Melissa. Gone to PTA meetings. Been a scoutmaster. Got drunk on New Year's Eve and sat there at the bar in the den, after everybody's left, wearing his little pointed plastic party hat, man, and looking out over the scatter of bottles and favors and maybe a forgotten coat or two and wondering where the hell his life had gone and where the hell it was going. Just a regular life, don't you know, Copper Joe? like everybody else's. But no, shit no, never be, sniper nailed him at nineteen, man, just above the right ear. Last words were, 'Don't take it all.' Well, they did, Jack, they fuckin' did."

"You keep it up," the pig said, "you apt to make me cry."

"You ever know a blood, man, name of Aloysius Royce? Grew up out at College Station. Seven brothers, three sisters. Daddy's doing a dime in Cummins. Momma's turning cheap tricks on Church Street. Big, sweet, tough motherfucker, man, Aloysius was. Kind of man you wanted at your side when the dark come in. We'd be holed up somewhere, dug in and damp, man, the goddamn rat rot eating at our skin, and when the incoming started in, he'd sing, 'Goodnight Irene.' Break your little silver-dollar American heart, man, and set you to hoping at the same time. Maybe you heard him sometime, Jack. You damn sure should've."

"Never knew him. And I always thought that song was overrated."

"You would. You just the kind. And you going on. But Aloysius, man that knew a song when he sung one, well, he caught friendly fire. Minor miscalculation by Marvin the fucking ARVN. Oriental calculus, Occidental death."

And as we drove north through the night, he went on, giving us a litany of the names and the deaths. Boys from Arkansas first and then, randomly, from other places. Boys black and white and yellow and one Cherokee sergeant, from Tahlequah, Alexander Waterdancer, who led the platoon into a village a few miles outside Saigon one morning, checked the charred huts, counted the village's blackened bodies, men, women, and children, radioed in his report, laid down his rifle, his belt, his pack, and walked, erect and silent, into the jungle.

"Don't know how far he got, man," Gunner said. "But if I'd had any balls, I'd've gone with him. Just walked the fuck away, Jack, to see if I could find an end to it."

"It goes on," the pig said out of the side of his mouth. "It's no different than it ever was. You just got to huddle up and call a new play." Gridiron wisdom in a blue uniform.

"Yeah, ain't but one end, man," Gunner agreed, "to the fucking 'Boonierat Blues' ":

While the fastmover's flyin'
My brother's here dyin'.
He's paid up the last of his dues.
And the body they'll be baggin'

Will ride the meat wagon
To the end of the Boonierat Blues.

The pig said, "Learnt you lots of songs and shit over there anyway, didn't they?"

"Learnt me more'n I can sing, man. Take that song there, Jack. I just sung the refrain. Motherfucker actually goes on about twenty years. The big pig fuckers in the five-sided house keep making up new verses, man. Ain't none of it got a end to it but that goddamn chorus. Don't none of it mean nothin', Ned. You just keep on singin' till the wagon comes."

Sadness had slipped into Gunner's voice now, perhaps even a little self-pity, and I think the pig may have become empathetic. They like to see themselves as soldiers, the pigs do: Wasn't for us the streets would fall to the enemy—that rap, you know. "I'd've gone," he apologized, "but I was a few years too old."

"Too bad," Gunner said. "You'd've probably been just the motherfucker that turned it around."

The pig gave him an offended backward glance, then turned his eyes back to the road. "Could've done my part," he said. "Way it's turned out, I feel bad I didn't."

And I realized there was something between Gunner and this pig I hadn't understood. Something male and proud. Something they just took for granted. Something to do with locker rooms and guns and lost causes.

"Been a damn fool to go, Jack. Ain't no light there. Ain't even no tunnel, man, 'cept the ones Charlie lives in."

They went on like that, talking back and forth, with, for the most part, a kind of gruff male ease, though, now and then, Gunner would sting the pig with a snapping jab. Gunner: bitter because he had suffered the bad war. The pig: guilty because he had not. Odd.

We'd ridden at least three hours when the pig turned off the highway and onto a gravel road, parked, got out, and opened our doors. "You're about fifteen minutes from Poplar Bluff," he said.

"The traveler's dream, man. The wanderer's rest. Poplar fuckin' Bluff," Gunner said. "Be still, my hopped-up heart."

"At least you ain't in jail."

"A bed'd be good, man. I seen them stars too goddamn many times."

The pig grinned. "Watch out for tornadoes," he said. He turned, closed the rear doors, and started back to the driver's seat.

"Sure you don't want to take that sap to me just once, man?" Gunner said. "God knows when I'll be back in Little Rock."

The pig stepped up into his seat, closed his door, poked his head out his window, and said, "Reckon I'll leave that to the next man, Jack."

"Lord God," Gunner said. "That's the meanest motherfucker on earth."

We walked back to the highway and then followed it three or four miles to a stone, glass, and beam building, which turned out to be the Call of the Wild Museum. Why it was built there, I don't know.

"Just the fuckin' place, Janie," Gunner said. "We can go around back and howl to our hearts' content."

So we slept together on the lawn behind the Call of the Wild Museum. But that night Gunner was impotent. When I had done all I could and failed, he said, "Try me again come morning, flower child. You never know when Ol' Blue'll come around."

3 MALEDON

Well, Wallace was right about one thing. The tornadoes came. One of them swooped down on Greenwood, Arkansas, killed eleven people, injured fifty more, and carried off about half the buildings in town. Dozens of other dark funnels were sighted across the state, and several touched down, ripping up trees and blowing down houses. One of them Old Testament kind of days, the wrath of God coming down on trailer parks and insurance companies and little Bible Belt towns in general.

But we got away again. Jesse and I drove north through air that was gray and perfectly still. Moving toward Missouri, we listened to the hearse radio, where the man was telling us there were other things going on. The FBI announced that Eric St. Vincent Galt, the man they suspected of killing King, was actually an escaped convict named

James Earl Ray. But, whatever he was calling himself, he was still on the loose. I figured his best bet was to slip down into Mississippi and announce for governor. Hell, J. Edgar Hoover would probably set up a residence down there so he could vote for him. Frank Borman, the *Gemini* 7 command pilot, criticized John Glenn for campaigning for Robert Kennedy. I guess he thought spacemen ought to be above politics (pardon me), or maybe he just figured you stuck with the man that had bought you your rockets. Out in California, Governor Ronald Reagan said that massive bombing was the best tactic for bringing Hanoi to the peace table. Wanted us to drop one for the Gipper, the bigger the better. At a New York City anti-war rally, Dr. Benjamin Spock was pessimistic: He thought peace was at least two years away. All the polls said Eugene McCarthy would win the Pennsylvania primary, but all the delegates were already committed to Hubert Humphrey, who was pleased as punch. Richard Nixon said he'd rather lose the election than mislead the poor. The solution to urban poverty was to bring private enterprise to the ghettos. If elected, he'd do just that. All we had to do was trust him. One of the world's great deadpan comedians. In Houston, NASA revealed that one of the first astronauts on the moon would set up a grenade launcher. One year later a radio signal from earth would fire the grenade. There might be some Cong lurking around up there, fucking with our dominoes. In Beirut, Yasir Arafat, a thirty-nine-year-old Jerusalem-born engineer, identified himself as the leader of Al Fatah. He was a short, pudgy man who didn't much like his name, wanted to change it to Abu Ammar. I told Jesse the poor fuck ought to just have himself a new set of cards run off. But then I had to allow that the Jews probably owned all the print shops.

There was some good news, though. In Lucknow, India, Ramu the Wolf Boy died, freeing himself from the clutches of scientists who had been studying him since 1954. And in Canada, Pierre Elliott Trudeau was sworn in as prime minister, replacing the retiring Lester Pearson. The man on the radio said Trudeau was handsome, urbane, and liberal.

"There you go," I said to Jesse. "Home, sweet home."

He looked at me, cocked an ironic eye. "I thought politics were irrelevant."

I shook my head. "Never said that. You got to know what they're up to, or they'll eat your lunch and arrest you for trying to poison them."

"When I walked out of their circle," he said, "they forced someone to take my place. I have to become part of a circle greater than theirs. I have to help others join that greater circle. It's the only way. Otherwise, I'm just another coward, just another kid who can be bought off with a college deferment or a court decree."

"Aw, shit, Son. They want a million men in Vietnam, there'll be a million men in Vietnam. The world's always been full of soldiers. Your job's not to be one of them."

"My job is to live with grace and generosity in a world almost ruined by technocrats. My job—your job too—isn't to escape the world but to be part of it. To be so clearly and purely a part of the world that even the soldiers will have to see. Otherwise, we'll be conceding that world to them."

"You can't beat them using honor, boy. They'll just have you certified crazy, slap you in the bin, say, 'Look at that poor son of a bitch. Thinks he's got honor.' Then they'll crack your door open just a notch so you can hear the visitors laughing at you."

He started to say something to that, but I held up my hand, stopped him, wanted to finish out my say. "The men that run things, Son, they're corrupt, every one of them, right through the core. There's no moral lesson anybody can teach them. The ones we got have dreamed up a war nobody understands, and they're sending eighteen-year-old boys over by the hundred thousand to fight it for them. You wonder why anybody ever does what the bastards say. I mean, Christ, if I pulled off this road up here at the next house and went in and told the folks there I felt like there was some bad men up the road a piece coming after me and I wondered would they mind sending their son up there to fight them for me, why, I figure them folks would throw me out on my ass, don't you?"

"Probably, but—"

"Oh, they might call the cops or ask me some questions so they might could make some sense out of what was going on. But they wouldn't just shove their son out the door and say, 'Go to it, Junior.' Ain't nobody fool enough to do that."

Jesse laughed. "God," he said, "the purity of outlaw logic." But I couldn't tell whether he approved.

"But you let Lyndon Johnson or Hubert Humphrey or Robert Kennedy or Richard Nixon or whichever cocksucker's next, you let one of them ask, and, why shit, it's all drum rolls and heroes, and they'll send poor Junior off humming 'The Battle Hymn of the Republic.' "

"They do that out of the impulse to do the honorable thing. They're misguided, they're taken advantage of, but they're not evil."

"All right. I'll give you that. They're just stupid. Okay. But let's say you go up to that same house and tell them you need a night's shelter because you're on the run, government's asked you to go to war for the Kennedy compound and the Johnson ranch and you ain't willing, you figure you got a right to make up your own mind what you'll kill and die for. Well, odds are real good they won't just turn you down, they'll turn your ass in."

"A lot of people would. Sure. Still, most of them would just be doing what they thought right."

"I'll grant you that too. But what the fuck difference does it make? They been thinking that way ever since the first motherfucker rounded hisself up an army and started telling folks, 'Look here, you know we're way better than them bastards across the river, but you know too we ain't ever going to be safe till they're gone. So God's called me to lead you on this crusade to wipe them out.' So all the able-bodied men and all their half-grown sons sign on with him, and off they go, over and over again. They do it partly because they think they ought to, because they think it's the honorable thing, a sacred duty, but they do it partly too because they're just real bored with the life they been leading there at home. But the point I want you to see is they been doing it forever, and for all that time they been hanging the few that wouldn't go along with them. And there ain't no sign they ever going to quit. You ain't going to change them, Son. They got too much history behind them, too many bodies. You take them on straight up, they going to ruin you. Ain't nothing scares them worse or pisses them off more than the sight of a free man being free. It's worse now than it ever was. The armies are way bigger and so are the guns, and it takes a smart man to find an open road. You can beat them, but you can't beat them being a priest. You got to be a gypsy. You can't let them get their hands on you."

"That it?" he asked, smiling at me.

"Yeah," I said. "I just figured it was my duty as a father to go all the way through it once."

"You know," he said. "I admire you. It takes courage and wit to live the way you have for as long as you have."

"But you think I'm wrong."

"I think you've given up on too much."

"Maybe so. I just try to hold onto what works and what makes me laugh."

He didn't answer right off. I thought about singing some then—ain't nothing like shooting through the dark on a springtime highway for stirring up song. But I could feel he had something more to say, and I wanted to honor him with the quiet to say it in.

I was right. After a few minutes he said, "I don't know exactly what all I'll do or how I'll do it. If I did know, I'd go do it right now, wouldn't be here with you. I know I won't serve in their army, won't go to their war. But I want to find the best way to make that refusal an affirmation. When the time comes, I won't run. I'll make my stand in Blue Mountain, where I belong. If they send me to jail, I'll return to Blue Mountain when I get out. I have a villager's heart. I won't let them deny me my home."

I let it go. We drove on into Poplar Bluff, rented a night's worth of dank room from an outfit called Sky-Vue Cabins, pulled the blinds to, and slept till an hour or so past daybreak. Or I did. When I got up, Jesse was sitting in a cross-legged trance on a cheap carpet. I showered and shaved before bringing him up out of it.

"Got to get Gloria," I said.

It took him a minute or two to come up from nowhere, but he made it.

When we got to Billie's Eat-Rite Café, Gloria was waiting for us. She had the big, strung-out hippie with her. I should have known.

"Gunner was just telling me about the war," she said when we sat down.

The waitress came, and I ordered coffee, two fried eggs, and a pork chop. Jesse wasn't eating. He sniffed at his water like a Bircher suspecting fluoride. It'd be an odd village he'll live in.

"I'm going to be part of the show, Jim. A mainstay in Maledon Productions. Make 'em laugh, make 'em weep, make 'em wait, man. Have Mom and Dad and little Amy on the edge of their seats waiting to see what's gonna come down on ol' Gunner. Classical theater, Jack. I can be the tragic hero or the *deus ex machina*, man. You name it. Don't matter to me. 'Cause you the boss, you the one, you the man, Stan."

"Why did you go in the army?" I asked him.

"I was a good shot," he said.

The waitress brought my coffee. I blew into it and took a sip. It wasn't bad.

"Now, you ain't thinking about turning ol' Gunner out in the cold, are you, man?" He leaned back in his chair, cocked his head, and, his mouth in a smirk, studied me. He didn't look like he'd ever again make the mistake of taking anything seriously. He said, "The nation turns her back on her fighting men. Ah me, Mr. and Mrs. America. *Dulce et decorum.*"

"Sam," Gloria said, her young eyes beseeching, "Gunner'd be good. He'd be a natural."

"Just one more cut out of the take," I said. "And your friend looks like he might be a doper. Might bring us the same kind of trouble Jimmy Song did."

"I think I'm in love with this chick, man. You don't give me a ride, I'll just have to follow along behind you, I'm a fucking heat-seeking missile, Jackson. Can't get away from me. Ol' romantic fuck like yourself, man, you must know how the heart is."

I had another sip of coffee. "Well, I'll tell you this, Son," I said, saucering the cup, "it's a damn-fool thing to follow."

"Yeah, but listen to this, man." He looked around, making a show of checking for eavesdroppers, then leaned forward, cupped his hands around his mouth, and said, like a conspirator, "Baby's old man is loaded, Jack. I land her, and, Lord God, I'm at the end of the rainbow."

Gloria laughed.

Jesse said, "If he isn't part of the show, neither am I."

The waitress set my breakfast in front of me. "You know what's wrong with this country?" I asked her.

"I've heard people say," she answered, "but I keep forgetting."

"Well, here's the answer. And you pay attention this time. It's that the young generation don't pay no mind to their elders."

"No," she said. "That's not it. Must be something else. I just can't think of it."

4 JESSE

Thus far we have been playing, on his ground, a game of my father's devising. None of us knows, for example, the precise machinations of his Wallace flimflam. We were paid by him, he was paid by them, and then, deceiving us, he robbed them. He used us to make arrangements with them, used them to make arrangements with us, used them and us to make his own separate arrangement. He draws attention here, money vanishes there, and he drives away in a hearse carrying their cash in a garbage bin. He says only, "We learned a long time ago, Villines and me, that people like them never pay attention to a janitor. You can always gig them by looking humble and being smart."

On his level he is far beyond any of us. He feels nothing but contempt for any form of ordained authority, feels little more for the millions who take that authority seriously. He has devoted the best part of a lifetime to mastering the at-once brazen and delicate art of hustle. Like some trickster deity, he gives you the illusion you have the upper hand, then works that illusion into his script.

And we ride on with him, Gloria and I, the revolution's child and the spirit's acolyte, ride on to his next gig. Motivated primarily by curiosity, by our fascination with his gall and cunning, we have become bit players in a carnival show.

I can tell myself that finally it doesn't matter, that he can have his way until the time comes for me to make my stand. And I will do that on my ground and in my way.

But why do I delay that time of reckoning? For the time is mine to choose. I could return today. I can only say that while I am certain, I am not ready. I need yet to further strengthen not my resolve but my spirit. I do not apologize. Even the best of men required their forty days in the wilderness.

But I must not succumb to the allure of my father's chameleon highways. Preparation must be but preparation, and it must have its natural end. I cannot allow it to become a pretext for repudiating responsibility. This I must always remember: For me the highway must ultimately lead home.

My father and I—

A child, I search for meaning and ultimate order. Who am I? Why am I here? What does it mean to be human? To be animal? To be possessed of life? What is my relationship to earth and cosmos and God? How can I be most fully alive? How does the fact of death affect the meaning of life? And what is my responsibility to others? Questions of faith and mortality, questions reason cannot answer, define me: seeker or fool—or both.

For my father there is merely the sun and the rain and the road. Meaning is the laughter at the end of the perfectly executed hustle. He is, in the realm of grit, the pharoah of flash and dazzle. Like a magician producing dove from hat, he lowers his hand into the abyss and produces meaning. But then—poof. Vanished. All of it. Hat and dove. Abyss and meaning.

Illusion.

And the magician becomes a good old boy behind the wheel of another man's hearse.

So, I issue the flat ultimatum: Gunner stays, or I go.

I am, I know, my father's one weakness. Whatever sense of obligation or responsibility he has focuses on me. He feels bound to rescue me from myself and the penitentiary. That is my power over him, and the ultimatum is a minor test of that power.

It is also a test of his ability to adapt and dominate. Will he be able to control a man as apparently unpredictable as Gunner?

Will the game remain his?

Again, curiosity. It is what yet binds me to this road.

It is perhaps my inheritance.

Its training is my preparation.

So we go on.

5 GLORIA

Gunner and I were walking through Brazos O'Flaherty's greening pastures. In the distance, acres away, we could see the wooden stage that had been built on a rise above the river. It would be another day before many of the musicians began arriving. Now there were only the few people handing out broadsides and the rings of freaks walking easily about in the afternoon sun or lounging on sleeping bags, blankets, flags. Everywhere joints passed from hand to hand. Our communion. Small nylon tents made bright, irregular patches of color against the spring meadow. I told Gunner I thought our generation would be different, would be the source of a new beginning. Because our parents had shown us what was supposed to be the American dream, and we had been appalled by it, by the geometry of its greed, the tight-assed exclusiveness of its order.

He laughed. "Y'all been spoiled, baby. That's all."

I started to say we were in the process of repudiating privilege, but I caught myself. He was still too much the calloused veteran to recognize hope. I told myself time and freedom would bring him around.

As we walked, we passed from song to song. Here we heard a quick-fingered acoustic guitarist accompanying himself on Dylanesque harmonica. Around him, happy, stoned people closed their eyes and hummed. A moment later we heard a flute and turned to see a boy—he couldn't have been more than fifteen, and already he sought freedom—a beautiful boy with dark hair and Irish blue eyes, sitting alone on his flannel shirt, his delicate hands holding the magic, silver instrument to his lips. The music was baroque and religious—Bach, I think, though it could have been one of the others—and we stopped, as others were doing, to listen. His playing seemed private, a form of meditation almost, and we seemed privileged intruders to be tolerated only so long as the intrusion itself was kept private. Strangely hypnotic, his music bid us come so far but no farther, drew us to him, then held us in limbo, but a beautiful, almost heavenly limbo. When he finished, he rose and walked away, toward the river, and a moment or two passed before those of us who had been listening were released from the spell and freed to continue our own wanderings. But then we walked, grateful for the interlude, toward other music, through air sweet and rich with the smell of spring and marijuana.

We were looking for Jesse. Maledon was working on the Hangman show and wanted to talk to Jesse about his part. The show wasn't to be a play, a drama, which is what I had in mind, but a series of interrelated monologues. Conrad Villines was to be Judge Isaac Parker. I would be Annie Maledon, the Hangman's doomed, wayward daughter. Gunner was to play Hugh Harp, one of Parker's deputy marshals. And Maledon, of course, always took the Hangman's part. Jesse? Well, he hadn't decided yet, hadn't shown any interest in any role. Maledon, who ordinarily delivers the last of the monologues, was willing to let Jesse deliver the final speech with a noose around his neck.

Gunner offered to fill that role, too, if Jesse refused. "Just cut a mouth hole in the hood," he told Maledon. "Let me talk through that hole, man. Or if you're worried about veri-fucking-similitude, I can just be Hugh Harp again, being hung now for going bad, Jack. I'm the one can tell them theatergoing motherfuckers about the incoming, man, about the outgoing, about the wagon master coming and choosing his load at random, laughing as he points his old, crooked finger at the next poor fucker on board."

Maledon had laughed. "Amen, Brother Grant."

"And in the gray air above your poor, fucked head, man, you can hear the incoming whistle a high harmony to the wagon master's outgoing song. I say, 'Look inward, assholes. I am the heart of the fucking mystery, Jack. Ain't nothing there but me. And this laugh." Then a lunatic's supernatural laugh. "You hang me while I'm still laughing, man."

Maledon said, "I'll say, 'Ain't nothing we can say but "Damn you, Hugh Harp." Ain't nothing we can do but keep the line moving.' "

Gunner was speeding, and Maledon had carnival blood, and they laughed together. And I smiled, thinking, The only ones fit to be with are the crazy ones.

We found Jesse where Maledon thought we would—on the eastern edge of Brazos O'Flaherty's land. He sat full lotus on the levee above the Mississippi. A few feet in front of him a small driftwood fire flickered and flared in the easy river wind. Beyond the fire ten or twelve dharma bums, yearning for the light requiring no tunnel, sat facing him. All but a couple had the Westerner's stiff joints and could only approximate the lotus. Master Jesse and the acolytes.

We climbed the levee, our steps cushioned by thick Bermuda grass, and stopped a few feet away from the meditators. I felt the promise of warmth in the gentle wind. The brown river rolled magnificently southward. The unblinking, unfocused eyes of the seekers stared into the small fire as if it were the very center of all. They looked as if the constantly shifting fire glow had both enlightened and blinded them.

The revolution of the spirit.

Perhaps, I thought, all the necessary revolutions can occur simultaneously. Perhaps this can be the revolution of pure light, perfect joy, and absolute justice. Perhaps we can have both Buddha and Che.

Gunner said, "Better get to circling up the fucking wagons, Lady Jane. Damn Injuns is on the rise."

"It's high time."

"Oh, lady, my love," he said. "It ain't but the old death dream. The dark night's coming, Janie Lou. Cavalry gonna chew 'em up, gonna chew us all up. Y'all ain't seen the cavalry massed yet, man, ain't heard the incoming coming in, ain't seen all the good men dead. Shit, my sweet, all y'all got's this faggot dream. Won't stand up. Word of God, it won't stand up. Cause they got ordnance, child, designed by little white-smocked men from MIT, does straightaway with the soul."

"Didn't get yours," I said.

"They put the slump in Ol' Blue, though, didn't they?" he said, showing the smile that was half leer. "Soul ain't nothing, pure heart, upside that."

I leaned against him, put an arm around his back. "We'll fix that."

"Could be," he said. "You can't tell about nothing no more."

I stared into the fire. "I know you think I'm naive," I told him. "I know you've had to take a lot harder look at the dark side than I have. But, Gunner, I really think we might win. There are so many of us, and the old world is so obviously rotten. 'An old bitch gone in the teeth,' like Ezra Pound said." I looked up at him. He, too, studied the fire. "Ten years from now, I think this might be our country."

His eyes moved from the fire to Jesse, then looked down at me. "I hope you're right, love," he said, tenderness in his voice now. "But that old world, darling, she may be a bitch, and she may've lost everything that makes a good dog but the teeth, but, by God, she's still got them teeth. I can't really blame you for trying. But they ain't never lost, man. Ain't never going to be. Every morning the headline ought to say, MOTHERFUCKERS WIN AGAIN."

"You're too much like Maledon that way," I told him. "When you look in that direction, you can't see anything but the machine. Well, people built that machine, and people can take it apart."

"That fucker Maledon," he said. "Way back yonder sometime, he caught a glimpse of that machine, and, man, he went straight into hiding. But not me, love, no ma'am. Dumb fuck I was, I joined right up with it, and it killed everything I knew."

He lowered his head and kissed me. "Now I got you. And all I got gall left to hope for is that I can work my way far enough back up to where I can do you some good."

Then, as if that were all the romantic sentiment he could tolerate, he let a tremor run through his body, and his face jerked into a grin. He ran in place for a few seconds, his upper body bending forward and straightening in rhythm with his pumping legs. Then, a B-movie Indian, he began circling the seekers, his palm pounding against his mouth: "Ooo, woo, ooo, woo, ooo, woo, ooo, woo, woo, woo."

It took him only two rounds to fully disrupt meditation. When he had their attention, he stopped, looked them over, walked calmly to the fire, and pissed on it.

I looked at Jesse, who had not completely returned from trance. There seemed to be no anger in him, no frustration. For a moment he seemed absorbed in the effect of piss on fire. Then he stood and looked out on the river.

He may be, I thought, the craziest one of all.

6 MALEDON

It was a big week, that one, that last week in April. For one thing (you remember, of course), it was when the New American Revolution began. This time there wasn't any of that slogging around in Valley Forge, eating boot leather and wondering whether the wife and kids were still alive back on the farm. Why, no sir, nearly two centuries had passed, and time had taught the freedom fighters how to work a thermostat. So they went straight to the heart of things, climbed right up into the belly of the beast. Wednesday night April 24, 1968—you got it marked somewhere, don't you?—two hundred Columbia University students commandeered the office of their president, Grayson Kirk, and seized Hamilton Hall, from the windows of which they hung poster-size portraits of Stokely Carmichael, Malcolm X, Che Guevara, and Lenin. The crocuses were blooming. Freedom was coming. A new world hove into sight.

I wouldn't've paid much mind to any of that shit, would've had no more than a mild laugh or two out of it, if it hadn't been for Gloria and all the damn fools littering up Brazos's pasture, who thought the by-God dawn had come.

"God, I'd like to be there," Gloria said that first night as all of us, even Jesse, sat around Brazos's big RCA color set watching the liberation on the late-night news. "I missed the free speech movement; I missed Selma. I've never really done anything."

"You know," I said, "I can't figure why anybody'd give a damn if they closed that place forever. Nobody lives there."

Brazos laughed. He was rich enough, with inherited oil money, and fool enough to see the world as a great amusement park. He didn't worry about anything but boredom. This looked like a revolution he'd fit right into.

Gloria said, "It's symbolic. It's a start. We've forced our way inside and tossed the ministers of greed into the street." And so on for some time. It was damn near unbearable. But sometimes you just got to forgive the young—especially if they're pretty.

The air over Brazos's pasture filled with excitement, exaltation, pot fumes, and wind chimes. The Revolution of Ecstasy has claimed its first tangible triumph. It was the dawn of the first day of the new Eden. Some of the campers abandoned the Missouri meadow, planning to hitchhike to New York City and lend direct aid to the besieged Hamilton Hall guerrillas. Some mailed ounces of Columbian Pride or little windows of God's own acid to the valiant, dope-starved heroes. And some simpy stayed where they were, stoned, composing ballads to Mark Rudd, plotting to seize this or that building on their own campus as soon as this pasture party ended.

My attitude toward them swung back and forth between amusement and disgust. There were so spoiled they didn't know the difference between storming the Bastille and camping out in a dormitory. They'd tell you their government was evil, ruthless, and monolithic, that it had at its command the largest, deadliest army in history, and yet they thought they could topple it by liberating student unions, chanting mantras on the steps of ROTC buildings, and singing "Maggie's Farm."

Maybe I was just another aging man, irritated by the vitality of the young. Maybe, but I don't think so. No, it was their need to be surrounded by a crowd that bothered me, their need to see a rock concert as an act of revolution. They were posturers, playactors. They'd never had to see the cost of choice—that when you choose one road, you give up whatever lies along all the others. They'd never had to know the nature of risk—somebody else had always paid for their mistakes, somebody they resented, somebody they rejected until it came time to pay another bill. And they had no real idea what this government they claimed to despise would do to them if they ever managed to get in its way. But I didn't think there was much danger of that. I thought, even then, they lacked both the sense and the courage to pose an actual threat. No, they would lose. That seemed as clear to me as the green in Brazos's pasture. And what's more, they'd lose without ever knowing they'd lost. Because they wanted to shut down Coca-Cola without having to give up Cokes. Because they didn't have the balls to take the risk that would cut them loose. Give them ten years, they'd be working on Wall Street, eating at French restaurants, buying season's tickets to the philharmonic, and voting their pocketbooks. They were just the spawn of privilege, out on a lark.

But I managed to keep my mouth shut most of the time, managed to keep from baiting Gloria, managed, at least part of the time, to enjoy Brazos's money and good humor, managed to see that they were all well on their way to having their monologues memorized, managed to get the gallows properly set up in town on the pier above the river three blocks from the Mark Twain home.

And I waited for Conrad Villines to come. He understood these campus guerrillas way better than I did. Maybe he could explain to me why I resented them so. Maybe he could tell me why these, of all people, seemed to me in some ways the worst of the American lot.

And maybe he would tell me again what I already knew, why it is that the few of us who choose to wander the edge come to judge so harshly the many who don't.

Meanwhile, I kept a lookout for Spoof Lyons or Homer Cantwell. I hadn't missed Mark Twain Days in years, and I knew one or both of them would be there watching. I'd planned on it. Because I knew this was the place I had to lose them for good. It was time to take my son into exile.

7 JESSE

In the beginning and the end and in the apparent arc between is the mystery, the circle that is microcosm and macrocosm, change and changelessness, order and absurdity, that defies reason and transends faith, that can be neither understood nor avoided, that is at once the seeker and the sought, that is the perfectly orchestrated chorus of chaos and the midnight jazz of ultimate harmony, that is the drumbeat of doom and the harp song of hope.

I am the medicine man and the medicine, and I am he who comes to be healed.

I am but man, part and whole, mortal and immortal, nothing and all.

I am the mystery whose source I seek. And I am the source.
I know nothing. And it is enough.

Commandments for myself:

Do not reject the world. To do so is to reject the mystery. Reject only that which is concocted or manufactured to allay the fear of the mystery: technological toys, Disneyland divertissements, political propagandizing.

Let fear make you humble and humility make you fearless.

Remain a citizen. Cosmos is also in community.

To know phenomena, observe the phenomenon. And vice versa.

Love not the idea of love. But love.

Make work and play indistinguishable, one. But work hard enough to understand the problem.

Follow no master. Master no followers. Walk alone, but do not abandon brotherhood.

Remember: When all else fails, call the darkness light.

Forbid yourself to issue commandments.

8 GLORIA

The first two nights at Brazos's, Gunner and I slept in a second-story, early American bedroom that had a private balcony and a state-of-the-art stereo system. There was a bar beside the bed and a mirror above it. The sheets were silk, and the lights could be lowered to moonglow-dim. The Sinners' Suite, Brazos called it.

But nothing I did in that room worked. We drank good wine, smoked good dope, danced naked to everything from Benny Goodman to the Dead. I played the virgin, and I played the whore. I played the frustrated housewife, and I played the high-fashion seductress. Homecoming queen and backseat slut. Schoolmarm and schoolgirl. I talked, and I attacked. I used my head, and I used my body, mouth, hands, tits, ass, and cunt. And, no matter what I did, there it was, hanging yet, beautiful but limp.

"Just like the hand of God," Gunner said. "Keeps dangling and dangling down in the darkness, man. Ever' once in a while, ain't no way of knowing when, the son of a bitch strikes."

I was tired and more than a little humiliated at having so determinedly offered myself and having been, on the purest level, refused. I knew it wasn't my fault, knew that I could walk out of the house and into the pasture and seduce the first man I met, but still I couldn't entirely overcome a feeling of personal failure. Gunner was the first man I hadn't been able to rouse, and this was the first time, really, I'd even had to think about it. I'd never doubted the power of my body. I'd always thought that if I said yes to mankind, it would form a line beginning at the foot of my bed. Oh, a man like Jesse might refuse me—or Maledon that time—but he'd have a hard-on when he did. It would be the mind's refusal, not the body's.

So those nights with Gunner made me see my power as conditional. I felt vulnerable, sexually vulnerable. And I felt confused, demeaned, debased—like a failed rapist. All that made me want him more than I'd ever wanted any other man. I wanted him as vindication. And that was so simple, so trite, so girlish, I became furious with myself. And with him.

I said, "Maybe like the hand of God, it's just dead. Maybe it always has been."

We were on the bed again, after trying carpet, rocker, love seat, and shower. I rolled over, turning my back to him.

"It's steady cock you want, sister," Gunner said, his voice seeming to come from oceans away, from some sandbagged bunker invulnerable even to a direct hit, "you done latched onto the wrong soldier."

"Evidently," I said.

9 MALEDON

"I'm going to make it permanent," Brazos O'Flaherty told us. "I'm going to turn the ranch into a full-blown commune."

"Hasn't been made into a ranch yet," Villines said.

"Aw hell, you got to call it something," Brazos told him.

We were in Hannibal, on the Main Street sidewalk directly across from the Mark Twain Boyhood Home. Tourists milled around us, sipping at literature's folksy fount. Brazos's thin, dark arms jerked around as he talked to me and Conrad, who had arrived just that morning. Several days of playing host to a field full of part-time dropouts had set Brazos's mind to doing even more than its customary amount of scat dancing. For as long as I'd known him, he'd run on the rich eccentric's faith that if you bought enough folks, a few of them were bound to amuse you—and one of them might even be just the man to show you the ultimate light. Brazos was a seeker, as Jesse might say. He wanted it all to be carnival, but he wanted it to happen on his land, and he wanted it to mean something. What he was telling us, more or less, was that he was going into the business of buying barkers. Nothing new about that, except that now he was going to hire them permanent, give them full-time shelter.

"You got enough money to support a pasture full of former humanities majors?" Conrad asked him.

"Man I bought the place from farmed it."

"Had it farmed," Conrad corrected. It irked him to hear mere landowners referred to as farmers. Conrad was your Jeffersonian democrat who was managing to survive here in the last third of the twentieth century by going a little crazy.

"There you go." Brazos nodded, gave Conrad's shoulder an admiring slap. "Always a man for clearing the scum off a sentence. I'll be needing a man like that. See, I figure I'll set up a school on the place too, Conrad. You might be interested in running it. Educate the offspring and all. See to it don't nobody's mind turn to mush, you know. Keep the fine edge on truth."

"Going in this counterculture business whole hog, are you, Brazos?" I said.

"Whole hog or none," he answered. "Always been my way." We'd reached North Street, having passed the Tom Sawyer Diorama, Aunt Polly's Handcrafts, the Becky Thatcher House, and Judge Clemens's Law Office. We took a right and headed toward the river. Brazos kept giving voice to his dream. "Be like a kibbutz," he said. " 'Cept not as serious and not as many Jews. All religions be represented, you know, and none at all."

"None at all?" Conrad said.

"I mean like a synthesis. No point in rejecting anything."

"Why not?" Conrad wondered. "Most of it's wrong."

"Ecumenicalism," Brazos explained. "You know, take over where the pope failed."

I said, "Brazos's going to fix up a place out there where everybody can eat, drink, dope, fuck, and see God."

He looked at me a second, nodded, cocked an eager eye. "Well, yeah," he said. "I guess that's about it. Ain't no reason it can't work, is there? Most everybody likes to do all them things."

"Pretty soon the fucking takes over," Conrad told him. "Every evening after that when you bow your head over the communal gruel, jealousy's saying grace."

"Nice way of putting it," Brazos conceded. "But ol'-fashioned thinking. Times are changing. These young folks, a lot of them, they don't think that way. Share their women like Eskimos."

"Best thing I can say about that," Conrad said, "is it won't last. If it does, we're in real trouble."

Brazos gave him a laugh. We came to the railroad tracks and took a left on them. There were a few folks standing down by the river's edge, thinking and talking about time and history or some such, but we had the tracks to ourselves.

"There's times," Brazos told Conrad, "when I don't understand what you're saying. Like this. Seems like you're saying jealousy's good. An old thief like yourself standing up for fidelity and virtue and all that old corsetted Victorian shit. I mean, I know you got your reasons, and I know they're properly convoluted, and if you gave it all to me full bore I'd be likely to wind up thinking, Jesus, the old fart's probably right. But your way you don't end up with anything but skepticism." He devoted a beat or two to considering that. "Comes from your being a teacher, I guess. Leaving a man with more questions than answers. Socrates and such."

"Probably it," Conrad agreed.

We walked a few steps in silence. Then Brazos stepped up on a rail and took off down the track at a run. He ran a good twenty-five yards, without so much as a wobble, then stopped, spun around on the toes of his right foot, and ran back to us.

A child. It was what made him tolerable company.

"Used to could do that clean across Texas," he said when he got back to us. "My daddy used to spend all his time going from oil well to oil well, whoring and hollering and counting his money. I didn't see him much, but when I did he'd tell me he was doing it all for my future. He bought Momma one of the first TV sets in Odessa, and she'd sit there all day, smoking L&M's and drinking highballs and watching *Search for Tomorrow* and *The Edge of Night*, whatever it was and whatever came on next on that one station she could get. And I'd go to school when I could stand it, where the other boys were always ragging me—sometimes hard, sometimes till I had to work to keep the tears down—because I liked to read, see, and because I couldn't catch a football right, and because their daddies worked for mine. So I got to where a day or two a week I'd pack me a sack lunch and instead of going to school I'd go down the tracks, spend half a day following them north toward Abilene and half a day following them back. But I was always back way before dark. The oil field spawn were right about one thing—I was a little chicken shit. I kept on coming back home. Came home one day, and there was a band of strangers with their hats in their hands telling Momma something about a load not being tied down good and something sliding off the side of a flatbed truck and Daddy happening to be standing there beside the road. Everybody shaking their heads, then looking down at their boots, and the TV still going. And Momma trying to come up out of the highball fog—or trying not to, I'm not sure which. And then, later, the funeral, and men coming by telling us he was the kind of man that made Texas what it was and me thinking, in spite of their sincere, wind-carved faces and in spite of myself, Amen to that.

"I hated Texas—still do—Jim Bowie and Davy Crockett and Sam Houston and Stephen F. Austin—ever' fucking founder one—ever' cow and ever' cowboy, ever' horse and ever' hero, crude oil and crude lives. So I took my high-school diploma and went to Columbia, Missouri, because somebody told me they had a good journalism school there, and I wanted to be a muckraker. But then one year I was home for Christmas, and Momma and me were watching *Miracle on 34th Street*, and she reached over for her glass and jerked twice and was gone. Last thing she said to me—and I think she said it a good hour before she died—I remember it because it was something she said a lot, because it was all she had of philosophy or religion—she said, 'It ain't much life, Son. Wasn't for my whiskey and my stories, wouldn't be no life at all.' I remember nodding.

"It was a lesson to me. I didn't know my daddy. His life was separate from mine. Maybe he enjoyed it, I don't know. But there wasn't anything I could take from it but the knowledge that I didn't want one like it. Momma, now, that was different. I knew her—or what there was of her. I understood what had sunk her into that darkness she lived in. She died in the biggest house in Odessa, and she left me more money than a man can spend in a lifetime. So I cashed in everything they had, down to the last barrel of oil, and I bought this place on the river, and there ain't been a day since when I didn't have somebody around me could make me laugh."

Nobody said anything right off. We veered off onto the spur that led to Riverview Park. The park was crowded for that time of day and week. Lots of people milling around in spring colors.

"So here we are," Conrad said, "laughing it up."

"You don't have to laugh out loud," Brazos said. "Though that's awful nice. It's just that feeling that life's a flying circus, all of us doing little turns up through the rainbows. Now and again somebody falls, but the circus goes on." He looked at Conrad, then turned to me, then gave us a couple of nods and a grin. "Y'all always give me that, the two of you. First time y'all came here and put on the show, it gave me a sense of what life could be. Farce and laughter and gall. For a while I thought maybe I'd go on the road myself, but then it came to me I had enough money to bring the road home to me."

"Doesn't count," Conrad said, "unless you go from scratch."

I gave that a laugh and said, "Conrad wants to hog-tie a meaning onto everything. Tends to make things go by slow, dragging a duffel bag behind them."

"Things matter," Conrad said. "A thing can't even be comic until it matters."

"Me, now," I said, "I remember, for instance, spending the night some years back with a barmaid from El Dorado. She carried a little too much flesh, and the years had worn some of the gloss off her features, and I got no idea now what her name was. Never saw her before, never saw her again. But goddamned if we didn't have us a night's worth of time."

"That matters," Conrad argued. "Two lonely strangers taking a night's brief comfort in each other. At the time it happens, that might matter as much as anything."

"I don't know about the woman," I said. "But I ain't ever been lonely to speak of. Fact, there've been times when just me was more company than I wanted to deal with. No sir, Conrad, what that was between me and that woman wasn't no more than just blind animal lust. Both of us was wanting to fuck, and we happened to run into each other. And maybe that matters. Who cares? Whether it does or not, praise God for it. Blessed be the mindless cock. All hail the vagrant cunt."

"Promiscuity is our only hope," Conrad mocked out the side of his mouth.

"One of them six-bit words can make paradise sound like shit," I said.

Brazos clapped his hands, threw back his head. "Ay, God!" he said. "You two. Just walking to the park with you boys brightens a man's morning."

Conrad gave him the sarcastic eye. "About one man out of three in Texas talks a lot like Sam."

"Maybe so," Brazos conceded. "But I damn sure had to leave there before I could hear it."

"Well," Villines said, "Missouri's not exactly civilization."

We'd crossed the south edge of the park by then, and up ahead of us more-or-less civilized commerce of various kinds was going on. Folks were loitering around, carrying rolled-up newspapers and little foam cups of coffee, sweet rolls and tourist guides. We passed a sizable cluster of Hare Krishnas, some of them doing their little tambourine stomp, the others begging alms. Brazos wanted to give them money, but I stopped him.

"Make them pull a gun," I said. No point in encouraging them. I didn't care for them anyway, but what especially set me off that morning was that I could just see ol' Jesse out there caught up in it with them, doing the skinhead dance, chanting for the Chinaman's chance.

But then, as we walked away from them, it came to me that that might not be a bad dodge for a while.

Jesse, Gunner, and Gloria had come into town a half hour before us, Jesse wanting to see the sun rise on the new gallows, I guess. Doom and immortality, the destiny of man and the mystery of God, now and forever, amen and etcetera. And ever since they'd got out of my sight, I'd been a little nagged by the thought that I might ought to've sat on Jesse. Spoof Lyons'd be here sooner or later, and I knew he might be operating on the word that it was time to rip the tracks out from under Jesse's train.

So when Brazos and Conrad stopped to talk to the springtime pacifists who were handing out broadsides against the war, I went on. Past the junk-food stands, the flag booth, the military recruiting stations, past the tourists and the dopers, the bikers and the narcs, past T-shirts saying LOVE IT OR LEAVE IT and T-shirts saying CHANGE IT OR LOSE IT, past campaign workers for Nixon and Wallace and Humphrey and Kennedy, past kids who got clean for Gene and kids who got down with the Dead. Everybody dancing to somebody's song.

Walking on through the park past them all, I began to hurry some as I neared the new-built scaffold above the edge of the river. And there he was, standing in the Hangman's place, one foot actually propped up on the lever. Ol' Spoof, jawing with the city heat. I slowed some, wanting to come in casual.

As I started up the gallows' steps, City Blue moved to block my way. "This is the stage for the Saturday night show, sir. No one's allowed up here right now."

"Why, Son, that's ol' Sam hisself," Spoof said. "Show's star. Come to check out the props, I reckon."

"You have identification, sir?"

I gave him a look. Spoof guffawed.

"Shit, Son," he said. "Identification? Ol' Sam here can reach in one pocket and haul out papers saying he's Richard Milhouse Nixon, then reach in the other one and show you some saying I'm a Secret Service agent. Fact, Son, something you been wanting to be, just give ol' Sam the nod. He's a damn equal-opportunity office all by hisself."

By that time, I was up there with them. I looked at the young cop. "How come you let this fat fuck up on my stage?"

He gave me a grin and a little jerk of his head. "He had papers."

"Got to where they're mailing out papers like Christmas cards," I said. "Damned if I know what the country's coming to."

"The brotherhood of the blue," Spoof explained.

I looked from Spoof to the local dick. "Brotherhood ought to up its dues," I said.

Spoof laid a big hand on the cop's shoulder. "Why don't you go on down, son, and spend a few minutes sizing up the gathering rabble. Get yourself a king-size Coca-Cola and a foot-long dog, maybe arrest one or two of them damn dancing be-sheeted beggars for vagrancy. Me and ol' Sam here need to work on the program."

The cop climbed down the steps, walked maybe ten feet away from the scaffold, then just stood there, his back to us, his arms folded across his chest. A guard.

I cocked my head and glanced aslant at Spoof. "How is it you got the Hannibal heat taking your orders?"

He took a Marlboro from the pack in his shirt pocket. "Man knows how to give orders," he said, drawing a slow arc with his Marlboro hand, "world's full of people ready to take 'em."

"You kind of in the middle, though, ain't you? Taking the big ones, giving a shit load of little ones."

"Yeah. Well, a man finds his place." He narrowed his hard, blank eyes. "Most damn-fool thing a man can do is misjudge it." He lit the Marlboro.

"I'll be sure to remember that," I said. "Wouldn't want to outsmart myself and fuck up my life's work."

He turned away from me, made a cool study of the morning crowd. "What you think of all this, Sam?"

I looked out there too, saw Brazos and Conrad coming toward us, saw Conrad touch Brazos's arm, saw them walk away. "Not much," I said. "Just the start of another small-town festival."

"Naw," he said. "Not that. I mean the young'uns. Always riding around all drugged up, keeping an eye out for a place to gather."

"Bad raising," I offered. "Slack education. Electric guitars. Cheap drugs. And then, just enough sense to see that the way most of their folks live is just a slow way of dying."

"They don't know shit from syphilis," Spoof said. "They just staying high and getting pussy."

"Figured a man like you'd go for that. What is it, Spoof? Envy?"

"I roll in a waller, I know it's a waller," he said. "These fucks want to make out it's a altar."

"Maybe it is," I said. "Maybe ol' bucks like me and you just want to poke at the darkness."

He shook his head. There wasn't much Spoof hadn't done in his time—he'd take a bribe, fuck your wife, spend the county jail's food allotment on blended whiskey, drink some of the whiskey, and then sell the rest of it in the dry county he sheriffed—but he'd always figured it had to be done on the sly. The daylight was for deacons.

"Now, Spoof," I said. "Tell me true. Wouldn't you like to slip that ol' calloused cock of yours up in one of them flower girls?" I gave him a sad shake of the head. "Here you are, you've reached a age and a size and a general state of ugliness that pretty well puts all but the most desperate woman off. Then you lost the sheriff's job, don't get to fuck the runaways no more." I made a clicking sound, shook my head again. "Damn, must be tough."

"How about your own self? Been fucking your son's piece?"

"Fine morning like this here, we getting awful grim, ain't we?"

"Getting tired of fucking around with you, Sam. Driving all over south Arkansas checking out them shows you advertised then took the shyster's farewell on. Running here, running there, knowing after a time or two you ain't going to show, but knowing too it don't much matter, 'cause you're bound to show in Hannibal. Always have. But then wondering about even that, thinking, well shit, maybe he's throwing it all over for that boy of his." He studied me a second or two. "You want to lose me, why show for this one? You go any other way, you're shut of me."

"I wanted you to earn your money, Spoof, but I didn't want you to give up and quit."

He looked at me, head cocked a notch to the right, then turned and let his eyes take in the park, surveying, thinking, seeming to prepare himself for some kind of summation.

"I'm getting tired, Sam. Like I said." He used a bedraggled old hound of a voice. "Ol'," he said. He sighed, flipped the butt of his Marlboro off the gallows. "Sheriffed for 'em awhile. Done it right. Then got to thinking about my golden years, you know, thinking I deserved more'n what the county had in mind for me. So . . . Well. Aw shit, I fucked it up. Man like me ain't much hand at doctoring books. Needs one of them boys buys their suits off a man that don't make many. It didn't take 'em long to catch me, same kind of boys, and, well, I'd've been living out my life in a cinder-block room with a one-hole shitter out back hadn't been for Homer Cantwell." He looked back at me then. Hard. "I owe him, Sam. He's a flint-rock motherfucker. And I don't like his kind. No color to him, no life. Adding machine for a heart. But I owe him. And I'm tired."

"What you wanting from me, Spoof? Sympathy? It ain't like you. Might be better off in that cinder-block room."

"What I want's that boy, Sam. And I seen him this morning, standing up here with the sun rising in his hair. Thought about grabbing him then, but there was folks around. Homer don't want no notoriety. And anyway I'm a reasonable man. So you got till Saturday night. Show's over then. We'd like him to come easy. He don't, we'll take him hard. Homer's got plans for him, you know. Homecoming and all."

"Sounds like you got some help here with you."

"Lots of it. Homer done moved this right up to the top of his list. Somebody eating on Cantwell money gonna keep within striking distance of Jesse's ass dawn to dawn. So ain't no point in you trying any of your finagling. Your kind of smart just works on the edges, Sam, and you're smack in the middle now. Ain't no way out. Ain't nothing for it but to throw up your hands and move back over where you belong."

"Well," I said, after a beat or two, "looks like the smart money done bought me out, don't it?"

He nodded. "They always win, Sam. Man can live off to one side like you done till you started feeling fatherly, or he can sink into the routine they've drew up for him, or he can sell out to 'em smart, piece by piece, getting a glimpse or a taste now and again of what they got. But sure, Sam, they always win. Surest bet there is."

"Jesus," I said. "I can remember back when there was something resembling a man inside whatever suit of clothes you happened to be wearing. Been awhile, though, I guess, ain't it?"

"We shit, Sam, just shit, and they shit stompers." He showed me his palms. "I like you, always have. Wish things ran your way. Life'd be way more fun. But one day a long time ago you decided to bet it all on some fool notion of freedom. Set your mind on never letting anybody tell you what to do. I don't know, maybe you got that, but it's cost you everything else."

"Everything else ain't much," I said. I gave him the smart-ass grin. "But then I never had the opportunity to kiss a ass as fine as Cantwell's. Might throw it all over for that."

He gave me a last shake of the head, reason to renegade, stepped toward the stairs, said over his shoulder, "Don't let this come to showdown, Sam. You got no chance."

I'll be here Saturday night," I said. "You coming? I'll get you a pass."

"You bet," he said. "Wouldn't miss it. Be sitting front-row center next to Homer and Mary Cantwell."

"By God, the show draws all kinds, don't it?"

Having climbed down the thirteen gallows steps, he stopped, turned back. "Quality's coming in, Sam, to carry off the trash."

"Be good to see 'em fouling their own hands with their work."

"Oh, they just be watching, see it's done right."

10 JESSE

My father has a plan. Always a plan. That is, of course, the way of the confirmed anarchist: no overriding order, only contigency plans.

"I saw my stepfather," I say to him. "He was just watching, letting me know he was there. We said nothing. There was only the reciprocal knowing gaze."

"And I saw ol' Spoof," he says. "Hell, we even talked. None of that silent, secret shit for us."

Whether I am ready or not, the time approaches. I have become the object of other people's games. That must end.

"Don't matter much, their being here," he says. "Just pumps a little blood in the game. I knew they'd come. Spoof anyway."

We say nothing more for a moment. We are on the sodded levee at the edge of Brazos O'Flaherty's pasture. A fire flickers before us. The great river, shimmering silver in moonlight, golden in fireglow, rolls by and rolls by. What can matter but this?

But I must move. I must move.

He says, "They're wanting you home real bad."

"Now," I say, "or soon. The precise moment of return doesn't matter. The merchant's punctuality is not truth."

But I must move. I must move.

My father laughs. "I'm here now, I'll be there then. But even there and then, it'll be here and now." He unscrews the cap from his pint of whiskey. "You don't start thinking past that firelight there, Son, the men with the clocks are going to be using you for a pendulum. Grab you by the heels and swing you back and forth, back and forth till you get so used to it you mistake it for peace, bong, freedom, bong, peace, bong, freedom, bong. Ain't nothing easier for 'em than handling some abstract motherfucker. Always predictable."

I am curious. "If you knew they would be here and knew they would be trying to take me home, why are we here?"

But this is enough of curiosity. I must not allow it to countenance indecision. I must move.

"I want you to see the choice clear," he says. "And I want to show you how easy it is to lose 'em good."

I think again, in the firelit silence, of his life, his way. His faith is in the moment, and if the moment proves bad he believes he can connive his way into the next one, the clean one, the moment of pure laughter. But the joy of that moment is dependent on the complications of its predecessor, the one from which he has just escaped. His joy comes from having accepted and survived risk. What meaning is his is there. In that, he differs from most of the rest of us only in that he has clarified his situation by repudiating many of the cultural buffers and restraints that tend to prevent our accepting (or even recognizing) risk. He has no home, little family, no real job. What routine he has is subject to whim. Each dawn he sees a new sun, each evening a new moon. He accepts them both.

There is much I can yet learn from him—but not, I think, how meaningfully to resist the draft, the war, my country's folly. His way would be mere avoidance, to slip the net and begin again. My way must be to stand, to say no, and to say why.

I must move.

Confronted by the machine of state, vast and evil, my father would hide in the underbrush until he could see his way clear to take to the back roads again. It is a sane reaction. He would be neither party to nor victim of the evil. But it is a limited strategy, its sole end being self-preservation. It offers no resistance to the progress of evil. It is time to begin to dismantle the machine. I must do my part. In my way.

So I must move. I must move now.

He asks whether I saw my mother.

"No," I say. "Why?"

"Spoof says she's with them. I doubt it. But if she is, it could make things easier."

"And why is that?" I ask, knowing his answer.

"Because she loves you and that cuts way down on their options. There won't be no gunpoint kidnapping, for instance." He gives himself another drink. "My guess is they'll try having her talk motherly sense to you. Play the ol' guilt cantata."

"That will be fine," I say. "I can make her understand."

"Maybe," he says. "But, remember, she chose Cantwell hoping it would give you order. Now here you are rejecting his order, and hers, rejecting the chance she sacrificed to make for you. There'll come a time when y'all going to have to bring yourselves to forgive one another, but it may not be here yet. You may have to give pain some time to work its way."

I think about my mother, about her being used. I say, "They'll try to fool her."

"There you go." He grins. "You're getting better. May make it yet. Smart thing for them to do would be to let her talk to you, see you healthy and sane and making your own kind of sense, then jerk you away without her seeing it. Fact, I figure that's just what they'll try. Then they'll lead her to think whatever happened to you after that was my doing."

"She's not stupid," I say.

"I know that. But she ain't devious, either. Has trouble even recognizing crookedness. And ol' Homer's turds come out looking like corkscrews."

"Homer's merely a small man with big money."

"He's not stupid," he says, grinning again. "Just wrong."

"About everything."

"Oh, yeah. No question about that. And, most times, he's got the means to get his way. That's why you got to either club the motherfucker or stay clear of him entirely."

"You took some of his money," I remind him.

"I robbed him," he says. "Took his money and used it my way. Just left him that much short. That's one way of clubbing him. Course, he ain't going to let you get in many of them kind of licks."

Silence again. The fire, the river, the moon. It is time.

"Well, Son," he says, getting to his feet, "you willing to take that ride in ol' Booger's raft Saturday night?"

"Yes," I say and smile. "I'm willing to see where it goes."

But I will make its destination my own. For it is time. I must move.

11 GLORIA

Booger Purifoy was Nigger Jim.

It was his job. And Jesse was going to escape civilization by rafting downriver with him, going to head out for the territories.

But first we had to set it up. So that Friday evening we got into the hearse, and Maledon drove us toward Hannibal and a meeting with Homer and Mary Cantwell. "The mock showdown," Maledon had said, "where we're going to show 'em how to win by losing."

I switched on the radio: Barry McGuire singing "Eve of Destruction." Maledon punched a button: the news.

At Columbia, the people still had control of Hamilton Hall. The administration had agreed to halt temporarily construction of the gym they were building in Morningside Park, land rightfully belonging to the citizens of Harlem. But Mark Rudd and the SDS were demanding amnesty, and the university hadn't yet agreed to that. Stokely Carmichael and H. Rap Brown had spent part of the day in Hamilton Hall as a demonstration of solidarity. The people of Harlem were preparing and delivering the protesters' meals. Soul food. We are all together. The people against the machine.

At Boston University three hundred black students had taken over the administration building. The people had seized Long Island University. It had begun. It would spread. We would not yield.

The ruling class, concerned only with the preservation of privilege, had taken notice. In Indianapolis, Robert Kennedy asked a crowd of student doctors why they were sitting in medical school blithely accepting their student deferments while thousands of poor blacks were being slaughtered in Vietnam. So, yes, a certain taking of notice. And, yes, a fair question. But they had not yet begun to face the essential message: Why were you, Robert Kennedy, heir to Camelot, living so grandly on your father's whiskey millions while a tenth of the nation went hungry and the government you served and were served by sent the sons of sharecroppers and the sons of ghettos halfway around the world to kill and die for corporate America?

Give the Hyannisport compound to the Iroquois!

Give your millions to the hungry!

Put your ass on the line, motherfucker!

Maledon said, "It's banana season in the United Fruit Kingdom." He punched another button and got Hank Snow singing "I'm Moving On."

"Wouldn't it be something," Villines said, "if they actually won? Won it all, I mean. A nation run by acid heads. Some Mercedes maharishi as the White House chaplain. Nobody knowing how to do a thing. Afraid to call an election because they'd have just sense enough to know that the people they claimed to stand for would vote them out."

"All of them thinking they hated what was here," Maledon added, "but none of them having any idea what to replace it with."

"Paradise," I said, giving them the Abbie Hoffman answer. "We'd replace it with paradise."

"Ah, paradise," Villines said. "Free pussy tomorrow. One orgy for all." He laughed. "Sex is the opiate of the asses."

Brazos said, "We'll make all America one great daisy chain. Everybody giving, everybody getting, giving and getting and changing places in the chain according to whim. Every citizen a link in the chain. The chain shaking and rattling to the earth's old song. Do-si-do. Be fun for a while. Sure beat lining up at the induction center."

"There won't be any essential change," Jesse told us, priest to parish. "Not this way."

"Ain't gon' change none no way, Jack," Gunner said. "Uncle'll get tired of these senior-prom guerrillas sooner or later. Fire a couple of shots, man, be over. Be over right then. Sight of blood do it in. Oh, they'll wail awhile and cry awhile and make a few last threats. But it'll be over right then. Comrade Joe College ain't seen no pain, Jane. It comes down, he rolls over, hoping they'll grade on the curve or give him a little makeup test. And they'll do it for him too, man, 'cause he's one of their own. And they know this shit here ain't nothing but a panty raid with a manifesto."

"The prince of pain," I said. "The fucking archbishop of agony. Why don't you give the Dostoyevsky rap a rest?"

He turned to Maledon. "She something, ain't she, man? This new woman? Mind like a file, tongue like a blade. Heart like rocking chair, pussy like a welcome mat. Goes off to school, first thing, she learn's how to give head. Let the black hats start turning screws, though, Jack, she's just another shakey-legged twat."

"We do threaten the impotent," I said.

"Ah, love," Maledon said. "Spring and all. Innocence going to seed. Little puffballs of lust blowing in the swamp winds. Touches a weary ol' fart like myself right to the quick."

"What quick?" Villines asked. "Nothing there but alligator hide and a carnival heart."

"Gunner's right," Jesse said in that irritating summary tone. "We know nothing of suffering."

"Still, I wouldn't go signing up for it, I was you," Maledon said.

"Where suffering exists," I said, using a summary voice of my own, "we should try to alleviate it. Eradicate it if we can. It's that simple."

Villines, sardonic, said, "If you're not part of the solution, you're part of the problem."

"Yes," I said, nodding. "I know what you're going to say, but I believe that's true."

"They start asking you to be part of the solution," Maledon said, "it's time to get off the pavement."

Gunner agreed. "Amen, Ben."

"Shit," I said. "Here I am with a hustler who cares about nothing but making sure there's always a way out, a part-time historian who's offended by anything that violates his strict definition of democracy, a mystic who devotes his life to concentrating on the mystery of the rise and fall of his own breath, and a soldier whose suffering in the name of one bad cause has stripped him of any faith in any cause." I looked at them, turning from one face to another. "Fuck, if everyone was like you all, it'd leave the country to Richard Nixon and Ronald Reagan."

"Some truth there," Villines conceded.

Maledon parked the hearse in a space reserved for festival staff. When we got out, we could hear music. Pasteurized folk music. You know, the chamber of commerce version of "This Land Is Your Land," The Young Rotarians singing "Ol' Man River."

The park was full. Cotton candy, snow-cones, caramel apples, popcorn, hot dogs, and Coke. Mom and Dad letting Susie and Johnny eat junk till they puke. Bobby Joe and Betty Lou holding hands in carnival light, their thighs flirting now and then, he looking for a dark spot and hoping for a hump, she deciding just how far to let him go. Campaign volunteers wearing straw boaters and passing out buttons and stickers and fliers for packaged thieves. The neutered music on a temporary stage.

The Mark Twain Riverfest.

Their version of the pastoral.

America.

"Not a bad crowd for a cold night," Maledon said. Always the ticket-taker's eye.

The air held a chill, but it wasn't as cold as it had been two nights earlier, when it had frosted as far south as Wilder Junction—a record late frost for down home. I hoped it had killed the pear blossoms in my father's lawn. He so prided himself on the trees. Had a man spray them every two weeks with a Dow Chemical poison. When the pears ripened, he let them fall and rot.

I thought about my daughter. I had to get her soon. Even now I knew I would have to wean her away from privilege. It is so quickly addicting.

Maledon led us through the crowd, toward the river and his stage, the gallows.

A fat red-faced man wearing a cheap suit stood at the gate in the head-high plywood fence built to enclose tomorrow night's audience. "Why, lookee here," he said. "The whole by-God shebang. Who'd've thunk it." He turned his face to one side and spat out a stream of tobacco juice.

"Y'all put the fear in me, Spoof," Maledon said. "We're here to cooperate. Always got to keep the big white folks happy."

"Who's the wasted fuck?" the man said, looking at Gunner. He shook his head. "Just keeps on getting on worse, don't it? Times I wonder what's gonna come of you, Sam. Your judgment's been fouled somehow."

"He's an old soldier," Maledon told him. "Stood off endless hordes of raging slants to keep the world safe for crooked sheriffs."

"That them?" a voice from near the gallows asked.

The fat man grunted an affirmation and opened the gate. "Now, Sam, you see to it the young'uns behave before the quality."

Homer Cantwell was a pale, small man with a bulbous nose and protruding eyes. He wore a rumpled brown overcoat and a worn fedora. When he spoke, his voice carried the raspy edge that thirty years of smoking gives. "Glad y'all could see your way clear to make it," he said. "Warms my old horse-trader's heart, having the family all together like this. Ought to do it two or three times a year."

"Yeah," Maledon said, "we could meet at my place. Turkey and trimmings in the hearse."

Jesse ignored his stepfather, walked around him, went to his mother, tall, slim, elegant. He asked her how she was.

They embraced, let go, stepped apart. "I'm fine," she said, looking him up and down, as if for injury. "I just worry about you."

"I know. I wish you wouldn't. I'm fine, too." Nodding slowly, he looked into her eyes. The generations.

"Homer was wrong to put you into the asylum. He knows that now."

"Your momma had nothing to do with that, boy," Cantwell told him. "I want you to know that. It was just me, covering my ass. Thought I had to do something to save us both."

"I'd have gotten you out," she said. "I wouldn't have left you there." She had both her hands around one of his now. "What you're doing is wrong, but I wouldn't have left you there." She looked from his eyes to their hands.

"I know," Jesse said.

Maledon said, "You always been a fine woman, Mary. It's that asshole you live with we been worried about."

Jesse turned on him. "This is mine. You rode away a long time ago."

It struck. Maledon gave him as hard a look as I'd seen him give anyone. Fathers and sons. The generations again. "All right, boy, you just go along with Daddy Homer. Desk job, easy money, think about your soul during the executive lunch."

"I'll do it my way. Not yours. Not his. And I want my mother to understand."

"I trust you, Jesse," she said. "And sometimes I understand. I always try to. I know you have to do what you think's right. It's just that the way things are now, that's not easy. And sometimes it seems like you make it even harder than it really is. You're so different. It scares me. The world doesn't run on honor, Jesse, and it hurts the people who want it to."

"I'm sorry. I'd make it easy if I could."

"I want you to come home," she told him. "But I don't want you to have to go to jail."

"I'll have to do both," he said. "Soon."

"You can get a deferment," she said. "I talked to a lawyer. He's sure you can get one on the basis of your religion."

"Accepting a religious deferment would be a sacrilege," he said. That tone again. But he caught himself. "I can't do that, Mother. I'm sorry. To accept their deferment is to accept their right to say who goes and who stays, who lives and who dies. If I do that, there'll be nothing left of me worth saving. It's not just that I don't think I should have to go. I don't think anyone should. I don't think they have the right to wage war. They can put me in jail for believing that, but they can't change my mind."

She nodded slowly, gently, sadly, then turned to her husband. "Homer, I want Jesse to drive me back to my room. He'll bring the car back for you all. I haven't seen much of him lately. Don't want to let the chance get away."

"Sure enough, hon. You do that. We be here. Ain't no hurry tonight."

She and Jesse took a few steps away from us.

"Ma'am," Gunner said. And they stopped, turned, faced him. "Ain't my place to be offering advice, I know. But you ought to do anything you can to keep them from fitting your boy's hands around a rifle. Nothing good you can say about that war, ma'am. I been there. There ain't a hell, why, they ought to make one up special for Johnson and McNamara and Rusk and all them fuckin' generals. You'll pardon my language, I hope, but it's the goddamn truth."

She gave him that long-knowing mother's look. "Thank you," she said. And they left.

When they had passed through the gate, Homer Cantwell said, "Now, let's see if we can't wipe some of the damn syrup up off of us and get down to business."

"If Jesse wants to go with you," Maledon said, "he's free to. Tomorrow night he can walk off that stage and leave with you right then, far as I'm concerned. Long as it's his own choice. But I won't stand for a kidnapping. And I want Mary sitting up here front and center, you on one side of her, Spoof on the other, so I can be sure ain't no force being used."

"Mary's got a tender heart," Cantwell said. "Lost her first love to war, you might remember. And a tender heart isn't always what's called for. But she'll be here tomorrow night, just like you say." He reached inside the overcoat, got a cigarette, lit it. "Anything to keep the family happy."

"Fine," Maledon said. "But if he don't want to go, he ain't going."

"Suits me. All I ask is that he tell his momma enough to ease her mind. Me, now, last thing I need's a damn hippie son preaching sedition in Blue Mountain. I want him gone, one way or the other. Nothing can come of him being home but pain."

"We're together there," Maledon said. "But what's your plan if he decides to take his stand where his stand is."

Homer Cantwell raised his smoking hand, seemed to study the burning cigarette, and half-shrugged. "Do what I can," he said. "Show him a little piece of paradise, most likely. Communes springing up around all over. See if I can't give him reason to think that's where his cause lies. Tell him he behaves, I'll give ten grand to Eugene McCarthy, or the Dalai Lama, whoever he wants. Give the goddamn Cherokees a thousand acres of Lee Creek bottom land. What the fuck difference it make to me? I just want to keep Mary happy and Jesse pretty well out of sight and trouble till he comes back around to seeing out of American eyes. And everybody's got some kind of price, don't they? Even Jesse. Buy him off with conditional philanthropy, you know. And a chance at the simple life. Purity and all. The life of the spirit. All these damn hopped-up kids gonna come around in a few years. Time being, we just got to find a way of buying 'em off and waiting 'em out. What do you think? Draft board's no problem, long as he don't call 'em on it. I know all them boys. They'll go cheap."

"Well," Maledon said, "we'll see. It's all up to him."

"That's right."

But I could tell that neither of them meant that. Each of them obviously intended to take Jesse in hand. This was merely some kind good ol' boy horse-trading game they played, both of them lying and both of them knowing it. And I understood then why Maledon had brought the rest of us along, Gunner and Villines and me. He'd said he wanted to be sure we'd be able to recognize the enemy tomorrow night. It might be important, he'd said, couldn't be sure when they might spring forth. None of us had said much, except for Gunner's few words to Mrs. Cantwell. Right then Villines was on the gallows, checking the stage, and Gunner and I were just standing there watching these two middle-aged men play their game. But that's why we were there. So that it would be a game. Maledon hadn't wanted it to be just him and Cantwell. The casual circling, the rough jests, the false bonhomie, all of them played better before an audience. By having us there, Maledon made sure he and Cantwell would come at everything obliquely.

Gunner climbed the steps to the gallows and joined Villines, who began showing him just where things would be, just where he would need to stand tomorrow night to deliver his monologue. On the river, near the shore, Nigger Jim went by, his motorized raft carrying parents and children downstream. I could hear the babble of the kids, excited, some of them frightened. The parents' shadowed faces, half-lit by the raft's lanterns, seemed sinister. A boatload of the doomed, I thought, going nowhere and paying for the privilege.

Maledon and Cantwell kept talking—veiled threats, mock plans, indirection and innuendo. After a while the fat man, the one Maledon called Spoof, approached us. "Mr. Cantwell, I got to thinking on Sam's manners, and it come to me he probably hadn't thought to introduce you to this young lady here. She's Jonathan Wilder's daughter, Gloria. Used to be a homecoming queen."

Homer Cantwell looked at me and smiled. "We met a time or two a year or so back when Jesse'd bring her home from school with him. Isn't that right, Gloria?"

"It is," I said. The truth is he'd never more than nodded at me. I'd been in his house twice, maybe fifteen minutes total.

"Well, I hope you won't take it amiss, an old man talking like this, but I believe you're even prettier than you ever was. You know, me and Mary, it's our fondest prayer that you and Jesse'll come round to your senses right quick here, two fine young folks like yourselves, settle down and bear us some grandchildren."

"I have a daughter," I told him. "I think that'll be all."

"Damn me, I forgot that. But don't you worry your pretty head over it. We'll be proud to take her in. Be just like our own."

"We could all be part of Cantwell Enterprises, couldn't we?"

"Best part of all, I'll tell you. Yes, ma'am, sure could. And, you know, one of these days, way times is changing, that daughter of yours might wind up running the company. Might even merge with your daddy's company. Lord, look at it that way, the sky's the limit."

"Yes," I said. "If you can look at it that way."

"You know," he said, "to be right frank, I guess I ought to tell you I been talking to your daddy some. Fine man."

"Must've been fun."

"Wasn't fun I was looking for, but what I was looking for I got."

He waited. So I asked. "And what were you looking for, Mr. Cantwell?"

"Company. Both of us worried about our children, you know. Got a lot in common, me and your daddy. Work all our lives carving out the good life for our children and, why, the children, soon as they grown, they turn their backs on it. Don't want what we give 'em, that's clear, at least for the time being, but the good Lord his own self don't know what they do want. You understand? It's hard. Makes a man wonder what it's all for. Makes him question his kind. Seems to me, a man knows what he wants, works hard all his life and gets it, well, it seems to me he ought not to do that. Such questions ought not be forced on him. Anyway, it was sure good talking to a man in the same fix."

"Just tell me what you have to say, Mr. Cantwell. Spare me the chamber of commerce pathos."

"Your daddy, he wanted me to pass on a message or two," he said. "Let's see now. What were they? Yes. Little girl you mentioned that I forgot about, well, she's been sick. Flu or something brought her down for a spell. But she's fine now. Asks about her momma now and then, your daddy said, but less and less as it goes on. Getting used to it, I reckon. Little kids, you know how they are, they apt to think, Momma's left, well, then, Momma's gone. So you needn't worry yourself over-much over that."

He watched my face. I started to say something but realized I didn't need to justify myself to him.

"Oh, and there was one other thing. That friend of yours, I forget his name, come to me any minute now, why, lo and behold, he's alive. Police just made up the killing and put it in the paper so he'd be safe while they set it up for him to turn state's evidence. Now, I ask you, ain't that something? Them boys is way smarter than some folks give them credit for. I can't say the whole thing made clear sense to me, not having any firsthand knowledge of the case, but your daddy, he said you'd catch right on."

"Jimmy Song?"

"By God, that's the name. The very one. I knew it was something queer like that."

12 MALEDON

The night had come. A circle of light found the gallows. I had become the Hangman. But first:

The circle of light searches the stage, reveals the thirteen steps, the trap, the lever, the beam, and the three nooses that hang from it. Then it finds, a few feet to the right and to the rear of the ropes, JUDGE ISAAC C. PARKER (CONRAD VILLINES) *sitting behind his desk. He looks up from some papers as if mildly, but not unpleasantly, surprised, and removes his glasses.*

Ah. You are waiting for the Hangman. *(He smiles, nods.)* I understand. A fine fellow. Dedicated, efficient, philosophical. And necessary. It would all have been much more complicated without him. *(He pauses, gently shakes his head, seems, for a few seconds, lost in thought.)* You will meet him soon enough. And I suppose, since this is his, uh, stage, shall we say, I should begin by talking about him. You will find that he speaks in absolute terms. Given the nature of his profession, that is to be expected. For George Maledon, like all but a very few of us, is not by nature homicidal. Yet he has executed sixty men. With his own hands tied the knot, fitted the noose, pulled the lever, dropped the trap. Now the proper hanging of a man is not simply a matter of technique—though, as you will see, George Maledon is the master of the art of the noose. *Science* of the noose, he would say. No, the art or science, for a reasonably intelligent man willing to apprentice himself to it, is relatively easy. It is the philosophy that comes hard. The ethics of legal execution. In order to execute sixty men, George Maledon, husband, father, cordial citizen of the community of man, had to believe that each and all of those sixty men deserved execution. A hanging could not be a mere act of reprisal or revenge. It had to be pure justice. It had to be necessary. It could not be simply an action against the lawless, or even against lawlessness in general; it had to be an action taken *for* law, civilization, the family of man. A subtle but vital distinction. Maledon made hanging a positive rather than a negative act.

(He leans back in his heavy padded chair, strokes his bearded chin, cocks his head.)

I disagree with him only in part. I have been the judge of this court for twenty-one years, 1875 to 1896. I have sentenced one hundred sixty men to death by hanging. Seventy-nine of them were hanged. One man, the Negro Frank Butler, cheated the gallows by attempting to escape from the jail the night before his scheduled death. But George Maledon, as expert with pistol as with noose, shot him through the heart as he ran across the green toward the compound wall. Butler fell dead at the feet of his parents, who had been waiting just outside the wall. They knew of Maledon's unerring accuracy, but Butler preferred this private death to the public one. I understand that. But I agree with Maledon that it would have been more dignified the other way. However you look at it, it's obvious Frank Butler didn't die running for freedom. He died running away from justice. And I find that there is something desperate, something futile about running for freedom. The free do not run. Freedom is not the absence of law; it is recognition of the law's necessity.

(A sweep of the hand.) But more of that later. I am digressing. And beginning to sound too much like my own hangman. Where was I? Yes. One hundred sixty men sentenced, seventy-nine hanged, one shot

while trying to escape. Three others died in jail before their execution date. Two were pardoned; two were granted a new trial, then discharged; forty-two were granted commutations, most to life imprisonment, by a higher court; and thirty had their sentences reversed and were then given new trials, where they were either acquitted or given but light sentences.

What is the point of those numbers? you might well ask. Just this: I represented justice on the last American frontier. I was the law west of Fort Smith. I was the embodiment, they say, of white justice on the Indian plains. I was, they say, hard but fair, wise but unforgiving. My word, they say, was in those territories The Word. And yet . . . and yet more than half the men I sentenced to hang escaped the gallows. seventy-seven of the hundred and sixty were given a second chance by a higher court. Nearly a quarter of the hundred and sixty eventually got off scot-free. So . . . if you committed a murder, were tried in my court, found guilty, and sentenced to hang, your chances of living out your full life span, of dying a natural death, were about fifty fifty. And your chances of evading any punishment whatsoever were about twenty-five percent. And I can tell you, my friends, that many—no, most—of that twenty-five percent who were pardoned or acquitted deserved the gallows every bit as much as any of the seventy-nine who died there.

So, I ask you now: Is that justice?

Well, yes. Human justice. I won't tell you I never resented the pardons, the commutations, the reversals. I did. I certainly did. I was once reprimanded for criticizing the Supreme Court, that little band of loophole lawyers. But I understood, always, that such was the nature of the game. Justice can be only a human concept, human laws enforced by human law officers. And justice, therefore, will always be more or less fallible, imperfect, inconsistent, unfair. The innocent, you see, will sometimes hang while the guilty ride laughing away. And that is too bad. We work to see that it rarely happens. Some of us even devote our lives to an ideal of perfect law, perfect justice. But unless we are fools, we know we will fail. For anything human will be quixotic. Justice no less so than laughter or love.

George Maledon, of course, would disagree. About justice. About love and laughter. About human frailty. There is an ideal, he would tell you. Divine love, pure laughter, absolute justice. And that ideal is the true reality. A frontier Platonist who sets the noose and springs the trap, he is an oddly saintly man, the angel of the gallows, death's technician.

Am I better than he? Or worse? I don't know. I do not make such judgments. I will leave Morality, capital *M*, to God. I base my judgments solely on whether I think—and on whether the jury thinks—the man standing accused at the bar has broken the law of our society. I would not presume to judge that man's heart. Nor would I dare question that law's morality. To do so would be to call the entire structure into question. It is not my place to determine matters of morality or constitutionality. I merely sentence the guilty.

Of course, my motives are mixed. I want to be feared; I want to be respected; I want to be loved; I want to be comfortable. Just like you. I'd like to be governor. Or senator. Or president. Wouldn't you? It's only natural. All accomplishment is derived from ambition.

Ah, now there's an attitude our prince of hangmen would detest. Our hearts should be pure, he thinks. We should free ourselves of ulterior motives. We should do work because it needs doing, and, for the same reason, we should do that work well. Nothing more, nothing less. There should be no ambition outside the desire to perform perfectly the work at hand. But that's ridiculous, isn't it? It denies our very essence. Look at me: I'm famous. But not for being a good, fair judge—which I am. No, I'm famous for hanging seventy-nine men. I am the Hanging Judge. That is not a fame I sought. I might prefer the fame of Newton or Tennyson or Washington or even your own Sam Clemens. But I am not scientist; nor am I poet, general, or storyteller. I am a lawyer, a courtroom judge. I was assigned by President Grant to the District Court for the Western District of Arkansas. There I did my duty, enforcing that more-or-less fallible law. Many of the men brought before me were murderers. The law makes hanging the prescribed penalty for murder. In accordance with the law, I had seventy-nine men hanged. It is as simple as that. Simple practicality, deserving neither fame nor censure.

But since fame has come, I will accept it. I am no fool. I also want to be remembered.

(He leans forward, folds his hands on his desk.)

And let me ask you this: Except as hangmen, of what use are the pure in heart? What good would a man like George Maledon be in any sensibly functioning society—other than as an executioner? Rational, civilized human beings do not want to be required to abide by a set of abstract, absolute ideals. We want merely to get by comfortably. We want to keep our ambitions, our dreams. We want not to have to work too hard. We want to be allowed to indulge our minor vices. We want our paradoxical hearts to be happy, even when we know happiness is an illusion. In times of crisis we need the hangman, the soldier, the dogmatist. In such times we will, indeed, see that the hangman is kept busy, that the soldier hears marching music, that the dogmatist speaks often of the glorious, ultimate sacrifice. But in other times, better times, most times, we want the idealists to stay out of sight, to leave us alone. The hangman's purpose is to punish our enemies. When our enemies are many, the hangman is king. When they are few, he is a gray man with an old rope. We tend to forget him. That is as it should be.

George Maledon, you see, could not have existed in a place other than one very like Fort Smith. Many men needed hanging. He hanged them well. But when it was over, he was done. What is he now? A mere historical curiosity. A relic of ruffian time. An avenger summoned during time of need, then quite sensibly banished.

On the other hand, you will always need me. I could have thrived in any civilization at any time. For you will always need a judge—not often a hanging judge, but always a judge. And certainly I can as easily sentence a man to thirty days for vagrancy as to hanging for murder. Oh, of course, you're right, I know that. Actually, I'm not displeased by it. I *will* be remembered because my time and its law required me to have seventy-nine men hanged. That's fine. I'm satisfied with it. But in another time, with a less stringent law, in a jurisdiction not daily threatened by the mad whims of desperadoes, I could have been the exemplar of mercy.

Whatever works, you see. That's all. Whatever works.

(He laughs, gently, avuncular. The light begins to dim.)

Pay no attention to the rest of this. The others are my subordinates. I have given my opinion. Further testimony comes too late.

He bends to his papers. The light dies. Some moments later it returns, finding GUNNER GRANT *center stage. He wears a dirt- and grime-stained yellow duster, sagging denim pants, wrinkled white shirt, string tie, dusty gray Stetson, old boots. A pistol is strapped to his waist. He cradles a rifle in his arms.*

I'm Deputy Marshal Hugh Harp. And it's all bullshit. All that talk about justice and practicality and civilization and community. You'll see soon enough that the Hangman's a damn lunatic, and he's way better'n the judge. Ain't nothing wrong with Maledon 'cept he makes way too much out of hanging a man. No hypocrisy to him. I had to be hung, I'd want him doing it. Got a code like a good outlaw. Man crosses him, man pays. And I like a man does his killing direct. Maledon does it hisself and does it right. A job of work. But Parker, now, he sits there all robed up on that bench and ladles out some overcooked lecture to some poor half-grown, half-starved, half-crazy half-breed ain't never had no teacher but ol' man Colt. Sits up there looking like the Reverend God Almighty hisself and passes down judgment on boys ain't never seen nothing but hard times and ambushes. Never hung nobody but small-timers, Parker did, scum spawn. Boys that was too dumb or too poor or both to buy 'em a lawyer or a way out. Ain't saying they didn't need hanging, just that there weren't much died when they went.

What I'm saying is that one time or another damn near ever' big-name outlaw in the West hid out in the territories, and it's safe to say most of 'em sometime kilt somebody there. Cole Younger and his kin, Bill Doolin, the Daltons, Belle Starr. You name 'em, they been there. And now you give me one big name Parker ever had hung.

Oh, we caught the Rufus Buck Gang. You're right. They was all about twelve, looked like, maybe fifteen, one or two of 'em. Bunch of damn kids gone wild on whiskey and women and blood. They needed catching, and they needed killing. Dangerous because there weren't nothing they helt to. Like killing a pack of bad dogs you had to trail a while first. You did it 'cause you had to, but it weren't work no pride could be got out of.

There was Cherokee Bill, too. There's about as big as it gets. And I knew Crawford—Crawford Goldsby, that was his real name. Kind of man it's hard to tell if he's got any sense or not. Didn't have none you could recognize right off. All he wanted was to just keep on killing till he died. Didn't care nothing about nothing 'cept seeing folks fall. Lot of people some like that. But Crawford was the only one I ever seen pure. Started out at twelve by killing his brother-in-law in a fuss over some hogs. And there ain't no reckoning how many he kilt after that. Shoot you for the pure ol' hell of it. Just like that. Like it was his calling. Like he was some kind of natural force. A cyclone or something. The hand of God twitching with a fearful palsy.

And he could've got away easy enough, if that's what he wanted most. He'd just rode out of the territories, wouldn't none of us followed after him, I can tell you that. 'Cause he scared us, all of us, ain't no getting around it. You see, he lived toward the end of things—'95 it was when we hung him, when there weren't much left of his way of life but him and memory. And that made it worse, Lord knows, and harder. A way was closing up on all of us, desperadoes and deputies too. Oh, there'd been a lot of lot better men out there than Crawford. Men that'd make you think today might be the last day, but that that was, by God, day enough. Don't get that much no more now, that glorying in the hour that's on you, that dancing in whatever light comes down, that dancing right on when the light goes out. Desperado grace, I call it. And Crawford had it. Ain't no doubt but that he had it. But give it to a man as mean as Crawford, and it makes him meaner. It don't make you good anyway, it just sets you free. He was the sure enough last of a kind, Crawford was, riding wild, abiding by nothing but his own appetites, living out the end of an age by galloping up and down the bed of a box canyon. Way up above, on the smooth road that led to the next century, you could hear his laughing, mixed now and again with pistol fire, echoing off the canyon walls.

Sure he could've got away. Probably wouldn't even've had to leave the territories. We'd never've took him straight on. Most likely, wouldn't even've tried. By then most of us had families and thought we had futures, and there weren't no future in going after a man like Crawford. Oh, we rode around deputizing volunteers and made a few runs at him, shot his horse out from under him once, but that was from a distance, and that's it really. He knew ever' draw and ever' waller, ever' hill and ever' hideout in that country. And there was some that liked him, some he was a hero to, some that would always take him in when he come by. No, he could've run till the running wore us down.

So we caught him with a girl and some turncoat kin. Girl name of Maggie Glass, half-red, half-black. Kin name of Ike Rogers, cousin if I'm remembering, that had him some white blood along with the mix of the other two. Rogers got word to Crawford he'd have Maggie there, so Crawford come in. Glass woman didn't know nothing about the setup, but pretty quick her and Crawford both had the suspicion. Crawford kept his Winchester handy. But he stayed. Stayed on after he finished doing what he come to do with Maggie, stayed on after he ate beans and corn dodgers with Ike and Mrs. Rogers, stayed on after he beat Ike at cards, stayed on past morning, past the time when the Glass woman left, stayed on 'cause he knew what Ike was up to and wanted to see if Ike'd ever work up the nerve. About midmorning, I guess it was, they was sitting there in front of the fire. Crawford rolled hisself a smoke and leaned over to take a faggot out of the fire to light it with, and Ike Rogers jumped up and grabbed a stick of cordwood and clubbed Crawford back of the head. But Crawford come to quick and fought back. And it took Rogers and his blood-nigger hired man and Mrs. Rogers too to finally get him down and cuffed. They put him in a wagon and drove him to Nowata to the deputies. Crawford broke the cuffs once, but Rogers was horseback beside the wagon, sighting a rifle down on him, and Crawford decided to make his main chance later.

We put him in a cattle car in Nowata and drove him into Fort Smith that way, and all along the track folks lined up to get a glimpse at him twixt the boards. We had to change trains in Wagoner, and while we was there at the depot this photographer come up wanting pictures. Crawford agreed to it long as they didn't allow Ike in the picture. So we rowed up for the camera man, Crawford smack in the middle of us, joking and laughing. He put his arm friendly-like around a deputy named Crittendon and then a second later made a grab for the deputy's gun, missing, but not by much. Sometimes think another piece of a inch, another edge of a second, and he'd be riding yet.

But we got him to Fort Smith, marched him from the depot to the jail, and word beat us there, so there was folks lined all along the way looking, wanting to be able to say they seen Cherokee Bill eye to eye. And Crawford nodding and prancing and flashing that big God Almighty smile. And when we got him to the jail, the prisoners was all up and cheering him. And it made you wonder what it meant, what it was in him that drew us. And it made you wonder too if he hadn't known it all beforehand, hadn't let hisself get caught just so he could be the center of this show while he was still young. 'Cause I never seen a man seemed happier with hisself. You'd thought we'd elected him governor.

And he gave us a show in the courtroom too. Hired the fanciest lawyer in town, J. Warren Reed, the one who'd been the first to prove you could beat Parker at his own game if you could pay the right money. Even then, even there. They got witnesses to say this and say that, and nobody believing 'em, and Crawford knowing that too, sitting there at the defense table swaggering without moving, just thinking the good citizens would enjoy the sight of pure gall. And when Parker sentenced him, saying, "I sentence you to hang until you're dead, dead, dead," Crawford said, "You can kiss my ass till it's red, red, red." And all of us stunned and then all of us laughing.

And he damn near escaped from the jail before we hung him. Somebody got a pistol to him, Lord knows who, could've been anybody. He killed Deputy Larry Keating, then tried to lead a general break, bust everybody loose. But there was too many of us outside. And most of the other prisoners lost their nerve, all of them knowing that Parker would've had the whole building blowed up, dynamited it to the ground, before he'd let Crawford get away. And I think when that failed that was the first time Crawford actually understood that he was going to die. 'Cause he sat on his bunk hangdog for two or three days after that. But he got over that too, commenced playing cards again with the guards and the deputies, always winning, which is what he was doing right up till the time we walked him to the gallows, made us all sign a paper saying we'd pay what we owed him to his mother. And we did. He deserved that much. And, 'cept for the two or three days of brooding after the failed break, only sign any of us ever saw of him preparing for the end was that turkey gobbling sound he'd make sometimes way in the middle of the night. The Cherokee death cry. Same cry he'd make when he shot a man, same one he was making when he was trying to bust out of jail.

And, tell you the truth, I hated to see him hung. Lot of ways he weren't no more than pond scum. And there weren't no way you could let him go. Not in a world like ours, where folks have a right to just get along. No, he had to be hung. But I knew I'd miss him. I knew I'd be thinking about him for as long as I kept thinking. 'Cause when he was gone, it was over.

And it was Parker that hung him, or had him hung. Parker, old and soft bellied, with his suits and his law books and his gold watch and chain and his trimmed-whiskered house-soft face, Parker with his spreading ass on that padded chair, Parker with all the piety of history and law separating him from any real blood, Parker that killed by signing his name to a crisp sheet of paper on a varnished walnut desk in a chandeliered office. Yes, it was Parker, with his pampered-woman hands and his merchant's law, that stood for the coming century.

And it was Crawford Goldsby, ol' Cherokee Bill, meaner than we can understand, that stood for the dying time, the lost way, the gone world. One of us ought to've took him face-to-face. That'd've been the way. I'd've liked to've done it—or tried. Done it right. Just me and him with a short stretch of Cherokee dust in between. He deserved that much—or his time and his way did. Oh, I know, like I said, he never cared nothing about nothing but what he wanted right then, nothing but the bright minute and the end of things. And he had no real honor about him, like some of the rest of them did. There weren't nothing to him beyond his own self. And it's a shame all of it come down to just him, but it did. And maybe there weren't no other way, maybe when it comes down to the last man that man's bound to be meaner than a swamp snake, full of nothing but his own way, knowing nothing but his own ground, master of nothing but the quick strike and the dark hideout. But fearing nothing either, not even knowing what that meant. Weren't that way, the rest of us would've took him out long before. Anyway, however it come about, he was it there at the end. And when he was gone, it weren't him I grieved for, it was me. Because there weren't no place to ride to no more, no man to ride after, no ground to stand on when you got where you was going.

I remember the last thing he said, standing there with Maledon's perfect noose knotted up under his ear. They always had a preacher up there, you see. Now and again, of course, some boy or other'd find the Lord standing on the trap. Always added a little something to a hanging. Made folks feel they'd had a hand in guiding a soul up on high—weren't no noose, wouldn't be no salvation, they could think. But most of the boys getting hung was way beyond any God you could box up and church. So some boys just took advantage of the occasion to make a long speech, hoping for rescue, hoping the boys they'd rode with'd ride up one more time, but knowing better really, really just putting off the fall as long as they could. A few apologized for the grief their lives'd caused. One or two confessed to other crimes, even going so far as to name the other boys they'd rode with. Quite a few were silent out of defiance. Quite a few more just plain too scared to talk. But Crawford, he looked out over the crowd, winked at his mother, motioned for the Hangman to put the hood on him, and said, "Let's get this done. I want to get to hell in time for dinner."

And I do reckon ol' Satan served him up a full plate come evening.

I like them for last words. They fit Crawford. And it was good to see a man up there again, somebody with the gall to go out with that kiss-my-ass grin. There'd been too many boys up there, too many kids, too much whining and repenting, too many knees buckling before the trap fell. Cowards, back stabbers, half-wits, that's pretty much what we caught and Parker judged and Maledon hung. Especially in them last years. So, yes, it give me pleasure to see Crawford go out like he done. But I seen better, back years before. Some too much show in Crawford's leaving. He wanted to catch hisself in the crowd's mind. And he done it, made that scaffold and that day his own. Nobody there then ever forgot him. But I preferred the men that didn't give a damn one way or the other, didn't care about being remembered by folks they didn't care about in the first place. Men that took their own hanging like it was just another something come down on just another bad day. Men that seemed to understand it all, seemed to take it like it come, all of it, even the end. I recall Aaron Wilson, big Negro man, standing up there looking off into the dead forever, saying, "By God, this ain't nothing when you get used to it."

What I mean to tell you here tonight, all these bad years later, in a time that's been corralled by settlers and shysters and government scum, in a age when there ain't a man left able to get by on his own, in a century that's turned all the territories into townships, turned the limberlost into lots, when everything's been surveyed and sold, when everybody's got a number and nobody's got a heart, when freedom ain't nothing but a merchant's dodge, when everybody gets by selling everybody else something nobody needs, when we live on bankers' terms and die in strangers' rooms—yeah, what I mean to tell you is this, I'll take Aaron Wilson's last words over all of Parker's laws, all of Parker's fine charges to all his decent juries, all of Parker's order, and all his reasoned peace. Yes sir, I'll go with ol' black Aaron Wilson. Because it weren't ever order I was craving, or peace either. Never cared about no future past tomorrow, never believed in mortgaging here for hereafter. All I wanted was a man to ride after and God's own ground to ride after him on. No fences, no roads, no bridges to the other side. Just the woods and the trails and the rivers winding free. And sometimes having it be one free man looking across that river at the other free man looking back—and both of 'em knowing there ain't no more to it than this, but that this was enough, this was God's plenty and more, that we had room to live in, both of us, and that death weren't nothing upside this, just that one last river to cross.

And what wears my mind now, here in my age, is the knowing I didn't understand any of that then, just saddled up and rode with it.

Took it all that one ride at a time. That's what let the best of us live so full, but that's what beat us too. So we just woke up one morning, and it was gone. While we was riding, chasing one another round and round in that man-sized circle, they was plotting and fencing and damming. While we was riding free, they was taming the ground we rode on. And I've had to live all these wrong years knowing that by wearing Parker's badge, I was part of the Sunday-suited scheme that ended it all. Yes sir, ladies and gentlemen, I was on the wrong side. And all the rest of it's bullshit.

But it's yours now. No way of bringing any of it back. Ever. No, I'm gone. It's yours. Welcome to it.

The light goes out. When it returns, it reveals GLORIA ALICE DAWN, *in a red satin dressing gown, lounging on a four-poster, queen-sized bed. The white bedcovers have been haphazardly turned back. She sits upright, her back resting against an overstuffed pillow, her legs outstretched, her bare feet crossed. On the nightstand beside her is a half-empty pint of bourbon. She holds a drink in her hand, absently swirls the liquid, sips from the glass.*

I am the one. The whore. The Fort Smith beauty. The Hangman's daughter. (*She laughs. It is the whore's off-duty laugh, mocking, harsh, apparently humorless, the laugh of one who has forgotten how to cry.*) Yes, the Hangman's daughter. Madame Rosetta Hegel's most wanted girl. The queen of the Riverfront Hotel. For a price—modest, if you're interested, two Yankee dollars and I'm yours for the moment, ten and you can have me awhile—I give myself to men my father may hang. (*She laughs again, drinks again.*) But he won't hang them all. The odds will be in your favor. There isn't that much rope.

(*She tilts her head to one side, runs a hand back across luxuriant hair, smiles.*)

Sure, I had every advantage, as they say. Beauty, enough money, a famous—or infamous—name, a lady's fine education. Latin, Greek, French, the piano, the art of fainting, the decorous tease. A girl's blush, a merchant's heart. The Fort Smith *Elevator* called me the city's most beautiful young lady, the area's most eligible girl.

Ah yes, but, you see, my father hanged people for a living. A hundred dollars a head. Once made five hundred dollars for a day. He hanged them well, and his pride in it easily passed vanity. Often he walked the streets of Fort Smith carrying his ropes in a wicker basket, the basket covered except for a noose dangling from either end. For years, on our drawing-room mantel, he kept a tintype of each man he had hanged. Finally, when there were fifty-three faces on the mantel, my mother, able to bear no more doomed eyes, took them down, stopped him. And until I was eighteen and met Frank Carver, who would murder me, my father and those faces and Charlie Parker—the judge's son, I'll get to him in a minute—they were the only men in my life.

Oh, I was beautiful, and I was prominent, and I had all the graces of a provincial Lady Astor. We lived in a respectable house in a respectable neighborhood—on Thirteenth Street, directly across from the great judge himself. But, I ask you, what kind of man would court the Hangman's daughter? (*The laugh again. She drinks.*)

My father did work you wanted done, you Rotarian swells. And he did it with an engineer's attention to detail, would talk about a particular hanging the way an engineer talks might about a bridge. And you didn't like that. You needed him and you paid him, but you wanted nothing further to do with him or his. He became, more so than any of the killers he hanged, a source of superstition. For—you see, don't you?—he would kill more times than any of the men he hanged. He has executed more men than any American. Only Deibler, the French Revolution's guillotine master, who decapitated four hundred thirty-seven, surpassed him. That is nothing, I know, to you citizens of the twentieth century, who will make the mechanics of horror absolute. But in the 1890s in Fort Smith, Arkansas, my father was death's legend. And, to court his daughter? That was not to court beauty or grace or even position. No, it was to court the scion of cold terror itself. I was death's daughter. (*She laughs again, swirls the drink.*) Scion? How do you like that? Fancy talk for a whore, huh? Oh, but I'm a special whore, don't you agree?

And you come to me now, don't you? Outlaws and merchants, lawyers and desperadoes come to me in the safety of Rosetta Hegel's brothel, where you can pay and rut and go. And you come to me now far less out of lust than out of superstition. When you finish, you think you have shot your seed into the abyss. It makes you feel brave.

But no one came to me then, no man. Except Charlie Parker, Isaac Charles Parker II, the judge's delinquent, dashing son. Charlie and I shared similar pain, walked parallel paths. His father, too, was a man both famous and infamous, a man both respected and avoided, an impossible father. We shared a heritage that was pure burden, and both of us fevered to escape it. He was handsome; I was beautiful. We were lonely; we were doomed. Trained to be exemplars of virtue, educated to become citizens of a new and decorous century, we abandoned ourselves to one another.

I was sixteen when we first made love. June 30, 1891. We did it at the very moment my father was hanging a man named Bood Cumpton. The great judge sat in his chambers, looking out the high window through which he could observe the death he had decreed, through which he could witness the culmination of his justice. Charlie and I sneaked into the empty courtroom and wordlessly undressed. Naked, I bent over the defense table, and he took me from behind. The moment he entered me, the instant I lost my chastity, felt the virgin's pain, is the closest I've ever come to freedom.

In the very place where men, our fathers foremost among them, spent their days attempting to impose a European concept of order on a vast aboriginal territory, Charlie and I repudiated the law and accepted the flesh. Oh, I know now—I knew nothing then except release—I know better than anyone that we didn't escape the prison of our heritage. We had merely chosen a new cell, a cell inhabited by those who can only hope for the redemption of the moment, those condemned to invest all faith in the fleeting grace of passion and laughter.

(For a moment she stares into her drink. Her index finger slowly, absently circles the glass's rim. Then she looks up again.)

Charlie Parker. I loved him, I think. But what is love? I needed a man, and he was there. He did what I needed done to me, and that increased my need. I did what he needed done to him, and that increased his need. So we kept on doing what we needed done. Orgasm is deliverance, dear customers. That instant of ecstatic oblivion is as close as we come to the white heart of the mystery.

So, Charlie, poor Charlie. We had each other for almost two years. And our having each other is about all I remember of that time. I wanted it to go on forever. And I think the best part of him did, too. We took insane chances, half-hoping to get caught. We made plans to run away together, but Charlie kept finding plausible reasons to postpone flight. I hoped I would get pregnant, believing that would force him to elope with me. But I didn't, and we stayed. Or I stayed. When I was almost eighteen, the judge sent Charlie off to Saint Louis to study for the bar. And the night I watched him board the train, as I stood there on the platform, I knew it was over. I knew that not even Judge Isaac C. Parker would let his son marry the Hangman's daughter. And I knew, too, that Charlie, finally, was too much the coward to save either of us from his father's will.

He became a gambler, a dandy, a drunk. Whoremonger to my whore. But we were doomed not to suffer our doom together. A kind man, but a coward. And I am worse. Overcoming cowardice, I lost all kindness.

Well, so what? What good would it have done me anyway? (*She laughs.*)

And only a few months after Charlie rode that train out of my life, I met Frank Carver, the man who would murder me but escape Ike Parker's judgment and slip my father's noose. I met him in one of those dirt-floor riverfront dives, the lowest kind of watering hole. You see, when Charlie left me, I gave up all pretense. But even there in the cheap-drunk saloon, down among the dregs, most of the men feared me. Men who seemed to fear nothing else feared me. They would look at the string of pearls around my neck and see my father's noose. Even those who took the risk rode away as soon as they sobered up.

But not Frank Carver. Not handsome Frank. Not Frank, so pretty and so stupid. You see, Frank believed he was destiny's child. He thought that any day, a great stroke of luck would deliver him into a life of luxurious ease. It would just happen because he was Frank Carver, the handsomest man in the Indian territories, and wanted it to happen. Oh, I knew better, sometimes even laughed at him, driving him into that rage that would be my death. But he was handsome, and when I wanted pleasing he knew how to please me. His mind was a joke without the punch line, but the rest of him—well, that was enough. That was all I wanted. A dependable sexual aid.

He saw me as luck personified. I had literally fallen into his lap, and he was certain I represented the fortune and luxury awaiting him. And maybe he could have used me to get what he wanted. But he was too stupid and too jealous to see how. I mean, he could have pimped for me, or he could have set up a show around me. You know, SEE THE HANGMAN'S DAUGHTER: SHE SINGS, SHE DANCES, SHE TAKES OFF HER CLOTHES. HEAR ABOUT THE NIGHT SHE SLEPT WITH CHEROKEE BILL. The kind of thing I'm doing here. The historical hustle. Catering to the voyeur trade. But not Frank, you see. No, not Frank. That would have required some work and a little sense, and Frank wanted it handed to him. Anything else would have offended his sense of honor. So what he decided, you know, my pretty, pretty Frank, was to blackmail my father.

(*She laughs again, raucously this time, until the laughter seems beyond her control. But then, abruptly, she stops it, drinks, shakes her head.*)

I don't know. Sometimes I think it's funny. But laughter is the result of a sudden, sharp sense of the absurd, isn't it? And while Frank's stupidity was profoundly absurd, it was too constant to often provoke genuine laughter. It was so constant I took it for granted, accepted it as just another obvious facet of the natural world: this tree, that river, Frank's stupidity. Now and then a branch fell from the tree, the river flooded, Frank came up with an idea. That's when he was funny. The ideas were always so dangerously stupid and so fantastically vain I couldn't keep from laughing. Then he would stare at me with those perfect, blank eyes until rage happened to him. He would come stalking at me then, and I'd tell him, "Oh, it's so perfect, Frank. This time you've done it. It's so pure and wonderful." Unless I'd waited too long he'd stop then, his eyes returning to blankness as his mind stumbled futilely toward thought. Then the satisfied idiot grin, perfect teeth, perfect mouth. I'd think, he'd be the ideal container for a human being. He'd say, "You knew ol' Frank'd do it, didn't you, woman? I'm going to be the king of Silver City."

You see, Frank thought Silver City was where you went if you had money. His idea of Paris or something. He was going to buy the biggest saloon in Silver City, live on steak and whiskey, and be forever surrounded by dancing girls. The big-time gambler, the high roller. Diamond Frank Carver.

Oh, he was a gambler of sorts, Frank was. Went to Muskogee the first of every month and cheated the Indians out of their allotment checks. Got them drunk and brought out the cards. And they would have killed him, I think, but he was married to one of their own, a full-blood Cherokee, and they had two children. They would have killed him anyway, sooner or later, as a favor to the wife and kids. But once he met me, Frank started spending almost all his time in Fort Smith, and the Cherokee weren't much for coming into Parker's jurisdiction. They were willing to be patient, content in the knowledge that it wouldn't be long before Frank screwed up.

Anyway, that's the kind of gambler Frank was, just a petty thief, really, unconsciously dependent on the protection of his abandoned squaw. What it came down to, I guess, even there, was that Frank was allowed to live because he was handsome.

But he was never gambler enough to have any realistic notion of the value of the cards he held. I mean, who else would have dreamed of blackmailing my father? George Maledon had been the Fort Smith hangman for over twenty years, and anyone who knew him at all could tell you he had no vices, didn't smoke, drink, swear, kept all the Commandments except the sixth. He thought being a hangman was not an occupation but a calling. He had no other ambition. He was where and what he wanted to be. He was unsurpassed at what he was. Because he thought his calling required more of him than lesser jobs did of other men, he was rigidly upright, steadfastly moral, absolutely incorruptible. Maybe that was his corruption: By purging himself of human weakness, he had purged himself of human feeling—he had become a perfect extension of his noose. Or maybe I'm just excusing myself—and you. Maybe he *was* better than we are. God forbid I be caught judging anyone. But either way, however you want it, he certainly was not a man to be blackmailed. Better try blackmailing Parker, whose political ambitions might have made him vulnerable. In fact, several times he did pay good money to buy Charlie out of Saint Louis trouble. (Ah, how bad we go, we children of the high minded.) No, my father could not be had. There was no temptation to which he was susceptible. As well try tempting Saint Francis by placing a bounty on birds.

And even if my father had been vulnerable, what did Frank have to offer? (*She laughs.*) My honor. (*She laughs again.*) That's all, my honor. In exchange for a dowry sufficient to set him up in Silver City, Frank would make an honest woman of me. The respectable Mrs. Frank Carver, queen of Silver City. (*She shakes her head, laughs again.*) An idiot, an absolute idiot. He'd divorce his squaw, abandon his children for good, marry me, and get me out of town. I'm surprised my father didn't hang him in the parlor.

Frank went to the house on Thirteenth Street several times. My father wouldn't so much as come to the door. So Frank finally confronted him outside the jail and made his offer. My father said, "She wants to be honest, she can come home. I've never thrown her out. She marries you, though, she'll lose even a whore's truth."

Frank returned, surprised and confused, of course. "What did he mean?" he asked, too astonished for anger, too stupid for understanding.

I kept from laughing. "He thinks you're no good, Frank. Thinks I'd be better off working for Rosetta Hegel."

He almost understood that. "I guess you'd like it that way, wouldn't you?" He had miscalculated my value. He could blame it on me.

"There's worse things."

"Like what?" he asked, coming toward me.

I decided to save myself, temporarily. "Like being a hangman," I said.

(*She sits upright, cocks her head, listening.*)

Ah, there's music downstairs. Business. Good. I'm about finished anyway. There isn't much more.

I followed Frank to Colorado, where he intended to prove himself. Well, actually, he intended to go to Nevada—Silver City, you know—but he got impatient and settled for Colorado. He made a little money rustling cattle. I made considerably more turning tricks in Denver—taking care not to let him catch me, doing it only when he was on the range, in hot pursuit of strays. It was Frank's belief, you see, that once a woman had had him she could settle for no other. (*She laughs.*) The purest kind of idiot.

Anyway, after a while, we went to Denver together, and he lost all of it, my money and his. Then we came back to Fort Smith. In a few weeks I'd go to Muskogee and let him kill me for what I'm doing tonight. He'd shoot me in the back, then come to me, roll me over, and lower his pretty, vacant face down to mine. We'd stare at each other in guttering, alley light.

"Do you know who done it?" he'd say.

"Oh yes, I know."

"It's Frank Carver, woman. Frank Carver."

And at last he will have made a name for himself.

(*She finishes the drink in her hand, screws the cap back on the bottle, takes a hairbrush from the nightstand drawer, and begins brushing her hair. After a few seconds she stops, looks again at the audience.*)

You're still wondering why. Why follow a man like Frank Carver? My father was right. There's nothing lower than that. But, well, of course. Can't you see? That's your answer. That's your answer right there.

(She brushes her hair a few more strokes, rises, goes behind a screen, emerges in a severe black evening dress, walks to the front of the stage.)

So, here I am, ready for another night's business. There will be only this and a handful more.

Oh, I don't know the precise hour. I know only its certainty. I have slept long with Doom. I have lain with hundreds. But it is Doom who stays.

(She turns, walks seductively away, a whore advertising. Then she turns again. The light is still with her.)

It's all inevitable, you think? The wages of sin, etcetera. And, of course, you're right, you smug deacon. Sure, she who lives by the flesh shall die by the flesh. Yes, I carry my fate between my legs.

But you would come up here and join me, wouldn't you now, Mr. Prim? To escape for just a few minutes from your obsessively ordered life, you would pay good money to lie with me, money you might otherwise set aside for your lovely daughter's education, your wife's anniversary dress, the family investments. Well, come on, then, come ahead. No one need know but you and me and Madame Rosetta. And we're the soul of discretion. Leave your wife at home, corsetted and ignorant. Slip away without disturbing your daughter. Let her sleep. She will need her rest. For she, too, carries her fate betwen her legs. And whether she decides to open those legs to many or keep them closed to all but the one banal Rotarian, she will need to be strong.

So slip away silently and and come to me. Only you and I know I am the woman of your dreams. Come on, now. Don't miss your turn. I'm ready for you. I'll be downstairs waiting. It'll be fine. You'll do all right. I've had worse men than you.

(She leaves. The light dies.)

When I appear, the stage is entirely gallows, no further adornments. I stand front, center, at the edge. Pasted to my face is the thick, gray beard that hangs to my chest. I wear a black wool suit. I have a rope in my hand. The light finds me.

I order my rope from Saint Louis. Cohen and Sons. Six strands of fine-grade hemp woven together. *(I hold the rope up, stretched between my hands, displaying it.)* When it arrives, new, it is an inch and a quarter in diameter. I carefully apply linseed oil and pitch and systematically begin the stretching process. When I have finished with the rope, perhaps a month later, it is but one inch in diameter. It is then perfect. (*I lower the rope.*) It will allow no slippage. I will then have eliminated play. For I am, you see, an executioner, not a torturer. When the trap falls, there must be no suffering, only deliverance.

Let me show you.

(The light follows me to the rear of the stage. I step on the edge of the trap. Three nooses hang from the beam above me. Each noose has been fastened around the neck of a large bag of sand.)

I am a scientist. This is my laboratory.

For the purposes of this demonstration, these bags have each been filled with one hundred fifty pounds of sand. A mere convenience. When preparing for an actual hanging, I weigh and measure the condemned carefully. Total body weight, head weight relative to body weight, thickness and strength of neck. If you have two men of equal weight but one has a thick, bull neck, that man will require a few more inches of fall. Simple, you say. And, of course, it is. But before me nothing was taken into consideration but death. And often even that was botched. When I am the hangman, death is swift and merciful.

The men I hang deserve hanging. But that is all. They do not deserve the grotesque decapitation or the slow strangling a hangman's incompetence can cause. And no man deserves to be hanged twice. None of those things happen when I am here. I am the best there is. I have mastered the science of execution by rope. I am the perfect instrument of justice.

(I make sure the first rope hangs directly downward and the first sandbag sits squarely on the trap. I move the second and third bags off the trap so that they will not fall. Then I step back to the lever, pull it, spring the trap. The first bag falls. The rope jerks, then swings limply. I step forward and draw the noose toward me. It holds only the upper end, the head, of the sandbag. Below me, JESSE *and* GUNNER *begin closing the trap, replacing the brace.)*

You see. (*I hold the head before me in my hands.*) Decapitation. With a human you have the squirting of arteries, the twitching of muscles. And then the head, like an obscene trophy. A scene more suitable to the Roman circuses than to constitutional American justice. Oh, you say, but this is the frontier, and, confronted by a world of brutality, justice must itself be brutal. Brutality, you say, is the only effective counter to brutality. (*Below me there is a tapping to signal that the trap has been secured. I lay the first sandbag head behind me, then step forward onto the trap.*) You are wrong. For when law is as brutal as lawlessness, the outlaw becomes hero. By murdering, a man forfeits his right to live in civilization. That is the first rule. Without that rule there is, in truth, small need for civilization. In the dark past men began to form more-or-less civilized societies because anarchy caused them to live in constant dread of random death at the hands of members of their own species. Without law, life would still be, in the words of the philosopher, "nasty, brutish, and short." But to be effective, law must be the clear opposite of anarchy. It must be ordered with logical precision; it must be absolutely predictable; it must be without loophole or exception; and it must be executed with dispassion. Otherwise civilization is but sham, a haven for cowards and cripples, an asylum for hypocrites and bureaucrats. And in such circumstances the man of courage will choose to live outside the law. And rightfully so, for the dictates of his own conscience would then be a better guide than the inconsistent, vindictive, unequally applied law of the civilization he has chosen to repudiate. He will then, as I say, become hero—even to many of the cowardly.

No. The laws of civilization must have the force and logic of the laws of science. Neither the judge nor the executioner can be the instruments of revenge; they must be the instruments of truth. And an execution must not be a rough reenactment of the murder; it must be that murder's direct contrast, the calm, stately restoration of the law so malevolently broken.

(*I set the second bag on the trap, then step back and pull the lever. The trap springs open. The bag falls. The rope jerks to a quick stop. I draw the bag back to the surface. Below me,* JESSE *and* GUNNER *once more begin closing the trap. I stand behind the trap, the second bag at my feet.*)

A widow, a seamstress capable of meeting detailed specifications, makes these bags for me. In 1866, when she was eighteen and had been married thirteen months, a gang of marauders, six men wearing Confederate cavalry uniforms, rode up to the cabin she and her husband had built on Caney Creek in the northern land of the Cherokee Nation. The riders were hungry. She fed them corn dodgers and beans. They ate, then brought the whiskey in from their saddlebags and began drinking and making lewd remarks. J. W. Chastain, the lady's husband, asked them to leave. They refused, mocking him. He turned, reached for the Winchester above the hearth, and was shot twice in the back by the gang's leader, Rayburn Painter. Then the six, each in turn according to rank, raped Mrs. Chastain. Their appetites sated, they set fire to the cabin and rode off with the couple's infant son.

Mrs. Chastain has never seen her son since. Rayburn Painter is thought to have delivered the child to his favorite Fort Smith whore, who, babe in arms, rumor has it, caught the next Butterfield stage out of town, on her way somewhere to learn how to be a mother. I suspect she failed.

Two years later, after another rape, another murder, Rayburn Painter and his gang were mutilated and hanged near Eufaula by Creek vigilantes. In the absence of law that was necessary. But it was not justice. The breach remained. No lesson was learned. Civilization did not prevail. Anarchy merely turned on six of her own.

Sara Chastain has never remarried, has never had another child, has never lain with another man. Since 1875, when I began to execute the sentences of the District Court for the Western District of Arkansas, she has sewn these bags for me. She is very good at it.

(*The tapping below signals that the trap is again secure.*)

Look. Can you see this? (*I loosen the noose, raise it, indicate the neck of the bag.*) Mrs. Chastain reinforces the neck, inside and out, with thin, four-inch-wide strips of leather. A difficult job, perfectly done. I hope you can see how this strip has just been scarred. And notice the black marks, the tinge of pitch. Signs of slippage. Had this bag been a man, he would have suffered. He would have died slowly, of strangulation. I might better, and more honestly, have simply used my hands on him. The noose was not tight enough, the fall was too short. The executioner who hangs a man in such a way has himself offended the law. Not to mention Mrs. Chastain.

(*I step back on the trap, stand beside the third rope.*)

Everything must be precise, clean. The trap must be oiled regularly and well. There can be no rust, no squeaking. The platform itself must be kept white and smooth with holystone. The necessary length of the fall must be accurately calculated and planned for. The rope must be treated and stretched until it is of perfect width and pliability. But all these things can be done, my friends, and the hanging still be botched. It is the knot that is the last secret. Some of you perhaps can tie the hangman's noose, the thirteen-loop slip knot. (*I kneel beside the third sandbag, touching the hangman's knot with my left hand.*) But few if any of you, I daresay, tie it well. And none of you, I'm certain, knows the proper way to put it around a man's neck. I'll show you.

(*I loosen the noose, lift it off the sandbag neck, hold it up to the audience. Then I put it back over the neck.*)

You put the rope around the neck and draw it up just tight enough to touch the skin all around without choking or interfering with the circulation of the blood. We want the condemned to be able to utter his last words without constriction. Then you make sure the big knot is under the left ear. You want it to lie in the hollow back of the jawbone. And now, here's a little secret that even very few hangmen know—and those who do learned it from me. To keep the knot from slipping out of position below the ear, you bring the rope up over the top of the head and let it hang down in a curve on the other side, down over the man's forehead. That holds the knot steady under the ear, and when you spring the trap and the man drops through, the rope snaps taut, and the big knot throws the man's head sideways and cracks his neck instantaneously.

If all this is done right—the fall perfectly gauged, the rope properly selected and properly treated, the noose properly tied and properly placed—if all this is done right, I say, hanging is the most humane form of execution. You will break the man's neck, and there will be no contortions. He will be unconscious the moment the neck breaks. He will hang motionless. Death will be painless and instantaneous. You will then have justice.

Before me executions by hanging were carnivals, savage frontier entertainments, a mere aspect of court-approved chaos. I changed that. Each of the prisoners who walks from the prison to the gallows wears a new suit of clothes. Each of the guards wears a uniform and must pass my inspection the morning of the hanging. When the hanging is done, each of the unclaimed bodies is buried in federal ground in a new coffin built at my expense. And the hanging itself is no longer occasion for festival. Some weeks before the execution date, I make out a list of persons to be admitted inside the gates. No one else is allowed to enter. Who *is* granted entry? you wonder. Family and friends of the condemned, newspaper reporters, officers of the court, and a group of thirty citizens, different each time, whose names I take from the list of registered voters. Everyone is granted access, but not all at once. A hanging in Fort Smith is no longer excuse for drunkenness, ribaldry, whooping, and hollering.

I have brought civilization to the gallows.

(I step back, pull the lever, and spring the trap a third time. The bag falls, stops. The rope seems to achieve immediate and perfect stillness.)

Bingo.

(I walk to the edge of the trap, lean forward, touch the taut rope with my fingertips, nod.)

The murderer died instantly, his neck broken, his spinal chord snapped. There was no choking, no suffering. The bowels have moved, but that is unavoidable. I have experimented with remedies to that sudden release of the sphincter muscle, but such remedies proved less humane than the simple, natural movement of the bowels. And I personally see to it that the undertakers, not all of whom are trustworthy in such cases, thoroughly clean the corpse before it is given its Christian burial.

(I draw the bag upward, allow it to rest on the scaffold floor. Below they begin to close the trap.)

With this rope I have hanged twenty men. Altogether I have hanged sixty. No American has done more. And for each of the sixty, death was immediate and just.

And I should have been required to hang more. Many of the guilty, especially in these last years when the lawyers have swarmed, have been granted various forms of reprieve. Some have been pardoned altogether. And you, the people of this civilization, should not have allowed that to happen. You should see that all murderers are brought here to me, without exception. A single exception, a single reprieve, a single pardon makes farce of all execution, of all justice. If you pardon but one, you must logically pardon all. And then, good citizens, the gates of hell are opened again.

(The braces now in place again, I step forward, onto the trap.)

But still I suspect you are not convinced. Hangings, you think, may be necessary, but, if so, they are also necessarily brutal. Why, you wonder, does a man who has murdered often and randomly deserve a clean, painless execution? How can I, in good conscience, continue to do my work when I am the servant of a system of jurisprudence that condemns one murderer and pardons the next? And who is this man, you ask, this long-bearded hireling who has killed sixty men, to be talking of logic, science, precision, and civilization?

Well, I have answered the first question, but I will do it once more. However dastardly the criminal, *society* deserves a clean, efficient execution. The gallows should be the place civilization demonstrates its transcendence over chaos. A hanging must have the order and the inexorability of law. It must be the embodiment of justice. Otherwise it is just another act of reprisal in a long blood feud.

In answer to the second question, I say that I have a necessary job, and I do it well. I deplore the inconsistency of the jurisprudence system, and I know, as do you, that in your century it will become more and more inconsistent, that the lawyers will multiply and so will the technicalities, and that you will have, finally, much more law and much less justice. But perhaps your children will grow weary with that, perhaps they will see that their world returns to the pure, the pristine law, the clear code of a strong, ascendant civilization that allows no exception, abides no technicality, grants no pardon. As for me here and now, I can but do my work. I am determined, in spite of all that lies ahead, to remain the exemplar of justice.

I think I can best answer the third question by telling you a story: On the nineteenth of August, 1880, near White Bead Hill, Chickasaw Nation, William Brown, a cowboy, ambushed and killed seventeen-year-old Ralph Tate. It was a case of mistaken identity. Brown had intended to kill a man named Moore, who had given him a beating after a quarrel over a horse race. Brown, disappointed but unrepentent, was plotting another attempt on Moore's life when he heard Ralph Tate's father was coming after him. Brown then ran, but neither far nor fast enough. Tate tracked him for six hundred miles across the Indian Territory and into Texas. After twenty-eight days, Tate caught him near Henrietta, a morning's ride from Wichita Falls. Now Tate could have hanged his son's killer then and there. Or shot him. And he was the kind of man who would likely have made a clean job of it. But he didn't do that. No. For all his skill on the trail, for all his passion for revenge, for all his grief, Tate was a man who believed in justice, the justice of the law of the civilized. So he manacled William Brown, locked a thick trace around his neck, and led him all the way to the jail in Fort Smith. Led him across two hundred sixty miles of anarchy to reach the law. And even then he wasn't finished. He stayed in Fort Smith until Brown was tried, found guilty, sentenced to hang, and out of appeals. Then Mr. Tate went home. He didn't need to wait for the hanging. He knew he could leave that to me. I was the one link in the chain of justice Mr. Tate trusted absolutely. He knew William Brown was in good hands.

He knew that logic, science, precision, and civilization would now take their inevitable course.

The light dims, dies. When it returns, Jesse stands on the trap. I am beside him holding a black hood. A single noose hangs behind us. In the shadows to our right, VILLINES, *dressed in a dark suit, reads from the black Bible he holds open in his hands.*

MALEDON *(to the audience).* Here is a man whose time has come. Perhaps he will be the last to die here. Perhaps you will be the final witnesses. Let us hope not.

VILLINES *(in a low, droning voice).* 'The Lord is my shepherd, I shall not want. . . .' (*He continues, in a barely audible monotone.*)

MALEDON *(to* JESSE*).* Do you have any final words?

JESSE. Just this: You are wrong, all of you. I am but a single man, and it has taken all of you to kill me. All of you and your law. This is no more than primitive blood ritual, the sacrifice of the outcast.

I am innocent. I have killed no one. I lived in peace on my own land until the deputies came to take it for the cattlemen. When I refused to go, you framed me for killing a man I never saw, a man whose death I know nothing of.

So I will die.

But I hope you will ask yourselves this: In whose name can you justify yourselves? Even if I am guilty, you are, by sanctioning my death, about to assume the same guilt. Do you act in the name of the state? Is that what makes you so certain of yourselves? Then remember this: On the roll of those executed by the state are the names of heroes, saints, and the God you say you worship. There is nowhere a more glorious list of names. But I am no martyr, no saint, no hero. My name will be just one more on your long list, and not an honored one. I wanted only to be left alone with my farm and my family, but you came and destroyed me with the law the cattlemen and speculators wrote to justify themselves.

There is no justice here. There will never be justice as long as these gallows stand. You pay this man, this hangman, to do your will, and he does it with a fanatic obsession. He calls himself the prince of hangmen, but he is merely your court's dogmatic killer. Even his daughter repudiates him. So should you. My last wish is that you will repudiate him, turn away from the grim mechanics of the state, and begin to seek grace and mercy and true freedom. Turn back to the light, my poor, lost brothers.

I am innocent of the crime you kill me for.

(*He turns to me.*)

Now.

(*I slip the hood over his head, carefully set the noose in the hollow of the jawbone behind his left ear, bring the rope up over the top of his head, adjust the curve of rope in front of his forehead, then step back to the lever.* VILLINES *reads the psalm more loudly. Offstage,* GLORIA *screams, "No! No! No!" The lights go out. I spring the trap. Jesse falls. Silence. Darkness. I wait until* GUNNER *has had time to untie* JESSE *and help him escape beneath the rear of the platform, wait until I hear* BOOGER PURIFOY *start the motor on his raft, wait until* JESSE *is on his way downriver.*)

No! Lights! I am not finished!

(*The light returns.*)

I am old. I am tired. But I am not finished. I will have the last word.

(*I walk to the front of the stage.*)

The hanged man was innocent, he said. Do not believe him. It is the common cry of the doomed. That will not change. And my daughter chose to become a whore, you think, rather than live in the shadow of these gallows. You condemn me for that? Why? She chose her path. Not I. You too will lose your daughters, your children. That will not change. Each generation condemns its parents. That will not change. It is the way of the cycle.

But much will change. The Indian Territory will become Oklahoma, a state like any other. Cherokee, Choctaw, Creek, Seminole, and Chickasaw will be assimilated and eradicated. And I will become a creature of legend, a figure larger and crueler than life, a dark character obsessed with the techniques of the noose. If you read of me at all, you will do so in the evening while you sit in the recliner beside the lamp you bought on sale. You will have spent your day making, buying, or selling objects or parts of objects the need for which must also be manufactured and sold. And as you read of me, you will nod or shake your head, approving or disapproving according to your politics. Perhaps you will ponder briefly the idea of progress. Perhaps you will think you have come a long way since 1890, you with your lights and your cars and your comfort. Perhaps you will feel superior to me, the Hangman whose only connection, finally, was to the men he hanged, the Hangman whose ideal of justice cost him everything but his rope. Perhaps you will simply feel removed from all that. I cannot know. You will live in a world I cannot fully foresee. But I ask you to remember this: Had I not been, you would not be as you are. There would be but wilderness, infinite danger, infinite freedom. Only a few of you, the best and the worst, could survive that danger, could tolerate that freedom. Remember this: I am the necessary guarantor of civilization. Remember this: Whenever your order is threatened, you will summon me back. Remember this: You are my children.

(*The light dies.*)

PART IV

1 JESSE

"We go soft," he says, as I board the raft. "We slip away, just like the man say, safe in the downriver dark."

And, hearing Booger Purifoy's voice, lilting, ingratiating, false, I know it is time.

He flashes the broad Tom smile. We drift into the current. He starts the motor.

"You daddy, he something. Always got them nighttime plans."

I am the white boy, then, his ride always planned and paid for. Another traveler on the packaged tour.

To escape, I must, tonight, think like my father.

"What about the others?" I ask. "Have they been taken care of?"

Rudder in hand, he studies me. "Sam Maledon, boy, I know him since the way back blue yonder be new."

Loyalty. So . . .

"And Homer Cantwell?"

The smile again, a shrug. "White man?"

"Very."

"Rich man?"

"Very."

He laughs.

This is too easy, and my father would have known that. Booger Purifoy has been paid twice, once and most by Homer Cantwell, but he will deliver me to a place other than the one openly specified, a place where Cantwell's men will not be waiting, a place my father chose.

"Keep close to the bank," I tell him. "I can't swim." There is one clear way. My own.

"Won't need to."

I wait until we are well beyond the festival lights, then dive into the river.

Surfacing, I glance back, see the raft making its slow turn.

My body is eager in the cold water. I swim well. I could go with the current, but I must seek the land.

The raft gains on me, but I am beyond its reach. I climb ashore, disappear into back brush. Behind me is Booger's voice: "Come on back here, white boy. You ain't hardly shut of town yet."

But I am gone. The path through the darkness is mine.

A few hundred yards downriver, I go over the levee, climb a hog-wire fence, step down onto pasture grass.

It is that simple.

2 GLORIA

We spent all that night and the next day looking for him, but there were too many roads, too many ways. The moment Booger told him what had happened, Maledon had become grim, determined—he even seemed a little haunted. So we drove systematically through the streets of Hannibal, checking alleys, playgrounds, motels, rooming houses, and parks. Then we returned to Brazos O'Flaherty's and sought Jesse's face among those of the freaks in the pasture.

"Gone to argue morality with the Selective Service System," Maledon said, when we had not found him in that field. "Dumb fuck."

And then there were Homer Cantwell and Spoof Lyons, who were sure this was all part of Maledon's plan. Maledon heard their ultimatums, tolerated their threats, and listened to their descriptions of Mary Cantwell's broken heart. After about an hour of that he told them to go on back home and start fucking their regular customers again.

I couldn't sympathize with any of them. Jesse's life was his own. Maledon, of all people, should have understood that.

The dutiful father, the lost son. Christ!

Each of us—Villines, Gunner, and I—told Maledon that neither he nor Jesse was suited to the role.

"He's got a right to fuck up," he said. "I got a right to stop him."

So we just rode around in the hearse with Maledon, waiting it out.

Several times, bored with that and wanting some rock or some news, I switched on the radio. Each time he immediately shut it off.

Just before sundown of the day following the show, a day we'd wasted driving up and down county roads and highways, we loaded up and headed south, toward Blue Mountain. It was a downer's trip. Not even Gunner said much. Running out of jump, maybe. After a couple of hours of it, I gave up on all of them and got stoned. Gunner took a couple of hits, then held up his hand and went pure on me. Said the dope reminded him of the war. Everything reminded him of the war.

So I just leaned back into the reefer cushion and let it all go. It was just as well, I thought. I'd learned what there was to be learned from Maledon. He was different, he lived on the edge, but, finally, he was just another middle-aged man trying to figure out how to be a father. He, too, was part of the generation that had fucked everything up and wanted to teach us how to carry on the work.

And, anyway, now I had things to do. Things I'd have to do on my own.

Free my daughter.

Find Jimmy Song and get back or get even.

If Gunner wanted to come along, fine. If he didn't, fine. It was up to him. I didn't really give a fuck. He could hang around Blue Mountain and fondle his dead cock for all I cared.

The people were in the streets, man, and it was time for me to join them.

3 MALEDON

Late that Sunday night, or early Monday morning, really, somewhere between one and two A.M., I pulled up in the alley behind the Full Moon Recreation Parlor in Blue Mountain and got out, leaving the hearse to Conrad, telling him to keep it or sell it, whichever suited him. Gunner said this was a hell of a way to end a run, Gloria opened her eyes just a slit and said something sharp about middle-aged men and their predictable little consciences, and Conrad reminded me that I knew where he lived. Then they drove off.

I picked the Yale lock hanging from the back-door latch and went inside. I thought Buster Odom might be sleeping in his bunk in the little back room. But he wasn't. Must've been getting along with his wife that night—or maybe just needing her some. So I pulled the cord that turned on the dangling hundred-watt bulb, stretched out on the bunk myself, locked my hands behind my head, and commenced studying the walls.

They were covered with forty-five years worth of calendars. Buster's daddy, Clyde, the parlor's founder, had started the collection back in 1923. He went for presidents, and he had them in order—Coolidge to Eisenhower. One wall was about half-covered with fourteen years of Franklin Roosevelt getting older. I never heard for sure why Clyde did it. He never voted, he hated politicians with a pure fervor, and every few years he'd been an issue in a local campaign—some Christer running for mayor or county judge or sheriff would call him a threat to the moral fiber of the community and promise to shut down the pool hall if he was elected. Far as I know, Clyde never responded, never even so much as reminded anyone that the community's moral fiber needed way more than threatening, just kept doing his business, leveling tables and shooting snooker, selling to those he trusted the good bottle of dry-county hooch, and, once a year, taking the old presidential calendar down from behind the till, replacing it with the new one, and tacking the old one in its place among all the others on this wall.

Maybe he did it out of some kind of perverse patriotism. God knows. Maybe it amused him to lay here of an evening and look at all them shined-up pugs. Or maybe it did for him what it was doing for me—maybe it reminded him of what he was up against. They made a grim sight, I'll tell you that. Set me to thinking on what all they'd done for us. In the forty-five years that had passed since Clyde pinned up his first president, they'd given us a good eighteen years of war, nearly thirteen years of Depression, which they finally stopped by going to war, twenty-three years of living with the bomb, and forty-five years of doing what was best for the Fords and the Rockefellers, the Du Ponts and the Mellons.

I say forty-five years, but actually Clyde didn't last through '59, had a heart attack in this very bunk. And when Buster took over the parlor and the room, he decided to leave his daddy's rows of presidents as is. A good decision. Enough is enough. There were already more than plenty up there for a good lesson. So 1960 to '67 were represented by naked women. This year's woman was up front, back of the till, hanging where Johnson would otherwise have been serving his last stretch. A vast improvement. It put a little something like life in the room.

I laid there awhile, letting my mind idle with Clyde's presidents and Buster's women. How would it work, I wondered, if we made all politicians go naked? There wouldn't be any way, not enough cops in the world, to keep the laughter down. Wrinkled necks, soft bellies, and sagging asses. The exposed, shriveled cock now symbolizing not power but mortality. Johnson, Humphrey, Nixon—they'd be through. Everybody would see them for what they were, three soft, vain, spoiled men who were nothing without their laws, their cops, their money, and their soldiers.

But then it came to me that once folks saw that, they'd fuck up again. They'd start electing Marlboro men and queer-bait. We'd have us a president pampered like a movie queen and hung like a gas pump. And come some rainy Friday, he'd call in the newsboys, and, holding himself at just the right angle, he'd say, "After due consideration of all the possible scenarios and contingencies with my cabinet and advisers and the chairmen of the pertinent committees of Congress, we feel that the glorious cause of freedom leaves us no recourse except to use our strength to assist the Tibetan people in their valiant struggle for self-determination. We assure the American people that once the Dalai Lama has been restored, free elections will be effected."

So it wouldn't make much difference, man or woman, naked or clothed, you give them an army, they're going to find somebody to use it on. No, once the young blood starts slowing in them, most folks are fueled by little more than a householder's fear and a storekeeper's hope. Now and again a good many of them get taken by a craving for adventure, which they try to appease with a bout of drunkenness, a spell of adultery, or a stretch of embezzling. But never the real risk, never the breaking free, never the taking hold of their own lives with their own hands. They've been trained from the cradle that that's the final sin, the ultimate treason. Every government and every religion comes down on real freedom like piety on laughter. So folks keep right on taking the same old lamp-lit street toward darkness, their progress measured on a banker's ledger sheet, their hopes bounded by alien prophets and dead soldiers. The men in power don't want anything but to stay there, so they'll keep the street lamps lit, keep the ledger pages turning, keep the alien prophets holy, keep the dead soldiers flying home. God and war, Easter Sunday and Memorial Day—that game has worked forever. They'd have us all in our Sunday suits and singing "Up from the Grave He Arose" when they drop their big ace on us. A man can't save himself until he turns his back on them.

What got to me about Jesse was that he knew all that, knew just how governments used people, knew way better than I did just how religion had been trimmed down and uniformed so that it would fit comfortable inside a tank or a fighter plane, knew how mystery and wonder had been put into formation at the head of platoons that marched for the doctrine of the glory of war. Yet somehow he felt he owed the people responsible for all this an honest stand, a straight-up confrontation. And what got to me maybe even more than that was that I cared. I wanted to stop him, save him, rescue him from his own damn-fool conscience. But I had no cause to offer him, no faith to share. And he was the kind of boy that needed those things, needed them pure and whole, and wouldn't have any truck with hypocrisy. That, I figured, pretty well cut me out. Didn't seem to be anything for me to do come morning but pick a direction and be gone.

But knowing that didn't bring me sleep, or even rest. I kept on laying and brooding, my mind scurrying for an angle, then scurrying back. Now and again I'd find I was feeling sorry for myself. Then I'd cuss ol' Clyde, blaming it on him, telling myself that anytime a man had to look at a wall full of politicians it was bound to set his mind to rolling down a bad track.

It didn't work, though. Images of people I'd lost kept coming back to me—my brother, John, and then Magdalen and then Mary and then Jesse. Outside of Conrad they'd been the only ones that mattered, and I'd lost all of them, except for John, because of who I was, pure and simple, who I was and how I lived. Here I was now, over halfway home, one leg over the ridgepole and the other swinging down, with nothing left but the steady slide to the drop edge, owning nothing but what I wore and a pocketful of carnival dollars, claiming squatter's rights to a pool-hall cot, and half-envying the men that had sold out to the predictable day, the patriot's faith, the lawyer's truth.

And feeling tired, Lord. And not just tired, but beat.

After a while it came to me that if I kept letting self-pity have its way with me, I'd be laying in this cot whimpering about the nature of things till I forced Buster Odom to call in the bug-house boys and have them wheel me off strapped to a gurney. So I made myself get up—went in and had a look at the worn face in the cracked mirror over the rusted sink in the foul john.

"Move, ol' man," I said to the hobo blackguard staring back at me. "You too ugly to stand still. Folks can't stand looking at you steady." And the bastard gave me a grin.

I splashed a double handful of tap-water in my face, dried off with the begrimed roller-towel, and walked into the Blue Mountain night, headed for the local outpost of the Selective Service System.

There's always a world out there, I told myself, and it's always run by fucks that need some hurting. You may not can stop their machine, but that's no reason not to go on and piss in its tank.

4 JESSE

J.D. Hannah, Margaret Salter, and I sit, legs dangling, on the edge of the porch of the log cabin J.D.'s grandfather built fifty-seven years ago. J.D. was born here, left, returned. He has a history degree from Arkanasas, marched at Selma, Montgomery, and Washington. Until they fired him for believing in love, he had been a social worker in Blue Mountain. Child welfare: foster children, child abuse, juvenile delinquents, runaways. Since his father's death, in 1963, J.D. has lived here.

And the land is his. Sunset Valley. One hundred sixty acres of clovered meadow and hardwood forest. And Clear Creek, which ten miles down-slope from here becomes Lake Shepherd Springs and another five miles from there becomes Lake Fort Smith, the first lake being the backup reservoir for the second and the two together being the water supply for Blue Mountain and Fort Smith. But here it still runs as it has always, clear and pure, twisting and falling through the ancient Ozarks until it slows to cross the gentle slope of this valley, this valley homesteaded a century ago, in 1868, by J.D. Hannah's great-great-grandfather and farmed long and well by each of that man's heirs.

"You begin by admitting you know nothing," J.D. says. "And then you learn how to feed yourself."

Sunset Valley is no longer his, or not in the sense that it was once. A community has formed around him, with him. From this porch, I can see a pole-house that stands at the creek's edge, an A-frame, Margaret's, just downstream from that, a simple frame cabin occupying the crest of a small rise across the valley, and, in the verge of the woods at meadow's end, three domes. At the top of the ridge, on the other side of Clear Creek, these people have built a meeting hall and worship center, austere and beautiful, of stone and glass. J.D. Hannah is, I think, one of the last of the faith. A Christian who believes in mystery, simplicity, love, and laughter.

"What we had to learn before we could do that," he says, "the first step in learning to feed ourselves, and I mean all of us, even me, and I grew up here, what we had to learn, what we had to overcome, was how completely we depended on the system we believe is evil. It fed us, clothed us, sheltered us, heated us, cooled us, doctored us, educated us, hired us, paid us, fired us, and buried us. And it did most of these things so well for most of us that we had to ask ourselves again why we thought it was evil. And the answer was that it had left us helpless. And not just helpless, but obligated. If our government decided to start a war in Korea or Vietnam, we were obligated to serve. Though, of course, it was all so corrupt that if you had the money or the right degree you could get out of even that. What we had done, without thinking, most of us, was to trade our birthright, our freedom, for a house with central heating and a two-car garage. Our role was to fill a niche, do work that was, in and of itself, worthless, to keep quiet while in systematic comfort we wasted our lives. Well, that was the bargain, and we wanted out. As I say, each of us was nearly helpless when he reached that point. None of us would've made it without the others. But then if you want to, if you keep at it, if you're willing to fail enough times, you learn. That's where the hope is. That's the basis of faith, and faith is the basis of everything else."

Margaret looks from J.D. to me, smiles, says, "And then there are those of us who came out here because we were too fucked up to make it anywhere else."

"Same thing," J.D. says. "Just a matter of emphasis."

* * *

This is not where I had meant to be. After swimming to that shore south of Hannibal, I spent a full day hiding in the woods above the river. Then I began walking due west, across fields and pastures, avoiding houses and people, fearing that my stepfather might have the police looking for me or that my father might have convinced Brazos O'Flaherty and his weekend communalists to help rescue me from the Cantwell Capitalist Goons who had kidnapped me and were transporting me directly to boot camp. But I saw no one, except at a distance, and on the evening of the second day I began following a county road south. An hour or so after dark, I was on a highway. A textbook salesman on his way home from a convention in Chicago gave me a ride to Columbia.

"Got a son about your age," he said. "Long hair and all. But a good kid. Played ball, made the grades. Never gave us any real trouble. Then about two years ago he went off to the University of Wisconsin. Good school, pretty town. His mother and me, well, we were happy for him. Proud he'd got in there. Feeling like it'd all been worth it, you know, all the working, all the saving. Not that we forced him into it, trying to make him live out our own dreams, nothing like that, you know what I mean? Because I don't think we did. We just wanted him to have the background for whatever he chose to do. I mean he had his choice, within reason, you know, a bright kid like him, and good looking, even with the hair. And even that was okay. We didn't like it, but we got used to it, it was his hair. And half the kids there at Madison looked worse. Real scraggly bunch. Smart, you know, but scraggly, real scraggly. We were getting used to it, a little at a time, and hoping he'd grow out of it, too, you know, the music and the drugs and the anti-American stuff, all that. It was hard, but we were trying. We didn't want to lose him.

"He got arrested for possession of marijuana a year ago Christmastime when he was home, and that was the hardest thing. Up to then. But I bailed him out, and our lawyer got him a suspended sentence. And, well, when I asked him, Billy said he didn't smoke much, a joint now and then, it wasn't as bad as alcohol. It's just a bad law, he said. And I think that's right. They legalize, it'll solve a lot of problems. The kids, they see one bad law, they think they're all bad. And it's the war, too, of course. A bad war, no question. Bad time to grow up in all the way around. For me, it was World War II, and you could always see the cause, you know, the reason. No matter how crazy it was day to day, you always saw that. But this one . . . it's like they just decided it was time for a war and picked a country.

"Then, a kid like Billy, he can get out of it by going to college and taking a deferment, he can stay out of it by marrying or teaching or becoming a doctor, any number of ways. But, you know, his mother and me, we raised him to have a conscience. So he takes a deferment, he knows what he's doing: He's saying he's better than the others, the ones that have no choice, that die. They leave you with no good choice; I guess they mean to. You go, you're fighting in a bad war, on the wrong side. You take the deferment, you're doing worse; you're letting a poor man go in your place, you know, you're really saying the war may be evil but if you spare me, I'll go along, I'll go to the rallies, the marches, may even make a speech; but you give me the deferment, I'll take it. And then, you just flat say no to everything, the war, the deferment, all of it, you're an outlaw. Then it's either prison or the underground or Canada. I understand all that. I wish I could say that to Billy, see him face-to-face and say that. 'I understand, Son, there's no good choice. You do what you have to. We'll help any way we can.' I just wish I could see him and say that."

"He's gone, then, sir?"

"Turned down his deferment last spring. Set fire to his draft card at a rally. Got arrested, arraigned. I put up bail, haven't seen him since. I keep waiting for a card or something, some word letting us know he's okay. Keep hoping he'll go up to Canada and we can drive up and see him. But word never comes. We just wait."

"I'm sorry, sir," I told him. "Sometimes we run to find out where we're going. Sometimes we just run until we stop."

He turned to me and, after a hesitation, said, "You shouldn't cut yourself off from home, though. I'm not the government. I wouldn't send him to war. I wouldn't send anybody."

He offered me his son's room for the night, but I knew that he had said all he had to say to me, all he needed to say to someone. I knew that breakfast the next morning would have been awkward, and that my presence, the presence of someone his son's age, might rouse the suspicions of his neighbors—and then the police. He had opened himself to a stranger; if I stayed with him long enough to cease being a stranger, he would feel ashamed, vulnerable, weak. We offer our hearts to passersby, but when they stop we withdraw the offer.

Perhaps I was wrong. Perhaps I could have eased the pain these times had caused him. But I doubted it then, doubt it now. Sometimes we find a stranger when his pain is spilling: Then we can but cup our hands and catch as much of it as they will hold. But when the spill subsides, we must nod, back gently away, leave the stranger his dignity.

So I asked him to take me to Highway 63, south of Columbia. He did. I stood beneath a bridge until another car carried me away. He returned to the house with the empty room.

"And you've got to be able to laugh at yourself," J.D. says. "If life is holy, laughter is its blessing."

The day nears its close. Only the upper quarter of the sun remains above the wooded hills we face. "My father would agree with you," I say.

"And you?"

"If life is holy, serenity is its blessing."

"Fine with me," he says. "Serenity is silent laughter." And very gently, serenely, he laughs.

"Only if you don't take serenity seriously," Margaret says.

I look back at the sun. What remains of it seems to flatten and spread. I am momentarily overcome by the conviction that all we know, or think we know, is an elaborate, but very nearly random, collage of ephemeral images held together only by the demands of the individual consciousness—the human need for a unified field. The world is not there, or not in the way we think it is, but we must move in it; therefore we construct one that will accommodate us, build ourselves a Tinkertoy world and move in.

Consciousness as a hindrance to actual knowing.

Mind as a tool by which to avoid the real.

Intelligence as an aid to cowardice.

Perhaps the very essence of what we are taught is wrong. Perhaps only the unexamined life is worth living. We examine the world bit by bit, trying to extract an intimation of meaning, a clue to God's nature, from each fragment, and when we are done with them, these fragments, when the fingers of the mind have explored the edge of each shard, we can never fit them back together. Each bit is altered, charged with a temporary, artificial meaning, and none of them can again be a piece of the whole. Then we, too, become fragmented, a collection of anomalous ambitions, insights, instincts, fears, alienated not just from the world, the mystery, but from ourselves. The paradox is this: To examine an object, a creature, a phenomenon, is to remove yourself from it, to separate yourself from the circle, to become an outsider. Thus have we become aliens on this planet.

"Let's go sit in the creek and wash this shit off of us," Margaret says.

And shit it is. We have been spreading chicken manure over a section of the communal pasture.

I go with them to the water. I like these people. There are dreams that merit preservation, hopes worthy of nurture. So little is ever rationally possible, yet so much *is*. Life itself is a grand wish, so fragile as to be terrifying, so beautiful as to be sacred.

Four rides and sixteen hours after the ride from the bridge, I was in Blue Mountain, with only a few blocks of street and sidewalk separating me from the Selective Service office. It was four thirty, half an hour before they would close. The town hurried to finish its day. Factory workers, come across the Arkansas River bridge from Fort Smith, rushed grimly down West Main toward the streets and highways that would lead them home. They work for too little in the riverside factories and foundries. They are used for the profit of those who already have too much. The objects they make are cheap, shoddy, designed for obsolesence, built to be sold to people like themselves. And yet they go on, and yet they breed and greet each new birth with hope. Is it but ignorance and habit that keeps them going, these people whose sons fight the war I repudiate? Or is there a kind of continuous courage here, so constant as to be unnoticeable, that accounts for their persistence?

I walked a block to an intersection governed by a traffic light, waited for the signal, crossed, abided by the sensible rule. The draft office was three blocks west. I had determined to enter it and announce to the secretary, Joyce Flowers, a girl who had graduated two years before me, "I am here. I am ready. I will not go." My fear was that because it was so near five o'clock they would be closed, that I would again have to wait. And they were. And I did. But not because of the hour.

A policeman I didn't recognize stood in front of the door. I went up to him. "Closed," he said.

"I have business," I told him. "I've been drafted."

"Nothing there," he said. "See for yourself." He stepped aside.

The room was empty. No desk, no chairs, no file cabinets, no bulletin board, no framed photograph of General Hershey, no venetian blinds, not even a light fixture, not even a bulb. Empty.

"What happened?"

"Middle of the night sometime night before last somebody picked this lock, went inside, and cleaned her out. Must've been a gang of them, and they must've had a moving van." He shook his head. "Never thought it'd come to this. Not here."

I stepped back to the door, peered through the glass again. Empty. And clean. I couldn't keep from laughing.

He pulled me back. "Now don't let yourself be getting all joyed up over this, Son. They'll be running you boys in and out of here again soon enough."

"I'm surc," I said. Then—"Any idea who it was?"

"Hannah and them hippies be my guess. We'll be finding out right quick."

We sit on large, smooth stones, our backs to the cool current. Margaret is a lovely woman. A few feet below us the rapids slow, spread, deepen, settle into a clear pool. Just above the point at which the creek curls out of sight, two blue herons stand poised in the shallows at current's edge.

"In an ideal world," J.D. says, "a world of tribes and villages, we would need your father to do almost exactly what he's doing now. We'd need the gypsies to bring us the news."

"I want to meet him," Margaret says. She lies back flat into the current, so that the water streams over her shoulders and around her breasts. "He sounds like life."

5 GLORIA

Adrienne Fielding, who had been my roommate in Hotz Hall our sophomore year at the University of Arkansas, the last year either of us spent in a dormitory, lived in a duplex across the street from General Douglas MacArthur's birthplace. Conrad Villines drove us there. From Little Rock he would go on, north toward Searcy and Harrold Smith College.

"A life of going from one disguise to another," he said. He gave us a good-bye nod. "Don't y'all be fouling the general's park now, you hear?"

Gunner stepped toward the brick building, snapped the rubber heels of his sneakers together, and saluted. "Old soldiers never die," he said. "Just young ones, you cocksucker."

I went to him, put my hand on his elbow. "Let's go see Adrienne," I said. "You'll like her."

I had called her six or seven hours earlier, from a filling-station pay phone south of Springfield. Told her we were coming down there, this dude and me, and needed a place to crash. Probably get there about three in the morning. "There'll be room," she said.

She paid her bills by writing obituaries for the *Arkansas Gazette* and, on her own time, publishing an underground paper, *The Word*. And, I mean, her own paper actually paid for itself and a little more. She sold ads to head shops, record stores, restaurants, bars, and bookstores. Each month she got dozens of review copies of books and records from publishers and record companies. She reviewed a book and two records an issue, but she simply sold most of them, unread, unheard, to secondhand stores for around a dollar apiece. And, for each of the last two years, she had gotten government grants. Each issue of *The Word* had at least one article about school integration in Little Rock, housing patterns, police attitudes toward the city's blacks, institutionalized poverty in College Station, or a muckraking profile of one of the state legislature's old segregationists. And Adrienne was one-eighth Cherokee, which tended to make the grant givers look on her with favor. She was a master of using the liberal establishment's guilt to her advantage. Thinking vaguely of Wounded Knee, the rich old Jews would give the pretty Cherokee a thousand bucks.

"What it means," she explained to Gunner as we sat on salvaged sofa cushions in her fiercely cluttered living room and passed a joint among the three of us, "is that the country's more complicated than most of us realize. Oh, it's repressive, finally, there's no denying that. All you have to do to see that is look around. Every city in the country with a population of more than fifty thousand keeps its blacks in a ghetto. And our foreign policy is brutal. There's not even any complexity there. Just the one goal, world domination. If there's any real difference between our foreign policy and the Russians', it's that, at least in the beginning, the Russians' tends to side with the poor. Oh, sure, you'd be better off living in France dominated by America than in, say, Czechoslovakia, dominated by the Russians. But that's only because of the ocean. If we shared a border with France and if we'd lost twenty or thirty million men because twice in twenty years Germany had crossed France to invade us, well, you can bet your ass and your first edition of *Swann's Way* that we'd've turned France into Czechoslovakia. Fuck self-determination, fuck culture, we want a buffer."

"Good dope," Gunner said, holding the roach at arm's length and cocking an eyebrow. "Carefully tended by Colombian slaves, man, kept at gunpoint."

"And subsidized by the CI-fucking-A," I said. "Otherwise it'd be legal."

"Nothing's pure in America," Adrienne said. "Not even racism, not even repression. That's why the establishment is, finally, so effective, why our work is so difficult."

"Putting out the paper?" Gunner asked. A drugged cynic's mockery.

Which Adrienned ignored. "That's one example of it," she said. "They give me grant money. They let me print what I want to print. They don't just tolerate domestic dissent, they encourage it, subsidize it. Only up to a point, of course. And there are all kinds of exceptions. They're much less likely, for example, to tolerate a black woman's dissent than mine. She has suffered their injustices every day of her life. Her testimony, her dissent, is, therefore, more likely to be believed. But they may choose to deal with her without smashing her press and throwing her in jail. They might just buy her off. Co-opt her. Offer her a job as director of a ghetto self-help project. A project they can be sure their corrupt, labyrinthine bureaucracy will doom to failure. They might even make her a White House adviser or a congressional liaison specializing in matters of race. Or maybe they'll just give her enough awards and grant money to take the edge off her anger." She snuffed the joint, dropped the roach into a small, red, Italian candy tin. "But then, if that doesn't work, they'll shut her off, shut her up, shut her down. Or try to. We have to remember, though, that that's when you can be most effective, when you've finally forced them to acknowledge you as their enemy."

"Well, now, baby, that's easy to do," Gunner told her. "You can get right to that. All kinds of laws you can break that'll make them sic their bloodhounds on you. Or, hell, love, you wanting to do good, you just pick you out any factory in the state and start organizing workers. Damn goons be on you like napalm on Nam."

With the back of her right hand, Adrienne absently pushed a strand of long, dark hair back over her shoulder. Then she tilted her head back slightly, studied Gunner's face with her glazed brown eyes, and awarded him a hint of a smile, apparently shy, very seductive. So she had not abandoned those arts. "You're right," she said. "We're too cautious. But we have to realize that we're governed by the most subtle tyranny in history. This government operates on the assumption that if it keeps seventy percent of the people relatively content, it can use the other thirty percent however it wants to. That thirty percent does all the dirty work, all the menial labor, and when there's a war, they're the ones that fight. The other seventy percent own homes, draw salaries, watch the network news, vote in the elections, and believe they're free. And when the poor rise—the menial workers, the uneducated, the wretched, the thirty percent—when they rise and demand justice, it's not just the government that suppresses them, it's the entire other seventy percent. And from their point of view, they're right. Because American capitalism absolutely requires a lower class. About twenty percent of the people in this system do the real work, about ten percent are just flat left out, and the other seventy percent get to play money games. Though, of course, the real money games are played by only about three percent."

"So, you going to lose then, lady. That what you saying? It is, then all you working for's good music at the funeral."

"No," Adrienne said. "Thirty percent is enough, more than enough, if they're organized. And if they all understand the stakes. That's why we have to be careful not to move too quickly. We have to be cautious until the moment comes, and then we have to have the courage to recognize the moment."

"So you while away the waiting time by putting out your paper? Rolling them presses, baby, and keeping that eye out for the moment. Hop to, sweet thing, and let's dance that mayday rag."

I had been ready to leave Gunner, had not asked him to accompany me here. He could've stayed in Hannibal or stayed with Maledon or gone with Villines. He could've chosen his own direction. I would've said nothing. I had tired of his cynicism, had been frustrated by his impotence. The resuscitation of maimed veterans was not my line. I was no nurse. He could, I had thought, just go his own way and return, if he cared to, when he had healed. It was up to him. But now that he was here, where he had, without either of us seeming to make a decision, followed me, I found myself feeling possessive, caught myself resenting Adrienne's flirting—the tough, efficient, radical woman resorting to the coy smile, the flickering glance, the casual play of hand in hair. The community organizer, pamphleteer, champion of good causes was obviously drawn, like me, to the nihilistic veteran. And I was unnerved by the suspicion that she might succeed with him where I had failed.

I hated the weakness in myself, and in her, hated whatever it was in Gunner—that male relish of doom, that skeptic's conviction that hope was but the source of comedy—that drew us so surely to him. We talk of hope and change and the making of a better world, yet yield, as soon as the opportunity presents itself, to the defeated soldier who calls us innocents and mocks our hopes. He appealed to both the whore and the mother in us: We would fuck him like he'd never been fucked, and we would make him whole.

And, as I rose from the cushion on Adrienne's floor, it came to me. It was not his maleness that attracted and held us. Otherwise I could simply have had him and let him go—no qualms, no jealousies—or shared him, could just have fucked him and forgotten him. No, it was his wound that captured us. The idea that our sexuality and our love could heal it, could restore him to full manhood—or full boyhood, really, the sort of two-hundred-pound boyhood we are all so charmed by—sexy, energetic, masochistic, and pointless.

So, fuck this, I said to myself. I'm tired. I'm going to find a bed and go to sleep. If she can get him up, she's welcome to him.

"You're hungry, there's gazpacho in the fridge. Some oatmeal cookies I made, too. In the jar by the sink."

The little homemaker. Hold the poor bastard's head in your lap, spoon him the chicken soup your grandmother taught you to make.

But—"I'm tired," I said. "I'll find a mattress."

She didn't stand. Gunner remained where he was, his curious, ironic eyes on me.

Adrienne said, "There's an extra mattress in my room. Ben's crashed out in the bed, You know Ben? No, you wouldn't. He's from Raleigh. Hitching to Boulder. Taking his rest here. About halfway. Gentle man."

Now she stood. She led me to the door and opened it. Moonlight entering the uncurtained window showed me a young man's form sprawled on the bed. He slept on his stomach, the lower half of his body covered by the sheet.

"He plays great saxophone," Adrienne told me. She smiled mischievously, as if we were a conspiratorial sisterhood out on a lark. "Sleep there if you want. It would make him believe in miracles."

I stood there, hesitant. I don't know what Adrienne saw in my face. "Whatever," she said. "He'll be gone tomorrow. Inconsequential either way."

She hugged me. The sisterhood again. "I'm glad you're here," she said.

"Me too."

I stepped into the room, then turned back to her. "He any good?"

She raised a mock-judicial eyebrow and made the so-so gesture with her right hand.

Then, from the other room, Gunner said, "Ain't none of us no good long, baby."

I got into bed with the man named Ben.

6 MALEDON

It was casy enough, the draft board job, and good for me too. Got my damn blood back to running right, set my mind in proper order, showed me again just how simple it was to strike a clean blow for peace and light and short tunnels

The work made me feel so good—you know how it is with work you do in the service of mankind, and work you're good at too—I thought about taking the crusade on the road, entering town after town by night and driving away before morning witth their draft board in the back of my moving van. But then I pulled myself up, remembered the important thing about good causes (all of them, finally, being lost), and told myself there was no point in making a calling out of it. I wouldn't just flat give it up, necessarily, just refuse to take it on as a life's work—or a half- or a quarter-life's work, or whatever part of a life it was I had left. But, now, if I happened to be somewhere feeling down, there wasn't any good reason I couldn't just hot-wire me another U-Haul mover and drive it over to the office your friends and neighbors sent their messages out of.

The one mistake I made on the Blue Mountain job was starting so late. Once I started in, I was determined to get it all cleared out, and by the time I'd done that, there wasn't much more than a little patch of gray between me and sunup. But the way it was, there wasn't any way around it. I'd wasted too much time laying on the flat of my back and letting the weight of all them dead or dying presidents come down on me. And even when I'd made myself raise myself up, I'd had no plan other than to just forsake that grim back-of-the-pool-hall room in favor of the freedom the night can lend a man. And as to the draft board office, I'm not sure what it was, but there was something not quite conscious in me that was pushing me there. God knows I had no plan. Maybe I'd've just stood there a few minutes, quietly consigning a few years of my son's life to the motherfuckers that ran the place, and then maybe I'd've left town, looking for a flow that would carry me to an eddy I could rest in. Or maybe just the sight of the place itself would've been inspiration enough. I might even have lost it altogether, commenced to busting out windows and setting fire to files. I don't know, you see, because when I slipped up close enough to recognize the man leaning, hands in pockets, against the parking meter in front of the place as Howdy Hardison—and not Jesse as I'd first thought, feared, and hoped—well, right then the plan came to me full formed.

I walked heavily up to him, shaking the ground good so as not to catch him by surprise, him being a deaf-mute except for the one word. I'm not sure he knew me right off, though I'd hired him a time or two years back to help me set up stage. But I faced him forthright and offered my hand and an easy nod. He seemed to balk there for a second, but then he took the hand and said his one word—"Howdy." A harsh, alien, animal sound that had the wilderness in it.

Howdy'd never been to school. It wasn't so much that the family was poor, though they were, as that they'd never been willing to consign him for nine months at a stretch to the hands of the strangers at the Little Rock deaf school. But his twin brother Billy Don taught him, over the course of a childhood, how to use the sign language, how to read and write, how to read lips, and how to speak the one word. They say Billy Don would've taught him more, taught him the saying of whole sentences and paragraphs—Billy Don, the golden farm boy, swift of foot and quick of mind. It's certain they were as close as two brothers get. Howdy's being both deaf and smart brought out not just the brother in Billy Don but the father too, caught him young and taught him early about the silence that sucks everything in but laughter, and, finally, takes that too. So that what Billy Don did for Howdy was done as much for himself—to give himself someone to share the brief but good laughter with, someone who was born knowing the silence. I like to think he got as good as he gave.

But why just the one word? I asked Billy Don that three or four years ago, when the two of them were doing summer work for me, helping me build gallows for a show I'd do near Younger's Bend.

"Don't know," Billy Don said.

"Must have some idea."

"Maybe got tired of being called Dummy."

"Couldn't hear it."

"Could see it. He knew."

"But why just the one word? Add one more, and he could be telling them to fuck off."

"And the rest of his life he'd've been Fuck Off Hardison."

So I guess Howdy, being friendly by nature and knowing he'd never talk right, just decided Howdy'd do. A simple greeting, anything more, especially farewells, being futile.

But it was the farewell that did them in. I've spent some time thinking about why it is people go off voluntarily to what stands a good chance of being their death. With some folks it's likely nothing more than being tired of life. Others, boys mostly, do it out of a lust for glory and foreign snatch. Quite a few, I guess, are actually simple enough to believe the government's cause is their own. Everybody knows all that. It's as old as the path from the first village to the second. Wave the flags and beat the drums, and there'll come folks barging out their door to join the parade. But I'd've thought Billy Don Hardison understood it all too good to go along with it. And maybe he did understand it, I don't know. Maybe a lot of folks go knowing better. Maybe he thought there was no point in resisting the general idiocy. Maybe he didn't want to go through life being part of the team of Howdy and the Dodger. Or maybe he thought his good head and his quick feet would see him through, carry him back to life. I don't know. But, whatever the reason, when they called, he went. Always a mistake. Less than a year later, in some place called the A Shau Valley, he was hit by what the men that run the world call friendly fire.

And now, in the middle of a night some two years later, here was Howdy, standing forlorn in front of the place that housed the fuckers that killed the brother who had taught him how to deal with everything but this final farewell. So I knew I had me an ally.

It took me a few minutes to make it clear to him what I had in mind, but soon as I did we set about our work. We walked up to Buford Pixley's Esso station on Broadway, where I stole us a dolly and hot-wired the U-Haul moving van. We parked in the alley behind the draft board office, and I picked your friends' and neighbors' lock, brethren. Took me maybe forty-five seconds. First thing we took were the files, in case we had to make a quick run for it. Then we got the typewriters, copying machines, and dictaphones. Then the desks and chairs, and we kept at it until, a good hour before dawn, we had it cleaned out, down to the toilet paper in the shitter and the portrait of General Hershey on the wall. As we drove off, laughing, I caught myself hoping this'd be a lesson to Jesse, show him a way, teach him just how to resist the bugle call and help your fellow man at the same time. If Howdy and me hadn't quite freed all the draft-age boys in Crawford County, we'd damn sure give them some space to make a move in, which is all any of us has a right to ask for.

7 JESSE

Howdy Hardison came into Sunset Valley the day before I did, the sheriff the day after. I didn't see the sheriff. He spoke only to J.D. But I knew. I made the connection. There is no question. The draft board burglary is my father's work. His hand is clear, the absence of a signature being his mark. But he would have needed, or could have used, help. And Howdy would have been there, almost always was when he wasn't here, would have been keeping his solemn vigil, a mute reminder of the consequences of war. My father, who can see little use for the silent, moral example, would have convinced him of the wisdom of practicality.

So Howdy has come, and the sheriff has followed. I bear a responsibility for that. My presence can only bring trouble here. I go to J.D. Hannah to explain, apologize, offer thanks, and bid farewell.

"You know the sheriff, don't you?" he says.

I do. Verlon Hooks, fat, bald, swaggering. And clever, in his way—knows the motivations of the hundred-dollar thief, understands the frustrations and the rages of the honky-tonk Saturday night. But he has no insight into J.D. Hannah, no insight into those driven by a cause other than the gratification of greed. I know the sheriff's brother, too, Lester, a deputy, thin, dark, dangerously uncertain, with harried eyes and a nervous hand that rests too often on the butt of his holstered .38.

"Law enforcement as therapy for delirium tremens," J.D. says.

"My father did it," I tell him. "It's what he would do, the way he would do it."

He seems to have gained energy from the sheriff's visit, is both cheerful and abrupt. "Sheriff drops by every week or so, sometimes more. Thinks he'll catch us conspiring with Ho or Castro or maybe even Brezhnev. When he gives up on unraveling the great conspiracy, he takes off walking fencerows, jerking up the ragweed he sends to the state lab to be tested." He is amused, almost laughing. "He's trouble, or can be, and you don't want to make any sudden moves around old Lester. But they're going to be here no matter what. Got nothing to do with you." He turns his face away from me, looks out across the long valley, turns back. "Anyway, we're not here to avoid trouble, we're here so we can stand together when it comes."

"I think my father had Howdy help him."

"Good for both of them. Howdy needed to do something besides just stand there."

"He wound up with the right man, then," I say. "My father never stands still. He thinks contemplation is a narcotic." Now I, too, let my eyes slowly outline the valley. How fragile community is, I think, in the world the planners have made. If you commit yourself to it, you are vulnerable—become, as my father would say, a standing target; but if you do not, you are less than human. Will the future be but a labyrinthine technocracy predicting and controlling everything except the random wanderings of a few resolute rogues and renegades? Is gypsy community our only hope?

J.D. says, "If you're worried about Howdy getting hurt, you've come to it a little late. That happened some time back. If he helped your father clean out the draft board, maybe he's on his way toward healing. Sometimes passive resistance is bullshit, man. Howdy did it, he did right. If it happened because of you, even indirectly, you can feel good about it. Fuckers on the draft board ought to have trouble sleeping. They don't, we need to be waking them up. Sending other peoples' sons off to war isn't honorable work."

Yes, yes, I think. Howdy is Howdy, responsible for his own actions. And I am I, responsible for mine. Or lack of action. Inertia. Responsible for my inertia. But each of us does what he must, or waits while he must, and bears the consequences. I am not responsible for Howdy, nor he for me. "Ask not for whom the bell tolls"—it's none of your business. Leave it to the undertakers. But I am overwrought. That is not what J.D. is saying.

"They arrest Howdy, man, put him on trial, it's fireworks time. One hell of a show. The counterculture rag, Blue Mountain style. Poor deaf man lost his brother in a bad war and in a fit of rage and grief does a second-story number on the local board. Long-haired lawyers'd be lined up from here to the Haight wanting to take the case. Be the biggest show that ever hit Blue Mountain. Hell, I hope it happens. Howdy probably does, too."

"That may be," I say. I hope you're right. Still, I think it's time I turned myself in again."

He meets my eyes, then offers a small shrug. "Up to you," he says. "You could wait, though, do it here. Won't be long till the sheriff'll be back. Do it then. Be best for everybody, unless you got reason I don't see."

"I wanted to keep you out of it."

"If you want to be the Lone Ranger of pacifism, go ahead," he says. "But we'd like you to think you're among friends, man. And it's not just you. We want people to see resistance as an act of community. So even if you don't need it, or need us, you might consider letting us help other people see that there's a place to stand, a way to go, that there are people here who'll hide you or help you stand, whichever you want. If we can't do that, man, we might as well all split up and move back to the suburbs. Because that would mean our trip is as selfish as anyone else's."

And then days pass. Warm, comfortable, not yet even hinting of the sure coming of the harsh summer. I spend some time with Howdy, fishing with him in the mornings, catching catfish in the creek, hooking spawning crappie in the lake shallows. Though he divulges nothing about the burglary, I am convinced something important has happened to him, something that seems to have brought him, finally, a measure of contentment. Perhaps J.D. is right. Perhaps Howdy has found a meaningful wreath to lay upon his brother's grave. But does he know the price of that wreath?

I wait without quite knowing what for, am indecisive, while believing I have made the necessary practical decision. Time. I look for the propitious moment, as if time were a finite series of consecutive instants, each of which can be examined, some of which can be predicted.

I am doing time.

Odd phrase, *doing time.* Implying punishment, prison, time as enemy.

How do you do time?

By waiting without noticing the wait. By waiting without waiting. By knowing that time is now and always, is timeless, has no motion and does not cease.

How do you do, Time?

I am. I do not do.

I rise early these mornings, rise from my pallet on J.D. Hannah's porch, rise into a darkness to which my eyes slowly adjust, a darkness promising light. Barefoot, I wade Clear Creek, pushing carefully through knee-deep current, my feet curling around slick, flattened, hand-sized stones. At stream's center, I pause, bend, splash water on my face, drink from cupped hands. From the opposite bank, I follow the path that leads through cottonwoods and then buckeyes and into the hardwood forest, oak and hickory and, now and then, even yet, walnut, and then along switchbacks upslope around the bluff, and, finally, across cliff top to the small temple, where I meditate until dawn.

But again this morning I cannot defeat thought. My mind will not cease its speculation, its interrogation. I catch myself, release myself, begin anew, concentrate on the candle flame before me, and thought returns. Then, thinking of the futility of both mind and non-mind, I laugh. I think; therefore, I am. I am; therefore, I fail. I fail; therefore, I am not . . . All the petty, ridiculous therefores. All the futile rationalizations. All the neat little circles being marshaled into an artificial line. Mind struggling to make sense of a world that already makes sense. Mind that must continually label the obvious and each of its obvious parts, that must contrive definitions and meanings, causes and effects, that deconstructs and reconstructs because it cannot simply accept, will not yield to wonder, refuses simply to be. I am; therefore, I am. That *is*. And that is all. Being as tautology. Leave out the specialist's words, the angels-on-the-head-of-a-pin jargon. Being as being. Enough. God's plenty.

Still, mind seeks its own justification. Though joy comes unbidden, laughter unearned, and grace as a gift, mind wants the universe to work on the merit system. I think; therefore, I matter. My thought is convoluted; therefore, I matter more. I am because I deserve to be. I have joy because I am good. I have laughter because I am clever. I have grace because I have earned God's love. We are made absurd by our vanity. We are fools, isolated from the world by the mind that seeks to understand the world. And I am but another of the fools.

Dawn comes, and I give it up, yield fully to mind, essence, and enemy, walk to a window and stare out over Clear Creek and its bordering woods, across the valley of meadow and into the green hills beyond. From here I can see it as natural, timeless, but I know that mind has built dams across the creek, cut roads into the edge of the meadow, forced highways across the hills. And the dams, paths, roads, highways intersect logically, so that you can begin on one road and go anywhere, so that nature will be, as much as possible, eliminated from the journey.

The constant tinkering, the congenital dissatisfaction, the groundless ambition. Houses, towns, cities—the new order superimposed on the old. Land becomes property, property becomes wealth, wealth becomes worth. Add to that our efforts, clever and various, to decorate and defend our respective properties, and you have it all: Western civ. Millennia of rebellion against what is.

I would step outside all that, return to natural rhythms. But morality, conscience, bind me yet to the world of planners, schemers, organizers, physicists of apocalypse, the society of reasoning men, the warmongers' world. For their world, that vast, bureaucratically managed complex of streets and machines, programmed patriotism and intercontinental missiles, is now so pervasive that to reject it thoroughly is to reject mankind, is to become, at best, a benign misanthrope.

Like my father.

So I remain a part of my society's order, which is actually a profound, fundamental disorder. I would be that part whose role is to point out the absurdity, indicate the existence of true order, the perfect beauty of simplicity. But I know my father may be right: In an order as corrupt as ours, that role, the one I would choose, may be the most absurd of all.

I leave the temple, descend the path, wade the creek. And I think again of my father, of him and Howdy Hardison. "Accomplice," I say aloud to the current, and am reminded again of the insufficiency of words. They will try to reduce Howdy to a category. If they succeed, they will judge him, find him guilty.

And I: traitor, draft dodger. Labels that aptly apply. I must bring honor to them. My refusal must be an affirmation.

One morning soon I shall come down from the temple, and the

sheriff will be waiting in the valley. And there, surrounded by a community to which I cannot fully belong until I have done with this, I will deliver myself to him, will try to stand with whatever dignity is human, with whatever grace is mine, unarmed and openhanded, against the progress of the machine, against the arc of the missile, against the death of the village.

I must purge myself of rage. It must be an act of love.

But, for now, I simply go to see Margaret.

8 GLORIA

He was all right, Ben, the traveler. And so, Adrienne said, was Gunner. Damn her. And me. Jealousy is the essence of the bourgeois. I must defeat it.

"Better than that really," she went on. Gunner was in the kitchen, frying eggs. Adrienne and I were on her bed, I still naked under the sheets, she, in Levi's and a Malcolm X T-shirt, sitting on the edge of the bed, her upper body leaning toward me. "When he gets it up, it stays up all night."

Ben had already left, was up on 40, backpack at his feet, thumb pointing west. Before leaving he'd given me a slow midmorning farewell fuck. "Never had anything like you just come to me before," he'd said afterward as he pulled on his jeans. "Beautiful and free. No names, no words, no past, no future. Just the one night pure."

"Just a man and a woman," I'd said, sitting up, the pillow behind my back. "It should happen all the time."

He'd slipped his arms into the sleeves of his flannel shirt. "It doesn't, though." He'd buttoned the shirt, pulled on his boots. "Maybe you have to be strangers." He'd stood then, bent over me, bracing himself with his arms, one hand pressing into mattress on either side of me, and studied my face. "I want to remember it clear," he'd said. Then he'd kissed me and stood. Another long look. He'd picked up his backpack. "Have a nice life," he'd said. And I liked it, trite as it was.

"You, too."

Adrienne said, "He wanted us to come in here and have a mini-orgy, but I wasn't in the mood."

"Might be the only way I'll get him," I said.

She smiled, then reached out and pressed my hand. "Let's not be jealous. I didn't know until too late just what you'd been through with him. Last night you looked tired of him, and I thought we could both do with a change."

"You were right," I said. "And Ben was good."

Gunner came in carrying a tray full of breakfast. He set it at the foot of the bed. "Should've seen Ol' Blue last night, baby," he told me. "Stood up like a German soldier, went off like a Roman candle."

"Hard to believe," I said.

He nodded toward the tray, glanced up at Adrienne. "Why don't you move them eggs, honey. Let me get a start here, and then you can crawl in with us. Or jump, if that suits you better."

Adrienne looked at him, at me, then picked up the tray. Smirking, another man who had found his weapon, Gunner unbuckled his belt, wide, cowboy leather, a big silver buckle with a map of Vietnam at its center.

I almost did it, almost gave him the spite fuck and then was through with him. But I didn't. I'm not sure why. Adrienne, I guess. And pride. Neither of them good reasons, I know, but then, how many are? When and if I made love to Gunner, I'd do it on my own terms, not with her at bedside serving him up to me like a Continental breakfast.

"No," I said. "Ben was enough. And I have things to do." I got out of bed and put on my jeans and blouse.

"Aw, come on, flower. You the one missing out." But I could hear bluff in his voice. "And any time now Ol' Blue, poor veteran, he's liable to be laid up again."

"Well," I said, "it won't matter much. None of you is much more than a few inches of serviceable meat, but almost all of you have that. I'm sure I'll manage to make do."

Adrienne laughed, confident and cool, and set the breakfast tray on the dresser. "Good morning, lovers."

Gunner shrugged and buckled up. "Used to be, soldier came home from the wars, Jack, everybody loved him. Womankind'd flop over on her back and spread herself open for him. They'd hold him a parade, and a big ol' brass band'd come marching down Main playing

'When Johnny Comes Marching Home,' and there he'd be sitting up on the back of a white convertible waving at the crowd and catching confetti. But, Lord, look at it now, children—ain't no heroes here no more, 'cept maybe them square-jawed fucks they shoot up into space." He looked at Adrienne. "How about it, sweetheart? Would you spread her open for ol' John Glenn?"

She seemed faintly amused. "If I had the clap," she said.

Gunner shook his head, turned back to me. "See there, love. What a sad state it's all come to. Woman here mocking our heroes. And look at yourself, too. Why, we got ourselves a generation of women that'll drop their drawers for a drifter but won't give so much as a hidey-do to a man that's come home after a year of shelling slants in the Asian jungles. Hell, y'all keep that up, won't nobody go."

A couple of hours later, after Adrienne had driven me, in her green 1952 Willy's Jeep, to Dillard's in Park Plaza, where I BankAmericarded myself into a cornflower-blue Bobbie Brooks summer dress, a pair of Italian sandals, and a string of cultured pearls, we were in the downtown cop shop talking to Detective Lieutenant Elijah Jones about the once and future Jimmy Song.

He knew Adrienne. After a Little Rock pig had murdered a fifteen-year-old black kid who had fled down the Main Street sidewalk carrying the Marvin Gaye album he'd lifted from Moses' Record Shop, Adrienne had written a couple of articles about the department's shoot-to-kill policy and its use of dumdum bullets. That's why they sent us to the black man's office. They decided it would take the edge off Adrienne's anger—let the nigger handle her, serve both of them right.

At first, Elijah Jones feigned ignorance. "Jimmy Song," he said, leaning back, seeming to search his memory. "Don't recollect the name. Man would, you'd think. Name like that."

Adrienne showed him the *Arkansas Gazette* report of Jimmy's death in the drug-deal shootout at the Hotel Marion. "Just that," she said. "No follow up."

"He was my fiancé," I said. "I meant to come earlier, to help with the funeral arrangements and everything. But my father, Jonathan Wilder, warned me to stay out of it. And I thought, Well, if Jimmy was into things like that, drugs and everything, like the paper said, well, you know, he couldn't have been the boy I thought he was, and, like, well, I don't know, maybe I didn't owe him anything anyway. And, see, I just graduated up at the university and was just starting to kind of sort things out careerwise, you know, and, well, I know I probably should've come in, but I was scared. I didn't want to get mixed up in a drug investigation and all, even though I didn't know anything about any of it, that was just too much for me to handle right then. But just last week Daddy told me he'd heard he was still alive—Jimmy, I mean—and, well, I had to be in town anyway, a job interview with the EOA and all—I thought, you know, working with the underprivileged might be good for me for a couple of years, and so when I finished that I decided to come on down here. I was curious, and, well, like I kind of wanted to find out what happened to him and all. Jimmy, I mean." I fumbled through my purse, took out a pack of Benson & Hedges menthols, fumbled some more, and looked up at Lieutenant Jones.

"Light, Miss Wilder?" He pushed a book of matches across his desk.

I lit the cigarette, inhaled, and coughed. "Excuse me," I said. "I just smoke sometimes when I'm nervous, you know. I guess maybe I shouldn't." I looked down at the matchbook cover. It had a drawing of a cop holding a crying, possibly wounded little boy on it. Below that was written SOME PEOPLE CALL HIM PIG. I almost laughed.

"Miss Wilder, you go right ahead and smoke if you want to," Elijah Jones said. "It was a free country last I heard."

"If you're a cop," Adrienne said. "The rest of us have to spend all our time trying to find out what the hell's going on."

"Oh, Adrienne," I said. "You promised not to get started on that." I turned back to the pig. "We just wanted to find out about Jimmy. Sometimes Adrienne gets mad."

He folded his forearms on his desk and leaned over them. "And how did you meet Miss Fielding?"

"We were Pie Fies together. You know, pledged the same time and all. Pi Beta Phi, but Pie Fie's what everybody called it. We were roommates until she quit the sorority. And, well, I guess that kind of started me thinking, and so the next semester I dropped out of it, too, and changed my major to politicial science. I wanted to be part of things, like, well, all the changes, you know. Civil rights and stuff. And we were in a vigil against the war together, too."

He nodded. "Good to know," he said. "Makes a colored man want to tap dance."

"Look," Adrienne said, "you think you might be able to dance over to one of the white boys' file cabinets and find out what the fuck y'all did to Jimmy Song?"

He shrugged, then stood. "I be makin' a try for you, Miss Adrienne, sho will. But the cap'n, see, he be watchin' ol' Lijah real close. I do right though, you think you might help get my sweet Barthenia in that Pie Fie house? She sho got her li'l heart all set on it. And me and her momma, Carolina be her name, see, we never got no schoolin' at all past that li'l dose they give us at Horace Mann."

"Some assignment they give you, isn't it, Elijah?" Adrienne said. "Entertaining the white folks."

He showed her a broad Tom smile, went over to the file cabinet, got Jimmy's folder out, and sat back down.

He opened the folder. "James Robert Sangster," he said. "Weatherford, Texas. Be my guess folks there called him Jim Bob. Born August 18, 1945. Graduated from Weatherford High in '63. Attended North Texas State in '64 and '65. Dropped out. Drafted in '66. Failed the physical, got 4-F football knees. Been arrested four times. Drugs. No convictions. Never even been brought to trial. Five ten, one sixty. Aka Jimmy Song. Got him one jim-dandy lawyer. That be him, Miss Wilder?"

"Yes."

He closed the folder. "Well, now, then, look like you know what I know." The broad smile again. He laid his big hands over the folder. "Ol' Jimmy, look like he be on them bricks again. Just as free as you and me and the mayor. Seem like we can't make nothing stick to that boy."

"So he is alive," I said. "Thank God for that."

"Ain't sure God be wantin' the credit for that, ma'am."

"And he's not out on bail?" Adrienne asked.

"No. Charges was dropped. Man went scot-free."

"Cut a deal," Adrienne said. "Who'd he turn in?"

He shook his head. "Oh, I hadn't ought to be letting on about that, ma'am." He stood, returned the folder to the file cabinet. When he came back to his desk, the games were over. "I'm going to tell y'all something. I don't like your friend Jimmy Song. He cut hisself a deal, all right, but it wasn't no two or three weeks ago. No, he cut hisself a deal way back when, kind of deal that lets him get by with burning folks." He looked from Adrienne to me and back to Adrienne. "Y'all catching my drift?"

"He's a cop," Adrienne said.

"Ain't got no uniform. Won't find his name on nobody's roster. Takes his pay in cash."

"Why are you telling us this?" Adrienne asked.

" 'Cause you're so pretty."

"Thanks. Now reason number two."

"Got all kinds of reasons I can't go into. All comes down to this, though. Law'd be way better off with him on the other side. He's one vile motherfucker—you'll pardon the nigger in me, I hope. He hurts a lot of folks ain't got no call to be hurt that way. Some of them's my folks."

I asked him if he knew where Jimmy was now.

"Not here. Don't reckon he'll be back for a while. Big summer coming up, political conventions and all. Big boys'll be needing him." He stood, went to the door, put his hand on the knob. "I was you, Miss Fielding, I wouldn't be writing any of this up in my paper. You see, it could all just be a pig's way of setting up a loyal revolutionary, couldn't it?"

"Yes," Adrienne said, standing. "That has occurred to me."

He nodded at her, agreeably, then opened the door for us. "Been awful nice meeting you, Miss Wilder. Hope things work out for you at the EOA. Folks out at Granite Mountain been needing some rich white lady to come out and do good for them."

9 MALEDON

If you have to make a stand, it's best to do it at night so you can be cleared out come morning. Unless you're like Jesse, that is, and want to make your whole life a stand. But, Lord, that's a grim way to get through. So after cleaning out the draft board, I wanted to put a good-sized state or two between me and Blue Mountain right quick. Problem was, I had to get shut of the truck and the files and the furniture and all the rest of them

Selective Service gewgaws, and that was the part of the plan that hadn't come to me right when I first laid eyes on Howdy.

The truck was easy. You can just pull over and walk away from one of them. And if you're the kind that worries about the ledger sheets of the U-Haul company, why, you can wait till another dark night comes along and park the truck right back where you took it from. But the files, now, that was different. A man wouldn't want to go to the kind of trouble I'd gone through getting them and then turn around and let them fall right back into the hands of the fucks he took them from. No, I couldn't just walk away from them files. Wouldn't be sensible. Wouldn't be patriotic.

I could've set them afire. But when I got to thinking about that, I realized it'd be quite a job of work involving more chance than was good. There was so damned much paper, you see. Drawer after drawer full of files, thousands of the fuckers. To make sure all of it got burned down to ash, I might've had to sit around for a day or two stoking paper into flame. It would've been both chancy and tedious. Hard to think of a worse combination.

I was driving Howdy north, up 71 toward Fayetteville, and we had to go past Lake Shepherd Springs and Lake Fort Smith, and I thought, well, I'd just let Howdy off down by the Hannah place, hide out somewhere till night cover came, then drive back to Lake Fort Smith and out onto the dam and just dump it all into the water right there. I could punch holes into the cabinets so they would sink and soak good. Some of the furniture would float, of course, but then it would've sure looked good floating there. They'd be able to fish the files out finally, but they wouldn't have much when they reeled them in.

Then just about the time I dropped Howdy off at the head of Sunset Road—he wanted to walk down into the valley, and anyway it was smart for us not to be seen together—I remembered Vestal Truax, the Winslow dump keeper.

As I was letting Howdy out, I thanked him for his help, said I thought we'd done ourselves proud, and wished him luck. He nodded, gave me a short laugh, stepped out of the truck, flashed me the peace sigh, and walked on down his road.

I sat there beside the highway watching him until he rounded the first bend and went out of sight, and then it came to me that there was a working commune in that valley and that if Jesse decided to do some more waiting that might be just the place he'd do it in. I stored that back and headed on up toward Winslow.

I parked the truck just inside the gate and then walked across the dump to Vestal Truax's trailer. He was a lively old drunk that for the past fifteen or twenty years had been tending to the Winslow waste in exchange for an Airstream trailor and just enough cash to keep him in whiskey, crackers, and Vienna sausages. When I came up on him, he was sitting on a fruit crate under a ragged old patio umbrella he must've rescued from the dump. He was reading a back issue of *Escapade* magazine.

"How you, Vestal?" I said.

He glanced up at me, then back down at the magazine. He turned a page. "Wonder what they pay these women?" he said.

"Why, you saving up?"

"Thinking about it," he said. He closed the magazine and dropped it to the raw, scraped earth at his feet. "But then they'd probably charge extra, don't you reckon, they had to come to a dump."

"Wouldn't be much future in it for them, I wouldn't think."

"Be a shit hole here and now, for that matter." He looked out over the dump, making a new survey of his domain. A half-dozen mange-riddled dogs were scattered about, nosing through the edges of the debris. "But then they might get to where they grow accustomed to it the way I done."

"Yeah," I said. "They might just take right to it. Might all of them be getting real sick of fresh air and young men and money."

He gave me that old gruff laugh of his. "And, Lord knows, I wouldn't be the kind that'd keep any of them long," he said. "You know, one could drop by, stay a night or two, and move on, leaving it clear for the next one. I don't kid myself it'd be the night of their life or nothing like that, but, Christ, Sam, looks like they'd take some pleasure from knowing how much joy they'd bring poor ol' Vestal. I mean how many of us here on this earth have the chance to do that kind of good for their fellow man. And, hell, if they thought it was too big a sacrifice for one woman to make, they could come two at a time." He looked up at me solemn and gave his head a slow shake. "And the God's truth is, Sam, whole lot of the time their pussy's just lying fallow. Damn shame, all the waste there is in this world."

He stepped out from under his umbrella. "Well, never happen, I don't reckon. Just going to keep on being me and them dogs." He flapped a hand toward the *Escapade*. "And them magazines," he said. "That's one thing about this job. Any time, day or night, a man can walk out over that dump and pick him out a whole armload of them skin books."

"Love's where you find it."

"That's what the big boys say," he said. "But then, lot of times, they don't know shit from Shinola." He cut himself a chew from the end of a Cotton Boll twist he took from his overall pocket. After he got it placed just so in his jaw and spit a couple of times, he said, "So, Sam? What is it you're wanting me to do for you? Bury that U-Haul?"

"Well," I said. "Just about."

10 JESSE

"Do you remember Norman Morrison?" I ask Margaret. I sit full lotus on a hardwood floor in an empty room, skylight above me, window to my right, white wall behind me and to my left. I wear faded jeans and a white orderly's shirt. She wears a mauve kimono. Painter's light suffuses the room.

She lifts her brush, turns her face from the canvas to me. "No," she says. "He from Virginia?"

"Baltimore. A Quaker. Been dead about two and a half years."

"Oh." Her eyes, her mind, her brush return to the canvas. "Strange eyes." The brush moves, small strokes, correcting my eyes, I guess. "Ever notice the resemblance between lechery and spirituality. Odd. I saw a painting of Saint Paul once. I can't remember where or who by. Just the eyes. Very convincing. He could've been a rapist."

"It's the obsession," I say. " 'Purity of heart is to will one thing.' You ever notice Kafka's eyes in the photographs? He almost has those saint's eyes you're talking about. But not quite. It won't quite come clear for him. There's no certainty there."

"Kafka looks like he's *been* raped. A victim's eyes."

"Twentieth-century eyes," I say. "But maybe that's better than that certainty, that obsession. That kind of purity can as easily be evil as good."

"The absolute need to impose your will on the world." She does not turn from the canvas. "You can see it in the eyes. From Jesus to Jack the Ripper."

"I doubt that Norman Morrison looked much like Jack the Ripper."

She turns her face to me, her brush poised. "All right, Jesse. Who was he?"

"He died November second, 1965, late in the afternoon. He carried his daughter, Emily was . . . is her name—she was fifteen months old then—to the river entrance of the Pentagon, just across the Potomac from the capitol building. Carried her in one arm and a can of kerosene in the other. He set his daughter down on the grass and walked about fifteen feet away from her. He was less than a hundred yards from Robert McNamara's office. He could see the windows. If McNamara happened to be looking out the window instead of at one of his graphs, he saw Norman douse himself with the kerosene, strike a match, and set himself afire. The papers didn't say anything about McNamara, but they did say that hundreds of Pentagon office workers saw the fire leaping six or eight feet above Morrison's body. An army major jumped a railing, ran to him, and tried to beat down the flames. But he was gone, Norman Morrison was, charred, black, unrecognizable, dead. Like the victims of napalm. Or like those South Vietnamese Buddhist monks. That was the point."

She has stepped away from the canvas, is facing me squarely. "What are you telling me, Jesse? You admire that? That martyrdom crap?"

"I wrote a paper about him. For ethics. It was the last thing I did before I dropped out of school."

"Well," she says, nodding once, her face hinting that it might smile, "we certainly don't want to shirk our assignments in ethics class, do we?"

"What I wondered about then, and what I wonder about now, is his daughter, Emily, fifteen months old, a baby, but old enough to be frightened by the fire. Why he brought her."

She shrugs. "He was like the rest of you, Jesse. He may have been a Quaker, but he wanted to be a hero. And he wanted his daughter to see it."

"I don't think so," I tell her. "I think he wanted her to remember, but I don't think it was your standard act of cowboy heroism. John Wayne on the sands of Iwo Jima."

"It's just the pacifist's version. One good man against the hordes of evil. The soldier armed with only a pure heart. The brave death for the good cause."

"But sometimes you have to make a stand. What we're doing in Vietnam isn't just wrong, it's evil. Unless you believe that evil is all-powerful, you have a duty to oppose it. Actively oppose it. Norman Morrison did that. He may have gone about it wrong. He may have been foolish. But he tried. And he had a legacy he wanted to pass on to his daughter."

"Oh, Christ! *May* have been foolish?" She lays her brush on her palette, goes into her small kitchen, returns with a glass of water, and sits on the floor, her back against the wall to my left, her legs outstretched. "So is that what you plan to do, Jesse? Go down to the Federal Building with a can of kerosene? Maybe stop off at the welfare office first and pick up a foster child so you'll have a proper witness, a little girl to leave your legacy to?"

"No." I unfold my legs, stretch them before me, turn my face toward window light. "I was only thinking about symbolic gestures."

"A person's life is not a symbol."

"Yes." I look at her, nod. "I agree. And that's where Norman was wrong, isn't it? You know, it always seemed to me to be an American attitude, or Western anyway: Nothing is, everything symbolizes. But Norman Morrison was inspired by the Buddhist monks. And his death changed no opinions. It can't offer us anything but sadness. The war goes on, doesn't it? It's much worse than it was when he died."

"Yes, and we may have Nixon next."

"Well." I smile at her. She is glorious, suffused with light. "He may be so busy pocketing the White House silverware he'll forget to send in more troops."

"The Joint Chiefs will remind him." She tilts her head back, letting it rest against the white wall, and closes her eyes.

"But maybe it wasn't symbolic," I say. "Maybe it was just Norman Morrison's suicide. Maybe the other is just us, our minds turning it into something it wasn't. Maybe it was just a man saying, 'I don't want to live here anymore.' "

Her eyes do not open. "Why do it in front of the Pentagon then, within view of McNamara's window? And why bring the little girl?"

"He could've done it there because that was why he didn't want to live, that building and what went on inside it. He could've been saying to them, 'You have robbed me of the moral right to the possibility of joy. The only pure way to resist you, then, is to die.' "

The blue eyes open. Head still resting against the wall, the face turns toward me. "That's crap, Jesse. He was a good Quaker boy, and those flames were his sermon. And that little girl, he didn't bring her there for her sake, he brought her there for ours. To increase our guilt. He wanted her to haunt us."

"Well, she does haunt me."

"Yes. You and his wife and his parents and his friends. Maybe a couple of hundred people all together. And I'd guess that most of you were already against the war. But Robert McNamara went right on about his business, didn't he?"

"Yes," I say. "We've already agreed on that."

But she goes on, calmly determined to make the point her way. "So he killed himself, Norman Morrison did, and two and a half years later the war's worse than ever. And God knows how much longer it'll go on before Washington decides how to surrender and save face at the same time. And twenty years from now there'll be a grown woman who can remember nothing of her father except a burst of flame before a massive white building."

"I think she'll know he meant well."

"I hope so," she says. "Because I'm sure he did."

"But that's not enough."

"No."

"Well then, ma'am," I say, "could you tell a poor, confused draft dodger what is?"

"Oh sure. Be glad to."

She stands, returns to her canvas. "Fold back up, bub."

I do. "So? You going to tell me?"

She lifts her brush to her right eye, sights down it at me, lowers it, and offers me a teasing smile. "That's easy. You live your life. Day after day. Honestly, carefully. You live it in such a way that, no matter what *they* do, you never forfeit the—what was it you called it?—the moral right to the possibility of joy. You recognize that despair is your enemy, and when you feel it coming, you fight it." She tilts her head coyly to the right. "And," she says, "you fall in love with a painter."

"In that order?" I ask.

Smiling, she shakes her head. "No, you start wherever you can."

"I've begun, then."

"Good. Now hold that damned pose."

11 GLORIA

"Boys in blue open their hearts and files for you?" Gunner asked us when we returned to Adrienne's apartment. "Give you a line on Genuine Jimmy Song? Let you see the general layout, ladies, the bullhead's theme, copper's dream, flatfoot scheme? Give you a glimpse of the Grand Hoover Plan, wo-man? Offer you a vision of safe streets and soothing nights, katydids and Christmas carols?"

So he'd found a connection.

"Something like that," I said. I wasn't up for one of his raps.

"Speed merchants on Granite Mountain say he be a narc, Mark, a brother to the other, Mother. Praise be the man that love both sides of the law, Maw, the man that do the dance, Vance, with the heat so neat between his feet, Pete. Oh, Sweet Jimmy Song, tiptoeing along the edge of either ledge! Be still, my pirate heart!"

I walked past him and into the bedroom. Rapping, he followed. Adrienne got a joint out of a Twinings tea tin and lit up. I started stuffing my things into a knapsack.

"We going hunting, baby love? Forge deep into the dark woods and commence spotlighting counterrevolutionaries?"

"Sure," I said, giving him a cold, dismissive glance. Then I fastened the knapsack and straightened up.

"You can crash here awhile longer," Adrienne told Gunner. Well into the joint, she was leaning against the dresser and wearing a weird, almost twisted smile.

"Ol' Blue always wants the one he can't get up for," Gunner said.

"Suit yourself," she said.

"Fuck Ol' Blue," I told him. I looked at Adrienne. "I'll trade him to you for a ride to the airport."

"Aw now, love. Don't be turning so quick on poor Gunner. You know you be needing a man to walk point on this. A knight what knows a land mine before he steps on it. Ol' veteran of the search-and-destroy life."

"Suit yourself," I said.

"There we go. Seems like that's the word today. Everybody wanting the soldier to suit hisself. But, hell, I reckon it's all the invitation a man could ask for."

So Adrienne drove us to the airport, where I showed the Hertz woman my BankAmericard and won a black Lincoln Continental. We could go first class until my father got the bill. It would be his contribution to the movement. He'd given me the card six months earlier, hoping that by making the delights of America accessible he could cure me of thought. Fight with the weapons at hand, someone had said. I'd been waiting for the right time to use this one. I wanted to be wearing elegant clothes and driving this diplomat's car, all of which I'd gotten with his credit, when I carried my daughter away from him, when I took her with me into the revolution.

As I drove out of the lot, Gunner ran a palm across the soft leather above the glove compartment, then began opening and closing electric windows. "By damn, ma'am," he said, "you sure right on this time. If you can't beat 'em, join 'em—or at least look like 'em. This here's your Park Avenue pimpmobile. We be servicing the Harvard Club vices now—name-brand narcotics, finishing-school whores. We en route to the palace, Gloria Alice—Dawn-Grant Escort and Pharmaceutical Services, Unlimited. We take a shit, we have a hired man wipe our fine Christian asses—refugee of some sort needing honest American work. My country 'tis of thee, love. Whoopee and amen."

I turned on the radio and caught another day's variation on the news of the death of America. A thousand New York pigs broke up the week-long sit-in at Columbia. A hundred revolutionaries and fifteen pigs were injured. Six hundred twenty-eight were arrested. It is only a beginning, a preliminary skirmish, an experiment in tactics. Next time we will be better prepared, more appropriately armed.

Dwight Eisenhower, the quintessence of the banal, suffered a mild heart attack. The suburbs were praying for him. Nelson Rockefeller announced that he was a candidate for president. He wanted Republicans to have a choice. Play the fascist combo—Nixon or Rockefeller. Justice Jim Johnson, the slapstick Nazi, filed for the U.S. Senate on the Wallace ticket, his wife, Virginia, for the governorship. I hoped they'd win; it would clarify things. The Pentagon said the Viet Cong were using squads of naked women to seduce and destroy American troops.

"It's time them boys learned," Gunner said. "Pussy ain't ever free."

I changed the station. Oldies. The Stones, "19th Nervous Breakdown."

"It's what happened to the Seventh Cavalry, love. Custer and all them fair-haired boys. Rode up over a rise, and there it was. Valley full of naked, writhing Sioux whores. Well, George Armstrong, now, never being one to ride off leaving a woman needing meat, he dismounts, brushes back his yellow hair, splashes High Plains Musk on his cheeks and neck and armpits, sprinkles ground sassafras root over crotch and crack, remounts, and leads his slavering troops down into the valley of the shadow of the Little Big Horn. And the last thing any of them heard, love, them boys that had lived too long on elk jerky and old mother palm, the last thing they heard as they humped away at fluttering, aboriginal twitch was the hoofbeats of Crazy Horse's descending cavalry and the sound, coming high and clear from the rim of the world, of Sitting Bull's apocalyptic laughter."

I glanced at him. He grinned, his eyes wide and wild. He looked as if he could go on, as if he could while away the afternoon, evening, and night regaling me with a slapstick, pornographic history of the West. I decided to encourage him. Why not? "I hope no unwanted pregnancies resulted."

He nodded, as if in thanks. "Oh, yes," he said. "It was the doom come down on them, babe, them savages. You bet. 'Cause the Crazy Horse cavalry come quick, but not as quick as the cunt-crazed Custerites. No ma'am. Them boys, salt of the earth to a man, why, I can tell you sure, Little Sisters of the Auxiliary, they'd all done fired once and were reloading without ever taking the short arm out of the breech when down come the tomahawks and the bootlegged long knives and the darkness. Praise God and amen. Life goes on. And, why sure, some of them, the dashing general for one for certain, had time to fire twice, my love, oh yes. And nine months later, O ye lovers of long-headed justice, the Sioux was rife with half-breeds, little baby boys and girls whose genes were tied to Pittsburgh and Richmond and Birmingham and New Bedford and who knows where all, had the DNA, Brethren of the Laboratory, that spiraled back to London and Dublin, and Kraków and Prague, the Black Forest and the Seine, the Po and the Alps, the Parthenon and the Colo-fucking-sseum. So they were doomed, them New World nomads, by the Old World gene. From then on, during the last dim years of raids and retreats, the Sioux was plagued with laggard youth.

" 'Why can't we stop here and settle down?' one of them'd say. 'I can't see any purpose in this wandering life. We could fence this in here, build a ranch house, dam the creek, raise some sheep, start a school, make something of ourselves. This shit here, man, this is the past, the fucking gone world, Daddy Bull. Romantic horse-soldier bullshit. War bonnets waving in the wind. Counting coup. Seeking visions. Smoking bark. Lords of the plain, my ass. It's time we wised up. Christ, man, we got to get over all that drag-time crap, Nap. Got to go with the flow, Joe. Got to change, LaGrange. Got to quit dragging these fucking teepees back and forth across all the wide Dakotas and greater Montana and build something permanent, something a family can live inside of. I'm sick of the wolf wind in the winter and the prarie-dog sun in the summer. We got to build us something we can air-condition. We just a ragtag bunch of desperados, and it's high time we adapted to the age, Sage.'

"Oh, the medicine men wept, and the warriors raged, and now and again Sitting Bull'd get a bellyful and slap one of the know-it-all little bastards upside the head, but it was over. Ol' Son of the Morning Star had done them in with the civilizing seed. They couldn't run, and they couldn't fight, not with the yellow-headed gene seeing home as a place that could be lined off and staked out, and they lost their religion by asking blue-eyed questions, so they let themselves get fenced into a reservation and commenced to drink their way into the bottle that holds every desperado's dreams."

He sighed, clucked, opened a limp, resigned palm. "Cong better listen up and learn, love. Long run that GI sperm gonna do 'em in, tie 'em down, give 'em a generation that prefers Rice Krispies to rice, hot dogs to Ho, Coca-Cola to communism. We ain't done nothing else over there, we spread the gospel of the dollar bill. Amen and forever for now."

"You're a crazy man," I said. "You may be right, but you're a crazy man."

"Years from now, love, man asks you, you tell him ol' Gunner told you so. We won't beat 'em, we just corrupt 'em. Hanoi wins, they done. Won't be no way to handle their own but give them a new war to fight or go all out after consumer goods—put Zeniths in them huts, motors on them bicycles, Coca-Colas in them wooden cups. Gonna have to put some Levi's on Mama San's wasted little ass. She done had her a look at them fancy goods she won't be getting over. Five, ten, fifteen, years, dream woman, they still there, they be begging us to bring in what they been fighting to keep out. We're lost, love, me and you, but you can be lost here, you can live a long, lost life, maybe even like living it, God knows. All you got to do is keep showing up at the job site. Don't have to do nothing, just show up, where they can keep track of you. And even if you can't do that, you might can make it by just staying out of the way. There's space here, you can drift a long time, maybe a lifetime, and never hit nothing hard. But them poor gooks, love, them raggedy, scraggledy, scrounging little slants, darling, they ain't just lost, they dead. Cause when it's over, they gonna be gone lost, one-way lost, and there ain't room there to be lost in. In Nam, ma'am, you got to have something to belong to. You lost there, baby, there ain't no road out."

We rode on south, air-conditioning and tinted glass sealing us from the bright day. Gunner's mouth never flagged, and by the time we reached Fordyce, his mind was flashing in all directions. He saw a Coke sign and took off: "Coca-Cola, RC, Ty Cobb, moon pie, razor spikes, marshmallow center. Whoa, baby, it all fits together. Man that invented Grapette lives right up this road in Camden. Bet you know him, don't you, love child? Gives the Coca-Cola boys a run for their money there in Ouachita County, I bet. Yes'm, Miss Scarlet, it's Ragged Dick and all the Alger boys. The American saga, children. Poor boy gets off his ass, he ain't poor no more. Worry the water and sugar the syrup till he's got him a bottled drink he can sell all over the world, ten cents a bottle, two bucks by the case. The human spirit, brethren. The American entrepreneur. Glory, glory, how-they-jew-ya. You got a dime, hon? I'd like a Grapette."

"They've gone up," I said.

"Fine with me. What's money to a mercenary? It's what I fought for, flower child. Make the world safe for inflation." He leaned his head back, swept a forearm slowly forward, and boomed:

Many fought and many died
Just to let the dollar ride.
Every gook gone helps to bring
Profit to the Grapette king.
Every bagged boy overseas
Helps ensure a price increase.
Every bomb dropped on Hanoi
Helps support a Harvard boy.
Every napalmed slant-eyed child
Makes the men at Dow go wild
With briefcase joy and sweet success
And scientific happiness.
We owe it all to men like that,
Educated, rich, and fat.
The scientists and merchants, too,
Who make the bombs for me and you,
And tell us, when they start a war
What the fuck we're dying for.
So, when they've all their maker met,
He'll give them boys a cold Grapette.

He let his head fall to his shoulder in a mock swoon.

I said, "His name is Foltz, the Grapette man, I mean. He has an azalea garden he opens to the public. Must be several acres. Azaleas everywhere, different patterns in different sections, and every time you go into a new section you go through an arch of wisteria. In early spring it's beautiful. We used to go there a lot when I was a little girl. I would slip away from my parents and follow one of the paths through arch after arch until I was alone. Then I'd just sit there on one of those white wrought-iron benches fantasizing that I was princess of a magic kingdom and that my prince was off somewhere riding at the head of a glorious army, defending us from a world I couldn't understand, a world without magic or flowers. Sometimes I'd go home and actually write him a letter, telling him of my desperate love and saying that no matter how long the wars lasted I'd always be there when he returned."

"But now you gone, ain't you, princess? When the dream soldier gets back, won't be nobody there but the Grapette king."

"No," I told him, "I'm still there. The dream doesn't belong to Mr. Foltz."

He shook his head. "All of you want chivalry back, finally, don't you? Simple as that. Fucking chain mail and scented handkerchiefs." With his head against the headrest, he turned his face toward me. His neck seemed vulnerable. His eyes were milky sad, yet still wild. "O, lady love, let us sit upon the ground and tell sad tales of the disappearance of the Grail, bemoan the fall of the kingdom of flowers, recount the crumbling of the hegemony of magic."

"Hegemony?" I laughed. "What did you do over there? Read poetry and thesauruses?"

"Thesauri," he said. Then he laughed, too. "Well, baby, I did get me an education. That's for goddamn sure."

He turned away from me, looked straight ahead. The ironic smile disappeared, then returned. "You know what I learned to believe in? What I pared it all down to?"

"Saving your own ass?" I said.

"Speed. But, well, sure, same thing, ain't it? Speed and saving my ass. I did the other shit, too. Lots of it. You just open your mouth up over there, and somebody'll stick some kind of dope in it. But speed's the only one you could live on. I saw too many floating boys get blowed away—or blow some poor slant away for giggling. They'd be drifting high, you know, or flashing high—potheads and A-heads, smack freaks and Seconal soldiers. But a man wants to stay alive, he needs him something he can focus on. Can't be shooting shit up, either, just a pair of white pills ever' so often. Every day you're on them probably costs you five at the other end, but you got to get through the one you're in before the others matter. A man's got no cause over there, love, nothing to believe in but getting through that one year one day at a time. You can't even think about that year, really, no matter how little or how much you got left in it. You just got to make the day. Then you got to make another one."

I looked at him again. He was still staring at the highway. But I don't think he was seeing anything. A blank sadness that seemed final had settled over his face.

"I don't care what you're using, Gunner. Just don't get strung out on me."

"I am strung out, babe." Even then he didn't turn his face back to me. "That's what I'm telling you, love. There still ain't nothing to believe in." Now he turned to me, opened his palm, showed me the two white pills there, and popped them into his mouth. "Naw, there still ain't nothing to believe in. Ain't even reason now to be careful with it. Nobody going to kill me but myself."

"Change," I said. "You can believe in change. And you can believe in helping change come more quickly."

He looked at me hard for a few seconds. Then he laughed, a loud, almost furious laugh. "Change, my ass," he said. "That's what's wrong now. The good's gone bad, and the bad's got worse. No, fuck, what we need now is, we need something worth saving, something worth keeping the same, something still around worth protecting from change."

"You change some things, you preserve others," I said. "And you try to pass the good on down. That's why I'm going after my daughter."

"Why, hell, yes, I see now," he said. "We going to take her out to the azalea gardens, ain't we?"

"We're going to try," I told him. "Or *I* am."

12 MALEDON

While Vestal Truax was bulldozing all those Selective Service files and knickknacks and that furniture into the landfill for me, I drove the U-Haul on up to Fayetteville and bought him two gallons of Four Roses, three boxes of crackers, and six dozen cans of Vienna sausages. I'd've been more generous with the crackers, but I figured any more would've gone stale on him before he got to them. When I got back, he was relaxing again on that crate under the patio umbrella in front of his Airstream.

"Aye, God," he said when he saw what I'd brought him, "if this don't beat that stunt the Master pulled. Loaves and fishes, my dump-stained ass. Here comes a man with crackers and Vye-eenas. And, Lord, all four of them roses to wash it down with."

"Ain't nothing too good for the director of the Winslow Township Sanitation Unit Number 1," I said.

"Ain't nothing much too bad, either," he said. "There's another unbroke crate leaning over there against the trailer. Damn dogs may've marked it, but you can just flip her over, be fine."

I went over after it.

"Might as well get them two tin cups out of the sink while you're up. I don't reckon there'll be any getting shut of you till you've had some of my roses, and a man could wear hisself out passing these gallon jars around."

I did like he said. The cups were old, dented measuring cups, marked here and there by spots of rust. Another little something else rescued from the archaeologists.

"Here," he said as I lowered myself onto the crate the dogs used, "you drink out of this number 2 tin. Got a little leak in her about halfway up. Keep you from getting too drunk for the drive home."

"How you know I ain't fixing to stay on for supper. Home has a wandering meaning for a man like me."

"Didn't bring enough of the sausages for both of us," he said. He scratched at his thinly haired, heavily grimed scalp. "No, what I'm figuring is, you'll lay about here till it gets dark good, then go on and take care of whatever night business it was brung you here."

"About it." I nodded.

"How's that boy of yours?"

"Seems set on doing hard time."

"Shame," he said. "World can sure mark up a principled boy."

We sat there a long time, ragging back and forth, watching the dogs sniff the dump, keeping half-track of the sun, and drinking on the Four Roses. It wasn't a bad life, for a while. I wouldn't've traded it for a banker's. If a man could've just moved from dump site to dump site every so often, seeing some country and picking up some women in between, it would've been within hailing distance of damn good. I guess the smell sooner or later would've either got to you or deadened your sense, but that's pretty much the way with any line of steady work.

We had ourselves some crackers and Viennas in honor of the sunset. Then I poured us another slosh of whiskey apiece, lifted my cup, and said, "Well, Vestal, it looks like highway time again. Sure you don't want to ride with me?"

"Can't," he said. "What'd them poor damn dogs do if I did?"

"Die, I reckon. But that's just good reason for you to come along."

"Naw. Lord gives a man a calling, it ain't Christian for him to turn his back on it." He drank. "Where is it you're headed, anyway?"

"Got to trade that U-Haul in on a proper car. Then I think I'll go looking for Magdalen. Remember her? Idea come over me just now as

I was sitting here. Seems like the summer for lost causes. I guess I'll just play it on out."

"Lord God," he said. "Ain't heard you so much as mention her in ten years." He looked into his cup and remembered. He'd met her once, way back before he took over the dump, when Dr. Ladders had hired him to come up and testify one night during a brush-arbor revival we'd put on outside the Missionary Baptist Church in Hogeye. "She was prime," he said. He studied the whiskey again, then drank. "But, Lord, that was back when Eisenhower had hair." He shook his head. "Pussy must be getting scarce," he concluded.

"Oh, I don't know," I said. "Looks to me like pussy's running wild all over the country. And that's fine too. Way God meant it to be. He hadn't wanted us getting laid regular and with whoever, he wouldn't've give us such a powerful hankering. It's just that I can feel myself coming under one of them spells where it seems like remembered pussy's the best of all."

"Well," he said, "it won't be what you remembered. Pussy maybe, but the trappings'll be different."

"That's why I'm going," I said. "That's the sure cure."

I stood, finished my drink, set the measuring cup on the disintegrating plastic that covered the patio table. "Anybody comes poking at my shit yonder, put the fear of the Sanitation Department in them. I figure to be back before summer's out. Might be some use for them files yet."

"Apt to molder where they are now."

"That's fine too. Ain't *that* much use for them."

He nodded, held his cup in salute. "You see Magdalen, you say Vestal said hidey, ma'am. She's needing a man and you still don't suit her, tell her I'm here and I get to pining lonely these long summer evenings. There's less Christian things a woman can do than ease an old man's age."

13 JESSE

Sheriff Verlon Hooks and his brother Lester have returned. It is Friday morning, the third of May. I am ready for them.

I have finished my cliff-top meditations and am eating a bowl of hot cereal on the porch of Margaret Salter's cabin when we see the official brown-and-white making its way slowly along the lane across the meadow of alfalfa.

"There are several thousand acres of national forest right behind us," Margaret says. "I don't think that car will climb the bluff. And the sheriff doesn't exactly remind me of Leatherstocking."

"They're only here to give me a ride to where I will do what I have to do."

She looks at me, her eyes dancing with doubt. "They're just instruments, then? A necessary part of the car that's come for you?"

"I didn't quite mean that."

"Why don't you quit patronizing people? Other people make choices, you know. To be a sheriff is to be making a moral decision."

"Verlon Hooks isn't my enemy," I say. "He's just another victim. He gets to be sheriff because they've seen to it that he's incapable of making a moral choice. He is a functioning victim, an ignorant tool of people he'll never see."

She shakes her head, glances at the approaching car. "Such humble arrogance. Practicing for the jury, I suppose, aren't you? After you've made your closing statement, after you've explained to them all about masters and victims, they'll all rise and burn their draft cards—or their sons' draft cards. Then they'll give their money to the poor and become spiritual pilgrims. The war will end, the established church will vanish, true religion will sweep the earth, the ghettos will become gardens, and throughout the land the voice of the turtle will be heard." Then her eyes harden, her mouth is tightly set. "Christ, at least have the grace to give them the dignity of an enemy. He's a *man*, probably a bad man. He's not just part of that fucking car."

I smile at her. "You'll visit me?"

"Oh, sure," she says. "I've never been able to resist the lunatic pariah."

Sheriff Hooks stops the car immediately in front of the steps to Margaret's porch. Saying nothing more, Margaret enters her home. The sheriff, his brother, and J.D. get out of the car.

As Sheriff Hooks walks around his car, his eyes make a systematic survey of the cabin's front and of the nearby creek-bank brush. As if he were leery of ambush. J.D. and Lester stand beside the car, J.D. looking lightly bemused, Lester looking determined but nervous, a timorous soul girded for dangerous duty, the conveyance of justice to the traitor's lair.

"Draft board got your letter, Son," the sheriff tells me. "Awful nice of you to write after all these weeks. Some of us was starting to worry over you. Thought you'd skipped the country maybe. Turned plumb turncoat."

He stops at the edge of the porch and looks up at me, waiting, apparently, for some kind of reply.

"I didn't want the time," I say. "But when it came, I realized I needed it."

He studies me for a few seconds more, looks down, shakes his head once, looks back up, and says, "Well, I thank you for clearing that up for me." Then he shrugs and extends open palms. "So? You ready now?"

But we stay there, neither of us moving.

He shakes his head again. "You know, boy, been easier on everybody you'd stayed gone."

"I know."

J.D. laughs out loud.

Sheriff Hooks turns to his brother. "Always some rich fuck's son, ain't it, Lester? Puts everybody in a hole nobody gets out of—'cepting maybe sometimes the rich fuck and his son. Damned ol' country sheriff, now, no way he can win this one, is there?"

"Fucker won't stand and fight with his own, Verlon, he's scum. You doing right. Ain't nobody won't see that."

"Aw, bullshit, Lester. Come next election, you and me, we'll be hoping to land work varnishing couch legs over to the furniture factory."

He turns back around to face me. "One goddamn draft dodger in the county, and he has to be Homer Fucking Cantwell's boy. Not only that, the son of a bitch ain't even got the good sense to dodge right. Sends us a letter saying where he is. Sees to it we got no choice but to come out here and arrest him." He folds his arms, cocks his head back, studies me again. "You know, boy, I don't want none of this. I never started that war, and, tell you God's truth, long as don't no kin of mine get shot up, I don't much give a shit who wins it. You understand what I'm saying, Son?"

"I understand the meaning of what you're saying, yes."

"By God, that'll do, for now." He nods appreciatively. "Now, you see, your daddy, Mr. Cantwell I'm meaning, he didn't hurt me none when I run for sheriff. Helped me considerable, truth be told, bought me several of them yard signs and bumper stickers a man has to buy that wants to get anywhere running for something. And, even so, it wasn't so much the money as folks just knowing he was backing me. Your daddy, Son, he don't lose much. Not here. You still following me?"

"I think so."

J.D. says, "Might even be a little ahead of you, sheriff."

The sheriff gives him a little sidelong glance. "Wouldn't be hard."

"Let's put the little prick in the car," Lester says.

Sheriff Hooks ignores him. "So, anyway," he says to me, "I seen I was going to have to come after you, I gave Mr. Cantwell warning. He's that kind of man, things're owed to him. And he gave me his say-so to go ahead. But he wasn't overjoyed over it, you see, boy? Wasn't happy at all. He don't approve of what you're doing, him being a man that loves his country the way he does. But I reckon he might rather see Ho Chi Minh elected president than have his family name drug across the headlines of the *Blue Mountain Banner*. And, tell you what, boy, case like this, lot of times what makes Homer Cantwell happy's apt to bring a little smile to yours truly, too."

"Yes, it would."

"Ought not be my job," he goes on, "coming out here after you. Ain't county law you broke, ain't state law, ain't county court you'll be tried in. Ought to be a pair of them FBI fucks out here in place of me and Lester. But it's left to me. They ain't coming. Apt to blow a goddamn tire on one of these country roads, apt to get lost, apt to get their suits dusted up. God knows why, but it's left to me. Me, that ain't got a damn thing to gain by hauling your yellow ass to jail. And could just have a shit load to lose. This whole son of a bitch liable to blow right up in my face. It's a nasty damn jail, Son. Winos howling all night. Hot-check artists lying all day. Every cell smelling like piss and puke. Head lice spawning on the mattress. Most times at least one damn maniac hearing the voice of the Lord telling him to walk in blood. No place at all for a educated boy like yourself."

He pauses, stares into my eyes.

"I understand," I tell him.

"They's killings go on in this county, pretty regular. Various kinds of robbery, all the time. Why just the other day, ol' boy walked into People's Bank and drove off with a nice little nest egg wasn't his. I got all kinds of shit I could be doing. Day gets slow, why, I can just step out on the courthouse lawn and arrest me a vagrant. That's my calling, Son, not this shit. I don't need to be messing with Homer Cantwell's boy, not as flighty as Mary is. No sir, whole thing's apt to turn upside down on me."

Again he waits and stares. J.D. begins laughing.

Lester gives J.D. a backhand slap across the chest. "Don't you be laughing at Verlon now."

"Might as well leave him laugh," the sheriff says. "This boy don't use his head, everybody liable to be laughing at all of us."

"I'm ready when you are," I say.

He looks down at his boots, shakes his head, looks up. "Listen, Son, I don't want to arrest you. That's clear now, ain't it? Far as I'm concerned, you can stay out here and cook your meals over burning draft cards. Don't make no never mind to me. But long as you're standing there calling me, I got no choice. So what I'm going to do, see, I'm going to turn my back to you, give you a minute, say, to think about the world of possibilities, pretty little woman in the house there, tens of thousands of acres of woods and hills right behind you, all kinds of places to go and things to do, whole countries, by God, that'd welcome you in and never ask you to shoot nobody. Yes sir, Son, that's just what I'm going to do, turn my back on you." And he does. "And if you're out of sight when I turn back around, well, me and Lester, we'll go back into town and tell folks. 'Well, the chicken shit cocksucker run off again.' That way everybody gets to keep riding along the way they've got used to."

"How much did my stepfather pay you?"

"Lots of times in this world, Son, a man don't get but what he earns. Lot of times he don't even get that."

We wait.

Finally, he turns to me again and says, "Well, I been as reasonable as a man could. Now get in the car, you self-righteous prick. We going to have to see how you like jail." He starts back around the car, stops, looks at J.D., and says, "Ought to just let Lester shoot him. Probably easier on everybody that way."

I step down off Margaret's porch and walk to the sheriff's car, reminded again how far my stepfather will go to keep me from taking my stand.

14 GLORIA

When his secretary had put me through and I had heard his voice, I said, "I got Aura and we're gone. She's happy. So am I. How's your day? Money rolling in?"

I had planned to hang up then, but I couldn't resist waiting for his response.

"There's a restraining order. I'll have your spoiled ass in jail."

"Too late," I said. "You're not paying attention. We're gone."

"You're always easy to find."

"Not this time. This time it's a new life for all of us. And not just us, either. The end's drawing near for all you money-fuckers, too."

"I'll have the police looking for you. You have no business with that little girl."

"I'm not in business," I said. "That's your line."

"I should've had you committed years ago. But it's a hard thing for a father to do."

"Yeah, I could've been homecoming queen for the Razorbacks. But I kept fucking it up for you, didn't I? Kept sleeping with hippies. Kept associating with niggers and traitors. If I'd've played it right, maybe I could've had Bill Montgomery—or whatever your quarterback hero's name is. You'd've been proud of me then, wouldn't you? Sitting up on the backseat of that white convertible as we circled the field, forty thousand idiots cheering me. Oh, you'd've loved that. I could've been Arkansas's whore."

"I realize you're still very young, Gloria. But, even so, you are extraordinarily full of shit."

A moment of Ma Bell silence followed, the humming of the wires between Paris, Texas, and Wilder Junction, Arkansas.

Then—"Gloria," he said, "bring Aura back. Whatever it is you want to do, she'll only be in your way. And you know as well as I do that Hallie is better with her than either of us is."

"Oh, I might have been willing to leave her at Hallie's house," I said. "But not at yours."

"She's just a baby. Don't do this to her."

Again the silence hummed.

"There's something I've wanted to say for a long time," I told him.

"Well, then, just say it, Gloria." As if he knew.

"Fuck you, Daddy." As soon as it slipped from my mouth, I wanted the "Daddy" back. So I said it again. "Fuck you."

And then I hung up on him.

This was, I kept thinking as we drove farther west, the final break. There would be no place now to slink back to. Gunner and I had spent the previous night in the Holiday Inn, Jr. (the great chain's way of bringing civilization to towns the size of Camden), and that morning I'd gone to the Merchants' and Planters' Bank and converted my savings account, nearly seven thousand dollars, to cash. I had trust funds, too, but restrictions were attached to them: To claim them I had to be either thirty years old or respectable—in my father's view. So I couldn't touch that money. At the Wilder Junction Baptist Church, where Aura had been spending every weekday morning, I'd walked into a room where Mrs. Myrtle Crump was reading a roomful of children the story of Joshua and the battle of Jericho, had taken my daughter by the hand, and had led her to daylight.

My money, then, was in my knapsack, my daughter was in the backseat, my father was in the past. I had cut myself free. There was no alternative to the future.

Through the afternoon and into the evening we drove toward the sun, stopping only for gas, junk food, and the john. Aura behaved well most of the time, pleased that her summer vacation had started early.

And when she did start to get irritable, just west of Oklahoma City, Gunner, who was driving, told her a long, elaborate tale about a little girl named Aura who was being hunted in the Dark Wood of Circumstance by the dogs of Fortune, named Fate and Skipper. Fate was the more systematic of the two—Aura knew that if he found her first he would lead her straight out of the wood and into a pen prepared for her by his master, Grunge, who would train them to be house servants. Aura's hope was to be discovered by Skipper, a whimsical mongrel who, though ultimately as lost as she was, would lead her here and there through the wood, showing her its secret meadows, healing springs, and magical caverns until he had not so much delivered her as made her feel at home.

By the time Aura had outwitted Fate and was following Skipper down the banks of the winding Happenstance River, I had fallen asleep. When I woke, it was dark and we were almost to the Texas Panhandle. In the backseat, Aura lay curled up in the pure sleep of childhood. Gunner was singing "By the Time I Get to Phoenix."

"We could get a room in Amarillo," I said. "Might be easier for Aura."

"Ain't nothing to do in Amarillo, for her or anybody else, but to get through it. Besides, I can drive forever."

"Just tonight and tomorrow will do."

"Maybe," he said. "But then we'd all probably be better off if we just kept on riding."

He eased us over into the eastbound lane and passed a gun-racked pickup truck. "The Panhandle Liberation Army," I said.

"Be my guess a handful of them boys could take San Francisco, darling. They make good soldiers."

"But they'd be too ignorant to know what to do with it."

"You wrong there," he said. "Right off they'd hold a big rodeo in the Cow Palace."

"Well, I take it back then. Everybody loves a rodeo."

The gun-racked truck went roaring past us, horn blaring. When he had pulled over in front of us, the driver looked back and gave us the finger.

"How about I pull up alongside Earl Wayne there and sideswipe him off into the long prairie night? Teach him better than to go to fucking around with a war hero."

I couldn't tell how serious he was. He would've probably thoroughly enjoyed playing highway he-man with the Earl Waynes of the world. I said, “We have Aura.”

“Ah, yes. We got to remember that, don’t we, Mom?” He slowed, letting the pickup grow smaller ahead of us. “Which reminds me, love child, what I been meaning to ask. Just what the fuck is it we going to do with that girl?”

“*I’m* going to give her a new life,” I said. “I’m going to be her mother now.”

“Right in the heart of the dope capital of the world?”

“We’re going to San Francisco to find Jimmy. After we’ve done that, we’ll make other plans.”

He shrugged. “Well, it don’t make a shit to me. Just seems a shame to let little Aura get wasted.”

“She won’t be wasted,” I said. “That’s why I’m doing this.”

“I see.” He nodded, mocking. “Sure eases my mind, knowing that.”

“When I want your opinion, Dr. Spock, I’ll ask.”

We crossed the Texas line.

“You sure he’s there?”

“Who? Jimmy? It’s where he always goes sooner or later.”

“Well, looks like good timing for ol’ Gunner anyway,” he said. “Only right, me getting there the summer after the Summer of Love.”

PART V

1 MALEDON

I took my time finding her. Nothing was pressing except getting properly shut of the U-Haul—and even that was easy enough. I waited until about midnight, then drove it down to Cherry Street in Blue Mountain and parked it in the driveway of one Dibrell A. Poole, head of the local draft board. Then I hot-wired the Oldsmobile I'd parked beside (It was Dib's car; his wife left her Oldsmobile in the garage), drove it to Fort Smith, found a space for it in front of the Como Hotel, went inside, spoke to Rita, the madame, signed Dib's name to the register, went back to a room at the end of a hall, and had myself a twenty-dollar piece of ass—a young whore, probably from some place like Blue Eye or Baptist Ford or Three Widows, that said her name was Gigi.

When we were finished, I asked her what a nice girl like herself was doing in a place like this.

"Just fucking around," she said out of the long end of a crooked smile. And I was tempted to see if I couldn't take her on permanent.

I stayed in the room, sleeping until, after maybe an hour, Rita came back and told me if it was sleep I wanted I'd have to get it someplace other than her hotel.

"Why, hell, Rita," I said, getting up buck naked, "I paid for the room."

"We both know what you paid for. You want more of it, you can pay again. I got a crowd out there waiting, and the cops frown on me letting them go at it in the lobby."

I thought it over. Then pulled out fifteen dollars and laid it on the nightstand. I'd already paid the five for the room.

"How about yourself?" I asked her.

"I'm retired," she said, "and married." She arched an eyebrow. "But what the hell?"

She led me over to the basin and washed my cock.

"Married," I said. "Got any kids?"

"Boy sixteen."

I gave her a look.

"He ain't my husband's."

"You don't look near old enough," I said.

Clean-cocked, I got on the bed, stretched out, and watched her undress. "You're still a beauty, Rita."

"I exercise."

She lay down beside me. "How do you want it? It's bargain night."

"Best way you can give it."

"We'll start like this." She kissed me, her tongue flickering. So it was bargain night. Then her face made its way down my body.

When she had me in her mouth, I said, "Christ Almighty," several times to show my appreciation.

Later, just after she had straddled me and had started a slow grind, I looked up into her good, professional eyes and said, "You know, Rita, that boy of yours, when he turns eighteen, you let me know."

She stopped. "Why's that?"

"Well, I'm chairman of the draft board over in Blue Mountain, and I might could do him some good."

"Yeah, and I'm secretary of state." Her eyes became slits. "But I tell you what, mister, I'll fuck every man in the Defense Department to save my boy."

"Show me how," I said.

She was a woman that knew her work. I was a man that wanted to be thoroughly soiled when he entered the Jacob Ladders Memorial Baptist Church. We had us a time.

When we were done, I gave her another five bucks and Dibrell Poole's name, address, and phone number. "I'm sick of what I'm doing," I told her. "This war's wrong." She agreed to let me spend the rest of the night in the room. "I guess we can work around you. Just don't be roving the halls."

In the morning, I walked down Garrison to Pete's Peep Show, where I bought a big brown grocery bag full of skin books and sexual paraphernalia. I put the magazines under the driver's seat of Dib's car, stuck a couple of dildos in the glove compartment, set the vibrator on the dashboard, and hung the artificial pussy from the rearview mirror. Then I walked the three blocks to the bus station and made a payphone call to Blue Mountain's queer lawyer, Tom Guy Hughes.

"Tom Guy," I said. "Sam Maledon here. I'm putting a thousand dollars in a locker over here at the bus station. I'll be mailing you the key special delivery. When they slap Jesse in the slam, you're his lawyer. Don't make a shit what he says. Done?"

"Done," he said. "By the way, that was pretty work somebody did in the draft office, wasn't it?"

"Place like that's always needing work done on it."

"I suppose," he said.

"Jesse's set on doing hard time," I told him. "Thinks it's the moral way. Don't you let him do it. You keep delaying them till the Cong's done conquered Asia. You need more money, I'll get it to you."

"Sounds like my kind of business."

"I mean it, Tom Guy. Do it straight up if you can, do some slithering if you have to. But get that boy out of jail, and keep him out."

"Of course I will," he said. "Jesse's too pretty for prison."

"You asshole."

"Godspeed, Sam."

After that I caught the midmorning Greyhound to Tulsa. I gave Dib's car a grin when we passed it. I knew ol' Dib, a man of such influence and reputation that he could send your children off to get killed without thinking of it as anything more that just another little something in another day's work, would be able to get it all sorted out without much trouble—probably cost him no more than an embarrassing afternoon. Still, any embarrassment you could cause him was all to the good—another chip you could set on the table come Judgment Day.

I stayed a week in Tulsa, spending my nights in a guesthouse at Oral Roberts University. I'd had Conrad Villines call and tell them I was the Reverend Dr. Dickey Bushmaier, professor of religious psychology at Harrold Smith College and that I was coming down to do research for a paper, and possibly a book, that would demonstrate the positive effects of Christian faith on athletic performance. Because I refused to be compromised by federal or corporate grants, I required whatever generous assistance good Christian people could find it in their hearts to provide. Oral's boys bought it and put me up in grand style. They knew that humble-pilgrim shit would never work in Tulsa, where salvation was something granted by oil companies. Unfortunately, Oral himself wasn't around—off curing Kansas of cancer, I reckon. So evenings, after sharing a side of beef with the resident evangelists, I'd borrow a university car, drive to one of the bars where the divorcees were in heat, pick me up one—or, if that failed, as it did twice, just buy me a whore—take her back to the guesthouse, lead her to the bed beneath the painting of Oral looking what passes in Oklahoma for beatific, and let her seduce a backslid preacher. Nothing they like better.

My days I spent establishing Tulsa credit for Dr. Bushmaier. Being a preacher helps, of course—especially there. The rest of it's a matter of having some cards printed up, along with a deed or two, then borrowing some money from a bank, paying it back two or three days later with the money you borrowed (you do lose some interest right there, but it'll work out for you in the end), setting up a checking account in a name that has a nice ring to it (say, Rev. Dickey Bushmaier, Doctor of Divinity), then paying a visit to whoever it is that's selling whatever it is you want to buy. On the morning of my seventh day here in Tulsa, I visited ol' Billy Don Pixley of Billy Don's Dodge way out on Memorial Drive, and I'm damned if that sly bastard didn't sell me a red factory-fresh Dodge van for two hundred down and a hundred a month.

I went to the courthouse, showed them Rev. Bushmaier's driver's license, paid the sales tax, screwed the tags to the back of the car, and headed for Sedan, Kansas, leaving a man who didn't exist to worry about making the monthly payments.

I drove from the Tulsa courthouse to the Heart of America Motel in Caney, Kansas. What attracted me to the place was its layout, fifty separate white-frame rooms arranged in a half-circle around a court of painted rocks, each cut into the shape of a different state and all put together so that they made a yard-sized jigsaw map of the U.S.A. The rock representing Kansas, at the heart of the puzzle, was oversized and the only one painted more than one color. It had red and white stripes. Caney itself was marked by a blue valentine with white stars.

"Hell of a deal you got out there," I told the man at the desk. "How's business?"

"Who gives a shit?" he answered.

So I just took a room and let it be. He gave me what was called the Kansas suite. It had roaches, and the water was sulfurous, but it sat at the center of the half-circle, and my window gave me a grand view of the big map. There wasn't a soul in the place except for me and the dreamer at the desk. I decided that what he needed to do was to smash up a few of the rocks and go to the cops and the press and claim he was being harassed by hippies and black militants.

Next morning I got up early, shaved and showered in the sulfur water, put on the good gray suit I'd got first thing after getting off the bus in Tulsa, and drove the twenty miles to Sedan.

The Jacob Ladders Memorial Baptist Church was about the size of the Pentagon—and was doing, I figured, the same amount of good.

The big sanctuary doors were locked, and I had to walk around the buildings trying half a dozen other doors before I found one that opened. I followed a long, tiled hall, cinder-block Bible-school classrooms on either side of me, and wondered what ol' Jacob Ladders himself would've thought of this shit—everything looking so shined up and respectable. He would've liked coming here, running a big, one-night con, and skipping town, his truck groaning from the weight of the collection. I was sure of that. He might've even got a laugh out of the absurdity of such a hospital-like place bearing his name. Oh, he might've been a little pissed that he'd fucked up so bad at the end that these people would mistake him forever for one of their own—no, worse, for one of their founders. But, at his best, in the days before the prospect of the end got to him, Jake had had a glad eye for the absurd, and I'm sure it wouldn't've taken this long to bring him around to laughter.

After what seemed like a half-mile of fluorescent hall, I came to an office and entered it. An assistant pastor, Rev. Tommy Finkbinder, the nameplate said, looked up at me from behind a desk, and I commenced to tell him who I was.

"My name's Dewey Dunham, sir," I said. "I was wondering if I might could see Dr. Jacob Ladders."

He gave me a good studying over. "Dr. Ladders is deceased," he said. "Over twenty years ago."

I nodded. "I was afraid of that." I cast my eyes down for a couple of beats. "He was a great man of God."

"Yes," he said. "Though I didn't know him. He wasn't from here."

"Didn't know that," I told him. "I knew he was a road evangelist, but I always thought Sedan was home base for him." I shook my head. "Don't know why, rightly. Could be he was the kind that had the gift of making every place seem like home. You know, sir, he led me to the Lord in them fairgrounds up the road yonder."

"Do say?" he said. "Praise God."

"Well, you know, I been meaning to come back all these years and thank him proper."

"I'm sorry," he said. "But, of course, you can serve his memory best by doing the Lord's work."

"Well, sir, I'm doing that. You bet. You see, about fifteen years ago come August, the wife and me, why we started up a little church in Ambrosia Springs, New Mexico. Little adobe church with a steeple on it no taller than a good-sized deacon. Not much to the naked eye, but the Lord lives in it."

"Amen," he said.

"Thank you." I nodded and showed him a humble-proud grin. "Nothing like you got here," I said, "but we do all we can to make the desert ring with Jesus' name."

"Dr. Ladders would be pleased."

"I reckon. He'd've done way more, I know. But I've done what I could."

He stood and offered me his hand. I shook it. Your uptown preacher's hand, soft as a beauty queen's. "We're honored you came by," he said. "Sorry I couldn't be of more help."

"Well, sir, if I'm not taking up too much of your time, maybe you could be yet. I was wondering, you see, if maybe Dr. Ladders didn't have some offspring of some kind?"

"No sir. Never married. He was a saint."

"I see." I rubbed my right hand nervous-like a couple of times up and down the outside of my right thigh. "Well, you see, reason I asked, sir, on the evening I was saved there was this woman singing, pretty as an angel she was. I'll never forget it. 'Just As I Am,' that was the hymn. In my church, I don't allow no other song sung come invitation time. That one says it all." I shook my head again, let a little mist fall over my eyeballs. Then I brought myself to again. "Well, sir, seems to me like—and I'm not meaning to question anything—but seems to me like Dr. Ladders made mention of that girl as his daughter. Magdalen, I'm thinking, is the name he called her by."

"Adopted," the preacher said. "Magdalen Abbey Ladders."

"That's her, sure enough, yes sir. I'm wondering if she might yet be around here somewheres."

"She founded this church, Mr. . . . uh . . .?"

"Dunham," I said. "Brother Dewey Dunham of the Ambrosia Springs Freewill Tabernacle."

"But she left us, Brother Dunham, about five years back."

"Oh my," I said. "I'm praying it wasn't a case of backsliding, sir. Surely not even Satan hisself would dare lay a finger on Miss Abbey. She was one of this dark vale's fairest sights."

"I wouldn't presume to speak for Satan, Brother Dunham. But Miss Abbey, she left here to start another church. The Lord called her south."

"South?" I said, going all thoughtful. "He has always favored the South, hasn't he?"

"Florida," he said. "We hear from her regularly. Her new church is doing quite well, from what she says."

He laid that last phrase on so thick I let an eyebrow raise up. "Well, sir, surely she wouldn't lie?"

"Of course not. I didn't mean that. I know she wouldn't. The church is doing well. I just meant I haven't seen it. We take up a special collection for her twice a year."

"The great commission." My head bobbed approval. "Some of us, you know, sir, good folks, I mean, too, why, some of us, we're satisfied if we can just accomplish one thing in life. Once we get that done—founding a church or saving a few souls or whatnot—once we get that done, well, we're ready to sit back and draw our reward. But that wasn't the Master's way, now, was it? No sir, not at all. And, I tell you, I'm mighty pleased to know it's not Magdalen Abbey's, either. Why, Dr. Ladders must be beaming down on her right this very minute, him being a man that traveled all over this great land carrying out the great commission."

He gave my face a slow going over, like maybe he was sizing up ahead of time the effect his next words might have. "Dr. Ladders shot himself," he told me. "Right here in Sedan. At the end of a sermon."

I took a step back, looked down, looked up, ran my hand through my hair. "Heaven help me, Rev. Finkbinder, but it's a struggle to believe it's the truth you're telling. Not Dr. Ladders."

"Magdalen always said it wasn't really suicide. She said it was his way of showing faith, demonstrating his certain belief in Paradise. He wanted people to see that we don't live until we die."

I shook my head, wrung my hands, played it up like a B actor in a C movie. "But we shouldn't force God's will. That's sin. It's through our own suffering in this shadowy vale that we show others the way toward the light."

"Magdalen said you could see him rising."

My eyes widened, my head went back a notch. "Whoa," I said. "That would make it different. Yes sir, that would make it different." I shuffled my feet, started to say something, cut it off, took a step back, took a step up, and, finally, said, "It was God that pulled that trigger, then, in a way, wasn't it? Dr. Ladders was just carrying out his will. That would set it right. Showing folks a miracle."

"I don't know," he said. "It's always troubled me. Sometimes I think there's too much of the snake handler in it. And I pray for Magdalen, Brother Dunham, because she's still under Dr. Ladders's spell. I pray every day of my life that she won't yield to the temptation to emulate him."

"Well, I'll join you, Rev. Finkbinder. Every day we'll be offering twin prayers. And when I find Miss Abbey—or is she married now?—why, I'll tell her that very thing. This world's a hard place, and Paradise is promised, but we must abide our time."

"Find her, Brother Durham?"

"Yes sir. The Lord spoke to my heart, telling me as straight as I'm talking to you now to find Dr. Ladders and Magdalen Abbey. He didn't tell me why, sir, but I don't question his will. I'm bound to find her. I think I know now why he wants me to."

He nodded, slowly, prayerfully. And then he told me where she was—an island in Florida Bay. She had named it Calvary Key.

2 JESSE

In the cell one thing becomes clear. This is where I belong, where I must be. To gain the right to persuade others seriously toward pacifism, I must have paid the price they will have to pay. I will do my time. I will be here. To do otherwise is aristocratic arrogance, like preaching the doctrines of Christ while living in a glittering parsonage.

The days are regimented, each almost identical to its predecessor. But in discipline lies freedom. I rise in the darkness and meditate until light and breakfast come. A trusty ladles oatmeal into a tin bowl. I do not eat lunch. For supper, there is beans and sometimes rice. Sometimes, too, thin strips of beef covered with thick, salty gravy. I give that away. What is here is enough. I read. I write. I am. I do not fear the men who put me here. For what I am remains inviolate.

Visitors come.

My mother: I am sure my stepfather encouraged her. She appears wan, betrayed. We sit on opposite sides of a table. She brings me a box of peanut-butter cookies she has made. "You used to love them," she says. "I didn't know what else to do."

"I'm content, Mother," I tell her. "This is necessary."

"There has to be another way, Jesse. Homer says you can get a conscientious objector deferment if you'll just apply for it. What's wrong with that?"

"I don't recognize their right to decide. And, anyway, what Homer means is that he can buy me a deferment."

"You *are* a conscientious objector. It isn't something they decide or he can buy. It's what you are. It's an honorable way out."

"I'm not looking for a way out."

"Leave me something to live with, Jesse. I'm not built to be a martyr's mother."

"I'm not a martyr."

"A . . . what is it? . . . A pariah, then."

"No, Mother, I'm not that either."

"Then just another damned fool."

"Maybe." I smile at her, reach across the table, take her hands in mine.

She looks at the four hands. "The world's bad enough," she says. "It's a sin to make it worse than it is." She slips her hands from between mine. Then she leaves.

Dibrell Poole: "We got no records, Son. Though, I suspect you know something about that. There'll be duplicates coming in soon enough, and we'll be right back in business. And all of us got memories, anyway. I mean, you set fire to your draft card in public, Son. Forced our hand, that did. Do it every time. But none of us want to see you rot in jail. And I thought maybe if we sat here together and talked it through like grown men, we could find a way out that would satisfy everybody. I don't mean I'm offering any special favors. We don't do that. But the Selective Service Act makes special provision for young men with strong religious feeling, so long as he's connected to some recognized church."

"I don't recognize the Selective Service System's right to choose either my church or my war."

"Whose right do you recognize? This is a democracy, Son."

"Nobody's. And no, it isn't. Not yet."

"I see." He takes a Parliament from its pack. "Mind if I smoke?"

In answer, I give him a light with my dead uncle's Zippo, the one I burned their card with. A reminder. A talisman. I had asked the jailer to return it to me just for the duration of this visit. He had.

He inhales. I lay the lighter on the table between us. He says, "I got my own light, Son."

"This one," I tell him, "always works."

"You'd be better off if it didn't."

"Who's to say?"

He looks at me quizzically, inhales again. "I guess that's the question, isn't it?" He leans back, absently watches the cigarette smoke rise. The Parliament's burning, I think. And am amazed again at the mind's affinity, under almost all circumstances, for the ridiculous pun.

He leans forward. "Let me see if I got it right. You're saying you're the only one qualified to decide whether you'll fight for your country?"

"I'm not sure I'm qualified. I know no one else is."

"You're a government of one?"

"With a constituency of one."

"And that's the way it should be for everybody? No government has the right to govern?"

"No government has an absolute right to govern. And the farther a government is removed from an individual, the less right it has to require his obedience."

He shook his head. "That's crazy, Son. Childish. Nothing would work."

"Nothing would work like it does now. That's its appeal."

He stubs out his cigarette in the Miracle Whip lid that has been provided as an ashtray. "I don't want to argue political philosophy with you, Son. That's not what I'm here for. And I don't have the benefit of your education. But let me say this. What you're telling me you believe may look good on the page of some college textbook. But in the real world, it's horseshit."

"It's possible we would differ over the definition of the real world."

"The real world, boy, is where folks live. There's streets out there and houses and jobs and bills to be paid. And there are millions of people out there, too, trying to make some kind of accommodation to all that. Here in this country most folks manage it all pretty well, even manage to make themselves a little room, a lot of them, for happiness."

"Those jobs and bills and streets, that's not a world. That's something imposed on a world."

"It's what's here, Son. And when you and your kind are finished, it'll still be here. The sensible thing to do is to compromise enough to get along in it. We're willing to make some allowances for your beliefs, you have to make some for ours. That's how society works, Son. And it seems pretty reasonable to me. Everybody gets along."

"Mr. Poole, I ask nothing of you. I certainly don't expect you to resign your chairmanship and begin picketing the Pentagon. And I'd like to remind you that it was you who sent me the draft card, not the other way around. It's you who demands compromise, not me. If you're overwhelmingly concerned about the war in Vietnam, go fight in it. You'd be wrong, but I can't stop you. As far as I'm concerned, you're free. What you have no right to do is to revoke the freedom of others. You have no right to require anyone but yourself to go to war. This one or any other."

"I see," he says. He stands. "I have great respect for your father. I told him I'd try. I have. I won't be back."

"My father?"

"Homer. I try my best to forget about your father."

"But it's hard, isn't it?"

"Some days," he says. "But he's never more than a minor nuisance. You tell him that."

He walks to the door, turns back, surveys the room. "You better get used to this, boy. It may be your life."

"There are, Mr. Poole, worse ways to live."

"You need to grow up, boy. Real quick."

3 GLORIA

When we got to the Haight that morning, a year (or more, really—Jimmy always said '65 and '66 were the good years) too late, it was the dark side of the acid dream. Bleary-eyed panhandlers and lost children. Grimed-over colors and sticky sidewalks. An ugly haze had descended over the head shops. The street people looked like real freaks now, true freaks, zombies who could do nothing but find the next hit, the next fix, today's connection. Gunner lowered his window and shouted a chorus of song to them:

Come on, people, now,
Smile on your brother.
Everybody get together,
Gotta love one another, right now.

"This doesn't look like a safe place for mockery," I told him, though the street-dwellers seemed to notice him and dismiss him with the same indifference. In fact, indifference didn't just characterize the scene. It was the scene. Everything had failed.

"Hophead heaven," Gunner said. "I could conquer the whole fucking town with a platoon of high-school cheerleaders."

"It is depressing," I said. "It used to be a place of such hope."

"Back when Owsley was God, man, and time an illusion," he said. "The truth is brought to you, Jackson, by the Quicksilver Messenger Service. Boycott every grape but Moby Grape. Take the acid test on the Jefferson Airplane with the good ol' Grateful Dead. Oh shit, yeah, I read the stories, flower child. The news, it do get to Nam, ma'am. All bullshit."

I turned onto Ashbury.

"The health inspector tried to close everything down last year," I said. "Maybe he should have."

"Poor fuckers," Gunner said. "Couldn't tell the Garden of Eden from an opium den."

We passed the old Dead house at 710. I remembered when Jimmy and I had heard them play at the Solstice Celebration last June twenty-first at Speedway Meadow in the Golden Gate Park. They'd all been there—the Dead, Big Brother, Quicksilver, using Fender speakers and amps they'd stolen from the Monterey Pop Festival. Bands played on wooden stages set up on two sides of the meadow and on the bed of a flatbed truck parked at one end. At the other end the Diggers barbecued a lamb and fried hamburgers in scoop shovels. People hung paper flowers on the park's shrubs. There were fortune-tellers, body-painters, astral projectionists, archers, jugglers, clowns, contortionists, holy men, thieves, magicians, and a Tibetan liturgical orchestra blowing on conch shells. The crowd played free-lance volleyball with an eight-foot canvas globe while chanting, "Turn on the world." And the Hell's Angels guarded the sound equipment. At sunset most of us danced west across the park to the sea.

That was my one previous time in San Francisco: the opening day of the Summer of Love. But even then, with everybody on good Owsley, you could tell. There were too many of the doomed, too many who lived only in the world of acid, unable to make distinctions. Gunner was right. Finally, innocence is a curse. This had never been even a dream. Just wishful thinking, fueled by electric Kool-Aid. Whimsical self-gratification, that's all. Urban children lost in the park. The Haight had been a psychedelic haven for runaways. Nothing more. The revolution had always been elsewhere.

I drove us around for a while, pointing out the landmarks to Gunner. The Diggers' Free Frame of Reference on Frederick, the Phoenix, the Psychedelic Shop, Blind Jerry's health food on Page, Wild Colors, Com/co, the *Oracle* office, the Fillmore, the Avalon, the Straight Theatre, the House of Richard, Mnasidika, the Blushing Peony, the Print Mint, Love Burgers in the Pall Mall Bar, the Trip Without a Ticket on Cole, Tacy's Donuts, the I/Thou Coffee Shop, the Blue Unicorn, the Drogstore Café, the Switchboard, and the Free Clinic.

Gunner started singing "My Country 'Tis of Thee."

"Why are we looking at all these places, Momma," Aura asked, "when some of them aren't even here any more?"

"I don't know," I told her. "I was just remembering. I was here when it was different. Everybody was young."

"Is this where we're going to live?" she wondered. ""Can we stay in the park?"

Gunner laughed. "Baby, don't you bet that's the first question every hippie here asked?"

Aura said, "Let's go see the big bridge."

"Tomorrow," I told her. "We have to find somebody first."

Jerry the Dealer lived in a condemned Victorian on Pine. He wasn't home, but two of his friends were. A thin girl, maybe sixteen, and a boy, about twenty, who had Wild Bill Hickok hair and wore a Navaho silver-and-turquoise necklace. They were sharing a big glass water pipe.

"Want some, baby?" the boy said to me. "It's organic."

"I'm looking for Jerry," I said. "I owe him some bread."

He looked at my daughter. "Groovy kid," he told me.

"Thanks," I said. "Is Jerry around?"

"Around is right," he said. "You better grab a toke or two. If God left early like the Frenchmen say, this'll bring him back home."

He and the girl laughed for a long time.

"Fact he left France," Gunner said, "ain't no reflection on the rest of mankind."

They laughed again.

"Jesus H. Owsley A. Stanley III," the boy said. "We got us a thinker here. Dude going to join the Mime Troop."

"Mime Troop play head games, bubba. I got the truth in the trunk of my car."

"Good place to keep it," Hickok said.

The girl was staring wide-eyed at Gunner. He walked over and patted her head. "You got pretty eyes, love child. You ought not tempt ol' Gunner with them."

"Are you an Angel?" she asked. "I like Angels."

"All of you like Angels," the Hickok boy said. "The choppers keep their dicks hard."

"I gave a foot of mine to science," Gunner told him. He looked down at the girl. "Still got God's plenty, though, hon. Just got a funny bend in it where they joined it back together."

"Oh," she said, nodding, serious.

"You know Jerry?" Gunner asked her. "I got business. Then we can play."

"We got some of the last batch Owsley made before they busted him in Orinda," I said. "But we have to see Jerry first."

"Owsley's dead," the girl told us. "The CIA killed him."

"But he rose," Gunner told her. "Baby, you can't snuff the magic man."

"Amen," Hickok said. Then, "Jerry's out. Doing business of his own."

"What time will he be back?" I asked, stupidly.

"What's time?" the boy wondered.

"Life," Gunner answered.

"Wow!" the girl said.

Aura let go of my leg, took a couple of shy steps toward the water pipe, and pointed at it. "What's that?"

Hickok, suddenly paranoid, darted his eyes toward me. "What the fuck is this?"

"She's been away," I explained. "I had to find myself."

His gaze softened, but he held my eyes a few seconds longer. Then he looked at Aura. "Little girl, it's time we enrolled you in High Kindergarten."

Gunner took two steps and kicked the water pipe across the room. "Now, listen up, cocksucker," he said. "Where's Jerry?"

"He's an Angel," the girl said to Hickok. "I knew it."

"Jesus, man," Hickok said. "You know how to fuck up a trip, don't you?"

"Ain't my trip," Gunner replied.

Hickok shrugged. "Dude's in the park, man. Does business at Kezar." He shook his head, stared at the shards of the water pipe, and shook his head again, as if all the world's sadness suddenly burdened him. "All you had to do was ask, man."

"I couldn't find the words," Gunner said.

The girl looked at Hickok. "Papers," she said.

"Acid," he answered. "The day's bumming me out."

Jerry the Dealer wasn't anywhere on the grounds around Kezar, but we found a Meth-head, tracks all up and down his arms, who said, "On the meadow, man, grooving with the guru."

He was—if Shiva Charlie Muldrow was what you wanted to call a guru. We found the two of them sitting under a tree at the edge of Speedway Meadow—Shiva Charlie full lotus, stiff-kneed Jerry only halfway there. They seemed to be in a trance Jesse might have envied. "Dealing their way to salvation," Gunner said later.

We stood before them for several minutes, apparently unnoticed. I sent Aura off to play in the sun a few yards away.

Gunner got tired of waiting. He squatted in front of Jerry. "We looking for Jimmy Song, bubba," he said. "He gave us your name."

Jerry the Dealer took no notice. But Shiva Charlie Muldrow did. "Have you seen the dawn?" he asked Gunner. "Truly seen it?"

"Seen the motherfucker just this morning," Gunner said. "Bigger'n shit."

"You are an Angel," Shiva Charlie said. "I can see your heart."

"You close, Jim Bob. I was," Gunner said, turning to him. "But I quit them when they hooked on with the hippies."

"You were wrong. There is much bitterness in you. Good and evil are at war. You must choose the light."

"Hurts my eyes," Gunner said.

Meanwhile Jerry the Dealer was coming to. He blinked rapidly several times, then grimaced as if the light of the corporeal world had, in fact, hurt his eyes.

"It will do that," Shiva Charlie said. "But you must persist. The eyes will grow strong. In God's time, they will see all and more."

"What they need to see right quick, Punjab, is Jimmy Song."

"He is a child, consumed by greed and folly. The flesh will draw you downward. Do not follow him. No good can come of it."

"Who the fuck's your friend?" Gunner asked Jerry, who told him, giving only the name. Then he, Jerry, looked up at me. "I know you," he said.

"Last year I was with Jimmy Song."

He nodded. "Arkansas," he said.

"There is hope in the Ozarks," Shiva Charlie told me. "You must go there. You must turn back. There are too many here. It must spread. We are the beginning. We will die. But it will live. I say to you now: It will live. Go."

As I watched him, his eyes lost focus and he reentered his trance. He had spoken.

"Always makes my day, talking to a prophet," Gunner told Jerry.

"He is," Jerry assured us. "The rest of them are bullshit. I've seen a thousand of them. Charlie's real."

"How about Jimmy Song?" Gunner asked. "He a prophet?"

Jerry paid no attention to that. He was studying me. "Jimmy gave me his rap about you," he said. "It got weird in Arkansas."

"Jimmy got weird."

"Said he had to die." Jerry the Dealer straightened his right leg, absently massaged the knee.

"Yes," I said.

"Reincarnation," Shiva Charlie said. He pronounced the word slowly, reverently, accenting each syllable. His eyes were still unfocused. His face bore a beatific smile.

"The very resurrection and the life," Gunner said.

"Grapevine says he turned." Jerry looked directly at me, his eyes narrowing.

"I think he's turned back," I said. "But I need to know for sure. He could burn me."

"Fire and water," Shiva Charlie said. "Earth and air." One eye now focused on Gunner. The other was cast blankly heavenward.

"Anything else, Reverend?" Gunner asked him.

"I cannot say. I have not seen the spiral's end." He tilted his head back. His eyes blinked one time each, separately, came together, then stared into the yellow haze of the city sky. "But soon," he said, "Soon. It will be finished."

"Yes," Jerry the Dealer said after a respectful silence. "It'll be over soon."

"It'll just be something else then," Gunner said.

Shiva Charlie's head jerked toward Gunner, his eyes suddenly hard and clear. "You have spoken truth," he said.

"It's my way," Gunner said.

Shiva Charlie looked at Jerry. "My heart tells me they have come for a reason. We must lead them to the peak of Mount Tamalpais." He turned to Gunner. "Jimmy Song will be there. We will know then. All and more."

4 MALEDON

I took ten days getting from Kansas to the end of Florida, stopping off wherever a roadside bar or a likely woman struck my fancy. The air all across the South was charged with the energy of fear.

The news came at me constant: On the sixth of May the good Lord Almighty hisself became the second southern governor to claim the body of Lurleen Wallace. Thomas Davis, from Marks, Mississippi, where twenty-five hundred blacks had gathered to begin their part of the Poor People's march, was arrested for firing his rifle, in support of all his state stood for, at a helicopter full of newsmen. Good southern politicians—George Wallace, Jennings Randolph, Lester Maddox, John Stennis—accused the niggers of being Communists. Stennis said he was tired of them that wouldn't work wanting handouts from them that would—a damned ironic thing for a senator to say, I thought. The first piece of violence on the march happened in Boston, where a man who described himself as a Polish freedom fighter got stabbed in the arm for carrying a sign that said, I FIGHT POVERTY. I WORK. TRY IT. IT WORKS. His name was Josef Mlot-Mroz, and he was unemployed. The leaders of the marching poor set up thousands of wooden shanties on the mall around the Lincoln Memorial and changed the name of their shantytown from the City of Hope to Resurrection City. Both Robert Kennedy and Hubert Humphrey went there and made a show of lending their support. They went on different days, of course—no point in depriving your own compassionate heart of its full spot on the evening news. In Mobile, four hundred blacks tried to march toward City Hall (claimed they wanted jobs there, of all damned things) but were turned back a block after they started by two hundred cops armed with nightsticks, shotguns, bayonets, gas, and grenades.

Ralph Nader told the Senate Commerce Committee that it was common practice for X-ray technicians to give blacks twenty-five to fifty percent more radiation exposure because they thought it took that much more to penetrate a black man's skin. In Hattiesburg, Mississippi, Kaley Duckworth, a member of the NAACP and the local Head Start Committee, was injured by a booby trap in the steering column of the car he'd just won at a benefit raffle for the high-school band.

Five hundred sixty-two died for the cause in Vietnam that week, setting a record, and bringing the toll so far to over twenty-two thousand dead and a hundred thirty-three thousand wounded, that is, if you cared to trust the men that did the counting. The Paris peace talks commenced, and the American and North Vietnamese negotiators, all of whom were put up in grand style, settled into calling one another names. The Viet Cong attacked Saigon, but the Pentagon said the attack plans were half-baked. Still, a couple of days later the Air Force had to bomb Saigon to save it from them same half-baked slants. Sunday night, U.S. jets dropped napalm and high-explosive bombs two miles from Saigon's center. Monday the Pentagon announced that that had crushed the Cong attack. Tuesday the Cong captured a Special Forces base atop Black Window Mountain, a little north of Saigon. Wednesday the bombers unloaded again. When it was all done, there wasn't anything left but rubble and Cong—and, of course, the Air Force, which announced that it planned to dump ten million gallons of vegetable- and crop-killing poison over South Vietnam. They figured that would strip the jungle, kill the crops, and expose and starve the Cong. The main concern over the plan was that it might cause American homeowners to suffer a shortage of lawn and garden weed killer.

Robert Kennedy won primaries in Indiana, Washington, D.C., and Nebraska and got hit in the neck by a rock somebody threw at a rally in Van Nuys, California. Eugene McCarthy supporters got beat up in Kansas City. Hubert Humphrey supporters made deals with Lyndon Johnson supporters. Richard Nixon supporters tried to make deals with George Wallace supporters. And Nelson Rockefeller supporters made deals with Nelson Rockefeller banks.

The Russians started working on tank formations at the Czech border. Thirty thousand French students fought police on the streets around the Sorbonne, and two of France's biggest unions called for a general strike. The Indian parliament broke up in outrage when the minister of food, Jadjivan Ram, said that holy beef had been eaten as a delicacy during the Vedic period three thousand years ago.

In Sweden nine AWOL GI's were granted asylum, bringing the

number there to forty-one, and I considered sending Jesse a card extolling the mystical qualities of the northern lights. In Catonsville, Maryland, nine people charged into the Selective Service offices, dumped six hundred draft records in trash burners, and set them afire. They were led by Philip Berrigan and Thomas Lewis, who already faced possible prison terms for pouring blood over draft board files in Baltimore the previous October. If I could've had a word with the Catonsville Nine, I'd've told them that with that many people and that much energy, a little common sense, and the cover of darkness, they could've emptied every draft board in Maryland and got clean away. There'd already been too many goddamn martyrs.

At Columbia, striking students fought with students trying to go to class. At Roosevelt University, Marquette, and Southern Illinois, police broke up student protests against the war. At Stanford, Vicky Drake, a topless dancer, won the preliminary election for the student body presidency. At Sacramento, Ronald Reagan called student demonstrators "revolutionary hypocrites who sing songs of freedom but dance to the beat of anarchy."

And, a few miles south of Valdosta, listening to Reagan on the radio of my new van, I said, "There ain't nothing revolutionary about hypocrisy, and anarchy, like it or not, Bonzo, is freedom. Everything else is a qualification."

But there wasn't anybody paying attention to me. Thank God.

Oh, the world seemed to be going to shit, all right. But it's been doing that, pretty steady, since God said go. And, anyway, in spite of it all, the Blue Mountain One was riding easy, cruising toward the tropics in his nice new loss-leader van, bound for the edge of America and the island home of his old love, lost and true, hoping that the orphan mother of two churches would consent to a little fornication with a pagan reprobate, believing always in just that kind of miracle.

5 JESSE

Another day, another visitor.

Tom Guy Hughes is twenty-nine—in, he says, the last year of his respectability. He has a degree in literature from Rice, one in law from Harvard. He is thin, pale, balding, and wears W. B. Yeats glasses. His law practice consists of civil rights work and charity cases. He is homosexual, a scandal to the town. For Blue Mountain High School football players, it is a rite of passage to give Tom Guy a thorough beating. It is easy. He does not strike back. He does not file charges. He is a pacifist. The town conscience. The town pariah.

"We'll do it any way you want," he says. "We can get you off, beat them using their rules. Or we can turn the federal courtroom into your forum."

"Tom Guy," I say, "I don't recognize their right to take me to court. And I don't owe them an explanation. They can carry me in and carry me out. But I won't utter a word."

He nods. "That would work," he says. "That's the purest way of taking the high ground." He stands. "You'll do time. But you won't do much. And the trial will be front-page news in Arkansas."

"Tom Guy—" I begin.

"Jesus," he interrupts. "I can't wait."

"Tom Guy, listen to me."

"No, Jesse, you listen to me. Sensible people are always asking me why I came back to this backward, butch town. Me, a queer and an intellectual in a place where either is sufficient to provoke confederated disgust and wrath. Well, Jesse, I can't give my sensible friends a satisfactory answer. But part of it has to be masochism, and part of it has to be revenge. And I'm stubborn, too, like you are. I intend to make this a decent place for a smart queer to live. Oh, I'm going to lose. But it'll be an interesting process. They'll beat me by letting me win slowly. A victory here, a victory there. Small changes. A step forward, a half step back. But I'm not going to miss any opportunities to take that step. Certainly not this one, Jesse. This kind of thing is what I'm here for—the virtuous lost cause. So don't tell me you don't need a lawyer. I'm not doing this for you. All I'll do—and I'll do it as your lawyer, or I'll do it on my own, but I'll do it—all I'll do is arrange this so that your silence is heard. So that it fairly fucking resounds, my friend."

"You can't sit at the defense table with me," I say. "I must be alone there."

"Good strategy. The lone man against the entire, ominous government of the United States of Armorica."

We stare at one another, deciding whether to trust. He offers his hand. "Done, then?"

I hesitate, then take the hand. "Done."

He nods, stands, turns to leave, turns back. "Oh, I'll have you out in the morning."

"No," I say. "I won't give them bail."

"Right again," he agrees. "We'll leave you in two or three more days while I arrange some publicity. Then I'll get you out on your own recognizance."

I start to say something more, that there will be no compromise, no deals, but he casually raises his left palm. "You can do good and be smart simultaneously, Jesse. You can make everyone who looks see that you're better than they are, that you're right. You can be an example, and you don't have to have nails and a cross to do it." He smiles, winks, flagrantly girlish. "And don't you worry, because, as the man said, 'I'm putting my queer shoulder to the wheel.' "

6 GLORIA

It turned out that Shiva Charlie Muldrow was the founder and guru of the Staff of Life Ranch, a commune on the Russian River in the southern redwood country, about seventy-five miles north of San Francisco. It also turned out that whatever was going to happen on Mount Tamalpais wasn't going to happen until Saturday night. We had two days to wait.

"Bastard just wanted a ride home," Gunner said as we were walking around the ranch that evening. "And we were fool enough to give him one."

Shiva Charlie walked just ahead of us, making an occasional sweeping motion with his right arm, as if offering a vista. But what we saw were ragged plants in crooked rows. And Gunner spoke as if we were alone, or accompanied by an idiot who couldn't understand the language.

"Potatoes," Shiva Charlie said grandly. A belated sweep of the arm.

"Might make one good mess of soup," Gunner said.

"In the soil lies the answer," Shiva Charlie told us. "Too many look only skyward."

"Worried about the incoming," Gunner said.

"And justly." Shiva Charlie looked skyward. "For the end is nigh. We must practice resurrection." He knelt, scooped up a handful of dust, stood, and extending the dirt toward us, said, "Whose secret lies here." He opened his hand, letting the dust fall through his fingers. "Blake," he said. "Who saw angels."

"Probably as good as we could do on short notice," Gunner told me. "We can sleep down by the river. Aura'll like it. I'll stand first watch."

"What is the mystery of the river?" Shiva Charlie asked us two mornings later. "Perhaps we have focused too fully on dust."

"The motion," Gunner told him. "The motionless. The change. The changelessness. Peace and the capacity for destruction."

Shiva Charlie stared into the river. "Our lives," he said. He looked long and full at me first, then at Gunner, as if participating in the conclusion of a ritual. Then he turned toward Aura, who was playing on the riverbank. "It is well," he pronounced. "We need more children."

"It's odd, ain't it, Punjab?" Gunner said. "How simple wisdom is."

Shiva Charlie looked as if he had heard an oracle. He went up to Gunner and placed a ceremonial palm on his shoulder. "You have truly seen. There are so few. Even here."

Gunner didn't glance at the hand, didn't change expression. He said, "I was born with the third eye."

Charlie gave him a nod so long and slow and studied that it was almost a bow. "As were we all," he said. "Sadly, most refuse to open the lid." Then he backed away a step and turned to me. "There's a meeting," he said. "You must come." Then he turned and looked curiously, respectfully, at Gunner once more, like Blake at an angel. And then he left us.

"You go," Gunner said to me. "I'll watch Aura. I've had about all the horseshit I'm in the mood to stomach this morning."

"But you're so good with him," I said.

"You do a year in Nam, ma'am, you get to where you got a way with your average lunatic." Then, grinning, he touched the middle of his forehead. "Besides, baby, I believe in this third eye, don't you? Ol' Gunner's got the gift of seeing. What everybody says. Why, once, seem like a age ago now, I beat Osceola with a last-second shot from half-court. Just threw her up and let the hand of God guide her."

"And, from all directions," I said, "cheerleaders leapt into your arms."

"All but the fat one. She wasn't much for leaping. But, riding home, she let me play telephone with her tits."

"Those were the days," I said.

"Tonight we gather at Mount Tamalpais." Everyone had had a hit of hash, and Shiva Charlie was opening the meeting. "To await a sign."

Not counting Shiva Charlie and me, there were a dozen people, six of each sex, sitting on the plank floor of the old farmhouse. They were the Staff of Life's original communalists. They wore jeans, granny dresses, tie-dyed shirts, tire-tread sandals, turquoise jewelry, diffraction disks, feathers. One girl had the image of Shiva Charlie hanging from a piece of buckskin she wore around her neck. Charlie, the perfect master.

Other people lived here, in various tents and sheds. But only these twelve were permanent. The rest were winos, hobos, roving hippies looking for a night or a week of rest and food.

"The skies are ominous. It will end soon." Then, for what seemed like at least five minutes, Shiva Charlie stared at his right foot, which he had folded into his lap.

No one spoke. The hash started round again.

Then he said, "You have seen the pilgrims who have come to us. The woman brings a child. The man has the gift of seeing. Their hearts have been revealed to me. It is good." He looked directly at me. "Peace," he said.

His eyes lost focus, and another silence followed. The hash pipe came to me. This time I let it pass.

"Deeper submersion in the mystery has confirmed what I have foretold. The asteroid Icarus will strike and destroy the earth on the night of Saturday, the fifteenth of June. We must prepare. Only the chosen will survive." He sighed. "I am weary. Tell them, Jerry."

So Jerry the Dealer took over. "There's not much more," he told us. "Tibet will be spared. But it can't be used as an ark. The master believes that the area around Boulder, Colorado, will be saved. But the signs aren't all clear yet."

"What has your friend seen?" Shiva Charlie asked me.

"He has not spoken."

"He watches the river," Shiva Charlie told his followers. "Soon it will speak through him."

"He waits for Jimmy Song," I said.

"Jimmy Song will come. Tonight that wait will end."

I nodded. "My friend says that then the signs will be clear."

Shiva Charlie returned the nod, then spoke again to his followers. Oracular. Hieratic. Saint Francis of Hashishi. "An end," he said, "a beginning. The closing of a circle, the rising of a spiral. In each death a new birth. This is the time of preparation, the hour before deliverance. Much will be left behind, and yet there will be nothing to mourn. The corpses of the unbelievers shall fertilize the fields of the faithful. The souls of the unbelievers shall be reincarnate in creatures of an earth suffused with divine light. And the Tao shall be made manifest to all." He looked around the circle, letting his eyes rest briefly on the face of each of the creatures around him. "All is well," he concluded. "Prepare for deliverance."

7 MALEDON

I drove through the Everglades to the end of Florida, took a room at the Flamingo Inn, and started asking questions. It didn't take long to get an answer.

A guide for one of the boat rental places said, "Yeah, Calvary Key. Used to be Calusa Key, after the Indian tribe. Nothing left of them but the name, and now it's going too."

He was a big man with a two- or three-day stubble covering his face. He didn't seem any too happy about making his living off tourists.

"Some kind of Christian outfit," he said. "Always amazes me." He looked directly at me, hard, like he hoped I'd take offense. "Sonsabitches are never satisfied to leave anything the way God made it."

"Kill off the Indians, fill in the swamps," I said. "And keep at it till the Second Coming. Can't have Jesus soiling his sandals."

It turned out he was drinking bourbon and was willing to share with a fellow heathen. We sat on a couple of crates, passed the bottle back and forth, and had at the tourists. "Fuckers sit in the boat snapping their Instamatics and talking about golf and real estate and the service at the inn and marveling at how brave them goddamn Spanish priests must've been way back yonder bringing the gospel to such a jungle as this. Now and then you'll get a pair of smart pricks speculating on how much oil there must be under the Glades. Or what Florida'll have to do to keep up with the population boom. Just this morning I had me a city planner from Charleston. Had a couple of half-grown boys eating Twinkies and jumping up and down every time they saw a gator or a snake. The planner, now, he was thinking about the *fate* of the Glades.

Only way to save them, he figures, is to make them profitable. Sensitive management. Small fish farms. Fertilizer factories. 'We have to be realistic,' he said, like me and him was in it together—two old swamp rats dealing with the world. 'We have to show the developer that these wetlands have some immediate utility. Otherwise, they'll drain it dry, and we'll have a national park consisting of several million acres of crusted earth.' 'Well,' I told him, 'we could just blow up Miami and keep the motherfuckers busy rebuilding over there.' Tell you what, by God, you hear a man say 'We have to be realistic,' best thing for it is to take him out to the far end of Limbo Slough and cut him adrift in a pirogue. Teach him realism."

"Give him a gross of Twinkies to tide him over," I said. "Drill a hole in the pirogue."

"Wouldn't need to," he said. "Sonsabitches'd capsize getting in."

It went on, him classifying the tourists and then damning them lot by lot, and me giving them all a good kick once he'd got them down and pinned. Then we looked up, and the darkness was on us, and the whiskey was gone, and we were drunk. The man's name was Mason Sloate.

"Just what was it you was wanting, anyway?" he asked, getting up. "I best be going off after another bottle."

He walked out to the end of the pier and started pissing in the swamp. Always a man to appreciate a good example, I followed suit. "I hear an old friend of mine's been living on Calvary Key," I said. "I was wanting to find her. She used to be something. I'd like to see firsthand what she turned into."

"She been there long?"

"What I'm told is, she's the one started the place, one runs it."

He'd concluded his piss and was doing that little flounce we do tucking our cock back in. But he cut it short and jerked his head at me. "By God," he said. "Not her."

"Magdalen Abbey," I said. "Though she could've changed her name for all I know."

He looked at me for a few seconds, his drunk face gone sober. Then he zipped up and walked slowly away.

I caught up with him after a few steps. "I was wondering if I could hire you to carry me over."

"You say sometime back you knew her pretty good?"

"Biblically," I said. I *had* been drinking.

"I be goddamned," he said. "The Holy Fucking Virgin of Calvary Key." He shook his head, gave me another look, and commenced to grin.

I said, "I heard she'd gone pure, but I wanted to see proof."

"I reckon you'll see it," he told me.

"Well, then, maybe I can talk some sense to her. Lure her into the bushes that line the straight and narrow."

He took a few steps forward, but I could tell he wasn't into a going-away walk. When he turned around, he said, "Tell you what, my friend, come morning you have a week's worth of whiskey and money enough to fill that cruiser yonder with gas, and we're off. I just canceled everything else. I feel me a vacation coming on."

"She may not be wanting a whole week of me," I said. "May not be wanting none of me at all, matter of fact."

"I'd just like to see whatever there is of it," he said. "And after that, hell, there's ten thousand islands out there, and you can't dangle your pecker in the water without some kind of fish latching onto it. Mother Magdalen don't have you shot soon as you step ashore, we'll be fine. Just fine. Have the time of your life. Guaranteed."

He started away again, shaking his head and laughing to himself. Then he thought of a business detail. "I cut down during vacations," he said, "so I won't be needing but a fifth a day. Jack Black. I'll leave you to figure your own needs. See you at six."

8 JESSE

It is the morning after my talk with Tom Guy Hughes, and I wake to the sound of a chant: "Free Jesse Cantwell." I go to the cell window and see them in the street between the jail and the welfare office—J.D., Howdy, Tom Guy, several people from the Fayetteville Switchboard (the local hippie crisis hotline) some people I know but vaguely, some I know not at all. Margaret is not among them.

I am still watching from the window when Sheriff Hooks enters the cell. "So," he says. "How's our little mahatma this morning? You be needing a loom, bub?" Without waiting for an answer, he comes to the window and yells down at Tom Guy, telling him to keep his hippies out of the street. Tom Guy and J.D. persuade everyone to get onto the sidewalk in front of the welfare office, and the chant continues.

"Got a preacher to see you today," the sheriff tells me. "One of them uptown fucks that wears a collar and needs the fear of God put in him. I believe you know him."

All the commotion has wakened the Cherokee Indian they brought in drunk last night. I had given him the bottom bunk so they wouldn't have to lift him to the top one. Now he sits up, holds his forehead in his hands for a moment, examines me through squinted eyes, and says, "Jesus, which one is this?" Then, focusing on the sheriff, nods. "By God, Blue Mountain. How'd it come to that?"

"Must've got homesick for your room, Gus," the sheriff says.

"I ain't sure what causes it, but it damn sure ain't homesickness." Then he turns his face toward the window, listens, seems to be having to make an effort to understand the chant. He studies me, then waves a thumb toward the sheriff. "These fucks been jacking me around for twenty-five years. Nobody says a word."

"You always guilty, Gus," the sheriff tells him. "This boy here, now, he's for peace and love and such. We just lock him up cause we're mean, gun-toting, bomb-dropping pricks."

"Always good to see a man understand hisself," the Indian says. He lies back on his bunk, folds his hands behind his head, closes his eyes.

"Door's open," the sheriff tells him.

"Lester's around, have him bring me a bottle." He does not open his eyes.

"Lester's on the wagon."

"Have him bring the wagon by, then. God knows what he's got in it."

"Soon as you get your sleep out, Gus, you go on. We can't afford to be feeding you breakfast."

"Just skip the food, and bring me the Rolaids."

I follow the sheriff to his office, where Justin Sayles is waiting for me in a straight-backed wooden chair on the visitor's side of the sheriff's desk.

"Here you go, reverend," the sheriff says. "Tell this boy how much the Lord loves war." He leaves us, closing the door behind him.

Justin Sayles stands, motions toward the wooden chair a few feet from the one he has just occupied, and says, "Not at all."

I sit and let my face ask the question.

He says, "Our Lord despises war. All war. But that does not tell us specifically how we are to act in regard to it." He crosses his legs. "Or does it?"

I have come without thinking much about it. Another visitor—so what? I left the cell so the Indian could more easily return to sleep. I wish I had stayed. Justin Sayles: pastor of Saint Paul's Episcopal Church, an educated man, a tolerant, liberal Christian, my mother's counselor, my first philosophy teacher. He sees himself, though he would not put it in quite these words, as an enlightened missionary to born-again bigots. He contents himself with small, personal victories, is resigned to the greater, general defeat. He believes that, to endure, faith must be practical, that the reasonable Christian can almost always find an acceptable compromise. He has been my friend. I like him. Directly and indirectly, he has helped me become what I am. But I know what he will say. I know who has sent him.

So, "How is my mother?" I ask him.

"Upset. This is difficult for her to accept."

"You told her, of course, that I am right."

"I told her the principle is right. And that you are young."

"You thought she'd forgotten my age?"

He takes a dark, bent-stemmed brier pipe out of his pocket, taps the bowl twice against the sheriff's Arkansas Razorback ashtray, empties the residue, refills the pipe from a leather pouch, and lights it with his tubular silver pipe lighter. "No," he says, "she knows your age. And I didn't tell her that your youth in any way discredited the principle." He puffs reflectively on the pipe. "Jesus Christ would not have been a soldier. That's simplistic, I know. But I reminded her of that, too."

"But maybe he'd've been a medic? Or a battlefield chaplain?"

"I was merely helping Mary see the principle."

"She understands the principle," I say. "She just doesn't want her son to have to go to jail for it. She wants there to be a way out."

"Yes," he agrees, puffing. "A perfectly reasonable desire."

"I can get out of it. I'm Homer Cantwell's stepson. People will make allowances. But I won't. That would be worse than simply obeying the draft board."

He sets the pipe in the ashtray, uncrosses and recrosses his legs, lays his hands in his lap. A sermon. I can feel it coming.

"These are bad times, Jesse. Young men, barely grown, are faced with difficult choices. I recognize that. The nation is experiencing almost cataclysmic change. We are gripped by violence, fear, and hatred. Black people, justly, are demanding complete equality. Now. Many white people resist that. Our government has involved us in a war we can't—and probably shouldn't—win. And a man your age looks at his future and sees a meaningless job, a tract home, a life regulated by technocrats and shadowed by the bomb. Or, even worse, perhaps, like Orwell, you see the future as a bootheel coming down on a human face. Forever. I understand all that. Very well."

This is the beginning of his sermon on despair. I know where it ends: special grace and general grace. I decide to shift his focus: "I could avoid all that by living in a rectory."

The sarcasm does not seem to surprise him. That kind of almost polite mockery is, I think, what he sees as his cross. The unbelieving unenlightened will not understand him. Nor will the resolutely ideological. But he will be patient; he has the inexorable force of liberal Christian theology behind him. In time all things will come 'round right. And if they don't, we will then adjust our thinking. He will not be shaken by the jabs of a doctrinaire draft dodger.

It occurs to me to wonder how he would respond to my father. The thought dismisses itself. It is impossible to imagine circumstances that would require either of them (my father or Justin Sayles) to bother seriously with the other.

"I'm not a saint," he tells me. "I merely serve my parish as best I can. In return, I receive a modest accommodation. It interests me that you see that as somehow wrong, somehow . . . mercenary."

"We must avoid purity, mustn't we?"

He nods, takes the pipe from the ashtray and puts it in his mouth again, puffs, discovers that the fire has burned out, lays the pipe back in the ashtray. "We must avoid a narrow dogmatism. As Christians we must realize that there are certain benefits, even spiritual benefits, to comfort, so long as that comfort is not seen as its own end. On this earth suffering will often enough come to each of us. There is no virtue in seeking it out."

"I see," I say.

He does not think so. "Saint Francis was Saint Francis. He honored our Lord in his own way. But his way is not everyone's; his way is certainly not the only one. There are those who choose poverty, those who choose flagellation and hair shirts, those who see sin at the heart of any joy, and there are those who seek martyrdom. But it seems to me that to choose any of those paths is to reject the earth, God's creation. To honor God by punishing oneself is, don't you think? an obvious contradiction."

"In the centuries between Christ and Constantine," I say, continuing his argument for him (how many times have I heard it?), "the Church was outlawed. Christians were persecuted, executed. The faith required a combination of sacrifice and cunning. Frequently martyrdom was necessary. But, since Constantine, ours has been the Western world's dominant religion—in many cases, actually the state religion. And during those centuries the faith has required a different kind of cunning, a different type of sacrifice. What is required of Christians in a Christian nation is not martyrdom, not fanaticism, but social tolerance and a certain political sophistication. The Crusades, for one example, and the Inquisition, for another, resulted from a disastrous misinterpretation of God's will, a general impatience with the status quo, and an epidemic of longing for a heroic martyrdom. Christ, it was thought, surely requires more of us than daily generosity toward our neighbors, than consistent tolerance of our enemies, than quiet acceptance of the mundane. Surely, he wants more than our small diurnal prayers. Surely, he expects more than the routine observance of ritual, the steady maintenance of his church. Surely, he most favors those whose sacrifices are the most spectacular. The Christian soldier. The glorious martyr.

"Vanity. From such thinking has come all the wars, all the purges carried out in the name of Christ. Martyrdom for the sake of martyrdom, martyrdom sought rather than merely accepted, is the ultimate vanity. One must always try to be certain that his or her sacrifice is not merely a strategy for breaking the tedium of the mundane. For a citizen of Germany in 1940 to have chosen public suicide as a way of protesting Nazi rule would have been folly. There was already too much death. For him to have openly courted imprisonment would have been pointless. There were already millions in, or coming to, the camps. No, the most virtuous form of resistance to evil is that which is most efficacious. What the brave Christian in Nazi Germany would have done was offer his home, as shrewdly, as cunningly, as secretly as possible, as a refuge to as many Jews and gypsies and Communists and homosexuals as could be hidden there. Always in such times what must come first is the direct rescue of human lives. Simultaneously, and as often as possible, he would have worked to undermine the machinery of terror. Acts of espionage, sabotage, rebellion. Acts as large or as small as seemed feasible and effective. The taking of risk not for the sake of risk itself, nor for the sake of penitence, nor even for the sake of vengeance, but for the sake of results. We must remember that for good to triumph it must be not only as wise, but also as cunning, as evil. We must remember that almost never can we be more effective in death than in life. We must remember that only rarely can we do more good in jail than out of it. We must remember that we cannot serve the cause of the good, the cause, in my view, of gentle Jesus, while yielding to either vanity or despair."

I look at him and smile. I have enjoyed myself. What began as parody ended as tribute. I am reminded that I have liked this man. I like him yet. "There now," I say. "Have I got it?"

He hesitates, lights the pipe again, puffs, sets the pipe back down, thinks. "Even if you are mocking me, I'm impressed by how thoroughly you remembered."

"Oh," I say, "you were why I chose philosophy. You remember how I would come by after football practice, and we would sit on the rectory porch and discuss . . . What? We began with Camus, didn't we? Maybe everyone does. And then, over the weeks and months, it was Pascal's wager, or Kierkegaard and the fear and trembling. Existentialism. Courage. Virtue. Ethics. The existence of God. Good and evil. I'm not sure it prepares us for anything, but God, I loved it. I felt like part of the world."

"Yes," he says. "Those were fine evenings, I thought. The exchange of ideas in the charged autumn air. It doesn't happen often here in Blue Mountain. There've been no other football players come to my porch to discuss fear and grace."

"Well, it isn't always the best way of getting up for the game."

He smiles. "Let's win one for Søren!" Then laughs.

"Well, why not? They win them for Jesus. 'Come on, boys, I want you to go out there and knock their asses off in memory of ol' Tom

Merton!' Or, 'Stomp them fascist swine in the name of George Orwell!' "

The door opens, and the sheriff is looking at us, a wry, good ol' boy grin on his face. "Don't look good, boys, a preacher and a prisoner laughing it up in the sheriff's office."

"We were discussing football," Justin Sayles tells him.

"Ain't no laughing matter, that. You know, preacher, first sign of this boy's going bad come back there five years ago when he quit the team."

"And quitters never win," I say.

"I'd tack my amen on that one, wouldn't you, preacher?" He closes the door.

"How do you rate the use of his office?" I ask Justin.

"Mary," he answers. "You know, whatever else we can say about him, Homer Cantwell does love your mother."

"He wants my mother. Wants to keep her, wants to keep her content. But I don't think he knows want from love."

"Who does?" he says. "And maybe want grows into love." He reaches toward the ashtray, absently fingers his pipe. "But I hear your goal now is to rid yourself of desire."

"Some days. I am not consistent."

"You know, I sometimes think it was desire that created the world. Desire in a very human sense. God's desire to show himself."

"Vanity?" I say.

He smiles broadly, seems genuinely amused. "There's a good deal of evidence to support that contention."

"It's heretical, though, isn't it?"

"Who knows? Anyway, we Episcopals are seldom defrocked anymore for speculating about God's motives." He shrugs, gathers his smoking paraphernalia. "Maybe we need a starker church. Too often now it does no more than insulate us." He stands. "But that has nothing to do with you."

I, too, stand. For seconds we stare into each another's eyes. "Well," I say, "I'm drawn to starkness."

"A sin?"

"Who knows? And surely we apostates have already been defrocked."

He pockets pipe, pouch, and lighter, then offers me his hand. I accept it. "I told your mother I'd come," he says. "And I'm glad I did.

Though it was futile, I suppose, by and large, since you know my little sermons as well as I do."

"It was good to be reminded of what I know."

The handshake ends, and we start together toward the door. "Tom Guy says you'll be released tomorrow. On your own recognizance. And you'll have some time before the trial."

"I suppose."

"Well, Jesse, use the time well. Be sure this is the right thing to do."

"In bad times," I say, "only evil is guided by certainty."

"The illusion of certainty," he corrects.

The sheriff leads me back to my cell, and the jail is in an uproar. The Cherokee stands at the cell window, waving his arms like some demented concertmaster. He, the people on the sidewalk across the street, and many of the county's prisoners are chanting "Free Augustus Riverwalker! Free Augustus Riverwalker! Free Augustus Riverwalker!"

When we enter the cell, he looks back at us, says to the sheriff, "By God, I never thought I'd see the day. It's a joy to my ol' heathen ears."

The sheriff seems more amused than irritated. "You a free man now, Gus. Elected official like myself can't be standing against the tide of public opinion."

"How about us making a day of this, and me leaving come evening?"

"Hell, they be tired of you by then, Gus. Liable to be howling for God knows who. Might be wanting me to fork over that ol' Chester gal filled her daddy full of buckshot last week. Mighty sad case."

"You probably right," Augustus Riverwalker says. Then, to me, "You ever go wandering the Winding Stairs boy, look ol' Gus up. I'll stand you to some 'shine, show you where we keep the Great Spirit hid."

Moments later he is on the street, and a cheer goes up for him. He stands with them for a while, laughing, chanting for my freedom, then goes his way.

I lie in my bunk thinking of him. His way. The Winding Stair Mountains. Poverty. Alcohol. Despair? Perhaps. But sometimes the laughter I saw, too.

And then of Justin Sayles. His way. Reason. Theology. Compassion. A kind of courage confined by the habit of his chosen role. Yet does he understand himself as well as does this Cherokee, Augustus Riverwalker, alive two centuries beyond his people's time?

What guides us? The illusion of certainty? The acceptance of uncertainty?

How do we go on? Any of us? And why? From what springs hope? When is it justified?

And I think that what I am doing, though right, is easy, a clear choice. Provocation and response. A measure of the certain abides in me, justifies my choosing this cell, will justify my choosing it again. It will be after the sentence is served that the difficult time will come.

But the wonder of faith is that in the difficulty lies the grace.

9 GLORIA

The word had gone out, and that night thousands of heads gathered in and around the huge, open-air amphitheater high on Mount Tamalpais. The ceremony began with sunset mantras, which were followed by three hours of acid rock by One-Way Ticket, Naked Lunch, Plutonium Squid, and Maximum Angel. There had been rumors that the Dead, the Airplane, the Fish, Quicksilver, Moby Grape—any one or any combination—would be there, but that may've just been Shiva Charlie and the other promoters guaranteeing a big audience for their apocalyptic prophecies and windowpane plans for salvation. There were a few Diggers there ladling out cups of soybean soup.

The music we did hear was more acid than rock. Eerie, atonal guitar solos, piercing feedback, minutes-long repetitions of a single chord, a general disdain for melody, and, with, Maximum Angel, unrhymed, irregular sadomasochistic lyrics.

While the bands played, Gunner and I—he carrying Aura on his back—worked our way systematically through the crowd, looking for Jimmy Song. After an hour and a half, during which we found nothing but the limits of my daughter's patience, Jerry the Dealer came to us and said, "Shiva Charlie says to tell you Jimmy's up on the peak, digging the lights."

"Not into music?" Gunner said.

"Hears his own." Jerry left us.

Just then, Plutonium Squid's lead singer howled, "Orgasm is love!" and totaled his guitar against the amphitheater stage floor.

"Why'd he do that?" Aura asked me.

"Been questioning the value of electricity for forty-five minutes," Gunner told her. "I believe he finally came to the right conclusion."

Aura looked confused and tired. A little girl in the wrong place. I reached up and squeezed her hand. "It's all right," I said. "He can't hurt anybody."

Jimmy, when we found him, didn't seem to be digging the lights. He was arguing with two men, a black dude with a goatee and a shaved head and a barrel-chested middle-aged white guy with an Allen Ginsberg beard. We heard enough to know that the argument was over money Jimmy thought he was owed. There were a few other people scattered around up there, sharing joints and blankets, huddling together against the cool and the light fog that was beginning to come in off the ocean, so Jimmy and the two men didn't notice us until we were ten or fifteen feet from them. Then they fell silent and turned toward us.

Gunner lifted Aura off his shoulders, handed her to me, then walked up to the black man, nodded toward Jimmy, and said, "Man's a narc. I was you, Jackson, I'd keep clear."

The black man gave him a slow study, cocked an eyebrow. "You looking for work, Booker. Ever since I'se just a little hookworm cotton-patch pickaninny, I been needing me a man'd do my thinking."

"This here's your day of deliverance then," Gunner said.

Jimmy, who had been looking at me, turned to the Ginsberg-bearded guy. "Tomorrow, man. My place. No fucking around."

"Whoa up, now, Mr. Slick," the black said to Jimmy. "This here be honkie guidance hour; I can't be leaving now. Nigger like me always searching for wisdom." Then, to Gunner—"What you say, Booker?"

"I was you, I'd be leaving. Then I'd remind myself there ain't never been no white man I owed shit to."

The black man smiled broadly, turned to Jimmy, made an elaborate show of his palms, and said, "I believe that there's the voice of the Master we hearing, don't you, Cool? Voice say go, we be gone." He looked at me and Aura. "Peace, children." Then he and his partner got on their motorcycles.

"Tomorrow," Jimmy said to their backs.

"Black man can't never tell nothing about tomorrow." They roared away.

Jimmy watched them ride off. "Bad timing, baby," he said, turning to me.

I asked Gunner to take Aura back to the amphitheater and wait for me. He shrugged, took Aura's hand, and left.

"Who's the asshole?" Jimmy asked.

"A friend."

"We all need friends." He spent a moment sizing me up, then came to me and put his arms around me. "Good to see you, babe," he whispered. "Glad you got Aura, too."

I stood stiffly in his arms, said nothing. He let me go and stepped back. "What came down in Little Rock, babe, I was lucky to get out with my ass."

"Lucky?"

He stared directly into my eyes. "What kind of shit you been hearing? I was set up. Framed. Marked and narcked. Met my man in the room. Next thing I know pigs bust in shooting. I go down the fire escape. Anything happens after that, they do it. I don't know shit about it. Bastard I was selling to set me up. That's all I know."

"Why aren't they looking for you?"

"Jesus!" He raised his hands as if I were arresting him. He looked at me hard, then took his hands down. "What is this? Interrogation by the Council on Revolutionary Purity?"

"I want to know what happened. Little Rock pig told me you worked for the government. The big pigs."

"What the fuck would he tell you, huh? Wise up."

"Gunner talked to some people, too. Street people. They said the same thing, Jimmy. I couldn't believe you'd do that. But I do now. I started remembering. Everybody you ever dealt with had to do time. You always got off. Odd, isn't it?"

"It's high-risk work. I'm smart, and I'm lucky."

"Fuck you," I said.

"That what you came all the way out here to say?"

"Yes. I wanted to start fresh. And I had to say that before I could."

"Well," he said, "you're free to think what you want. Now go on home and be the Emma Goldman of southwest Arkansas."

"I'm spreading the word, Jimmy. You're through here."

"*It's* through, baby. All of it. Over. Never was anything but a bunch of rich white kids' dream. You're just another one of the dreamers. Another debutante throwing a tantrum at her daddy. None of you ever been a threat to anything but each other. And I'll tell you something else. Simple fucking truth. You ought to send your daughter home before you ruin her."

"Fuck you."

" 'Fuck you, fuck you.' " That the new slogan? Peace Now and Fuck You?"

"I don't know. You're the one who kept up with the slogans. That's all you knew, isn't it? All you needed to know. Mouth the slogans, and we'll accept you because we're children and we need friends. Especially in Arkansas, where we were so few and far away all we had were the slogans. But you'd been around, hadn't you? You could show us things, teach us something about nerve, about living on the other side of the line. Christ!" I shook my head slowly, looked away from him, looked back. "You're scum, Jimmy. Shit. Just another pusher who cut himself a deal with the man." I turned from him and started away.

"Babe," he said. And something in me made me turn back. Curiosity. The memory of infatuation. The foolish hope that I had misjudged him—not then, but now. Weakness. "I like you," he went on. "You were fun. But you were never more than a high-spirited piece of ass. All that shit you got in your head is just that—shit. The revolution never was, never will be. Just a word people use to glorify their appetites. All you are is a rebellious girl that likes to fuck. And that's cool, babe, if you'd just accept it for what it is. I mean, the streets are full of people that'd love fucking you. Casual, you know. Nobody going to take you serious till you grow up. But by then, you'll be fucked out."

"If you need money, Jimmy, my father'd probably hire you back. He thinks like you do. You could talk him into dealing drugs in a big way. Pay the pigs off with petty cash and street dealers. Haul the shit in by the truckload. Be just the thing for both of you. Capitalism and cynicism. Always pays well. Costs you nothing but your soul. Which isn't worth anything anyway."

Then I left him there—forever, I thought.

* * *

I followed a path downhill into a redwood grove and sat in the fog at a picnic table. I wanted to think, but I could only feel—and remember. My men. Pregnant with Aura, I had married John O'Leary when I was eighteen. My first real act of rebellion. He was twenty-eight, had been a freedom rider, had marched with King. He was from Camden and had a house there, but he was gone a lot, organizing for the NAACP, going to every big march, everywhere. When I met him, I thought he was my way out, my way up. And I loved him the way a girl can love a male example—not with passion but with pride. We married because I was pregnant, but maybe I was pregnant so we could marry. And we had almost two years together, or parts of two years. He wanted me to go to college, and he wanted to carry on with his work. And the idea of that kind of sacrifice for that kind of revolutionary marriage appealed to me. So he lived in the house in Camden and I in the dormitory in Fayetteville, and we saw each other weekends and holidays and summers, and he kept Aura in his house when he was there and his mother kept her in hers when he wasn't. So I could be a college-educated civil rights worker, so I wouldn't later regret having missed my youth, so we could have a marriage that wouldn't be an excessive burden to either of us.

In October of my sophomore year, his mother, a widow in her early sixties, died of a heart attack. After that he started leaving Aura with my parents. I was sick of college, was willing to be a mere placard bearer, even a secretary, in the movement. But he wanted me to finish and then he wanted me to go to law school, become a good, dedicated countercultural lawyer. Finally, he believed in the system. But I didn't. I didn't want college, I didn't want law school, and I didn't believe in the system. I wanted us to be radicals together—John Reed and Emma Goldman or something. So he joined the Peace Corps. Just like that. I came home one weekend that February, and he told me. The civil rights movement was a black movement, he said. A white liberal was an interloper, a special kind of impediment, a man whose primary goal, finally, was the placating of his own conscience. A SNCC organizer named Buford Travis had told him that his—John's—place was with his own people, changing the minds of the Klansmen, the White Citizen's Council members, the Southern Baptists. He should organize white liberals and work to change the minds of white racists. "The problem ain't with black folks," Buford told him. "It's with white folks. They the ones need changing." John had yielded, had come to accept the argument. But he wasn't yet strong enough, he told me, to devote his life to converting the Klan, the councils, the segs. "Change the young, and wait for the rest to die," he said. "No more confrontation. I'd be going door to door proselytizing like a Mormon. I'm not ready for it. It would be like starting all over."

So he joined the Peace Corps and went to India. Alone. I wanted to go with him and take Aura, but he wouldn't allow it. Maybe the government wouldn't have either, I don't know. Anyway, it was a personal mission. He wasn't going for the Indians, he was going for himself, to find himself. A spiritual quest, a search for the courage to accept his role in America. This would be his time spent in the wilderness preparing himself for his American mission. And he had to be alone.

He had been gone months before I completely accepted the idea that, whatever else going to India was, it was his way—the impeccably moral way—of getting rid of us, his wife and daughter. Simple as that. So I wrote him a letter setting him free, his answer expressed gratitude, and that was over. If I'd still believed in the bourgeois institution, I would have divorced him. As it was, I didn't need to. I would certainly never marry again. If he wanted to, he could divorce me. He could pay the bourgeois lawyer to file the bourgeois papers and get the bourgeois decree. I was a free woman.

In his way, I guess, he was a good man, John, a lot like Jesse, bright, moral, dedicated, but, finally, ineffectual. I had a lot of men after John left, some of whose names I can't remember now, some of whose names I never knew: spite-fucks, pity-fucks, drunk-fucks, habit-fucks, spectacle-fucks, you name it. One of them was Jimmy, who came into Fayetteville every few weeks with a load of pot. But the next man I stayed with was Jesse, younger than John, spiritual, and less overtly political. But a radical with soul, an apprentice intellectual devoted to the study of morality's fine print, a study that led him systematically to religion, mysticism. God, holiness, a divine order—whatever—greatly simplifies things, justifies inaction, sanctifies patience. What we needed then—and what we need now—were action and impatience. America was racist, materialistic, imperialistic, militaristic. Confronting that made John want to leave, Jesse want to meditate, and me want to start manning barricades.

Instead, I took up with Jimmy. A rebel, I thought, an outlaw. A man who spends his life and makes his money on the renegade side of the line. He was cunning, daring, exciting. For months, I slept with both of them—Jimmy, when he was in town, Jesse the rest of the time. Jesse was too spiritual for jealousy. Jimmy didn't know Jesse existed. I even helped Jimmy get the job driving for my father. I loved the idea. Smuggling dope into the country on a Ouachita Best Freight eighteen-wheeler. Sometimes I traveled with him. It was, I thought, the definitive step across the line. I was an outlaw. They could put me in jail. I liked the feeling.

And all the while, Aura was with my parents, growing up in the plantation house. I told myself that any day I would rescue her, that Jimmy and I would begin using our dope profits to pay for our revolutionary activities. But it went on, and we did nothing. Oh, I joined SDS, and, on the green in front of Old Main, I demonstrated against the war and threw rocks at the ROTC boys. Campus pranks for radicals. I did nothing. Except provide a cover for Jimmy Song.

So, I had failed. I had left my daughter too long with my father. And I had yet to find a method of rebellion other than the illegal use of my father's trucks—and, as Jimmy had said, the flagrant use of my sex. And I had let my sex limit me. I had always found a man to give me definition, to determine my role in the movement. Flower child, dope moll, or ammunition bearer . . . I could be anything; it depended on my man.

Christ! And now I had Gunner. Impotent and angry. Maybe it all fit.

When I got back to the amphitheater, the music was over and Shiva Charlie was on stage dressed in a dhoti, sitting full lotus at the center of a turquoise spotlight, and staring reverently at the basketball-sized meteorite a few feet in front of him. Inches above the meteorite was a microphone. We could hear Charlie breathing.

Looking for Gunner and Aura, I walked around the edge of the crowd, most of whom, following Charlie's example, had folded up and were meditating on the meteorite. I had stopped and was waiting for Charlie to begin speaking of the world's end when I heard Gunner's voice behind me.

"Ain't nothing you couldn't get these poor fucks to believe in."

Then, from speakers that had been placed everywhere, came Shiva Charlie's voice: "It will end." For a moment, nothing more. Then sitar music. Then Charlie's voice again. "I have heard the sky and the river. They sing of the end." Sitar music. The tinkling of bells. The spotlight widened and went white. Behind Charlie the sitar player and the bell tinkler appeared. Then the whole stage was illuminated, and, behind the sitar and the bells, was a semicircular row of young women dressed in saris; at the center of each forehead, a diffraction disk. Softly they chanted a mantra.

"Shiva Charlie and the Shivettes," Gunner said. He sat down. Aura lay beside him, rested her head in his lap. I sat down, too, took her hand. "What's that man doing?" she asked me. She meant Charlie.

"It's a carnival game," Gunner said. "Pretty soon he'll take everybody for a ride."

A kid sitting on the ground near us told Gunner that skepticism was evil.

"I doubt it," Gunner told him.

Blissed out, the kid nodded. "Evil," he repeated.

"As has been foretold," Shiva Charlie said, "the asteroid Icarus will strike the earth on the night of Saturday, June 15." Now his voice had become that of a military strategist—clipped, objective, factual. "Tibet will be spared. And perhaps Colorado. Other than that, all predictions are questionable." The saried chorus line turned Colorado into a mantra. Most of the crowd, Aura along with them, joined in. "Col-o-ra-do. Col-o-ra-do. Col-o-ra-do."

"That is where we must go," Charlie said. "We shall gather in Boulder. And then we shall ascend the mountain."

For several minutes after that he spoke of endings and beginnings, circles and spirals, apocalypse and resurrection. The crowd began to show signs of restlessness. Joints were lit and passed. I could hear bits of conversation, laughter. Off to my left, under a Navaho blanket, a couple began fucking.

Charlie had just circled back to a new beginning when a mime troupe, androgynous in tattered tuxedos and heavy white makeup, rushed onto the stage. They circled Charlie, pointed at him, slapped their thighs, and broadly mimicked laughter.

"Salvation," said Shiva Charlie, who seemed not to have noticed the mocking troupe, "lies in meditation. Goodness has its own force, a force as measurable as gravity and far more powerful, a force that can either attract or repel." The mimers flung themselves belly first to the stage and writhed in paroxysms of mock glee. The couple to my left slackened their pace and turned their heads toward the show. From somewhere behind the stage came the sound of an engine starting, and, seconds later, a man rode a motorcycle up a ramp and into the light. He stopped beside Charlie, letting the motor idle. A huge man wearing jackboots, blue jeans, a sleeveless black leather jacket, and what looked like a crown of thorns. Without getting off the bike, he pulled the thorns off his head and flung them, Frisbee style, into the crowd. "God is joy," he said. "No more suffering." The mime troupe circled him, whooping rhythmically, bobbing dramatically up and down. "Fuck this somber shit," the cyclist shouted. "Let's go to the End of the World Orgy. Anybody wants to fuck, I'll be in the woods." He revved his engine, put the bike in gear, lifted his boots, circled the stage three times, and roared down the ramp.

Unperturbed, Shiva Charlie said, "The estimated population of the world is three billion four hundred eighty-three million two hundred sixty-three thousand. The square root of that is just over fifty-nine thousand. That's how many we'll need at Boulder to save the world. The square root of the power of good meditating on a mountaintop, each in his own way, will emit a force that will cause Icarus to change direction, and the world will be saved."

The saried chorus line gathered around the meteorite, and each woman assumed the lotus position. Arms outstretched like those of children imitating airplanes, the mimes began to circle the stage. They gradually increased their speed and decreased the radius of their circle until they were spinning round and round, their fingers touching above Charlie, the chorus line, and the meteorite. Lights flashed on and off, each flash a different color, and all the rock bands began playing again. Pulsing drums, shrieking guitars, screaming voices. This went on for several minutes, everything getting louder and faster. And then, from the center of the whirlwind, Shiva Charlie's voice boomed: "Om." And them "Om" again. The mime troupe circle began to widen and turn more slowly, the music grew softer and more melodic, the lights flashed and changed color less and less frequently until finally the mime troupe was tiptoeing gracefully along the edge of the stage, the bands were playing soft background while the chorus line sang, beautifully, the Doors' "Crystal Ship." And everything was bathed in a clean white light, through which the words to the song passed on their way to the darkness.

Then the song ended, and it was lights out and silence, followed by Shiva Charlie's voice softly repeating "Col-o-ra-do. Col-o-ra-do. Col-o-ra-do." Then the chorus line joining in. Then the mime troupe. Until "Col-o-ra-do. Col-o-ra-do. Col-o-ra-do" boomed and boomed from the dark peak of Mount Tamalpais down toward the lost cities of the sea.

"Won't be long," Gunner said, "Shiva Charlie be working Vegas."

10 MALEDON

Well, I had to hand it to Magdalen. She'd worked the grand con right to the ground, right down to where she'd made herself the priestess-queen of a tropical island. Most everybody's dream, that—the year-round sun and the evening breeze, living on palm fruit and seafood, being waited on and worshiped by the lithe and the limber, having them all stop short, cock their heads, and still their hearts every time they heard you talking, all of them thinking that in the sound of your voice might lie the source of the mystery.

Yes sir, Lord God, she'd worked it all the way, the grand con, the God con, the answer to every question, the cause for every quest. Ol' Jacob Ladders, in his prime, would've been proud of how far she'd gone, how she'd named the game and played it out. But then he'd've seen the other too, seen the thing that drove him to the gun and made him point it backwards. Because the one thing you can't do if you're running a con is con yourself. You start believing, it's over. You got to always leave that back door open. You don't know that or forget it or just can't accept it, well, the con's going to take you down, drag you under, like it did Dr. Ladders, because it's you you're running it on. You've become your own sucker. There won't be no road out, no other con. When the game gets real, the times grow grim. And that was what was wrong with Magdalen's little paradise. First time I saw her on that island, she was stretched out on a hammock and suffering from Jacob Ladders' disease. The hard knowledge was coming to her late. It's the old trap: You got to be a believer to make the grand con grand, but you can't get the good out of it without seeing it for what it is. And poor Magdalen, my old dream of love, hadn't ever got over being a believer.

The north coast of the key, which couldn't have been more than three or four miles in diameter, was sandy beaches, the south coast was coral. Coconut palms just beyond the beaches, then starting a few yards back, mangrove swamp, palmetto thickets. There were frigate birds and herons and gulls and birds by the thousands I didn't know the names of.

There was no path to the heart of the island. They had dug a canal, Magdalen's Christians had, and Mason Sloate found it, anchored the cabin cruiser, and lowered a canoe overboard. The canal wound through a midday darkness, limbs and vines joining just overhead, the thickets filling with the calls of birds, the thrashings of scurrying life. What Magdalen's believers had done was to cut through the gaps between dank pools of swamp water. But we made our way smoothly along the narrow canals, across the thick sloughs. And the air was so rife with rot and waste I caught myself thinking there wasn't any form of life that couldn't've sprung from this source and that maybe Magdalen had been right to come here, maybe here where life was so varied, death so constant, resurrection so common, you could find a religion wild and rich and changeable enough not to dishonor life. No more of that goddamn desert doom.

We entered a broad, open swamp and, in the gloom at the far end, saw a pier, thatched houses, movement. As we neared that, we began to see a lot more, a village, houses on poles, narrow streets covered with crushed coral. The land rose gently from the swamp. The jungle had been cut back. Fruit trees and flower and vegetable gardens made a bright patchwork on the slope. At the far end of the village, at the island's height but still no more than maybe fifty feet above the sea, was a huge structure. It too was thatched and built on poles, but towered over all the other buildings. The Vatican, I thought, of Calvary Key.

Three muscled-up, long-haired boys Jesse's age or younger waited for us at the end of the pier like guards—which, I guess, is what they were. Swamp guards of the Christian keep. Mason Sloate ignored them. We rowed right past, got out, and pulled the canoe ashore. The three boys hurried back down the pier and caught up with us. Mason lifted two bottles of Jack Daniels from the canoe, took a drink from the one he'd already opened, and held the unopened fifth out to the largest of the guards, who had a gaudy parrot on his shoulder.

"No liquor allowed here, sir," he said.

Mason drank again. "Too late," he said. "And once it's here, you might as well make the best of it." Again he offered the bottle.

"Do you have business on Calvary Key?"

He was asking Mason, but I answered. "Come to see Magdalen Abbey," I said. "I'm an old friend. Sam Maledon's the name."

"Sam Maledon?" The main guard looked at the other two. They looked at him.

Mason grinned, drank, said, "Sam here used to be her main man. One that led her to God."

"Even God grows weary," said the parrot.

To say the least, it caught me by surprise. I gave him a look and said, "Yeah, but he's been at it way longer than me."

The parrot nodded.

"Who was Jacob Ladders?" the guard under the parrot asked.

"Dr. Jacob Ladders," I told him. "Magdalen's stepfather, my teacher and friend. The great evangelist who ascended to heaven." What the hell? These boys were bound to be fools.

"Perhaps," the guard said.

"Jacob Ladders was pure example," said the parrot.

"For man and parrot alike," I agreed.

The big guard thought a minute. Then, to Mason, he said, "I wish you wouldn't drink."

"Me too," Mason told him. "But any second now I'll change my mind."

"Well, come on," the guard said. "We'll see."

We followed them up the coral road to the big house. They had us wait on the front porch while the one with the parrot went in to check things out. Going through the door, the parrot said, "There is no mystery."

Mason said, "No, it's all birdseed and cages."

The parrot made the sound of raucous laughter.

Mason and I sat in rattan chairs. The two remaining guards stood, backs to the wall, on either side of us.

"You boys don't want a drink?" Mason asked them, glancing up, looking from one to the other. "We got God's plenty."

They ignored him. But one of them addressed me. "Do you drink, Dr. Maledon?"

I liked that "Dr." It seemed to hint at a good future for me there. And the truth was I'd earned it the same way Ladders had earned his.

"Only in connection with certain rituals," I answered. "After weddings and funerals. Before a healing." I looked at Mason. As if on cue, he drank. I shook my head sadly. "I'm afraid my friend Mr. Sloate abuses it. The tropics disagree with him."

"We've been having fevers," the boy said. "But they pass."

"As do all of Satan's workings," I said. I reached over the arm of my chair and patted the guard's leg. "Have faith," I told him.

It seemed like a half-hour passed before the big guard came back down for me. "She's pleased you've come," he told me. And he said Mason was to have the freedom of the island.

"What's that like?" Mason asked him.

"Sir?"

"The freedom of the island. What's it like?"

"A blessing," the guard said. "To those who have sufficient spirit."

"Spirit, spirit," the parrot repeated. He threw back his blue head, his orange beak, and again came the mocking, raucous laughter.

I followed the guard inside, and he pointed toward the stairs. "All the way up," he said.

Four flights. The place was built like a Japanese pagoda except that each level was surrounded by a wide porch rather than sloping eaves. The top level was covered with a thick, thatched roof, but there weren't any walls, just a waist-high railing around the edges. The place looked to be about fifty feet long and fifty feet wide, and it had no furniture in it except for perches, swings, cages, and feeders for the dozens of birds making a life there—mynahs, parrots, canaries, crows, doves, toucans, and God knows what all. And there was Magdalen's hammock, of course.

She was sunk in the white netting. The birds were silent. A light breeze sidled across the wide covered deck. We were well above the trees. The skies looked as if they'd been clear forever. In the distance the sea glistened under the morning sun. Here and there, against the horizon, you could see the outlines of other islands. Nothing limited vision except the curve of the earth.

She didn't stir—or if she did, I saw no sign of it. I walked to the hammock and looked down at her.

And for that first moment it was like all the years, almost twenty-five of them, had worked together for the sole purpose of making this instant pure. All my wanderings, all my cons and scams and hustles and all her search for meaning, purpose, religion seemed to be the two parts of a long, elaborate dance that had just now come together, had suddenly made absolute sense. Everything seemed inevitable. All the scattered strands wound into a fabric. The random pathways of half a lifetime merged. Coincidence assumed purpose. Accident became fate. Everything either one of us had done seemed a necessary part of destiny's pattern. There was order, there was purpose. Chance was but the illusion allowing a benevolent God to work his way with us.

Well, you know how it is. You've had these moments, I'm sure, when everything seemed to tie together so neat even the knots disappeared. When everything made sense and seemed just. When a minute of good luck conquered a lifetime of doubt. When you thought you saw all the puppet strings and, because they'd brought you here to this good place, you liked them. When fate seemed so much finer than freedom.

It's all bullshit, of course. Whatever order there is is so old and vast and set that it takes no more account of us than it does of Vestal Truax's dogs. And, hell, I wouldn't have it any other way. But you know what I mean. Just for that long minute there, looking down at her after all those years, I lost my head. Seeing her made me want to believe in everything.

She wore a white silk robe. Rich black hair framed her face. Her dark eyes were wet and round. The good bones, the wide mouth, the languid body. The very picture of prime woman perfectly seasoned.

"Well," I told her. "I got to thinking. I ain't dead, and you ain't either. We might as well try it again."

She held a hand out to me. I took it and sat down beside her in the hammock. "I knew you'd come," she said. "I prayed for it."

I tried to ignore that. I didn't like being the subject of anybody's prayers. And it was making the moment fade. "Nice setup you got here," I said. "Beats the hell out of Kansas."

"Will you stay, Sam?"

"I'd like to, Meg. But I'm not sure I can stand all these birds."

She smiled. "They talk to me, Sam," she said. "They talk to all of us."

"I know." I nodded. " 'Even God grows weary.' "

Several parrots immediately repeated the phrase. Others said, "There is no mystery." Others, "Jacob Ladders was pure example." The canaries sang. The mynahs began reciting the Beatitudes. The crows squawked threats from Jeremiah. The doves flew away, circled the building, returned. Then, gradually, all the birds lapsed again into silence.

"You have to be careful," Magdalen said. "We have them trained. If you say any of the words they know, it triggers them."

"We could make us a fortune," I told her. "Taking them mynahs on the road, having them deliver the Sermon on the Mount at revivals."

Her smile returned. "You haven't changed, have you?" And then, the smile not entirely faded, but her face serious, she said, "I *have* a fortune, Sam. Did you know that? I didn't want it. It was the last thing I wanted. But people kept giving me money to keep being what they thought I was. After we built the church there in Kansas, I had no further use of money. But it kept coming. I had to do something with it, use it wisely. So . . . well, it's been easier to accumulate a fortune than to use it well."

"Trouble with that kind of fortune," I said, "it makes you plan for the future all the time. And the future starts happening while you're planning. Only solution is fiscal irresponsibility. You want to enjoy your fortune, you got to start pissing it away."

She was laughing. "How I've missed you, Sam. I never hear anyone talk like that. I've made everything too somber."

"Well, if it's somber at all, it's too somber. Every religion needs a strong dose of heathen joy."

"We do need something," she said. "Everything has worked perfectly here, and that's made us all a little weary."

That set the birds off again. Watching them, watching me, she laughed gaily, girlishly, and I leaned down and took her in my arms.

And we were young again.

11 JESSE

I am free again. Back again at Clear Creek. Posing again for Margaret Salter.

Waiting again.

I had expected, had prepared myself for, a change. But change is illusion. The oldest wisdom. The first cliché. Why do I forget?

When I was released from jail, the demonstrators cheered, celebrating as if for a great victory. But it was, I knew, no victory. It was at best a delay, at worst a defeat. It is a deep flaw in our character, the young, the American. We know so little, have so fragile an understanding of what we want that we will interpret the slightest conciliation as a victory.

A week passes. Days of pure light, unfiltered, and then rain, thundershowers, a night of drizzle. Luxuriant pastures. The strong, clear creek rolling, rippling, hissing against its banks. Freshets springing from the hillsides, rushing to the creek, the lake, the river. In the gardens, English peas, carrots, lettuce, spinach, mustard greens, Bermuda onions, asparagus, cabbage, cauliflower, strawberries. The cultivated earth damp underfoot, the plants heavy with health. Howdy Hardison catches crappie, bass, catfish, perch, bream. There is fresh cream, butter, cheese, good bread.

It is enough. It is everything. And yet I am not content. I am not here. I am waiting. I am wrong. Expectation emanates from ego. I wait for what I know will not be what I wait for.

Before, I did not simply wait; I prepared. The anticipated time came; I was ready. The time passed. Nothing. Nothing happened, nothing changed, nothing mattered. The preparation was vain. Vanity. I should have known. I should have believed. Even then. And now . . . now I do know, but I will not yield. I cannot fully rid myself of frustration. Have they defeated me by setting me free?

And why do I let them determine my mood? I had wanted to make a clear stand. They would not allow it. Delay. Complication. Accommodation. Is Gloria right? Does nothing but violence, open rebellion truly gain, fully focus their attention? Otherwise, will they merely wait, granting token concessions, making irrelevant conciliatory gestures, until your own frustration defeats you?

If, finally, I make them, they will imprison me. If I don't, they will ignore me. They believe nothing I do can interfere with the war. They are right. I must learn to expect nothing from them. They are the outsiders.

Politics, materialism, the science of dividing the spoils. Why do I bother? Freedom lies not in the province of the lawyer. Enlightenment is alien there.

I cannot allow my pacifism to become political. War is the ultimate expression of human evil. To assist in the waging of war, in however small, in however involuntary a manner, is to contribute to evil. Always, without exception.

What justification can there be for slaughter of the innocent? What justification for the slaughter of the guilty? Who decides? Who has the right? Certainly not the men who have accumulated an arsenal capable of obliterating creation.

It is simple, then. War is wrong; I will not go. I have known that for years. So why does it obsess me? Why do I not simply live? Gather the vegetables, fillet the fish I will not eat, walk the hills, bathe in the creek, make love with Margaret?

Be here now. The old admonition. The one way. How simple. How difficult. The mind remembers, plans, expects, defeats itself.

Am I but something waiting for something to happen? Something wanting to be something else?

What is now is all.
Be satisfied. Want nothing.
Christ, man, BE HERE NOW!

How many times do I have to say it?
Until I believe, yield. Until the voice becomes the silence.

12 GLORIA

There was nothing for me to do about Jimmy Song except finger him. So the day after the Mount Tamalpais ceremony, Gunner and I talked to Shiva Charlie and Jerry the Dealer, and then we all drove down to the Haight and laid the line on Sugar Hillstrom, a junky who had been a printer for Com/co until the Diggers took it over from Chester Anderson and gave all the equipment to the Panthers. Sugar still had access to an old offset machine and a copier, and I paid him to print up a thousand flyers with nothing on them but Jimmy's face and the words THIS MAN IS A NARC.

After that it was time to leave. The Haight had become a kind of doped-out Dodge City, the Bay Area communes were financing themselves with food stamps and drug deals, the Diggers had ridden a calculated anonymity to countercultural fame and ceased to do any useful work, the would-be revolutionaries were all seeing with their third eye, and the few people still capable of organizing anything were busy founding cults. It was over, here. Whatever would be happening would be happening elsewhere.

Probably not in Colorado, I thought. But it would be on the way, so it was where we went. Except for the few vagrant winos Shiva Charlie left in charge of things, the Staff of Life Ranch packed up and headed east to await the end of the world. That was three or four days after Mount Tamalpais, a Wednesday or a Thursday, I think. At sunrise, Shiva Charlie led us in a safe-journey mantra—one composed thousands of years ago, he said, to subdue the demons of the Nepal mountain passes.

It took us over three weeks to get there. Charlie simply pointed us east out of the commune and from then on chose whatever road seemed to match his karma. The Staff of Life bus was a rusted, coughing version of the Prankster's notorious one, but, unlike the Pranksters, the Staff of Life had neither a mechanic nor a long-haul driver. They did have enough LSD to see them through any seige of rationalism, however, and Jerry the Dealer hadn't driven half an hour before taking the bus down into a ditch, jerking it back up onto the shoulder, and, in the process, clipping a row of mailboxes off their stand.

We were following them in the Continental. Jerry the Dealer stopped the bus, and the Staff of Life piled out, laughing at the scattered mailboxes. Shiva Charlie solemnly eyed the damage. "Mail," he said. And dismissed the postal service with a sweep of the hand.

They got back in, and Jerry the Dealer drove for another hour, weaving randomly back and forth across the white lines. Then the bus went into a ditch again. Shiva Charlie got out, looked up at the morning sun, and decided to call it a day.

"Fuck this," Gunner said as we pulled up behind them. "Let's cut loose from these half-wits."

"Don't you want to watch the world end?" I said. "What else have we got to do?"

"I'll drive that goddamn box, then."

We got out.

"We have to get straight," Shiva Charlie told Gunner. "We'll start tomorrow."

Jerry the Dealer showed us his resigned palms. "I'm fucked up," he explained.

"Ain't nothing here," Gunner said. "Bad place. I'll drive."

Shiva Charlie examined the sun again. Then he nodded.

Gunner drove the bus as far as it would go. Just west of Sacramento the brakes went out. We were there two days waiting to get them relined. After that it was the clutch, the transmission, the radiator, the generator, the drive shaft, the universal joint. A water line burst while we were crossing the Nevada desert. We threw a rod in Moab, and, after three days, a Mormon mechanic replaced the engine just to get us out of town.

And, to make it worse, Shiva Charlie traveled like a child. He had to see this, he had to see that. This road looked interesting, that one promising. Hippie faith and juvenile curiosity were our guides. How could you get lost in a land so large all directions were general? How could you despair when all around you were wonders too magnificent for the telling? In the Great American West there was no such thing as a wrong turn.

We visited communes, Indian reservations, artist colonies; slept in ghost towns, old mining camps, sparkling little Mormon cities. We parked the vehicles and climbed buttes and mesas so Shiva Charlie could get a good vantage of God. We danced in the desert and sang into bottomless canyons.

At the end of the fourth day, Gunner was again ready to leave them, but Aura was sleeping well just then, and, by the next morning, we had decided to give it another day. After that we were hooked. It was adventure—ridiculous, idiotic, spontaneous, incongruous, and fun. We were headed to Boulder to await the world's end, and nobody seemed to care how or if we got there. It was all a joke, pure and glorious and absurd, as only the best of life can be. Irresponsibility as a credo.

By the time we did get to Boulder, the bus, except for its Day-Glo shell, was almost completely new, nearly every part having been replaced at least once. And Gunner, who only three weeks earlier had known only the barest rudiments of engine repair, had become a first-rate mechanic. Shiva Charlie came more and more to seem like an amiable holy fool. The Staff of Life was a collection of happy, haphazard childlike pilgrims. My daughter was brown and happy and free. America, wide and beautiful, was a land of endless possibility. And, as for me, well, I can't remember how long it had been—years—since I had felt so completely unburdened. Five days into the journey, while we were waiting in a Nevada campground for someone to find another radiator for the bus, I said something to Gunner about the strike in France and he simply walked over to the Continental, reached under the dash, and ripped out the radio wires. After that all I heard from the great world was the rock music—the Dead, the Airplane, Dylan, Quicksilver, Moby Grape, the Stones—howling forth from the half-dozen speakers on the Staff of Life bus. For nearly three weeks, then, I was free of the news, politics, guilt. I knew it wouldn't last, couldn't last, shouldn't last, knew that this could be no more than respite and reprieve, but that knowledge only heightened my sense of liberation. The times would catch us again, but for those weeks I was free.

We entered Boulder carelessly, reveling, like a kaleidoscopic troupe from another, younger, happier land, a place so fertile responsibility was not necessary, a place where joyous freedom was everyone's birthright, the America of our dreams. But, Boulder, one of the nation's half-dozen hippie capitals, was solemn. The freaks on the street looked up at us as we passed—the psychedelic bus blaring rock and the

Continental carrying several layers of desert—as if we were an affront to propriety. The kind of looks—resentment, disgust, anger—we might have expected from our parents.

There was almost no traffic. Stores were closed. The few people we saw were silent, grim. Something had happened. A flag was at half-mast. We saw a woman wearing a black armband.

We stopped at an Esso station, got some gas. The attendant told us.

Ten hours earlier, in Los Angeles, at a victory celebration, a man named Sirhan Sirhan, had, as a blow against the nation of Israel, assassinated Robert Kennedy.

I don't know how long we sat there, scattered along the verge of the filling-station parking lot, confused, dejected, lost. Somebody bought a transistor radio somewhere. The news clarified nothing.

It seemed like hours later when Shiva Charlie came up to Gunner and me and said, "It's a sign."

"It sure the fuck is," I said.

He was an idiot again. Pure and simple.

The idyll was over. America had welcomed us home.

PART VI

1 MALEDON

They had it all there, Magdalen's Christians did, or should've had. Drag a net across the surf and you had supper. Shake a tree and down came dessert. Yeah, the food came to you almost of its own accord. Shrimp and oysters, grouper, mackerel, mullet, flounder, cobia, bluefish, bass, porgies, snapper, and wahoo. Coconuts, bananas, various kinds of roots and berries. Two freshwater springs at the heart of the key. While I was there, the weather never got so bad it couldn't be put right by a thatched roof, a hemp hammock, and a cardboard fan. You could sit on the beach and watch the sun go down in glory somewhere over Mexico. Morning, if you were still there, you could watch it come up clean over Cuba. You could sing, you could dance, you could tell stories. Your time was all yours. The place required nothing of you but just enough sense to get out of the hard rain. Well, nothing but that and the gift of liking life.

But it was the old story, friends and neighbors: Here's Paradise, and here come the Christians wanting to straighten it up. There's nobody hates the Lord's own handiwork like folks that need a church to worship him in. Even in the worst of places there's never enough suffering to satisfy them. And here, why, hell, the ease of it all damn near drove them to doubt. Everything they tried worked. They couldn't have that—wasn't any credit in it. If they didn't try anything, that worked too. They damn sure couldn't have that. They needed some thorns in them bushes, needed the snake that lurks behind the Word in the first chapter of Genesis, needed ol' Satan to give it all meaning.

So they brought in the birds. But who can take a parrot seriously? Then here I came.

This is how it started: I was lying up in that high hammock one night with Magdalen, and she asked me if I thought Dr. Ladders would've liked it there.

"Here, next to you?"

"The key. The church."

"Ladders never was much on churches," I said. "Never saw them as anything more than a ready source of suckers. But you let him build a still, he'd've liked the island."

She stared at me, curious. We were talking about different men. She'd spent so long dressing up and brushing down a memory that what she remembered was something that wasn't ever there. She'd devoted her life to decorating a disintegrating coffin. There was, for her, nothing left of Jacob Ladders, the clever old reprobate. There were only the decorations honoring not a man but a wish.

So I said, "Ever' couple of weeks, he'd probably need to make a run up to Miami and bounce a scam off some God-fearing patriots. It was what he lived for."

She looked away. "You didn't know him the way I did."

"No," I said. "I knew him the way he was."

She got out of the hammock, walked across the deck, leaned against the railing. "It's been my life," she said, her back to me. "Finding what he wanted there at the end."

"You find it?"

"Yes, Sam. Yes, I have."

"And what is it?"

She turned, faced me. "The community of God," she answered.

What can a man say to something like that? I let the parrot answer for me. "Even God grows weary," he explained.

Magdalen looked at him. "Yes," she said, "I think that may be true."

The mynah bird said, "Truth varies."

"No." Magdalen set her jaw on that.

"I believe the birds are getting the best of it," I said.

"Doubt is easy," she replied. "Faith requires courage."

"Aw, Meg. Is there anything you ain't got backwards? It's easy to believe ol' Jake died searching for God. What's hard is knowing he killed himself cause he could't get no more pussy."

"Puussssseee," the parrot practiced.

"Don't teach them that, Sam."

"It's all we heathen got, love. I'm teaching him our holy word."

"Jacob Ladders was pure example," the parrot told us.

"There are no heathen, Sam," Magdalen said as she came back to me. It looked like it was that thought that had driven her back to the hammock. "God is in the search for God. And each of us in each of our ways is a searcher. You in your way, me in mine. Everybody."

"What about all the men all suited up?" I said. "All the boys in uniform, all the scientists searching for the last big bang, all the briefcase boys trying to clear-cut everything they can't regulate?"

"They're victims," she said. "They've been frightened away from the search."

"That's dreamland thinking, Meg. The world's full of motherfuckers, and all that gives the rest of us hope of keeping clear is that most of them are idiots."

She got back in the hammock, rested her face on my arm. "Anyway," she said, "this is dreamland."

"God!" I shouted. "Ladders! Mystery! Spirit! Truth!"

And the birds squawked their messages.

Magdalen laughed. "They're yours," she said. "I don't need them now. You can be the Birdman of Calvary Key."

"Well," I said, "it'd be honest work."

So I did it, became lead bird, head mocker, church jester. And I liked it. A man needs something to do in a paradise remodeled by Christians. And there's no higher calling than trying to teach them how to laugh. Even if they learn hard. Even if they won't learn at all. The very sound of it's good for their souls. High, raucous, mocking laughter with the dark edge to it. It's what they've forsaken, and it's what they need.

It wasn't hard. A few mornings, a few evenings with the birds, and I had them behaving. I could say, "God" or "Truth" or "Salvation," any of the big words, and Magdalen's rooftop aviary would resound with the cackle of laughter.

After about a week, I started taking them out with me. I'd get a sack of birdseed and lead them down the four flights of stairs and onto the porch and out into the day. It was a sight. The stairwell fluttering with dozens of fat, bright birds, so eager for food and so conditioned to laugh that sometimes, in flight, descending the stairs, one or another of them, usually the big parrot I'd met first, would say "God," and the house would grow riotous with laughter and its echoes.

Outside they followed me in the proper way, in no formation, some hovering above me as I walked, some circling, some flying ahead and waiting on a perch until I caught up, some lagging behind and then catching up in a rush, some veering off into the bush to return whenever, but always to return. For they were loyal, my birds. They were loyal.

I'd wander the crushed coral pathways linking houses and workshops and gardens (oh yes, on this island of fish, fruit, and flowers they cleared little plots and raised vegetables and more flowers; a Christian yard isn't meant to open up to the world—it's meant to close it off), the birds flying above, around, beyond, and behind me, and I'd stop when I felt like it and talk with one of Magdalen's believers. They were good people, bright, serious, hardworking. Most of them were young, all of them were possessed by the kind of simple, driving faith that changes things. They were calm, generous, considerate, certain. Even tolerant. Magdalen, their founder, could welcome an old lover into her hammock, and that was fine. It was natural. It was good. They saw nothing perverse or obscene about sex. So they weren't beyond redemption, these particular Christians. And Mason Sloate could sit on the porch, cranking himself up on bourbon, and that was fine too. It was wrong, a sin, because it was a waste, but Mason was free, man was free, and they would forgive every drink. They were the kind of people—it was the kind of settlement—Jesse would've liked, though he might've quibbled with them over specifics of doctrine. I even gave some thought to seeing if I couldn't get him down there. I believe he'd've fit right in. And, to be honest, I liked them better than I expected to.

But, still, they did need the mockery. So I'd stand there talking sociably to them, and sooner or later somebody—I always made sure it wasn't me—would say one of the big words, and the air and all the bush would ring with hilarity.

"Why that?" Magdalen asked me.

"It's what Eve should've done to the snake," I told her. It was an answer I'd planned, one using their own language. "If she could've done that, the ol' bastard would've been through."

"Laughter is the product of the Fall," she said.

True enough. "Well, God bless the Fall, then," I said.

"And if the serpent had come to you, you'd have teamed up with him, wouldn't you? Put a show together, taken him on the road? Toured Paradise with a medicine show?"

"Could be," I agreed. "It'd sure been better than sharecropping for a landlord that wouldn't let you eat the good fruit."

* * *

But, by and large, we got on good, me and my Meg did. We were both grown and pretty sure of ourselves. Each of us had made our mark in the world—though I'd always been careful to erase mine. Each of us had the kind of confidence that comes from living your own life in your own way for a long time. In a world of shyster evangelists, priggish pastors, faggot youth directors, timid tithers, bucolic censors, worn-down wage earners, Old Testament warmongers, Bible-quoting racists, bitter, brittle-cunted old matrons, and all the rest—Lord, all the rest, all the fearful faithful whose main belief is that all that lives is suspicious—Magdalen had managed to keep both her faith and her intelligence. A miracle, that. No question. And me? Well, about all I can say is that in spite of all the roadblocks, I'd always managed to find a road. And I was confident I could do it again. And again. That I'd keep on finding a road and finding a road until all the lights went out, until it was over, until my heart quit pumping and my mind quit turning, and all the roads came to an end. After that, I'd be content to do like damn near everybody else had begun by doing—settle down on a nice little plot of ground.

So we were equals, each of us needing the other, but neither of us desperate, both of us knowing that neither of us could ever be converted to the other's way. But knowing that was all right too, that was part of the power of it. Twenty-five years ago she had feared the anarchy in me, had fought to resist the wayward road, the long succession of days promising only what chance and mother wit could bring to them. And I had been furious at myself for losing her, furious at her for choosing the world of the one big answer over the one of infinite possibility. Oh, I know. She saw it different then, sees it different now. For the believer, the searcher, the pilgrim, the one big answer was like a bridge leading from what seemed to be land's end to another land, one much like this except seen through knowing, hallowed eyes, a land where possibility gladly yields to certainty. The promised land, where all roads lead to the depot for the last train to glory. Amen.

Sure, I understood that. And, while the belief itself seemed to me to be idiotic, a denial of the variety and richness of all the roads, it may have made Magdalen even more attractive to me. Like the flaw that can take a woman well beyond beauty. And it seemed to work the other way too. For whatever she thought of my way of life, Magdalen welcomed me, warmed me, loved me. And what's a fundamental, philosophical disagreement up against that?

We talked about it. Times it seemed like that was all we talked about. Sometimes we talked about it straight on, and sometimes it edged into our discussions of other things, other people, especially Jacob Ladders and Jesse. One night in her bedroom in the main house she was telling me again how she thought my concern for Jesse had changed me for the better, made me more responsible, given me a clearer sense of the values most people lived by. Then she said she'd like to meet him, maybe there was something she could do to help him find an honest way out of his moral predicament.

"Oh, he knows the honest way out," I told her. "That's the trouble."

"Going to prison?"

"Yeah."

"To openly hand the key to the jailor," she said, "is clearly to place the moral burden on him, where it belongs."

"Yeah, y'all'd get along," I said. "Trouble with both of you is ain't neither one of you ever known any jailors. Them boys don't give a shit about moral burdens. They did, they wouldn't take the job. You give them a key, they'll lock your ass away. Nobody comes for you, they'll leave you in there till the corpse rot gets to them. A good man's job ain't to teach them pricks morals; it's to run them out of business."

"I mean *jailor* in a broader sense," she explained. "The jailor as representative of society."

"Oh, me too," I said.

She laughed. "You reject so much more than we do, Sam."

"No," I told her. "It's the other way around."

"Well," she said, smiling, "maybe you accept more too. But all the traditional things, the traditional ways—family, community, work, religion, country, all the things almost everyone needs to get through a day, much less a life—you turned away from them when you were sixteen and have never been tempted to turn back. I don't see how you do it, how you've done it so long. I'd be weary. No matter what you say, it's what finally killed Jacob—the emptiness of it."

"I got some friends," I said, "a son I care enough about to want to keep him from fucking up hard; I got a show I put on when I feel like it; so far I've picked every lock they've put up in front of me; and there's days I'm driving down the road singing some old song, the sun warming me, and every face I see looks like the Judgment's come down on it hard. I want to yell out at them, 'Listen up, fuck heads, just move a little one way or the other and you're free.' I don't, though, 'cause if I do they'll have me picked up as a public nuisance. And I ain't never wanted to be nobody's savior."

"Except Jesse's," she said.

"I guess," I answered. "But he's my son. And, anyway, there's some folks matter more than others. I'll put myself out for my son, Meg, and my friends, but you see me doing something for the sake of mankind, you can have them haul me off."

" 'Who begins in behalf of mankind,' " she quotes, " 'too often ends as chief of his own police.' "

"Ol' Jake," I said. "He knew."

"I knew you'd remember," she said. "But 'too often' isn't always. And that tendency results from arrogance, not love."

"That kind of love is arrogance," I said. " 'My love will change the world.' What's more arrogant than that?"

"We don't say that," she said. "We simply say, 'I love.' Because of everything. In spite of everything. 'I love.' "

"And why do you need God?"

"He gives love form," she said.

I looked around the room. "Where's them damn birds when I need them?"

Her smile flickered in the candlelight. "You said it would be all right here. Remember? 'You ought not talk about God except when it's dark and you're locked in your room.' "

"Or when you're trying to raise money."

"Oh, I've mastered that," she said. "I even have old freebooters coming to pay their respects."

"I don't know," Mason Sloate said. "It ain't what I expected."

We were sitting at the end of the pier, sharing a bottle of whiskey and watching the moonlight silver the slough. "I thought they'd run us off. You know, be standing on the beach with their faces all twisted up in fury and their Bibles bristling in their hands while we stood at the back of the boat, trolling speed, laughing and slinging empty bottles at them." He shook his head, hangdog, and spat in the slough.

We'd been there a couple of weeks—me, the whole time, Mason, off and on. Twice, for three days each week, he'd gone back to Flamingo and done his guide work. But he seemed to be losing what interest he had in that line.

"Well," I said, "they may turn on us yet. A voice could sweep in through the mangroves and say, 'Smite my enemies.' And I reckon we'd be the ones."

"No," he said. "It ain't that way here. You know that better than me. They just keep letting you be till you want to be something else. Something better." I handed him the bottle. He held it in front of his face like he was reading the label. "This here, for instance, is the first bottle I've drunk on all day long."

"Not thinking of quitting, are you?"

"Not thinking about it at all," he said. "That's what's strange. Used to be on my mind constant unless I was drunk enough to be satisfied. About a year ago I got unzippered drunk and beached a boatload of corporation fishermen. Passed out at the wheel, by God, and peeled the bottom right off that motherfucker. Coral reef. I hadn't been in them waters more than five, six thousand times. But, shit, I come to, you could've told me I'd run aground on Guam, I wouldn't've known. Coast Guard had to come get us." He took a drink, laughed. "You should've seen it. Reef full of shit-scared insurance executives. Coral cutting their feet to shreds. Little, sunburned, spindly legged, fat bastards squeaking out threats that they was going to file suit. I told them, 'You win the suit, you get that boat.' Hell, I don't know. Good day, all in all, I guess. Watching them fucks and listening to them whine. Boatload of beauticians would've handled theirselves better. Damn near cost me my license, though. Had just enough money to bribe my way out." He passed the bottle back. "Scared me too. Hell, captain gets to where he drinks so bad he can't keep his ship on the ocean, he's in some trouble."

"So you thought about giving up the liquor then?"

"Yeah. Sure did. Or cutting way down anyway. I told myself, 'Mason, ever' time you want a drink, ask yourself do you really need it.' "

"That one don't work, does it?"

"No. Sure don't. Answer'd always come back yes. Over and over till I got tired of giving the same answer to the same damn-fool question. Ain't much test, that."

"But it's different here?"

"Yeah," he said. "Sure is. Scares me some. Maybe I'm just tired; I don't know."

He shook his head again, spat again, took the bottle back.

"Seen the light here on Calvary Key, have you?"

"Well, not the big one," he said. "Just a kind of dim glow ever' so often when I cock my head right."

"Might be the onset of the DT's," I said.

"Sure might," he agreed. "But I've never knowed them to come on so calm."

"Got the Paradise DT's."

"Well, that's what they are, I might just take them."

I gave him the bottle back.

"How about you, Sam? Found you a home?"

"Found me a resting place," I said. "I ain't sure I can get my mind around home."

"You and Magdalen, there, that's a good thing."

"No love like first love," I said.

"I'd never've believed it. What I heard of her, you know. The virgin queen of the Christian Quim, all that. And then when we first come ashore, why, I thought, That's it, they going to cut us adrift. But they take you up to see her, and it all changes, just turns right over. She greets you like . . . Christ, I don't know what. I mean, she was wanting you. I could see it soon as I saw her."

"I must've caught her coming into heat," I said.

He looked at me, damn near appalled. "It ain't right to even talk like that," he said. "A fine woman, damn fine. It was me, I wouldn't ever leave. Wouldn't even think about it. No sir, taking up religion's a small price to pay for a woman like that."

"I take up religion, I won't be the man she likes."

He thought that over. "Probably take her awhile to notice," he said. "Then she'd probably find it in herself to forgive." He took another drink, handed me the bottle, thought again, and disagreed with himself. "No," he said. "You're right. Thing for you to do is keep looking tempted by it. Religion, I mean. Let her all the time be seeing hope. But don't ever give plumb in to her. Yeah, that'd be the boat to ride, all right. Woman like that, keep her interest up, you got to keep showing her a soul it'd be a life's work to save."

"And you?" I said. "You found you a woman here?"

"No. Everybody's pretty well paired up." He watched me drink. "You know," he said, "times I thought there ought to be a religion founded on this right here. Sitting on the end of a dock, drinking good whiskey with somebody you can talk to, the moonlight slipping across the slough."

"Trouble is," I said, "we'd be drinking up the sacrament eight, ten hours at a stretch."

I passed him the bottle again. "Well," he went on, "you a believer, ain't nothing wrong with being real religious. Comes way closer to the blood, that's sure, than them grapes do. Got some snap to it."

"Amen to that, Brother Sloate."

He stood up and pissed in the water.

"So what *are* your plans, Mason? You really thinking about staying on?"

He zipped up, sat down. "Got me a Cuban woman in Little Havana I'm thinking about bringing. Lives above a fish market on Flagler Street. Isabella, that's her name. She ain't one for the halfway measure, and I'm afraid once I bring her here there won't be no leaving."

"They ain't going to quit making boats, are they?"

"It's not that easy," he said. "I bring her, I'll be intending to stay. That's why I'm having to think."

He drank again. "Be nice if you was staying on," he said. "The rest of them, they been good to me. Tolerant, you know, let me drink, don't say nothing about it, talk to me friendly, all that. But I can feel the tolerance. One way it's good. I've damn near quit the drink, speaking relative. But I'd hate to give it up cold. Come the right clear evening I'd miss the easy talk, the good bottle. Maybe just on a Saturday night. I bet you even the Lord God hisself, all the shit he has to put up with during the week, I bet you even he likes to get a little buzz on come Saturday night."

I took the bottle from him, held it up to the moon. It was half gone.

"What you say, Sam? Think you might stay on two or three months anyway? Help me kind of ease into it? I'll keep the boat. Hymns get to us, we can go for a ride."

"Might," I said. "I don't know. I got things need doing. Tell you the truth, Mason, I'm thinking about seeing if I can talk Magdalen into going back out into the world with me."

"Oh, God," he said. "You ought not try that. That scares the shit out of them."

"Maybe not Magdalen," I said. "Maybe not now."

2 JESSE

"So," he says, his face cocked against a shaft of light, "this is the holy ground, is it?"

A week after Robert Kennedy's assassination my stepfather has come to see me. He wears his roughneck ensemble—new Levi's, handmade alligator boots, a blue cotton work shirt. His sleeves are rolled to his elbows. *Esquire* in the Ozarks.

"It'll do," I say. I look at him, try not to think of the disorder he brings with him, so neatly packaged. I turn back to the window, let my eyes go out of focus. For a moment, I make him disappear.

He walks to the window and sits on the sill. The light is broken. I try to stare through him, into the world. But I cannot. Not this morning.

"Nice looking woman down there in the valley," he says. "The one you've been living with."

I give up, let my eyes focus on his face. It carries a patently false, ad man's good cheer. "Did she ask you for my hand?"

He smiles, confident. Confidence—there, in all its meanings, is the great secret behind money. A confidence that approximates faith. A faith that brings assurance. An assurance that drives doubt and doubters before it. Ask and ye shall receive. Believe and ye shall have. All things are justified in the name of the faith. Capitalism and mother church. Greed and sanctimony. Usury and Eucharist. The till rings and rings in the name of God. The Lord giveth and the Lord taketh away, collecting interest, compounded daily. Shall we gather at the Savings and Loan?

"She didn't ask," he tells me, "but I certainly offered my approval. I worry, though. She doesn't seem the type to be a martyr's mistress."

Nimbus. Corona. Halo. The morning sun frames his head. An incongruous sight.

"The musk of the martyr," I say, "is the surest aphrodisiac."

"There must be easier ways. For both parties."

"Depends on the parties," I tell him.

The temple has ceased to be sanctuary. I rise and leave.

He follows, of course. Persistence is another attribute of the confident. As we take the path downward, he talks.

"It'll be Nixon now, won't it? It would've been Kennedy. But from here on, the Democrats will be busy eating their young—or being eaten by them. They won't give it to McCarthy. You can bet the store on that. He broke the rules. And if they did, Johnson would have him assassinated. So it'll be Nixon. Humphrey and Nixon and then just Nixon. He'll probably have J. Edgar Hoover be his vice-president. Him or somebody harder. Somebody who'll make Nixon look reasonable."

I do not respond. The man is but a nuisance. An irritating irrelevance. Unlike my father, who represents a genuine alternative, my stepfather represents only a slick, cynical accommodation. All that endures is money. Rock of ages. It serves him well, requiring nothing but his conscience, a negligible thing, at best.

At the edge of Clear Creek, I remove my clothes. Then I wade to the center of the stream, sit in the rapids. At first I can hear the sound of his voice, but, as I lie back into the current, the rush of water cleanses the air. I can outwait him. That will be easy.

But he will not allow it. I have been in the creek but a moment when he is standing beside me, smiling, naked. A body slim but soft. The light lunch. The brisk ten-minute walk. He sits, puts his hand behind my head, and lifts it out of the current.

"We're going to talk, Son."

"You're going to talk."

"All right. But you sit up and listen. You'll have to hear me out sooner or later. Might as well be done with it."

I sit up. "Go," I say, like the starter for a schoolyard footrace.

He feels behind him for steady ground, then leans back on his hands. "Well," he says, "we'll begin with politics. That's in order, wouldn't you say? The nation still in mourning? The future uncertain? The war raging on?" He pauses, glances at me, nods, continues. "Yes, politics and reality. The role of a conscientious individual in a turbulent society. All that."

He shifts his weight onto his left buttock and removes a rock from beneath the right, which he then lowers back into place. "This year, 1968," he says. "It'll be the end of it, really. The big year, but the end of it, too. King, Kennedy, Johnson. Riots and fires. The young going wild, the old getting desperate. The solid money turning anxious. Yeah, the big year, all right, but the end of it, too. Sure. You know why?"

Another glance, another pause.

"Nixon," he answers. "He knows what everyone else seems to have forgotten. He's got you outnumbered. Most people want to believe the good Lord smiles on America, where all wars are just and everyone who isn't lazy or larcenous makes a good living. So he'll win this election, and then, you know what he'll do? He'll wear you down. A half-million of you can demonstrate against him every day. He won't give a shit. It's what he wants, in fact. He needs you. He'll just call you a few names, order more bombs, give Main Street a good look at his persecuted face, and the millions that like him will like him even more. And he'll have you, Son. Because your people are going to get tired of it. You'll quit. None of you have ever worked that hard. Hell, if it hadn't been for all the hippies and Black Panthers, Nixon would still be working for Pepsi-Cola. America needed him."

"Men like that lose the ability to distinguish their ambitions from the nation's needs."

"No question. But sometimes they coincide. And almost anytime the American voter will decide he'd rather have a crook than a crusader. Americans like to think they're idealists, but they're not. Oh, there are exceptions, of course. And this is a time of exceptions. There are probably more idealists loose in the land now than there ever have been. Or, at least, they're more visible. But you're all young, you're arrogant, and you don't have much idea of what you're up against." He slaps at the horsefly biting his shoulder. He looks at his hand, then lets the current wash the blood away. "You want me to tell you what you're up against, Son?"

"It's what I've been waiting for all these years," I say. "The guidance of a cynical stepfather. I was just too shy to ask."

"Well," he says, "I may be wrong sometimes. Hell, I may be wrong as often as not. But what saves me, boy, is that I'm always wrong in the practical way."

"Yes," I say. "You never risk anything but money."

"All right. Have it your way. But money's what you're up against, Son. Big money, little money. Corporate money, wage earners' money. Tight money, risk money, Saturday-night-dive money. All the money there is. The man on the line in Detroit hates you more than the president of General Motors does. Because his money's more vulnerable and he sweats to get it and he doesn't like being told he's a fool for doing it. So, yes, money. That's our idealism. That's what America believes in. And you'll all come back to it. Two years, five years, no more than that. You've all had it, and you'll all want it again. You've just backslid for a while. A temporary lapse of faith. And you're young enough now to let energy get you what you'll need money for later. But you'll be back. That's sure. Back in the great temple of the dollar, boy. Give Nixon one term, and you're done. You'll be hustling for the car, the house, the sound investment. A comfortable living, a secure future. The man who can't be bought is an outsider, a heretic, an infidel. Nobody trusts him. The best he can hope for is to preserve himself, his private, ascetic ideals. To do that he has to move out, find sanctuary, some place like . . . well, like Clear Creek. Because he can't change anything. Not here. The game'll go on, Jesse. Dealing for dollars."

"And you, of course, like it that way."

"Sure. Most of the time I'm the host. And when I'm not, I'm smart enough to know it."

"Let me see if I can summarize all this wisdom. What you're telling me is to either get back in or get well out."

"Yeah. I'm telling you that going to jail to stop the war is like jacking off to protest against women. Nobody cares. It's just one less man they have to fuck with. There are plenty left who'll go along."

"Quite an analogy."

"Well, make up your own. What I'm telling you is that if you go to jail, all you'll be doing is going to jail. It's that simple. The war will go on until the politicians figure out a way to either win it or make it look like they've won it. There's nothing you can do about that. This is a democracy, and you're a minority. The man who says, 'We've been wrong about Vietnam for fourteen years, and I'm going to get our troops, our equipment, and our money out of there the day I'm inaugurated,' is going to lose. This is America, Son, and a voting majority always thinks of their country as a Winner. Capital W. God's people. The chosen land. The City on a Hill. The Nixon people, the Wallace people, the Humphrey people, the Kennedy people, most of all. Hell, nobody believes in dreamland like the Kennedy people. And the McCarthy people, they believe in it, too. The Liberal Arts College of Moralistic Winners. America the beautiful, America the strong, America the good. It's horseshit. You know that. I know that. But there it is. You can either accept it and deal with it—make a living off it like

I do—or you can reject it, live outside of it, the way your friends do here—or, hell, even the way your father does. So, yes, you get in, or you get out. But you don't do both. You can't. Not unless you're just trying to satisfy some perverse need for punishment. Nobody wants you in jail, Jesse. And whatever small hope you have of changing anything lies in that very fact."

"What most provokes people to revolution," I say, "is the arrogance of their oppressors."

He laughs. "There may be a revolution in this country someday, but it won't come from your people. If the Wallace people ever learn to shine their shoes and stop saying 'nigger' in public, America will be theirs. For a while. And that's what you're up against, too, finally. You could spend the rest of your life in jail; they wouldn't care. Make them happy. You'd be like some exotic animal in a zoo—the unregenerate sixties hippie. They'll come by and look in your cell just to remind themselves how much smarter they are."

He waits for a response. After a moment I say, "Well, in such a world a prison cell would seem an honorable place to be."

He sighs, stands, shrugs. "For Christ's sake, Jesse, use your head. It's your heart's only hope."

"And what does it matter to you? You carry your heart in your wallet."

"I love your mother," he says. "I don't want you hurting her."

He wades to shore, gathers his clothes, crosses the stream again, disappears beyond the creek-bank brush.

I lie back, lower my head into the water. It splits the current. I hear water roar, see a splintered sun. Slowly, slowly the rapids wash me clean. I close my eyes, open them. Directly above me now the sun displays itself whole. It is good, I yield. Mind, body, and world are one. Spirit. Flesh. Spirit-flesh.

A moment, an hour, a half-day later, I rise and reenter the world of phenomena. Which, at this moment, seems sound to me. Seems good. Feels good. Is good. Like my father, the carnival existentialist, I can wonder what an assassination half a continent away, what a war half a world away, can have to do with me. I live here. And if I am not doing much good, I am doing no harm.

But it is that very assassination, along with my stepfather's practical analysis of the state of the world, that has led me to this feeling. A sense of the futility of the grand act. A sense of the necessity of starting over, beginning here, remaining here. A sense that in order not to become delusion, hope must have fixed horizons. Oh, I know: Robert Kennedy was a career cold warrior and was one of the dozen or so men most responsible for the American invasion of Vietnam. He did not choose to run for the presidency until after McCarthy had frightened Johnson out of the way. Like any other candidate, he was driven by ambition, the greed for power. And had he lived and been elected, little would have changed, except a few superficialities of style. No, my stepfather is right, he would not have simply, clearly, and on the day of his inauguration ordered the troops home, leaving Vietnam to the Vietnamese, the strongest and most determined of whom are Communists. He would not have allowed himself to be perceived as the kind of man who would decide to lose a war. He was, except in the glamour of his name, like all the others. I know all that, have known all that. But he had come to represent (falsely, I know) a dream of a purer America, a vision of the politician as a practical idealist. And it was that dream, that vision, toward which the true idealist, the uncompromising politician, the obsessed patriot, Sirhan Sirhan, aimed his small, sure weapon. And when Robert Kennedy fell dying, there in the artificial California night, the nature of American hope changed, lost some of its naïveté, drew in on itself, erected sensible barriers. To let another man, a man you do not know, carry your dreams, represent your vision, embody your ideals, issue your orders is the purest kind of folly. We must live where we are. We must love the earth we walk on, the people we share it with. We must worship the particular. We cannot look elsewhere, longing. Truth, like God, is a local thing, homegrown, hand cured.

Is this the avoidance of responsibility? Should we merely tend our gardens and ignore the sound of approaching jackboots? No. For we must remember, too, that great evil always covers itself with the elegant cloak of an ideal, an ideal allowing no exceptions. And we must remember, then, that all life is a local exception. We must recognize that each living thing is the miracle, the source of wonder, the way. And we must know that there are times, times such as these, when, in order to preserve the local, the particular, the various, we must stand our ground against the jackboots of the general, against the armies of the ideal. And, always, we must remind ourselves, even as we stand, that what we would die for is but the simple right to remain peculiar.

3 GLORIA

"Kill what kills you," Manny Munn said. "Anything else is cowardice." He glanced down at us from the driver's seat of his command vehicle, an army jeep he claimed to have stolen from Fort Sill. "Put a sergeant's uniform on, rode the bus in, drove the jeep out."

"Ain't nothing killed me yet, General," Gunner said. "Anything does, though, I'll snuff it quick."

"Laugh," Manny said. "Go ahead. Join the chorus. They'll either ignore us or laugh at us—everybody will—until we've won. We know that. It's another weapon we use. Their condescension gives us time. And truth is patient."

In a meadow between Little Shaman Creek and the foot of Shadow Mountain, we were watching the Rocky Mountain Liberation Army, ROMOLA, go through combat exercises.

"Twenty years," Manny said. A quarter-mile away, a bomb exploded, and an old shack in a small grove of aspen roared into flames. "Maybe twenty-five. But we know we've just begun, and we know we'll win. Meanwhile, we're free."

The Staff of Life Ranch owned this land. Shiva Charlie had bought three hundred twenty acres two years ago, when he decided California was not the new Eden, merely a doomed precursor, and that he and his followers would need a retreat, a refuge on which to await the end and the beginning. He had dispatched one of the most devoted of his disciples, Emmanuel Munn, to oversee the formation and development of the new commune. Manny, however, had taken up arms. Now Shiva Charlie and the Staff of Life were fifteen miles away, meditating beside their tents in a national forest campground.

Manny raised a pair of binoculars to his eyes and watched the fire for a moment. Then he withdrew a police Colt .38 from his quickdraw holster and fired it three times into the air. The exercise had ended. Manny started the jeep and drove briskly toward field headquarters, a family tent shoplifted from J.C. Penney's.

Gunner and I stayed behiind and watched the shack burn. We could see several small figures scurrying around, keeping the fire from spreading into the grove. Gunner laughed. "Grab the vittles, Lady Jane," he said, "hide them chillun under your skirts, and clutch the family Bible to your sweet, heaving breast. The goddamn rock 'n' roll boy scouts are rising. And all the world's a-shiver.

We had come to negotiate with Manny Munn. Or that's what we were supposed to be doing—Gunner seemed mainly to be indulging his taste for American exotica. Shiva Charlie had wanted the Staff of Life to wait here until the eve of the end of the world and then climb the mountain for the great gathering of the faithful, but Manny, in his current commando leader incarnation, had no use for mystic peaceniks. Charlie would've just let it be, I think—apocalypse was coming, anyway—if he hadn't been worried that because of their appearance and their open use of dope, the Staff of Life would get busted in the national forest campground at Arapahoe. He didn't want the end of the world to catch him in a Colorado jail.

And he hadn't had any luck when he'd tried to talk to Manny, who had treated him like the neighbor's overindulged child—ignoring him until he had tired of the irritation and then ordering him off the place. When Shiva Charlie had simply sat there, smiling beatifically and saying things like, "Emmanuel, have you forgotten that Little Shaman Creek is sacred?" Manny had given a military nod to the most muscular member of his cadre, who had thrown Charlie over his shoulder, carried him out from under the mess-hall canopy and across the meadow, and dumped him in the sacred creek, which marked the property's edge.

"So Emmanuel the Dreamer turned into Sergeant Slaughter, did he?" Gunner said, after Shiva Charlie told us about the encounter. "Well, Cap'n, it's a lesson. There's a little John Wayne in the best of us."

Shiva Charlie thought that through, then nodded solemnly. "It's the mountains," he declared. "They turn the weak toward weirdness."

"That's the sure enough truth, there, Pandit," Gunner agreed. "When God goes to climbing, there'll be demons on the slopes."

Charlie nodded again, this one stiff, formal, almost a bow. "Too often the gentle forget that," he said. "Emmanuel was a pilgrim. This saddens me."

"Road forked on him, Guatama. Ain't no predicting that."

Charlie squatted, looked gently up at Gunner. "Will you talk with him? You were once a soldier."

Gunner made a clicking sound, winked, and grinned. "You bet, Mr. Charlie. Ol' Gunner'd been going anyway—just to see the show. And I'll tell Manny, soldier to soldier, he keeps fucking around up here, somebody's apt to send an army after him. Or a posse, anyway. And where'll he be then, poor bastard?"

That night, as we sat around the guerrilla mess table eating jackrabbit stew and hardtack, Gunner, posing as a Yippie organizer, told Manny the movement needed both the Staff of Life and ROMOLA. "We going to make Chicago a circus, man, we need all kinds of acts. This ring here, Mr. and Mrs. America, doing their number for truth and justice, we got the Rocky Mountain Liberation Army; to your left we got the Aggrieved Ghetto Burn and Loot Minority Blues Band; and yonder, wearing tie-dyed dhotis and rhinestone diffraction disks and bringing you all the magic and laughter of the cosmos, is Shiva Charlie Muldrow and the Astral Projection Good Time, Rag Time Bebop Whores."

"We're not part of the circus," Manny said.

"Ought not be making purges till you win the war, man."

"Whimsy is not revolution."

"Revolution needs a starting place, place to show itself. Chicago, Comrade Emmanuel, going to be our Boston Tea Party."

"It'll be a TV spectacle, interrupted for deodorant ads."

"TV's there, man, use it. Why not? Don't be a fucking puritan, Cap'n Mather. Plymouth rock's a shrine for the dead. Anyway, what you going to do? Whup the world with this eight-man army?"

"We are a cadre, a beginning, a spark."

"And Chicago, Sparky, that's going to be the fuse. You can hunker down out here with your hands cupped around your little match, always having to worry over whether it's going to come up a rain, or you can go to Chicago, Jack, and set something afire. Purity's a pretty thing, Nikolai, but it's a bauble you got to keep boxed up."

"Shiva Charlie'd be in our way here."

"Christ, man, this is anarchy. Everybody doing his own thing. You torch the buildings, Shiva Charlie plays the celestial fiddle. Everybody got a part to play."

We were under a canvas canopy in a grove at the foot of Fiddler's Hat, a shoulder to Shadow Mountain. Manny's tired eight-man army seemed impervious to the discussion. Their attention focused on the stew, which they spooned up methodically, as if eating were but another tactical necessity. It may, however, have simply been the food. The jackrabbit was old, tough, stringy. The broth tasted of salt and rust, the hardtack of sweat and mold. Moths flailed against lantern globes. A cool wind soughed through aspen and spruce. Little Shaman Creek hummed its night song. No one had spoken but Gunner and the general.

"I'll consider it," Manny said.

I thought he had just tired of the discussion. But two days later everybody was there.

4 MALEDON

Time glided by, full sail in an easy wind. I had my birds and my woman. Sometimes of a morning I'd go out fishing with Mason. Sometimes of an evening I'd sit on the end of the pier with him and share a bottle. Sundays there was church, but it was mostly singing, old hymns and folk songs. Magdalen's voice had lost nothing of its beauty and had gained something in power. Its sound, by itself, was almost enough to make a man believe. Some of the hymns were a little grim and blood-drenched for my taste, but its the sound and not the sense that draws most of us anyway. And I'd get a kick out of ol' Mason, lifelong whiskey drifter, sitting beside me there on the pew and bellowing out "Love Lifted Me." Of course, I sang right along too, keeping the chords tuned, honing up the memory. Down here, anywhere south of Cincinnati and east of Tucumcari, you never knew when being able to sing a verse or two of something like "Amazing Grace" might be just the thing to save your old rogue ass.

It was at one of those Sunday morning services that I first saw Isabella Atienza, Mason's Little Havana love. And not just her, but her parents too. Salvador Atienza, short and round, wore a tight, sharkskin suit, iridescent loafers, slicked his hair back from a receding hairline, trimmed his mustache into a dandy's thin line, and walked with his upper body cocked back a notch—if his legs hadn't been so insubstantial, the walk might've passed for a swagger. He looked lecherous, gluttonous, and crooked—like, say, the president of Honduras or Nicaragua, like he could've walked into the White House at noon and come out at one with several hundred million dollars, a Marine honor guard, a dozen fighter planes, and a brace of new women.

Luisa Atienza was a solid woman with good bones. She had her rich, graying hair back in a bun and wore a white cotton dress whose simple elegance was the precise opposite of Salvador's flamboyance. And she had smart eyes. On their dark surfaces you could see both the gentle laughter and the steady calculation. Behind that was something else—a hint of the great tolerance that comes from an understanding deep enough to know how much can't be understood. Hell, I'm going overboard. I didn't know the woman then, don't know her now. But I liked her right off, just looking at her. And I enjoyed sitting there in Magdalen's church wondering just what kind of predicament life must've forced Luisa into so as to make her choose to settle in with a man like Salvador.

And Isabella? Well, Christ Almighty, she was beauty itself. Looked the way her mother must've looked twenty-five years earlier. The kind of woman that can just walk into a room and change all the talk, who would be, whenever there was a man around, the focus of awed desire. You know, the kind that, by doing nothing more than look like she did, made you suspect you weren't quite worthy.

Mason introduced me to them after the service, when we were all standing out on the crushed coral under the tropical sun. Magdalen offered to take Salvador and Luisa on a tour of the settlement, and they agreed, Salvador making a little bow and remarking on Magdalen's beauty and generosity. He looks like a porn king, I thought. Then it came to me how often right-wing dictators resembled pornographers, pimps, peep-show entrepreneurs. Yeah, the right-wingers looked like sex merchants and the left-wingers looked like the James Gang.

"So what you think of her?" Mason asked, bringing me back.

Isabella stood there beside him. I looked her over good, my right eye cocked. "Don't see how you could beat this, Mason," I said. "But, then, a man has to wonder about *her* judgment."

Isabella laughed. And, Christ, for a minute, I thought about seeing if I couldn't talk him into trading her for Magdalen.

"I love boats," she said. "And Mason, he has one."

"Well," I said to Mason, "the sea's full of ships these days. You better keep her belowdecks."

"And you," said Isabella, "Sam, you are the man of Miss Magdalen?"

"Yeah. For the time being anyway," I said. "There ain't no end to wonders, is there?"

And she laughed again, Mason's beauty did, a laugh that carried the sound of real amusement. I decided that she knew just what she was doing, that she was aware that the absurdity of it, of her and Mason, me and Magdalen, men and women, was what made it sometimes worth doing.

I said, "So, you young'uns thinking about putting the ring 'round one another?"

Mason said they were. Her parents were checking out their daughter's possible future home.

Apparently they approved—or, at least, didn't disapprove strongly enough to tie their daughter down till the heat wore off. A week after the Atienzas's inspection of Calvary Key, I went with Mason to Miami and Little Havana. In the apartment above the fish market, they made wedding arrangements—Salvador the Venal, Luisa the Wise, Isabella the Beauty, and Mason the Smitten. Bless them all, I thought. Then I decided it was moving time again.

So I found me a phone booth in front of a bean house and called Tom Guy Hughes. It was a Saturday, but he was in his office. He lived there.

"Sam," he said. "How's the great world?"

"I believe Columbus was right," I told him. "It keeps a man going in circles."

"Illusion," he said. "Pure illusion. You keep going, you'll fall right off the edge."

"I suspect as much. It's why I always keep a parachute within reach."

"There'll be nothing to land on."

"Yeah. But a man might as well savor the fall."

He laughed. "I'm not sure an entirely reasonable man could like living as much as you do."

"So much for reason," I said. "But speaking of reasonable men, how's Saint Jesse the Martyr?"

"He's been to jail, got out, wants to go in again. Nobody wanted him in, the first time. Nobody wants to put him in again. But he's determined to make a stand. He won't be able to live with himself if he doesn't."

"Where is he now?"

"The Clear Creek Commune. You know, J.D. Hannah's place? J.D. tells me Jesse may be in love."

"Well, then," I said. "There may be hope yet. Times pussy can do wonders for a boy."

"I wouldn't know," he said.

"Aw, pardon me, Tom Guy. I got no manners. Keep forgetting you're queer."

But he had too much business on his mind to be taking time out to take offense. "Listen, Sam," he said, "I've been hearing rumors around the courthouse. Matter of fact, they've been making sure I hear them. The sheriff has been working with the feds, trying to make a case against Howdy Hardison." He paused. "The draft board burglary. You remember?"

A black guy in a pimp's costume and a young, hard-looking Cuban girl wearing hose, hot pants, and high heels stopped behind me and started arguing. I turned around and looked at them. The girl talked in Spanish. The pimp just kept thinking of new adjectives to go with 'bitch.' He was good at it. Finally, he noticed me and said, "How's the fucking phone, dude?" Then he winked and swaggered away. The girl fingered her hair out of her face, gave me a long look, and then hurried after him.

"I remember," I told Tom Guy. "But it didn't seem much like Howdy's kind of work."

"What does Howdy's work look like?"

"My guess is he'd've had to break in. Man that did that job knew how to pick locks."

"Howdy used to stand on the sidewalk in front of the office for hours almost every day. He hasn't been there since the burglary."

"Don't mean shit."

"It may be enough to let them bring him in on suspicion."

"They do, you're his lawyer."

"And you?"

"I'm paying. And I'm coming back."

"Fine," he said. "And one other thing. I don't think they want to bring Howdy to trial. That would embarrass them. They'll just use him."

I waited, thought. "Jesse?" I said. "He wasn't even in town."

"Oh, not the burglary, Sam. There's no one fool enough to think Jesse had anything to do with that. Jesse would've made sure he was caught. He would've been making a point."

"I see," I said. And just then I did. I saw it all.

"They don't want to bring either of them to trial, Sam. Howdy or Jesse. They want to arrange it so that everyone will have to go along with the deal. Right now, they're busy setting up the deal."

Neither of us spoke for a few seconds. Then he said, "You have to remember that in the law nothing matters except appearances."

"Well," I said, "you go tell Homer Cantwell I got a suit to fit ever' occasion."

"And do you?"

"I got one for this one," I said. "And you tell Howdy not to give them the time of day. I'm coming."

"Oh, I think Howdy's well beyond intimidation. I almost hope he makes them try him."

"No," I said. "You want to be damned careful about playing the bastards on their home court."

After that, I called Alvy Wolfe to tell him I'd be needing a new set of papers and tags for a red '68 Dodge van with such-and-such a serial number. Then I rang up Conrad Villines and warned him that in a week or so I'd be dropping by to check on the quality of education at Harrold Smith College. "I think maybe I'll have Miss Magdalen Abbey with me." I couldn't resist saying it. You know how love is.

"Lured her from the Lord, have you, you asshole?"

"Aw, come on, Conrad," I said. "You know the Lord's always been way over here with me."

"I suspect you've been misjudging your company."

* * *

The Sunday after that, Mason and Isabella got married on Calvary Key. Magdalen performed the ceremony. That was what the negotiations in Little Havana had finally come down to. Salvador had wanted a big Roman Catholic bash on his home ground, where he could make a show of his fishmonger money. Luisa, Mason, and Isabella had talked him into this, a simple ceremony at the place Mason could feel he'd finally come home to.

Everybody wore white, including Salvador, who came in a seersucker suit and a planter's hat and who kept throwing calculating looks into the surrounding bush like he was gathering material for negotiations with the United Fruit Company. Magdalen said the few necessary words, gave the couple God's blessing, and welcomed them into the community. Then we all sang an old English hymn—"Morning Has Broken" I believe it was—and Mason and Isabella disappeared into the thatched house the Calvary Key Christians had built them.

That night, in the hammock with Magdalen, I said, "I'm going to have to go for a while. I stay, I might end up like Mason."

"What's wrong with that?" But she asked the question calmly. She had prepared herself for this.

"Nothing. For Mason. But he's tired, and I ain't."

She said, "I'll never understand you, Sam." Then she caught herself. In candlelight I saw her smile—sad, resigned, beautiful. "Oh, of course I understand you. I just wish I didn't."

"Everything here works too good," I said. "It's not that I'm the one doubter. Everybody's been good about that. And it gives me a role—me and the birds. It's just that . . . I don't know . . ."

"You like it out in the world, don't you, Sam? Corrupt as it is?"

"Yeah," I admitted. "It's a comedian's paradise."

"The corrupted world . . ." She said it like the phrase itself might contain the threat.

"Come with me, Meg," I said. "Come see Jesse. He only heard the stories. He needs to see the flesh."

She said nothing. I could feel her breathe. Gentle, regular. The interior order. If she came, she would be forsaking an earned content.

"Just for a while," I said. "Look on it as missionary work. For me. For Jesse. We ain't all suited for Calvary Key, but maybe you can bring some of us partway there. It's worth a week or two anyway, ain't it?"

Still the silence. I could feel her considering the temptation.

"Is he at all like you, Sam?"

"Jesse?" I said. "I don't know. He's stubborn."

Silence again. But this time I waited. I'd said my say.

"I *would* like to see him," she said. "Sam Maledon's saintly son. How strange." She turned onto her side, laid her head on my shoulder. We choose between love and freedom, and we live with the knowledge of what we've lost. But we have to choose.

"For a while," she said. And I wished I'd taught one bird to shout hallelujah. "I believe in fairness. You've visited my life. I'll visit yours. But I have to come back. I *live* here. You have to promise not to ask more than I can give."

"We'll just do the one show, Meg. The one last road show."

5 JESSE

I am in the cliff-top temple. I have completed my exercises, my meditation. The sun has risen. I sit and feel my five senses returning. There is a sound outside, on the path. Footsteps. The door opens. J.D. Hannah enters.

"They came and got Howdy this morning," he says.

I turn, look, stand. Our world's confusion returns. "Who?" I ask. "The sheriff?"

"Him, his brother, some low-level FBI fuck, and Tom Guy Hughes."

"Tom Guy?"

"Took it on himself, I guess. What difference does it make? He's the best there is here."

We stare at each other, questions between us.

"Howdy's fine," J.D. says. "I think he was wanting this. You ought to understand that."

"I'll go to the jail with you," I say. "I can get bail money if we need it."

"No. I'm going in. But you're not. They took Howdy's brother, remember. So this is his deal, man. Let him play it out. There's nothing you can do but fuck it up."

"I'm going," I say. "You can let me ride with you, or I can find another way. But I'm going. I have some part in this."

"Well," he concedes, "maybe just enough to get a ride. No more. We do it Howdy's way. You understand?"

I say I do.

"As fine a piece of work as you ever saw," Tom Guy tells us. We are in his office, an old storefront on Main Street, two blocks from the jail. Tom Guy has been with Howdy all morning, and now he is showing us Howdy's confession. "Our friend, Mr. Hardison, proudly takes credit for everything."

J.D. and I read it. A solemn, notarized form. Howdy's words have been typed onto the white space. Then there are signatures, his, the sheriff's, the deputy's, Tom Guy's, and a seal. The typed words give name, date, time, and method. They say Howdy worked alone, picked the lock, loaded the contents of the office into a borrowed flatbed hay truck, and drove away.

"Yes," Tom Guy says, "an ingenious, transparent lie." He walks to a file cabinet, opens a drawer, removes a bottle of whiskey, two glasses, and a pewter coffee mug. "A drink, gentlemen? In honor of Howdy's trump card."

"Are you sure?" J.D. asks.

Tom Guy pours casual shots into the two glasses and the mug. "Oh, yes. It was the perfect maneuver, gentlemen. Mr. Hardison has been thinking while in yon dark forest. I take no credit." He leans forward, taps the confession twice with an index finger. "It's pure Howdy, lovers of the bar. What we have before us is a clear case of a young man so aggrieved by the loss of a dear brother in a bad war that he has confessed to a crime he *wishes* he had committed. But he couldn't have done it: He knows nothing whatever about the picking of locks, he never learned to drive, and it is inconceivable that this burglary was committed by a lone man. In addition to all that, there is strong circumstantial evidence suggesting that Mr. Hardison was engaged elsewhere during most of the night of the robbery." He lifts the pewter mug, poised for a toast. "So, dear brothers in the fraternity of justice, today a deaf-mute redneck has brought our local bureau of the establishment to its virginal knees." He is beaming. "My friends, here's to democracy."

J.D. takes a glass, says, "I do believe I'll drink to that."

They drink.

Tom Guy lowers his mug, looks at me, cocks an eyebrow. "And you, my mystic client?"

"I don't drink. But I am in favor of democracy." I smile. His good humor is contagious.

"In drink, good fellow, *is* democracy."

"Then why," I ask, joining the spirit, "do so many bars have bouncers?"

"Because, dear soldier of conscience, at any given moment a common laborer is likely to be inspired to rise and strike the owner." He turns to J.D. "Another drink?"

J.D. shakes his head, rises. "We got a commune to tend to, counselor."

"Yes, yes. Return to the earth, O ye idealists. All is well here in Jeffersonia."

When I stand, he says, his tone now serious, "Howdy will be free within forty-eight hours, Jesse. He caught them by surprise, and they botched it. And this case has nothing to do with you. Remember that. No matter what the sheriff or one of his friends may tell you in the next day or so. They thought they'd get your father through Howdy and you through him. And they've misjudged everybody, except maybe you. They've fucked up, and Howdy's called their bluff. And that's that. This part of it's over."

6 GLORIA

After two days of what Shiva Charlie and the Colorado press had begun calling the gathering of the tribes, Manny Munn was reveling in the role of guerrilla commander. He gave interviews to both underground and straight journalists. He gave the latter hooded. One evening, knowing that an interview with Manny would be a featured spot on the Denver TV news, Gunner and I left Aura with the parents of the precocious little girl she'd played with all day, dressed up straight, and drove to the American Legion bar in Boulder, where we watched him on the set above the register. A soulful woman with Marianne Faithfull eyes asked the obvious questions. Manny, wearing his hood, his fatigues, his bandolier, and holding an M60 across his lap, did his best to sound like a Rocky Mountain Che Guevara while looking like a hangman who sought both anonymity and celebrity.

"Woo-eee! What we got here, baby love? The Grand Fucking Imperial Wizard of the Rockies."

"Well, he's made it now," I said. "Mission accomplished. He's been on TV."

"Got to make the networks, Miss Luxemburg. Man ain't nothing till ol' Walter puts his stamp on him."

"We tried nonviolence," Manny told the woman. "It doesn't work. Not here, not now. I don't like violence, but it's the only way. Fidel proved that. And Mao and Lenin and Ho. George Washington and the Panthers. You have to kill what kills you."

"Got him that one line down good, ain't he?" Gunner said.

"We're through marching for the man," Manny said. "We're marching at him."

"And what," the woman wondered, "do you plan to replace the establishment with?"

"A socialist workers' paradise." The Abbie Hoffman noun modified by the Karl Marx adjectives.

"You got to work, my man, it ain't Paradise," Gunner said. "Motherfuckers never learn that, do they?"

"Do you truly believe you pose a serious threat to the most powerful nation in history?" the woman asked. "Isn't this just another publicity stunt?"

"No," Manny said. "This is a declaration of war."

The bartender, bringing Gunner another beer, said, "Damned hills are full of them. I bet you a dump truck against a doorknob that hooded bastard talking about a workers' paradise hasn't hit an honest lick in his life."

Gunner nodded, poured the beer into his tall, tapered glass. "Yeah," he agreed. "I know him. He used to tend bar for the VFWs."

The bartender, a big man with a hard, round stomach, pushed his face toward Gunner. "What's with you? You need trouble, drink somewhere else."

Gunner sat up straight, tilted his head back and to one side, displayed two docile palms, and flashed his hypocrite's grin. "Just talking shit, man. Just another Tom from Nam talking shit, Loo-ten-it. Don't mean nothing. You want to frag me with a Article 15, Mr. Charlie, I go back to humping them boonies titi time, leading them Zippo raids."

"Jesus," the bartender said, his tenseness turning into resignation. "Viet-fucking-nam."

I tried to get Gunner to leave after that, but he kept drinking, beer after beer, as if performing ritual penance. The others in the bar stayed away from us. The bartender served him without saying anything, just brought the bottles and ignored us. Then, finally, Gunner turned on his stool and faced the room. There were maybe a dozen of what looked to be World War II and Korean War veterans quietly drinking beers and shots. Gunner started to say something to them, but stopped, stared a moment longer, and turned to me. "Shit, baby, these poor fucks done seen it too. Didn't quite recognize it, maybe. Or been working to forget it. But they seen it. Too many longtimers out with the Lurps, love, when everybody ought to've stood home."

"You ready to go?"

"Yeah. Take ol' Gunner on to wherever it is ol' Gunner got to go on to."

* * *

But he was fine the next day. Or, anyway, back to what, in his case, passed for normal. Back to playing the salty veteran with the third eye for Shiva Charlie and all the others.

All the others, the myriad others. The counterculture fair. All of *us*, I suppose, though I found it hard to think of myself as one of the group, which had become so large I couldn't feel myself to have a role in it, to be essential, or even useful, to it. It had been easy back in Arkansas, where we were few, the small cult of the radical. But here were all kinds of cults, transient, overlapping, interchangeable, contradictory, and, I began to feel, irrelevant. The MOBE—the National Mobilization Committee to End the War in Vietnam—and the SDS, Yippies and hippies, Malibu maharishis and Harley thugs, street thieves and tree freaks, Zen acolytes and switchblade queens, apprentice demolitionists and ersatz Gandhis, Taoist drifters and schizoid guerrillas, Betty Friedan feminists and motorcycle molls, cooled-out heads and burned-out veins, fantasy cowboys and allegory Indians. The whole freak show, the psychedelic circus, the anarchists' bureaucracy. They talked of McLuhan and Marcuse, Norman O. Brown and Bronislaw Malinowski, Jung and Reich and Laing, Ginsberg and Dylan and Blake, Eldridge and Huey and Rap, Martin and Malcolm and Marcus Garvey, Ho and Che and Danny the Red, the Stones, the Dead and the Airplane, hash and smack and Owsley.

And, all the while, surrounded by murmured conspiracy theories and joyous utopian scenarios, Manny Munn drilled his troops. Rifle cleaning, target shooting, demolition seminars, hand-to-hand combat exercises, climbing, rappeling, crawling, digging. After evening mess the soldiers studied Che's *Guerrilla Warfare*, *The Special Forces Combatant Manual*, and *The Marine Corps Field Manual on Physical Security*. An hour or so before lights out, Manny would give them a written test on the day's assigned material:

"List the body's vulnerable points," which are:

1. Eyes
2. Nose
3. Adam's apple
4. Temple
5. Nape of the neck
6. Upper lip
7. Ears

8. Chin
9. Groin
10. Solar plexus
11. Spine
12. Kidneys
13. Collarbone
14. Floating ribs
15. Stomach
16. Armpit
17. Instep
18. Knee
19. Shoulder
20. Elbow
21. Wrist
22. Fingers

"Describe the most effective blow an unarmed man can deliver to each of these points."

"Twenty-three, brain," Gunner said to me. "The most effective way an unarmed man can destroy his enemy's brain is to seduce that enemy into making lists consisting of twenty or more items."

After appearing on Denver TV, Manny continued to wear his regulation fatigues, but he did begin to sport a red bandanna around his neck and, on his head, a black beret with the ROMOLA insignia. And he bought a mimeograph machine and a portable generator, so that each morning he could issue, often still wet from the machine, copies of statements; polemics; instructions (including illustrations) for making Molotov cocktails, homemade grenades, book traps, gate traps, road traps, ballpoint pen traps; directions for tamping explosives, formulas for calculating the amount of a particular explosive necessary to do a particular job (for instance, if A is the area in square inches of a steel beam to cut with explosives and P is the number of pounds of TNT, then $P = \frac{3}{8} A$). And on and on. Manny working hard to convince us he was serious, that he knew what he was doing, that he was certified in the algebra of death.

But, however he perceived himself, however he wanted to be perceived, the rest of them, the rest of us, saw him as but another aspect of theater, another act by another mime troupe. After a few days even Shiva Charlie, who had at first worried that Manny's martial exhibitions might cause Colorado, come Saturday night, to forfeit its exemption from doom, began to view Manny and his troops as just another little something else, a comic diversion, one more wild strand in freedom's random fabric. When you are awaiting the end of the world, the collision of the asteroid Icarus with the planet Earth, what are a few rifle shots, a few booby-trap explosions? A kind of preparation, perhaps. A whiling away of the last hours. Nothing more.

As far as I could tell, no one other than Shiva Charlie took the end of the world, the oncoming Icarus, seriously. For most it was just another excuse for a party. For some it was a way of making the point that there was no point. The world was a gloriously absurd place that had been fucked up by men who took their roles in it too seriously. It could be put right again only through instinct, whimsy, caprice, anarchic celebration. Even Apocalypse can be cause for celebration. The end is but a concept, an illusion. Laugh at it. Celebrate it. Set it to music. All that lives is holy. All that dies becomes part of the dance floor.

But I think Shiva Charlie did believe. It was his vision, his scene. He had the kind of childish, energetic faith that embraced everything. To him contradiction was but cosmic proof of the gods' good humor. The end would come Saturday night for all but the chosen—and maybe for the chosen, too. And if it didn't? Wow, here's Sunday morning. Let's believe in that. It's all illusion anyway. Believe in that. Believe in everything. Believe in nothing. You are a child of the universe; orphan, where are your parents?

That attitude made him the perfect organizer for the Shadow Mountain End of the World Convocation of the Tribes. He had handbills printed up and pasted on every lamppost and window in downtown Boulder. He gave interview after interview to the underground press. He was quoted by the straight press, who treated him as an amusing human interest story. "Do you actually believe the world will end Saturday night?" a Boulder newsman asked him. "Yes," he said. "But, fear not. Everything will go into syndication." He was one of the panelists at a University of Colorado forum on eschatology. "Celebrate everything," he said. "Embrace the earth even as it disintegrates. The shards of the old will be the molecules of the new." And then he climbed onto the table and danced like Zorba.

People came from everywhere. Vanloads, busloads, groups of hitchhikers. By Friday night only the center of the meadow beneath

Shadow Mountain, that part Manny had reserved for his irregulars, remained relatively free of camping pilgrims.

That night, lying in my sleeping bag between Gunner and Aura, between my impotent soldier and my neglected daughter, I became so depressed I considered leaving, going home, enrolling in law school, becoming a legal aid attorney. I don't know. Anything. Something. Something useful. Marrying a decent, corduroy liberal. Being a mother to Aura. Sending tithes to Cesar Chavez, the NAACP, Ralph Nader. Living the conventional, responsible life. A little home, a little garden, a little conscience.

I said as much to Gunner.

"What you got to learn, love, is just because it don't matter don't mean it ain't worth doing."

"This, you mean? Shiva Charlie, Manny the Great, the Be-In for the End of the World? Or that? The other? The straight life?"

"Either one," he said.

"Thanks."

He bent his elbow, rested his head on his palm. "Feeling lost, flower child?"

"I just told you that."

"And you looking to ol' Gunner for answers? Shee-it, baby, if that ain't one for the hoo-raw boys."

"Yes. I must've lost my head."

I closed my eyes then, but I could feel him looking at me. From behind me, on the other side of Little Shaman Creek, I could hear music. A guitar. A male, southern voice singing Dylan's "Song to Woody." I listened to it, straining to make out the words. Alternately it made me homesick and gave me wanderlust. Could Woody have longed for Okemah and the life the wind blew away, Dylan for Hibbing and the lost Bob Zimmerman?

Gunner said, "I ain't been much good to you, lady, probably ain't going to be. All I can tell you is, you don't keep going, you going to stop. But, then, times stopping might be just the thing."

"Gunner," I said, "let's zip the bags together. I want you to hold me."

"You bet, love. Why, even ol' Gunner can do that. Yes, ma'am. Even ol' Gunner."

We lay there together for what must've been more than an hour, saying nothing, hearing scattered bars of music, the wind, the water.

Out on the meadow there were campfires, lanterns, candles, the red tips of joints. But Gunner had laid our camp away from the others, and I couldn't hear conversations. I knew the men from MOBE and the Yippie organizers would be moving from fire to fire, talking of Chicago, trying to persuade people to come to that festival at the end of August. And many of them would go, I knew. Many of them would go anywhere there were many others. And why shouldn't they? I asked my self-righteous self. What else is there to do? Chicago is where they will give us Hubert, Lyndon's little puppy. So, why shouldn't we all be there protesting, mocking? All that was wrong with me, I thought, was that I was tired. Yes. And wanted clarity. I wanted it all to be clear. I suppose that, too, came from being tired.

Sex could have substituted for clarity then, for the night. Could even, maybe, have been clarity. But I made no effort to seduce Gunner, who was being gentle, compassionate, brotherly. Why try again, fail again? No wonder I feel alienated, I thought; I've come to the freaks' ball on the arms of a eunuch. In the middle of the Revolution of Ecstasy, I've somehow allowed myself to be quartered in the ascetics' tent. There was a flyer the Yippies were handing out. It invited everyone to come to Chicago, stay in Lincoln Park, VOTE PIG IN '68, and it outlined the seventeen basic points of the Yippie party platform. Point fifteen was: "We believe that people should fuck all the time, any time, whomever they wish. This is not a program to demand but a simple recognition of the reality around us." Well, not my reality. Not now. No, my mate here on the gay fields of Gomorrah was strong, dark, tough, smart, and, at least with me, impotent.

But, even though I wanted to, I felt no anger toward him, and only a little resentment. Mostly, it was just resignation, a feeling that, whatever I had wanted, hoped for, I belonged here now, zipped into these bags with Gunner Grant. I didn't think it would last. It might end. It might change. Passion might come to him. Who could know? The one certain thing was that soon he would change or I would split. So, I told myself, it will get better. One way or the other. Ignore this insecurity, this dislocation. You're young, and you're only beginning to learn to adjust to freedom. This man here, having seen death, having caused it, is both stronger and more pessimistic than you. That's only natural. Forgive him. But don't let him hold you back.

I know, I know. Lassitude is too easily disguised as patience and then seen as an aspect of maturity. But if that's what I did, it got me through the night. And I needed sleep.

In the morning, while Gunner cooked bacon, eggs, and campfire coffee, Aura sat beside me on the ground, her head resting on my breast.

"On the morning of the last day," Gunner said, "the infidels ate fried pig fat and cold-storage eggs. They washed it down with coffee made from beans harvested by slave laborers. Nor were they moved by the sun, which rose in glory over the great mountains of America."

He forked the bacon and eggs onto paper plates. All of us, even Aura, drank the strong coffee.

"What will happen today, Mom?" Aura asked, grimacing at the heat and taste of the coffee she had just sipped.

"I don't know," I answered. "But the world won't end. Tomorrow we'll go somewhere else."

"Where? Will we go back home?"

"No, Aura," I told her. "Not that home."

But, as it turned out, I was wrong.

Midmorning, Shiva Charlie, white-robed and playing a flute, began circling the meadow. People broke camp and followed him. By the time he was finishing his third circle, all of us were behind him, holding hands, dancing, singing, playing guitars, harmonicas, and horns, ringing bells, banging pans, buckets, and tambourines.

We crossed Little Shaman Creek and found the path we would follow to Fiddler's Hat and up Shadow Mountain. We stopped there and waited while Charlie made a short speech about our "pilgrimage to the sky." Toward the end of it, he started sounding like a southern Baptist preacher. "Be strong in your faith. Rejoice in the certainty that the last day shall be the first." He raised his arms, displayed hieratic palms. "We go upward, then, one by one, two by two, tribe by tribe. Believers all, we ascend into the mystery." He raised his face to the heavens then, and when he lowered it he was smiling, as if another piece of the answer had been delivered to him. "And a little child shall lead us," he said. "Aura, come here."

She looked at me, her eyes a question wanting yes for an answer. Gunner said, "What the hell? It might be fun."

Shiva Charlie knelt, took her hands in his, and said, "Here is the path. Lead us along it. When you are tired, rest. And then so shall we all."

"Okay," Aura said, and started up the trail.

Shiva Charlie stopped her. "The flute," he said. He held it out to her.

"I can't play that."

Charlie smiled again, knelt again. "Put your mouth here, like this. And move your fingers over the holes like this."

She took it, tried. No sound emerged. Then a high note. Then a lower one.

"It's your music," Shiva Charlie said. "Lead on, child."

She did, experimenting happily with the flute. Charlie walked immediately behind her, humming, singing, occasionally making odd, clucking sounds. Gunner and I walked just behind him. Frequently, especially at first, Aura turned around to let me see delight on her face.

We climbed the path for four hours, following it to Fiddler's Hat, across the plateau, and, finally, to the rounded crest of Shadow Mountain. Aura, consumed by the joy of leadership, never stopped.

Every half hour or so we passed one of Manny Munn's guerrillas standing guard beside the path. Each of them wore green fatigues, a black beret, and a red bandanna. They had both Sam Browne belts and bandoliers, and carried, in sheathes and holsters, knives and pistols. As we wandered by in standard hippie disorder, they stood at attention, submachine guns across their chests.

From the mountaintop we could see how the long file had scattered. People were clustered together in small groups. Some sat beside the path smoking joints, some had left the path and were gathering mountain wildflowers, some, far behind, were resting on Fiddler's Hat.

Shiva Charlie, facing west, assumed the lotus position on the peak of Shadow Mountain. The rest of us formed ragged, semicircular rows in front of him. We shared nuts and dried fruit. Aura stood beside me, looking around at the throng she had led up the mountain, feeling proud of how much she had outdistanced so many of them by.

At first her delight pleased me. A good, simple thing. But, watching her as she explored the mountaintop, as she talked with the people who had followed her, as she basked in the favor of the benevolent Shiva Charlie Muldrow, I thought how seldom this had happened, how rarely my naturally ebullient daughter had been really happy this summer. Oh, there had been moments. There had, the last few days, been other children for her to play with, enter collective fantasies with. Once—the night Gunner and I had gone to the Boulder VFW to watch Manny on TV and had left her with her playmate and that girl's parents—she had had a happy evening fantasizing with adults. The parents were drop-outs from the psychology department at Berkeley and were engaged in an effort to become children again. Aura had liked them. They had, they told me, spent the evening sitting around a campfire fabricating tales about a world ruled by children, a world in which skepticism was criminal and the goal of all rehabilitation, all therapy, all social programs was the restoration of innocence.

"Aura was great," Johnny Bliss, as the former psychologist now called himself, had said. "But children always are, aren't they? The instinctive spontaneity, the inherent goodness, the innate openness." He had taken me in his arms then and given me an open-mouthed kiss. "The unguarded expression of emotion," he continued. "All the things we adults are programmed to repress. Western education conditions anal-retentives. We must save our children so that they can save us. Since the day she was born, Kali has been re-educating Anita and I—since before that, really, well before that. The instant of Kali's conception was the instant of our rebirth. We began shedding our inhibitions like old lendings." He had stopped and offered me his smile.

"You seem uptight," Anita had said. She had come to my side, taken my hand, showed me her eager, innocent eyes. "We can help you. It's so easy, so natural."

Ordinarily, I would have either fucked them or told them to fuck themselves, but that night I had merely told them I was tired. They had nodded sympathetically, condescendingly, and I had taken Aura and myself back to Gunner, who, after I'd told him about it the next morning, had said, "Oh, it's easy, love. They all done decided to look inside, explore the inner space, Jim. And what they see when they look in there, man, is Swami Manyfingers' Massage Parlor."

But Aura had obviously enjoyed the evening with them, the would-be children and the child, their parent. So they had given her more than I had. I was losing faith in both hip whimsy and revolutionary commitment. But all that was left was uncertainty, confusion. And Gunner. Who had simplified everything by believing in nothing. I had wanted to make Aura a child of the revolution. But she had become a bored, summertime vagrant. I had wanted to show her, teach her, commitment, sacrifice, radical love. We would find the way together, I had thought. How to live for the cause. How to be both a revolutionary and a dancer.

No, the truth is, I hadn't thought at all. I had merely wished. I had simply hoped that someone—Christ, anyone—would recognize the revolutionary in me and accept me into the cadre. Comrade Gloria, Comrade Aura. Do you play the electric guitar? Well, here's a tambourine, a kazoo. Have a hit of Owsley, baby. Somebody start the strobes. I feel like fucking somebody—how about you? Wow, baby, you blow my mind. How about this? Ever took it there? This is fucking religious. We get through, we'll go picket something. Everybody'll be there. We'll score some mushrooms. That your little girl? She can come too. Kids, wow, you know, they really know where it's at.

So here we were, Aura and I, part of the mountaintop gallery for Shiva Charlie Muldrow's end-of-the-world gig.

I said it out loud to Gunner. "We're irrelevant. All of us are just fucking irrelevant."

"Well, love," he said. "Thank God for that. If any of this mattered, babe, we'd really be fucking up."

"I'd like to take that chance," I said.

I got up, went to Aura, took her hand, and together we explored the slope, showing one another colorful rocks, talking to other children, experimenting with her flute. We walked down again to where the flowers grew, began picking them, exchanged bouquets.

"Hallie used to give me a flower every morning," Aura said.

Hallie, maid and mother. The rich little white girl's one hope. "Yes," I said. "When I was a little girl, she did that for me, too."

"Momma," she said. Wide, homesick eyes. "Sometimes I miss Hallie. Grandma and Grandpa, too."

I knelt, my knees on broken stone. I took her in my arms. "I know," I said. "I know. But it'll get better, darling. It'll get better. Mother's just finding her way."

And I held her until she didn't want to be held anymore.

It was evening when we climbed back to the top of the mountain. Shiva Charlie was leading the crowd in the chanting of "Om."

"Been going on a good hour, seems like," Gunner said. "Vocabulary building."

Shiva Charlie kept chanting until well past dark. By then most everyone else had given that up and gotten stoned. The sky had clouded over, and there was lightning in the west. Gunner decided to walk down the western slope and see if he could find a place that would both shelter us from the coming rain and allow us to watch the storm. "Got to keep an eye on the incoming."

Aura and I sat together quietly, listening to Shiva Charlie's "Om's" and watching the sky. She asked whether the comet was causing the lightning, and I told her it was just lightning.

"Won't it strike Charlie?"

"Jesus," I said. "It might."

I was trying to decide whether to warn Shiva Charlie, who was here, after all, to greet the end of the world, when the rain came and the lightning, absurdly, began to strike all around, but far below us. Whatever doubts Charlie might have had earlier were now surely gone. For that moment we did seem to be on a protected peak. Backlit by storm light, Charlie looked enchanted, wild, holy. Though we couldn't hear him now, we could see that he was still chanting.

Gunner, drenched, came running back to us. "Let's get out of here," he said. "She don't need to see the mahatma get blowed off his perch."

I took Aura's hand, and we began following Gunner through the crowd, most of which was still sitting, stoned, and perhaps stunned, in the downpour. Then I heard Shiva Charlie scream, and I glanced back. He had stood up and was clapping his hands behind his head. He yelled again. "Dance! Dance!" Then the shout was lost in a clap of thunder, and a bolt of lightning struck the mountainside below and behind him. Charlie began dancing a Hare Kirshna jig round and round the peak. A moment later others were doing it, too. People joined hands, and the communal dance embraced the mountain like a windblown spiral.

Just as we passed through the circle, lightning flashed behind us, and the valley to our east—Shiva Charlie's valley, Manny Munn's valley—started exploding. We stopped, turned, watched. The chanting and dancing ceased. Then resumed, frenetic. There were several more simultaneous explosions in the valley, then, after some seconds, three more. Then there was darkness. Then more explosions. But these happened one at a time and seemed to be climbing the path up the mountain.

I had Aura in my arms. "What's happening?" I asked Gunner.

"It's God blowing claymores at the mule deer," he said.

The explosions, each separated now from the next by maybe thirty seconds and five hundred yards, ascended Fiddler's Hat and then stopped. I noticed then that the rain had ceased. The storm had moved eastward. Shiva Charlie, his voice suddenly clear again, seemed to have been given the power of tongues. Glossolalia, loud and clear and indecipherable. The Hindu Holy Roller. His dancers joined hands again. The spiral turned again, each member of the chain singing or chanting in his own language. The hippie day of Pentecost.

I realized I was laughing.

I set Aura down, assuring her that everything was all right now. The storm had passed, the mines had exploded. She wanted to know what had happened. Gunner answered her. "Maybe Shiva Charlie and Manny worked it out together so that both of them got to show their muscle. Or it could've been that the lightning detonated all of Manny's little traps. Who knows? Soldiering's a loose art." A voice just behind us said, "Could've been me."

I turned around. I'd recognized the voice, but in the darkness I couldn't make out his face. When Gunner stepped toward him, Jimmy hit him with something, and Gunner fell. I think it was a piece of metal, a length of pipe or a tire tool, something like that, because of the way it sounded and the way it reflected glints of the little light there was.

Screaming, I leaped at Jimmy. His fist hit my forehead, and I fell to his side and rolled. The rolling seemed to last a long time, and the thought that I would go off a precipice panicked me. But finally, I stopped rolling, and, then, bruised and bleeding, scrambled back up the mountain.

Shiva Charlie and the end-of-the-world tribes were still dancing and babbling. Gunner still lay where he had fallen. I knelt, rolled him over, and saw that he was breathing.

Then I ran down the mountain. But I never saw them. Jimmy Song had done what he'd come to do, what he'd been paid to do. He had kidnapped my daughter.

7 MALEDON

We made it an easy trip, a honeymoon tour of the Deep South. Florida, Georgia, Alabama, Mississippi. We slept in motels, stayed in the van, camped out in parks. We walked on city sidewalks, sat on benches beneath the Confederate soldier in town squares, followed highways and back roads headed generally east and a little north. The heat was brutal, the air was charged with change and the fear of change. Magdalen and I knew we were traveling a world, watching a way of life, that was ending. I had no strong opinions about that. It was just people moving to town, really, changing from cheap labor on the farm to cheap labor in the factory, a little more money and a little less ground to stand on. And, of course, the boys that ran things were going to have to figure a new way of shitting on the niggers. But they would: that's what they were in business for. Few years, I might have to change my act, put a little uptown sheen on it, but that would be easy enough. Anyway, when they all got huddled up in the cities, there'd be more room in between clusters for the men that drove the side roads. That was fine with me. It wasn't that way with Magdalen, though. Now and then it'd all come together and make her sad. I don't mean she went plumb fool over it. She had the sense to know there never had been any good ol' days down here. But she did think that there had been the basis for a good life—small towns and farms, dirt-road communities and backwoods villages, barn dances and corn shuckings, front-porch sing-alongs and dinner on the grounds. Get rid of the racism, she figured, and keep everything else pretty much the same, and you might have a world you could live in. The way it looked now, though, everything was going to be replaced by an organized, standardized greed. And Mobile would be just like Milwaukee, except for the weather.

"Well," I told her, "they apt to make joining up, signing over, look a lot better than it used to. We've just got to keep reminding ourselves it's our lives they want. And we don't get but one apiece."

She thought I was being oversimple. And I thought the same of her. But we got along just fine. She could live in my world, for a while at least, and I could live in hers. All either of us needed was some leeway.

We finally got to West Memphis, where I bought me some new papers from Alvy Wolfe. And then, at the North Little Rock warehouse, I traded the papers and Billy Don's two-hundred-dollar red Dodge van for a black '64 three-quarter-ton pickup with a camper shell over the bed. After that, we drove up to Conrad Villines's little brown home in the wildwood, where I traded him the camper for my ol' Hangman's van.

Even though I'd warned him, Conrad was more than a little surprised to see Magdalen.

"Hell, Conrad," I said. "You know how it is. Love conquers all."

He hugged her, then held her at arm's length and looked her up and down. He said, "I thought that once a woman got away from ol' Sam, she'd stay away."

"Some of us never learn," Magdalen said.

Well, if you look at it that way, Conrad never learned either. We spent the night at his cabin, next morning he hired a man to take care of the place, and we headed west toward Blue Mountain and Clear Creek and the Winslow dump.

We stopped first in Blue Mountain, hoping to find Tom Guy Hughes, but he was out somewhere, so I drove across the bridge to Fort Smith, bought a couple of half-gallons of Four Roses at Boog's Package, drove back to Blue Mountain, got some crackers and Viennas at the Piggly Wiggly, and headed on up the road.

It was late afternoon when we got to the dump. Vestal Truax and a pair of black mongrels were having themselves a nap on a mattress he'd rescued and rolled out in the shade of the persimmon trees that lined the far edge of the landfill. Vestal, sleeping on his back, was making loud, irregular groaning noises. He had his face covered with an opened, thoroughly fingered copy of *Caper.* I gave him a nudge, and we waited while he took his time waking up.

"By God, Vestal," I said. "Them damn dogs done took leave of their senses. They could get heartworms off a mattress like that."

"They're test animals," he said. "Whatever kills them, I don't eat. Or sleep on."

"Well," I said, "it's worked so far."

Then he took notice of Conrad and Magdalen. Me and him and Conrad had been drunk together several times, so he knew Conrad better than he did Magdalen. But it was her he spoke to. "God Almighty," he said. "I was beginning to doubt you'd ever come back to me."

A true follower of the sweet Jesus, she hugged him. It must've tested her faith.

You could see pleasure make its way up Vestal's begrimed face. "You boys can go on," he said to Conrad and me. "Be a nice walk through that gap yonder. Take them damn dogs with you. Me and the little lady here, we got some tenderness to share."

"Aw, now, Vestal," I said, "this here's my woman you're messing with."

He let his head twitch a little to one side. "Well, then, surely you didn't come all the way up here without bringing a spare for me."

"Ain't no spares no more, Vestal. All the extras have started taking to one another."

His neck went slack, and his chin fell down on his chest. Then he gave his head a half-shake, pulled his gaze up again, and said, "A man works day and night and tries to keep up with things by reading the latest periodicals in his spare time, and, come the dark days, he tells hisself, Well, things can't get no worse, and then you drive up with news like this."

He looked me square in the eyes, and I gave him the laugh he'd earned. "No cause for laughing," he said. "It's the Judgment come down on me. I took to drink, and the good Lord, why, he's commenced turning the whole world to shit just to spite me." He turned to Magdalen. "I think that was a little heavy-handed of him, don't you?"

He walked past us, heading uphill toward his trailer. I was enjoying the show he liked to put on. So was Conrad. Magdalen, I'm sure, didn't yet know quite what to make of him. "Odd, ain't it," I said to her, "what one little turn in show business can do to a man's life?"

Vestal stopped and looked back. "Well, come on, goddamn it. Surely you brought me some Roses. If the Big Judge his-own-self is set on marking up the world on account of my drinking, like I suspect, well, I'm going to sink all you sonsabitches."

He trudged on up the hill. The dogs limped after him.

Magdalen said, "I'm sure you know what you're doing, Sam. But I can't keep from wondering what he has to do with Jesse."

"Aw, love, I thought everybody knew. Vestal, there, he's the man that keeps the county records."

Villines laughed, and we followed ol' Vestal up the raw hill to his home.

8 JESSE

So, my father returns. And, as though in proof of something—his power to reorder lives, perhaps—has brought Magdalen Abbey with him.

They find me meditating in the cliff-top temple. I have only begun—it is perhaps an hour after sunrise—but it has been good. It is one of the few mornings when I have almost immediately transcended consciousness. During the last few days, I have, with Margaret Salter's help, rediscovered peace. I am prepared for whatever the government might choose to do to me, but I am also content to wait. I have made a statement, committed myself irrevocably to a course. Now, while the government stalls and threatens, I will make another statement. They can carry me away, lock me up, but until they do I will be content to live in this good place with that good woman.

So, enter my father, intent on change.

Even in my trance, I feel the force of him when he enters the room. An energy distinctly his. He comes in behind me. I do not see him. But I know it is he before he speaks.

"By God, Son, you can shut her down now. All your prayers have done been answered." Then a laugh, void of malice. Pure energy. Delight. His, of course. Not mine. He is drawing me away from mine.

Without turning to see him, I say, "Father." And hear the word as if it were new, its attachment to meaning as yet tentative, probationary.

Then the voice of a woman, whose energy I had not yet felt, says, softly, "Sam, wait outside with me."

"Hell, Meg," he says, "ol' Jesse's a good working-class boy. He knows to get his chores done by sunup."

And then I know who she is. Though I have never met her and

though he has seldom spoken of her to me, he has said enough. I have heard enough to know.

I turn.

She is lovely. Her grace seems to bless everything around her. She smiles. I see understanding in her face. I tell her, "I'm glad you came. I'm glad he found you."

I stand, walk toward them. Then she and I, a step apart, look at one another. "So you're Jesse," she says, smiling again. She takes the step, embraces me. "Who would've thought he could've had such a son?"

"Or such a woman," I say, returning the embrace. His two women, I think, this one and my mother, neither of whom could have seemed the kind to choose him. My mother, a woman who needed security, and Magdalen Abbey, a woman who needed purpose. And he, my father, who thought security a trap, purpose a joke.

"Good to see the pair of you hitting it off like this," he says. " 'Cause I figure we'll be doing a right smart of traveling together, next few weeks."

Magdalen and I step away from each other. I look at him. "I'm staying here. I've done what I need to do."

"Hell, Son, we got to go to Chicago."

"Chicago."

"Patriotic duty. Why, we can't let our party nominate a man like Hubert Humphrey without standing up for ourselves. This here's a democracy. We got to make our voice heard. I'm all for McCarthy. How about you?"

Because his tone is one of broad mockery and because I know he believes nothing of what he has said, I assume he is joking. But, an hour later, in Margaret's cabin, I am having to come to terms with the fact that he has already organized the trip. Conrad Villines will go. And Magdalen Abbey. J.D. Hannah is thinking about it. Margaret has decided to join them.

"Why?"

"It sounds like fun," she answers. I can almost hear a shrug in her voice. "I need to get away. As long as we don't take it seriously, it can't do us any harm."

"To go, to participate without taking any of it seriously, is pure mockery."

"Maybe it needs to be mocked, Jesse. Everything. Them and us. Let's go laugh at everything. The politics of farce."

"The war isn't funny."

"If enough of us laugh at it, it will end."

"That'll never happen. They'll grant a few laughter deferments and keep right on drafting the millions of poor bastards they've drilled the laughter out of."

"Well, then. We're back where we started, aren't we? Let's just go for the hell of it. We can't do any harm, and it'll be fun. Simple as that. And, besides, twenty years from now everybody our age in America will be saying, 'I was there. The Democratic National Convention, Chicago, 1968.' We might as well be telling the truth. When I'm asked what I did during these times, I can honestly say I danced in the street while the Democratic party committed suicide."

"You'll get Nixon," I say, frustrated. "He'll be dancing with you."

"You must be getting desperate," she says. "This is an incarnation I haven't seen before. Jesse, the practical politician." She smiles at me then, takes my hand in hers. "But I can play the politician, too. Watch." She releases my hand, rises, backs away from me, and, pedantic, says, "You see, don't you, that at this particular moment in history it is the Democratic party that is, because of its pretensions, vulnerable to us. Simple revolutionary logic, then, requires us to attack them first. The Republicans, on the other hand, have no pretensions. They are clearly what they are—servants of money. But when they nominate Nixon, they will become vulnerable. He's a man who trusts nothing, not even money, except the cash he can carry in his own pocket. Give him four years, and he will destroy his own party. Nothing will be required of us except patience. Establishment politics at its simplest and coldest, comrade: Give them what they think they want; then be patient while they suffer."

She has been charmed by my father. The happy, arrogant air of mockery. How quickly he works. In only a couple of hours he has changed everything. No, be accurate. In only a couple of hours he has temporarily changed the surface of life at Clear Creek.

All of it because of me, to get me to follow him to Chicago, where he hopes something will happen to cause me to choose to resist authority in his way—to take up the life of the alias. I know all that. Therefore I resist. But what is especially irritating—and he would have known this—is that the idea itself tempts me. I want to go. Yes. I want to go. If it had been my idea—or J.D.'s or Margaret's or anyone's except his—I would have accepted it eagerly. So I am merely being stubborn.

And, I tell myself, I have gone his way before (to Little Rock, to Hannibal) and managed, when the time came, to do what I had to do in the way I had to do it. I can do it again.

Margaret sits beside me. This time I take her hand. "All right," I agree. "We'll go. I can't will the world to end at the mouth of Clear Creek, can I?"

"Not until after Chicago," she says.

9 GLORIA

By the time we were able to do anything, Jimmy had a half-day's start on us. He had, of course, taken the Continental. My father would have received a BankAmericard bill by now; he would've ordered the car either brought to him or returned to Hertz. If the bill were too high, he'd have just bought the car. It's all simple if you have enough money and no conscience.

I was sure just how it had worked and why. After seeing Aura with me at Mount Tamalpais, Jimmy had called my father and made a deal: Aura for cash. Otherwise, Jimmy wouldn't've bothered. Otherwise, I was nothing to him; Aura was nothing to him. He did everything for money. And no one but my father would've paid for this.

Gunner and I bought a '65 Mustang in Boulder. It was a special deal for veterans, a hundred dollars down and low monthly payments. I forget just what the payments were. Neither of us planned to make them. I put up the hundred, and Gunner agreed to risk his credit rating. Shiva Charlie, pleased that he had saved the world from Icarus but visibly disappointed that we—especially Gunner—were leaving him, saw us off and wished us well. "Perhaps we will meet again when we are younger," he said. Then he om-ed us out of sight.

We didn't hurry. Jimmy had the start on us, and I knew where he was going. If he had driven hard—and he probably had—he was over halfway there already. My father had won this round, and right now he would be carefully rigging the next one. I wasn't even quite sure why I wanted to go to Wilder Junction. I wouldn't be getting Aura back, probably wouldn't even be allowed to see her. My father would've gotten an injunction against me and hired a guard for her. I had no plan—for myself, for my daughter, for my father, for anything. I was confused. All I knew was that if I didn't do something, I'd stay confused. So I'd go home and start again, even if it made no sense. But there was no rush. We could drive slowly, stop for a night. I needed time to think.

"Best way to get her back," Gunner said in the Oklahoma City motel room, "is lay low and stay gone. Let it go for a while. Couple months, maybe. No calls, no visits, no word, no sign. Lull them. Let them go lax again. Then, come September, maybe October, you just ride in quiet one last time and haul your little girl away."

"Maybe I'll find out where Jimmy went," I said. "Chasing him may not make much sense, but it'll be something to do."

"By God, woman, there it is," he said. "Makes plumb sense to ol' Gunner." His right eye was black and closed, and that side of his face was swollen. "I love revenge," he said. "It's so fucking simple."

When we drove into Wilder Junction early the next evening, I was dressed like a Radcliffe woman applying for work at corporate headquarters, and Gunner, in seersucker, looked like he might be a social worker or maybe a volunteer canvassing for McCarthy—bruised and rumpled, but a man trying to give respectability another shot.

My father had hired a guard to stand at the door of the plantation house. I knew him—Joe Fred Shondell. Burly, small-eyed, about forty. He'd been the football coach at Fairview until integration. Then, a point of honor, he'd quit and started making his living as a bouncer, a strike-buster, a private guard—this thug for hire. The kind of man who helps keep America strong.

"Well, look what's coming here now," he said when we had walked to within a few feet of him. "I believe it's the homecoming queen slinking back for her crown. Lord knows how I hate to be the one to tell you, but it's done been passed on, sweetness."

"I need to see my father," I said.

"He's sure been expecting you," he said. "Fact is, he figured you'd be here way before now. That's why he hired me, you see, wanted me to deliver a message for him. He don't want to see you, don't even want you on the grounds. Got nothing to say that ain't already clear. Don't want you here, don't want you coming back. You don't go right quick here of your own accord, I'm authorized to run you off. Lots of folks don't much cater to it, but it's my line of work. Suits me, you know."

"Yeah," Gunner said. "But I don't think you up to the job this time, are you, puss gut?"

Joe Fred, his hand on the nightstick attached to his belt, hesitated, sizing Gunner up. Then he said, "You better be getting gone, bub. Else that other side of your face going to be all swole up too."

"I'm going into that big house there behind you," Gunner said. "And tomorrow morning you going to be looking for new work. You can't ride this one, cowboy. You in the wrong chute."

He took a couple of steps toward Joe Fred, who jerked the nightstick out of its sheath and swung. Gunner blocked with a forearm and, almost in the same motion, hit him hard in the stomach. Joe Fred bent over, gagging. Gunner stepped back and kicked him flush in the face. Joe Fred flew backward, in a half-somersault, onto the ground. Out. "Well, there went reason, love," Gunner said. "But it never had much hope anyway, did it?"

He bent over Joe Fred, who was bleeding from the mouth and nose, took the pistol from his holster, picked up the nightstick, and threw them both on the roof of the house. Then he rolled Joe Fred onto his side. I walked to the door and rang the bell.

Hallie answered it. She looked at Joe Fred, at Gunner, at me, then shook her head resignedly and let us in. "All of you set on making everything worse," she said. "Nobody got patience for nobody else."

We followed her into the den, which my father, martini beside him, commanded from a high-backed leather easy chair. "Joe Fred needed work," he told us calmly. "I shouldn't be so sentimental. It always hurts everyone involved."

Hallie went into the kitchen.

On the wall to our right, above the sofa, were the framed family photographs. Dozens of them. Old patriarchs. Bridal portraits. Group shots of children. Gunner walked over, leaned across the sofa, and began studying them.

"Bad taste, I'm told," my father said. "Too many of them. No particular pattern. Very 'country' of me. But I'm attached to them. Can't help it. History doesn't often arrange itself into a sensible pattern. That big one on the far right there? That's my daughter when she graduated from high school. Not too long ago. Who would've ever thought?"

First I went through the motions. "I believe you have my daughter," I said.

He took the martini from the reading table, sipped, set it back, let his head go limp against the chair back, closed his eyes. "Your daughter; my ward," he said.

I walked over beside Gunner, who was still studying the photographs, and sat on the couch.

"Some sort of visiting rights might not be entirely out of the question," he said. "You'd have to go to chancery court, naturally, and convince the judge—Audit Kincaid, you remember him?—that you'd pose no serious threat to the child's welfare. You'd have to demonstrate some sense of responsibility—get some kind of job, establish a residence, that sort of thing. Not much really. You behave yourself until Thanksgiving, say, and there's a fair chance the court would let you see her. Supervised visits, probably, the first few times. Maybe you could see her here for an hour or so. Or, if that didn't seem appropriate, we could arrange a visit at the welfare office. The court can't be too careful, can it? Judge Kincaid certainly doesn't want to have to worry about checking that little girl's arms for needle tracks."

"He used to be your lawyer, didn't he? Audit Kincaid?"

"Years ago," he said. He sipped at the martini again. "The company's lawyer, not mine. And not for long. Not much lawyer, really. Far better judge."

"Yes," I said. "Now all he has to do is remember to decide in favor of the party with the most money."

"Not a bad system, all things considered," my father said. "Encourages initiative in the poorer classes. Rewards those most responsible for the preservation of order. Oh, I'm sure Audit didn't think it through. Just has good instincts."

It was his way of torturing me, I knew. Playing the urbane conservative. Showing me how safe his world was from mine. He was prepared to accept any accusation I might make against him and his and then coldly nod it away as if, behind everything, there were a vast, incontrovertible system of logic I was simply not mature enough, not realistic enough, to see. He knew just how deeply it irritated me, this particular pretense that the system was, if not fair, resolutely logical and that he and his kind, the ones who ran it, America, had done nothing more devious than recognize the logic and adjust to it. If the system rewarded those with money, then get some money.

"I'd like to see her now," I said. "Just to make sure she's not hurt."

"Hurt?" he said. "After all you put her through, a thousand-mile ride home should seem relatively safe."

"I want to see her. She is my daughter."

"A mother's love. So very touching. How could I have forgotten?" Again, the martini. "But surely you don't think I'm fool enough to have her here, do you?"

Gunner turned around, sat beside me on the sofa. "You like it here, Jack?" he asked my father.

Who, raising his eyebrows, hesitated but an instant. "It's where I began. It works well enough."

Gunner nodded. "Yes sir. Scab labor. Low taxes. Seldom any ice on the roads. That's Arkansas. Shit, you got her knocked, don't you, Jack? You don't mind me calling you Jack?"

My father said nothing.

"Good. Now, you take a man like me, Roy Don, come back from Nam, Sam, stained neck deep in gook blood. Why, short of going back and sinking all the way under, he can't hardly find hisself fit work. But I just got to thinking here, if there's one thing I can do, it's drive a damn truck. You know how things sometimes just flash clear for you out of nowhere. Like the Lord hisself just up and hollered out, 'Yo, bub! This a-way.' Well, Bob, that's the way it was for me not a minute ago. God's truth now, Jim, all bullshitting aside—I can take one of them big trucks of yours right down into the heart of hell and come back with a tight load of fire. What you say, my man?"

My father looked from him to me. "God, incredible as it seems, They keep getting worse. Who is this asshole?"

" 'Fore we get to that," Gunner said, "I was wondering couldn't I have me one of them gins you're hogging down? I won't spill nothing."

My father, reminding himself, I guessed, to stay in character until the scene had ended, stared at him. Then, "Hallie," he called. And, pointing at his glass, "A drink for Gloria's gentleman." He looked at me again. "After the drink, it's over. My humor only goes so far. When I start feeling fatherly, I remember our last phone conversation. Good therapy."

"Hell, Wayne," Gunner said, "she was safe with me. I'm impotent, you know. I don't tell that to just anybody. But Ol' Blue, goddamn him, he got real down on hisself over in the demilitarized zone. You ever been to war, Willie?"

"This one," my father said to me, "is stark raving mad."

"I take that for a no," Gunner said. "Which is fine. Don't matter. Ain't much can be said for it. Everybody's got to die, might as well do it in clusters. Sometimes the company does them good."

Hallie brought Gunner the drink.

"You the one was watching at the picture window, ma'am, when me and ol' Buford come to blows there in the yard?"

"Yes," she said. "Seem like I have to see everything."

"I was you, I'd let Mr. Jonny there do his own looking. He may not can see. But he ain't never going to learn till he has to look for hisself."

"I was you," she said, "and cared one bit for Miss Gloria, I'd be driving her away now and telling her to be thinking on what it means to be somebody's momma."

"Hallie," my father said, "you go on back and finish supper. I can handle them."

"I don't know, Mr. Jonathan."

When she had reached the door, I said, "Hallie, I was learning. I was. Then he took her away. She's not his; she's mine."

She stopped, turned back, looked at me, looked at my father, then went on into the kitchen. It was white folks' business.

"You ain't going to hire me, are you?" Gunner said to my father. "Always the way it is. Everybody shits on the veteran." He brought the glass to his mouth and swallowed half the martini. Then he turned to me and asked, "Where's your momma, love? Maybe I can reason with her."

"Oh, I'm sure he has her securely locked in her room, with her bottle and her pills."

"Don't matter," Gunner said. "That's the kind of woman I can understand." He took a far more moderate drink of the martini. "What kind of pills?"

"So, is this the plan?" my father asked me. "Bring this man in and see how long I'll sit back and watch him make a fool of himself? Or is he going to babble awhile and then attack me? Torture the information out of me?"

"We were going to do that second thing," Gunner said. "But then I come in and right away I liked you. Took the edge right off. Probably can't do it now."

"Anyway, I can save you the trouble," my father said. Leaning forward, elbows on his knees, as if he were being solicitous, he looked directly at Gunner. "I'll tell you where Aura is. You see, when she arrived here, she was quite upset, sometimes even hysterical." He leaned back. "She'd been through so much, and we weren't sure exactly what to do for her. So Gloria's mother and I decided to seek professional help. Diagnosis, therapy, counseling. You know. We took her to the Child Therapy Center in Little Rock. They'll run some tests, evaluate her, do some counseling. Very thorough, the professionals. Just the thing. Probably be good for any child. After that they'll see her on an out-patient basis. Once a month, once a week. Depends. No visitors now except her grandmother and me. We may drive up for a visit tomorrow evening, if I get through at the office in time. I'll call the center first, of course, and see if they think it's advisable." He folded his hands in his lap and, still looking at Gunner, said, "Well, I guess that's that, isn't it, my man? Finish your drink."

Gunner did, but made no move to leave.

"You prick," I said to my father. "You Goddamn prick. You'd do anything, wouldn't you? One thing's sure, though, whatever happens. When she grows up, she'll hate you as much as I do."

"One takes one's chances."

I stared into his eyes for a moment, then felt tears covering mine and turned away.

"Looks like you got us there, General," Gunner said. "Yes sir, you done picked up that little girl and broke our backs with her. We going to have to wave the white flag on that one sure enough, for the time being. But I was wondering about your man Jimmy Song. Surely you got no need to protect him now—man been using your trucks to haul Mary Jane across the line in, and all. Man ain't doing nobody no good now. Neither side. You done got what you wanted from him, and I expect he gouged you pretty good for it. Might as well tell us which way he went. I owe him a good beating, but I might lose. You never know. Hell, man, we find him, whichever way it turns out, you win."

"I know all about Jimmy Song," my father told him. "I make it my business to know what I need to know. And I realized some time back I needed to make Jimmy Song a project of mine. You see, he had his uses, but he was dangerous. I had no way of knowing when someone would make him a better offer. You see, don't you, boy, the times are ideal for a long-haired mercenary. Jimmy must've been one of the first of you to understand that. He's been drawing back-door money for a long time. And, you're right, he's of no further use to me. In fact, he could cause me trouble. Not much, really. A minor embarrassment, at worst. I've been careful, protected my interests. Still, if I knew where he was, I'd tell you. Because, sure, I couldn't lose." He looked at me then. "This may be the only thing left you and I can agree on, Gloria, but I don't want Jimmy Song to get his hands on Aura again."

"So where is he?"

"I said I didn't know." He cocked his head at a smug angle.

"So what do you know?"

"I'm told he works for the Nixon committee. He's been hired to create disturbances for the Democrats, though you wouldn't think they'd need any help. If you can't find him between now and then, I'd say he'd be in Chicago the last week in August, wouldn't you?"

"Well," Gunner said. "That works out. I'm going to be there anyway. I'm a delegate."

"I'm sure," my father said. "Odd, isn't it, Gloria? How, finally, we'll all be working for the same cause? And Richard Nixon, of all people to be bringing us together. Though, of course, your people won't even know they're working for him, will they?"

I stood, walked out of the den, up the stairs. I went to my mother's room and knocked on the door. After a moment she appeared. She wore a silk robe, loosely tied. Her stiff hair was neat except at the very back of her head, where it stood straight out behind her as if it had been pasted there while she was moving. She was pale and drawn, absolutely haunted.

"Oh, Gloria," she said. "You're back." Her right hand felt her face. "I just wanted you to know I've joined AA. But it's hard. I didn't know it would be this hard."

She seemed completely gone. I didn't know what to do or say. My father hadn't stopped me, so he wanted me to see her. But why? Was it a threat? Or just his cold way of asking me to come home and help? I went to my mother, held her in my arms, and said, "That's good, Mother. I'm glad you joined. I hope it gets easier."

She began crying, then pushed me away, saying, "Your father." I backed up, stood in the hallway for a few seconds, and stared at her. Still silently crying, she reached out and closed the door between us.

"You're killing her," I told my father when I reached the foot of the stairs.

"I don't think so," he said. "You're the one she loved, and you're the one she lost."

PART VII

1 MALEDON

Well, they buried Bobby Kennedy, and the summer slowed down for a while. Oh, the war went on, and the riots, but they slacked off just enough to make you feel that everybody was getting ready to let it all fall down.

Sirhan Sirhan stretched out in his cell and read *The Secret Doctrine* and *At the Feet of the Master*. In London, Scotland Yard arrested James Earl Ray, who was traveling with the Canadian passport of one Ramon George Sneyd. The Patriot Legal Fund of Savannah, Georgia, offered to defend Ray free of charge. And there were other offers. The man who killed King was a hero to many. He'd've made a strong vice-presidential candidate, stealing the Wallace vote, on the Nixon ticket. The Poor People's mule train had trouble getting through Georgia, having to deal with Lester Maddox, the state troopers, and the Humane Society, which didn't like seeing mules dragging a load down the highway—hell, that was nigger work. But the mule train entered Washington on the twenty-fifth of June, a day after the capital police had torn down Resurrection City and the very day Ralph Abernathy was given a twenty-day sentence. Cops arrested poor people by the hundreds—good practice for all concerned, I guess.

Trudeau won his election in Canada, which seemed, I told Jesse, quite a fine country. De Gaulle won his in France, then closed the Sorbonne and evicted the students who had occupied it for over a month. Simple as that. The Russians kept threatening the Czechs with tanks. Fifteen thousand Japanese students demonstrated after a U.S. jet fighter crashed on their campus. Protesting against the Vietnam War, thousands of Australians smashed all the windows of the U.S. Consulate in Melbourne.

In Boston, Dr. Ben Spock and three others got a two-year sentence for conspiring to violate the draft laws. Meanwhile, General Hershey endorsed George Wallace and announced that he'd lined up eighteen thousand three hundred marks for the August call. The marines pulled out of Khe Sanh after weathering a seventy-seven-day siege and losing twenty-five hundred men. Nguyen Van Thieu said there'd be peace in '69—not this year, unfortunately, "but we will see the light at the end of the tunnel next year." Major General Edward G. Lansdale (Retired) sent the White House a secret report, which was leaked to *Newsday*, saying that the Cong, goddamnit, would win any free election in South Vietnam. Ronald Reagan came out in favor of winning the war. Richard Nixon had a secret plan. Hubert Humphrey said that "poor President Johnson gets blamed for more blamed things." Congress passed, and Johnson signed into a law, a bill making the desecration of the flag a federal offense—a thousand-dollar fine or a year in jail or both. And Gaylord Nelson was the only senator to vote against a bill giving the big boys another six billion dollars to blow Vietnam away with.

And me? Well, a man with a career to think of can't afford to lay about too long. So I went back to work. On the Fourth of July we did the Hangman's show as the prelude to the evening performance of the Rodeo of the Ozarks in Springdale. Jesse's new woman, Margaret Salter, played Annie Maledon, the whore, but without near the feeling for it Gloria had. Course, it may never again be played with that kind of feeling. But we did add a voice to the show—Tom Guy Hughes did a little ten-minute spiel as J. Warren Reed, the Fort Smith attorney who defended a hundred thirty-four men charged with murder and lost only two to the gallows—the one man who, day in and day out, beat Judge Parker. Tom Guy took right well to the role.

Jesse wouldn't have anything to do with the show, so J.D. Hannah took the part of the young man who gets to have his say just before being hanged. I dressed it up to suit him, making him a half-breed teacher who traveled the territory saying that Parker was the Antichrist and that the Five Civilized Tribes ought to cease being civilized and return to the holy state of nature. He did it with conviction, and while he spoke his dying words Magdalen was at a piano in the stage-left darkness playing "Shall We Gather at the River?" It went over good, everybody being so sentimental about all the Indians their grandparents killed.

For a while, I thought I'd have to play the Deputy Hugh Harp role myself. I'd done it many a time, and I could do it justice, so to speak. Fact is, it's been a one-man show about as often as not. I have to leave out Annie Maledon, of course, but I can do the rest of them. Still, though, it's always better not to have to. So about a week before time, I went up to the Winslow dump and offered the part to Vestal Truax. I had my doubts about doing it, worrying mostly about the carrying power of Vestal's voice. There was a chance too that he would show up so drunk he'd nod off right in the middle of the son of a bitch. But I could make allowances for that, turn it into part of the show if I had to. But I didn't have to, by God. Soon as I mentioned the idea to him, the old fart started grinning like an arsonist having a smoke on a can of kerosene outside the fireman's ball. And when the time came, he played the role—I mean, claimed the night for himself. He sat in a rocking chair, a drugged dump mongrel at his feet, drank from a pint Mason jar of pure shine, sponged up every few drinks with a Vienna sausage he'd eat from the can he'd lift off the floor to his side, and had his say. The more he drank, the clearer his voice got, until at the end it was all anger wrapped in sadness for the lost world of the lone rider. By the time he was done with them, I could've sold many a man in the crowd before us a sway-backed gelding and a man-sized stretch of Mexican desert. There's still a whole lot of folks that, now and again, want to be free. Of course, it ordinarily doesn't take them more than a ride home and a cup of black coffee to get over it.

Anyway, it went over so good there at the rodeo that we were asked to do it again two weeks later in Muskogee. Some kind of official Indian celebration—by official, I mean the Indians didn't have much to do with it—just politicians wanting votes. But there was beer and barbecue, and Indians enough, I guess, and, what the hell, you do whatever gig you got on whatever ground comes open. The show played well enough that time too—though Vestal, still a little flush from first success, overplayed the role, took to acting, you see, long sweeps of the arm, sudden falls from shout to whisper, and elaborate, high-school Hamlet facial contortions. It occurred to me once to walk out there with the Hangman's long pistol and shoot his dog just to bring him to, but the crowd seemed to be liking it, and I let it go. They knew they were seeing acting, I figured, but they thought that was what they were supposed to see. Still it irks me to watch a man fuck up that way, and when it was over I told Vestal, "Goddamn it, don't play the role, be the man." And I kept on him over the next week or ten days, whatever it was, reminding him that while Uncle Hugh was angry at being part of what destroyed the life he loved, he was also old, fatalistic, and damned sure there wasn't much of anybody left who could fully understand what he was talking about. What he had to give them, he'd give them cold and dry.

"Just say it plain," he said, "and let them take it or leave it. That how you want it?"

"Yeah," I said. "Like you were sitting in the shade on a crate at the dump and finally saying your piece to some dog that had been nosing around in the leavings for years."

"That's what you want," he said, "that's what you get. Me, I got to figuring my fan club was wanting to see me strut some."

"May have," I said. "But then fan clubs're always wrong."

"Depends on what you want out of them," he told me. "I'm in this for the pussy."

"How's it working?"

"Bob Motley's bitch goat was here the other evening eating the labels off canned goods and eyeing me up right coy. But she's all Bob's, you get down to it. And other than that, love's just been a memory and a magazine. Hell, Sam, I been thinking about taking out an ad—Well-hung sanitation engineer seeks casual sex. Offers rustic mountain home with sweeping view. Large groups welcome."

"Tell them you're Jewish and like Mozart. Otherwise, you'll just be drawing road whores."

"Road whores be just fine," he said. "And it ain't a quarter-mile, here to the highway."

And, in Sapulpa, next time we did the show, he was good—almost as fine as he'd been that first night. To show my appreciation, I sent the others back in the van, borrowed J.D.'s pickup, and drove me and Vestal to Fort Smith, where I bought him the love of a Como whore. "The actor's life," he said when he came back to the lobby. "Ain't nothing like it."

"Immoral admirers in every hotel," I agreed.

But I could do nothing to get Jesse to take any part in this. He wouldn't even come and watch the shows. Just pure stubbornness. The kind of resistance that had to be constantly willed. The others loved being in the show, on the stage, in the spotlight, and often in the evenings at Clear Creek it was what we talked about. Laughing at one another, poking light fun at this or that aspect of someone's performance, and wondering sometimes how long you could keep at it before it started pulling back on you.

"Oh, after a while," I told them, "it gets to be like any other job.

Some of your freedom starts leaking out into it. Difference is, though, with this job you always got you a boss you can quit easy on."

"Someone who appreciates the full glory of giving up," Jesse said. He said it hard, irritated, I'm sure, at how gladly his fellow communalists had taken to me and the show.

Magdalen, bless her wonderfully packaged heart, tried taking up for me. "Jesse," she said, "your father is the one man I know who has never given up. It's what's most exasperating about him. He is going to go his way. Always."

"But to go his way, he's had to give up on too much."

He left. Magdalen followed him, it being her Christian duty to keep families together. I shook my head, looked at J.D. Hannah and Margaret Salter. "He's probably right," I told them. "So why don't we all go on down and lock ourselves up in the jail so they'll end the war. Christ, I could've stopped the Korean War if I'd've just thought."

So I pretty much left Jesse to Magdalen, and they seemed to get along—no surprise, both of them being believers and, as believers go, fairly tolerant ones. They took walks together along the creek, sat in that little church on the bluff and watched sunsets, hoed and watered and harvested together in the communal gardens. Sometimes Margaret was with them, often not. There may've been an edge of sex to it, the way there tends to be between any man and any woman, but that was all, I'm sure—the unacknowledged animal attraction. You may not believe me, but I'd've taken it as a sign of Jesse's good health and high spirit if he'd made the hard play for Magdalen. Even if he was just doing it to revenge himself on me. I'm not saying I'd've liked it. I wouldn't've. But I would've understood it and dealt with it. Lust and revenge, I understand those things. It's the desire for the pure, moral heart, the longing for the spotless soul, that stumps me. I can't make any sense out of that whatsoever. It seems way too much like wanting to be dead. You live, you're going to get stained. And, Christ, it's the impurities, or what a man like Jesse sees as impurities, that makes the good laugh possible. It was Satan's one tree that made the orchard. Otherwise, there is no story.

Magdalen grew quite attached to him, the honorable son who wavered between renunciation and affirmation. I figured the problem was that he couldn't tell the two things apart, that he tended toward thinking the best way to affirm life was to renounce it, and that this came from him wanting to make his life an example.

"He sees the contradictions," Magdalen told me. "He knows that to seek to be an example of humility is to cease to be humble. He knows that being nonviolent is not a means of protest but the way to remain human. He knows that the spirit cannot deny the flesh. It's that knowing that makes him indecisive, that makes him matter. You should be proud of him, Sam."

"Hell, I'm here, ain't I?"

"Yes, but you only confuse him. You're older and stronger and surer of yourself. He has to will himself to resist you, and it's hard for him. He respects you, respects the life you live, but he knows you're wrong."

"Wrong?" I said. "It's that simple?"

"Wrong for him. Wrong for most of us."

I thought about it. "Maybe," I said. "But I'm not asking him to give his life over to being a barker for the Hangman's show. I just want him to see that the choice isn't between going to jail and going to war. Hell, Meg, there's a world of ways out there."

"Not for him, there isn't."

"Well, then, goddamn it, it ain't me that's given up on too much."

There was a silence. I could hear the wind behind me making its way through the creek-bank brush.

"Let's not argue," she said. "I'd like to think I understand both of you. At least a little." She hesitated. I looked away. She placed a palm on the back of my hand. "Sam," she said, "I'd like to take him to Calvary Key."

I turned back to her and smiled. "Shit, that was the idea," I said. "They'll never find him there. God's truth is, they don't want to find him. Ought to suit everybody. Far as I'm concerned, we can leave right now."

"Not *we*," she said. "Just Jesse, Margaret, and I. And not for long either. A week, maybe two. He's not going there to hide. We'll be back. We'll go to Chicago. But he wants to have everything clear by then. And to do that he needs to get away from you."

"Aw, well, then, go on," I said. "Hell, who knows? Just that little feel of the road might do all of you some good."

2 JESSE

It is only at the eastern edge of the continent that I can feel, fresh, the power of the old explorer's song, the call to adventure, the beckoning of the vast, the wild, the lure of limitless promise. And it is for me best felt in Florida. Others, I know, feel it elsewhere. The great prairie, the stark mountains, California. But, for me, while the midlands seem most American and the mountains most beautiful, they do not evoke the sense of infinite possibility. And California is not the land of promise, but the land of promise thwarted, the place where the great dream died and new ones have to be daily willed, manufactured. When God was not there, we became desperate hedonists. And, sure, I know, Florida has been ruined. There is now no pristine stretch of beach. All of it is now but a warm place for the young to breed, for the middle-aged to profiteer, for the old to die. Except for parts of the Everglades, we have destroyed the wilderness, bought it cheap, sold it dear. It is perhaps our most depressing state, with its roadside alligator zoos, its ramshackle cities, its exclusive, iron-gated sanctuaries for the rich. It believes, like so much of America, in growth for its own sake, the pure ethic of the cancer cell. But, standing on the beach at Calvary Key, I can hear it yet, in spite of everything, the forgotten call of the lost dream, America.

Somehow it strengthens my desire to go to Chicago. I try to explain it.

"Do you know the story of Álvar Núñez Cabeza de Vaca?" I ask them.

Margaret does not. Magdalen knows only the beginning. So I tell them all of it, tell them of his wondrous journey from Florida to Mexico, the walk from the Gulf of Mexico to the Gulf of California, from the land of the Apalachee, the amazing archers who used bows of oak, six feet long, that none of the Spaniards could even bend, across the Texas plains, where the ragged tribes lived on prickly pears, rodents, and reptiles, past the mesas of the Southwest, the sacred lands of the

Pueblo tribes, and down into Mexico, finally, where he met his own kind again, capturing Indians for the slave trade, and was infuriated. Four of them, the survivors of Pánfilo de Narváez's disastrous expedition to Florida, made that journey. Alonso de Castillo, Andrés Dorantes, and Dorantes's black slave, Esteban, were the others. But it was Cabeza de Vaca, with his endless curiosity, his Chrisitan compassion, his European cleverness, and his great gifts for navigation and language, who, over and over, saved them. He learned languages so quickly and so well that, in Texas, he served as interpreter between tribes who had before communicated with one another by means of hand signals and grunts, tribes who spoke not merely different dialects, not merely different languages, but languages deriving from different roots. That trip across America took eight years, from 1528 to 1536, during which Cabeza de Vaca was trader, slave, interpreter, botanist, zoologist, sailor, anthropologist, physician, and priest. A man whose mind could accept so many possibilities and never lose course, he was the ideal conquistador, the perfect American.

Three years later, in 1540, Cabeza de Vaca, then sixty, accepted Charles V's offer to make him *adelantado* and governor of La Plata, insisting only that the contract forbid any lawyers to enter that territory. His fleet of three ships carrying four hundred men and forty-six horses landed, after a five months' crossing, at the island of Santa Catarina off the west coast of Brazil on March 29, 1541. After he had thoroughly reconnoitered the area, he, two hundred fifty soldiers, and the twenty-six surviving horses set off on an overland march, six hundred miles through jungle to Asunción. The horses carried food, equipment, trading goods, and the sick. The healthy walked, cutting a narrow path through undergrowth. One day they built eighteen bridges so that the pack horses could cross small rivers. Whenever their food ran low, friendly Indians provided more. A tribe living on the banks of the Río Iguaçú gave them not only food but also dugout canoes. The Spaniards rowed to the great falls of the Iguaçú, where they were met by Indians dressed for war. Cabeza de Vaca, speaking gently through an interpreter he would need but once, distributed gifts and complimented them on the beauty of the place they had chosen to be their home. The dozens of friendly Indians who were by then accompanying him told these hostile ones of this conquistador's gentleness, of his fairness—how he took nothing without paying a fair price for it, how he treated them always with respect, and how he punished any of his men who did otherwise. The hostile Indians, appeased, allowed the Spaniards to make the eight-mile portage from the gorge of the Iguaçú to the banks of the broad Paraná. There Cabeza de Vaca ordered that rafts be built with decks of hewn wood stretched between pairs of dugouts. When that was done, he sent thirty sick men and fifty harquebusiers down the Paraná and up the Paraguay to Asunción. He and the rest continued cross-country and were greeted everywhere by friendly, generous, even cheerful Indians. They entered Asunción in triumph on March 11, 1542, four months and nine days after leaving the island of Santa Catarina.

It was an unparalleled march, not so much because it crossed dense jungle, navigated difficult rivers, and encountered tribe after tribe of natives, but because it was accomplished without a single battle, without mistreating a single Indian, without abusing a single soldier, without ever descending to greed.

In Asunción, Cabeza de Vaca declared slavery illegal, freeing the Indians who had already been captured, forbidding any further slave hunting, and imprisoning two friars who had set up a harem of native girls in what they called their nunnery. He then led a huge expedition into upper Peru, another six-hundred-mile journey. The flotilla, four hundred archers, a thousand friendly Indians, ten vessels, and a hundred twenty canoes, stretched for a mile along the Paraquay River. They went hundreds of miles upstream to Los Reyes, where they built a small settlement. Cabeza de Vaca left a garrison there, then continued westward. This time he failed. His provisions ran out, there were no natives to provide more food, and, when he returned to Los Reyes, he found that his men there had alienated the Guaicuru, who attacked the garrison and killed about sixty Spaniards. He ordered the hundred captured Indians girls returned to their families.

A few days after Cabeza de Vaca and his army returned to Asunción, he was deposed—by the old governor, the soldiers angered at having to relinquish their concubines, and the priests. He spent ten months in an Asunción prison cell, three months in irons during an Atlantic crossing, and, after being convicted of charges brought against him by slave traders, politicians, and priests (the old alliance), six years in a Spanish jail. After serving that sentence, he was banished to Oran. In 1551, Charles V revoked the banishment, and in 1556 the ideal conquistador, the one explorer who deserved the America he found, died obscure and destitute in Seville.

"All of it is there," I tell them. "In one life. America." I stare out over the night sea.

"The lost dream of Eden?" Margaret says. The words are flat, dry. I cannot tell if she intends sarcasm.

"No," Magdalen Abbey answers. "Sam Maledon's always been right about that. To long for innocence is to wish to be less than human."

I nod. "It's freedom," I say. "Not innocence. The freedom that comes from tolerance instead of power. That's what Cabeza de Vaca represents to me. Over and over again, America chooses power instead of freedom. The reason's simple, I know. For most of us fear is stronger than love."

Again and again the sea strikes the shore. The stately waltz to the moon's soft song.

And Margaret says, "But it was still a conquistador's dream, wasn't it? Even Cabeza de Vaca's. He needed a world to conquer. I mean, if all he'd wanted was the mystery of America, he could've just kept walking from tribe to tribe that first time. He wouldn't have required a license from Charles V. He wouldn't have needed anything. It was all here."

Magdalen stands, steps toward the surf line, stops. The ocean wind lifts her moonlight-burnished hair. "He had to think of those who would follow him. He wanted to find a place he could save from them." She turns back to us. Her hair is blown across her face. She pulls it back. "It's what I want to do here. I still think it's possible."

"It may be," Margaret says. "This may be small enough to survive."

Magdalen nods. "Yes. I've come to understand that. But I've never been quite satisfied. There ought to be more we can do."

"Yes," I agree. "There's a world out there."

A world. A war. And Chicago. Where the dream will die. Will die because the old men who rule fear it above all things. Will die because its adherents are now but children, decadent innocents.

We must go, then. Be there to witness its death, plot its resurrection.

3 GLORIA

"Fuck it," I said. "Even when you don't know anything else, you know you have to try to save your children from the Goddamn machine."

"There it is, love," Gunner said. "You learned that much, it ain't all been a waste. Now you just got to learn the machine's going to get them anyway. Do that, you got it all. The unexpurgated wisdom of man."

So, knowing that it was futile, knowing that there would come a better time, we drove to Little Rock to try to rescue Aura from the Child Therapy Center. I don't think direction or destination much mattered to Gunner then. One way was as good as another. Little Rock would do. I had a reason, he had a ride. That was that.

We stayed in a truck-stop motel just south of Little Rock that night, and, out of masochism, I guess, I tried to seduce Gunner. No, that's euphemistic; rape is closer to it. He finally brought me off with his mouth. I ground myself hard into his face, pulling at his hair, calling him names, smothering him with my anger, my frustration. He took it well enough, the mutual humiliation. The self-flagellation of the impotent and the unbelieving. He probably needed it too.

When we were finished, I felt like the slut my father thought I was. There was some gratification in that. I was able to sleep.

"Ain't exactly love, is it?" Gunner said the next morning. He was sitting naked in the vinyl chair by the window. He may have been there all night.

"I'm sorry," I said.

"Well, maybe it is, then."

As soon as the receptionist at the Child Therapy Center told me Aura wasn't there and never had been, I believed her. Where I had expected to be confronted with a restraining order, I was met with a studied, professional politeness. The center was young, in the process of trying to establish a reputation. And this was Arkansas, after all, where, to their credit, most people were still suspicious of any institution whose function began with the removal of children from their homes. Consequently, the receptionist and, later, the psychologist I talked to were noticeably worried about image. They and their center had been created by liberals. They were dependent on government money and the goodwill of the enlightened. They didn't want to be seen as something that could be manipulated by a south Arkansas millionaire.

The psychologist, Dr. Mary Price, went so far as to give me a tour of the facility, introducing me to staff and children. All but three of the children were there on a nine-to-five basis, she said. The other three spent their evenings and nights just across the way, on the psychiatric ward of the University Medical Center. "This is a research facility," she said. "We're very particular about who we accept."

We entered a small, huggy-bear classroom, where a young child psychologist patiently explained the benefits of positive self-image to two twelve-year-old boys, one of them black. "If you like yourself," he told them, "you won't feel the need to ridicule others. You'll have lots of friends because being around you will make other people feel good about themselves."

"Shit," the black kid said. He opened a cool palm toward the white kid. "Kevin here, he like hisself. But that just because he such a stupid motherfucker." Kevin began sobbing. The black kid shook his head. "Look at this shit. Little Kevin be needing his momma. She stupid too."

Dr. Price touched my arm and nodded toward the door. But I stood there a moment longer.

"Roy Lee," the psychologist said. "You have no good reason to deliberately hurt Kevin's feelings. You do it only because you haven't learned to feel good without making others feel bad."

"Come off that shit, Jim," Roy Lee said. "You all be wanting me to feel good, how come you always be throwing my ass in jail? I just a little nigger boy. Why don't you let me be, motherfucker?"

Kevin, his face all snot and tears, screamed, "Nigger! Nigger! Nigger!"

"Whooee!" Roy Lee said. "Honkie boy be liking hisself now."

"Roy Lee's a special project," Dr. Price told me after she had politely maneuvered me out of the room. "He was in foster care for a year and then was sent to the Boys' Training School at Wrightsville as an incorrigible. They gave him a battery of aptitude tests, and he scored the highest of any child in their history. We agreed to assume custody of him. and, despite what you saw a moment go, we've made considerable progress with him. At first, he wouldn't even speak to us."

"What about his parents?"

"His father's in prison. His mother's a prostitute. No hope there." We were walking toward the lobby. "Adoption seems to be the best hope. But he'll have to learn to modify his behavior significantly before we can recommend him to the agencies. Last Christmas, for instance, he was in a group home in Pine Bluff. Quite a good place, actually. Baptist, but far more enlightened than you'd expect. While they were singing carols Christmas Eve, Roy Lee set the tree afire. Poured scented lamp oil on the tree and struck a match to it. Pointless defiance. He sees any type of conformity as a weakness, any display of affection as a threat."

We reached the receptionist's desk, and Dr. Price stopped. "I'm going to be perfectly frank with you, Mrs. O'Leary. Mr. Wilder's attorney did call us and request treatment for your daughter. But when it became apparent that we would be used for no reason other than to strengthen his case for permanent custody, we declined. The attorney threatened legal action. But that was a bluff." She gave me a confident look. "That's all I can tell you about it."

"He doesn't like to be turned down, my father."

"Oh," she said, "I've known your father a long time. You see, *my* father, until his retirement, was a dispatcher at Ouachita Best Freight."

"Jesus," I said. "Old Henry?"

"Yes. *Old* Henry."

I didn't know what to say. I didn't understand what she was doing.

"So," she said. "You can see, I'm sure, that we had good reason not to accept Aura. And, I promise you, Gloria, she's not here. I have no idea where she is. What I'm fairly sure of, though, is that the problem isn't with her. It's with her family. You and Jonathan. Each of you so proud and stubborn you'd use a child to get back at the other one."

She walked to the door with me, held it open. "I'm speaking to you as a human being now, Gloria, not as a psychologist. Up against the life of a child, politics is bullshit."

I stepped past her, through the doorway, then turned back. "Why did you show me Roy Lee?"

"I'm a teacher," she said. "I wanted you to see the question. I'm sure you think we don't have the answer. And maybe you're right. We *are* conventional. We *do* encourage conformity. But we know that Roy Lee is the question. I wanted you to see that. It's the least I could do for my father's former employer."

"My father asked you to do it?"

She uttered a short laugh. "God no," she said. "He's less interested in the question than you are."

"Aura's not there," I told Gunner a few minutes later in the medical-center cafeteria. "I should've known. He wasn't about to tell me where he was keeping her. I don't know what the fuck I'm doing anymore."

"He told you the perfect lie, love," he said. "The one he knew you'd believe. The one that'd make you so mad you couldn't think."

He went to the serving line and got us each a cup of coffee. We sat for minutes without speaking. There seemed to be no place to go, nothing further to do. Aura could be almost anywhere. Another psychiatric facility, the home of one of my father's friends or employees, any one of his several vacation houses. Wherever she was, she would be heavily guarded. Gunner got us each another cup of coffee.

I told him about Roy Lee. He said, "He ain't the question, he's the answer."

"I don't know," I said. "All I know is that we've lost."

"For now," he said. He touched the back of my hand. I looked at his fingers. "Ain't nothing ever plumb lost, love, till they zip you in that fucking bag."

I said, "Take me somewhere."

His mother was the manager of the Woolworth's in West Helena. We got there a few minutes before closing time. She was at the back of the store, in her office, a cubicle whose walls didn't reach the ceiling. In front of her, on the gray, metal desk, was an adding machine and a stack of checks. She had a hard face made harder by its frame of long, straight gray hair.

Gunner said, "How you, Momma?"

She looked at him, at me, at him. "It's summer," she said. "I'm hot and tired. Winters, I'm cold and tired."

"At least you ain't lost touch," Gunner said. "That's something."

"Something," she said. "Not much."

He introduced me to her. She said, "You must be real lost, girl."

Before I realized it, I said, "I'm in love with your son, Mrs. Grant." I don't know why I said it. I didn't know whether it was true. I hadn't really considered it before. Maybe I just wanted her to take notice.

She said, "That's what I meant.'"

She looked down at a check, punched out a number on the adding machine.

"How's business?" Gunner asked her.

"The K-marts're coming," she said. "So we're about done. Everybody down here's about done."

"Ain't just down here," Gunner said.

And she looked up again. "You're too young to quit, William. There ought to be good between here and there."

"You'd think so, wouldn't you?" he said.

"You in love with her?"

He nodded. "In my way."

"She satisfied with that?"

"No. But she ain't give up either."

"Might be a lesson there," she said.

"Might be several," he said. "None of them clear."

A girl, high-school age, wearing the aqua Woolworth smock, tapped lightly on the door twice, entered the cubicle, saw us, and said, "Oh."

Mrs. Grant said, "It'll just be a minute, Vera."

Vera left.

"Eighteen," Mrs. Grant explained. "Her biggest problem's making the register balance out at the end of the day. The way it ought to be."

"I been needing me a register like that," Gunner said.

"The God's truth," she agreed. "Though, for you, it's just something else to say."

"If you don't keep talking," Gunner said, "the silence gets you."

The secret's not in talking," she told him. "It's in saying something you believe."

"I was afraid of that."

They stared at each other for a few long seconds. I could feel the power of whatever was in the air between them. Then Gunner took the two or three steps to the door, touched the knob, hesitated, and turned back toward her. "We going to the island, Momma. I'm going to get straight."

"You do that, William, you come back and let me see you. I can't stand this. I'm sorry."

He opened the door. "Ain't none of it your fault," he said.

We took State Highway 20 south from there to Elaine, then followed a gravel, county road to Baptist Ford, where there was a dilapidated boat dock, a gas pump, and an old tin-roofed general store that had once been painted white. We went in.

Behind a worn counter covered with boxes of candy bars and cartons of cigarettes, a big, young black man sat in a rusted lawn chair and read the *Commercial Appeal*, which he had folded down to the size of a paperback book. He lifted his eyes slowly from the paper and, seeing Gunner, nodded. "I be damned," he said, "if the motherfucker that lost the war ain't done come home."

"Ain't plumb lost yet," Gunner said. "But I done my part to get it there."

The black man laughed. There was no threat in its sound. I knew they were friends.

"Yeah, I just bet you did. And I'm wagering too ol' Sam ain't never had him no soldier the like of Private Gunner T. Grant."

"Didn't make a shit to Sam," Gunner said. "He done solved his problem over there, Marcus. Treats everybody like niggers."

Marcus nodded again. "Step in the right direction," he said. "Band us all together, we get that motherfucker." He laid the paper on the counter. "Look like that white boy from Detroit might win thirty, don't it?"

"Ought to be Gibson," Gunner said.

"No justice." He leaned back. "Y'all fixing to stay. I'll commence firing up the grease. Catfish do?"

"Going over to the island," Gunner told him. "Need a bill of groceries, some ice, some tackle, and a ride over before dark. Lady here, she's got money."

"Look like she might." He reached under the counter, handed us a cardboard box. "Going be getting back to nature, are you?"

"Part way," Gunner said, walking toward the shelves of canned goods. "Then I'll stop and look her over careful, see if I want to go on."

"Don't be looking too hard, bubba. Ol' bitch, she'll take you down."

We stood at the edge of the island, a rod and reel, some hooks, a twenty-gallon Igloo watercooler, and two boxes of food at our feet, and watched Marcus guide his boat toward the sunset, back across the river. "Well, love," Gunner said. "Here's to me and you and Captain Henry David Thoreau."

"You think H.D. lived on pinto beans and cornbread?"

"Waldo said he kept a pot going all the time. Man was high on fatback."

He took a vial of pills out of his jeans pocket, ate two twenty-milligram beauties, poured the rest into his palm, held them out toward the sun, and said, "Farewell, ol' friends." He turned his hand over, and the speed fell into the Mississippi.

"Catfish be jumping tonight," he said. "Be swimming to New Orleans for the hell of it."

The island had been formed during a flood a hundred years ago, when the river had dredged herself a second channel, separating a small peninsula, Renegade Strand, from the eastern bank. For much of the last half of the nineteenth century it had been sanctuary for river pirates, vagabond cardsharps, bootleggers, and unreconstructed sons of the Confederacy. In 1879 a man named Washington Monroe Hobart, former colonel in the great gray army, declared the island's independence, renamed it, and, for the next year, he and his last band of the gallant collected a stiff toll from the Memphis–New Orleans river traffic. Confederate Island was their headquarters, but they moved up and down the river—right-wing guerrillas, as Gunner said, in the belly of the beast—and managed to evade the soldiers, marshals, and posses pursuing them. On April 14, 1880, the fifteenth anniversary of John Wilkes Booth's leap onto history's stage, they robbed a bank in Memphis, and, after that, nothing was heard of them until Colonel Wash Hobart and the pick of his raiders returned to Confederate Island sometime in the spring of 1883. By the next spring they had built a great house. Three stories; a saloon with dancing girls and gambling tables on the first floor and, on the upper two, bedrooms for the dozens of whores—white girls stolen from the streets of Memphis, black girls kidnapped from cotton farms, and the expensive octoroon and Creole beauties bought at market price in New Orleans. The house thrived. All white men were welcome, brigand and banker, deacon and desperado. Over the next thirty years there were some killings—gentlemen dueling, fathers and lovers trying to rescue their women from the house—but they were surprisingly few. A man was less likely to be shot here than in the French Quarter in New Orleans. The prostitutes were paid well, and, after the house's first year or so, allowed to leave when they wished. Others happily volunteered to replace them, waifs and widows, the defiant and the lost. The paradise of lust and money, patrolled by the last soldiers of the doomed cause.

"The American utopia, flower child," Gunner said. "Yankee money, Confederate glory, and the love of a whore."

We were eating hot dogs off of paper plates on a metal card table in the rusting, sheet-metal shack that now stood on the ground once occupied by the grand gaming house.

"The old bastard died in 1914," he continued. "Seventy-nine years old. People claim a heart attack took him while he was in the saddle giving a new whore a trial trot. A death concocted, most likely, by folks not wanting to believe he died like any other crooked baron, old and fat and rich. Wanted to have him riding love's bronc, you know, off to that Great Confederacy in the Sky. But whatever it was took him, took the house too, really. All the original soldiers were either dead or just gone, and the new ones, the ones knowing nothing about nothing but hot gash and cold cash, well, they commenced feuding. Folks started getting shot. Whores started slipping off in the dead of the night, headed for Memphis or New Orleans, where these things were still done proper. Couple of years was all it took, wasn't nothing left but one paranoid pimp and two or three whores a Tijuana pony wouldn't've had. In 1918, at the climax of a revival held to properly fuel the spirits of the the boys they's sending off to make Europe safe for America, a band of foot-washing Baptists came over by barge and torched what was left of the place.

"And that was it. Nobody much came here after that. Maybe now and then a runaway from Parchman or Cummins. Ever' so often a fisherman. But seldom. Word was it was haunted, so folks stayed away and told the story. And, like you see, there ain't much here but the story, and you don't have to be here to tell it. Just a little mudbank river island nobody ever really wanted but the ol' fool that was going to build a new Confederacy on whorehouse money but then come to decide that just the whorehouse and the money would do." He looked at me, grinned, took the last bite of a hot dog. "So, about four years ago, me and Marcus came over here and built us a home. You know, the old story, sheet-metal dreamers."

We lived on stories during those weeks of our mud-island, sheet-metal dream. In the beginning it was all we had. For the first several days, squeezed in the grip of the memory of speed, he talked of Vietnam. Bitter, disjointed, booby-trapped stories of fear, betrayal, death. Being led by incompetent ROTC lieutenants into treacherous villages—Zippo raids. Tossing hand grenades at water buffalo to ease the boredom, chase the fear. Never seeing a foreign face that wasn't obsequious, aggrieved, or vengeful. The mutilation of the dead, the malevolence of the living. The repudiation of all causes save survival—and sometimes even that. And now and then something like conventional combat, a real battle. "Come like salvation—or doom, Lady Boom. Same thing over there. The long waiting over, the blood rush come. Easy time, Brother Slope, me and you now. M16 and AK47, yeah, me and you, motherfucker. Your country, my ass, all I Corps to me. Ain't even that, Mr. Red. Just a hole to hide in while the bags go by. So don't you be digging here, Dr. Dink, don't you be shoveling in on ol' Gunner. Got to have me a place, Uncle Ho, got to fight for that, something to die for, Cap'n Cong, makes me mean. I be a fucking hero, man, you don't let me be, get me some decorations. You be good, though, shoot me in the ass, I be gone. Back in the world, General Giap, eating Frosted Flakes. But all right, okay, don't listen to nothing, come at me, freedom fighters, come on, all of you, bookoo gooks, don't mean nothing to me. Chung He, fear done got bored with ol' Gunner, man got nothing to lose but ammunition."

Then he'd stand up and say, "Quit feeding me the belt, baby. The gun's gone." And he'd walk out of the shack. Walk around the island, sit beside the river, I don't know.

I cooked the meals—beans, cornbread, rice—and ate with him when he was there, ate alone when he wasn't. Evenings, Marcus came over with ice and water and milk. But he stayed only a few minutes, kidding briefly with me or Gunner before leaving. The time wasn't yet right for friendship. They were long days, those first few. Mosquitoes and heat and time. But I waited. Swept the rotting plank floor and waited. Gathered wood for the cookstove and waited. Sat in the humid silence and waited. Because I knew I needed this man.

About noon on the fifth day he came into the shack and said, "War's over, flower child. Gunner done got her licked. Chased the Cong back home. Fragged all the fucks needed fragging. Found shelter from the friendly fire. Turned all the incoming round wrong-side-out. Done come the last klick home." I was lying on the old mattress in porch shade. He walked toward me smiling, proud of himself. "River done washed all my sins away. Blood's pure, head's clear, peace is at hand. Ain't no light in the tunnel so, I got out of the motherfucker." He sat beside me, took my hand. "And, tell you what, love, I was down at the river just then, thinking about you, where we been and why and how we going to get out again, and, well, by God, don't you know, Ol' Blue, he stood up like the torch on the Statue of Liberty. So I jumped in to get him clean for you."

I could have cried, but I laughed. "Let's have a look. The madam needs to see if he's acceptable."

"Romance," he said. "Goddamn, there ain't nothing like it."

He was good, Gunner was, as, I told myself, I'd known all along he would be. Passionate, uninhibited, playful. Sure, part of the joy resulted from this being the end to so much waiting, so much frustration. And, for him, it was, at last, the soldier's proper welcome home. But, still, he was good, I was good, it was good. Often the naked man is a child, alternately arrogant and insecure—"Baby, you've never had a man like me . . . or, uh, have you?" And Gunner, God knows, had real reason to be insecure. He wasn't, though. Ol' Blue got hard; the rest was easy. The most natural thing in the world. So this was everything it was supposed to be, an end and a beginning, the gratification of desire, the affirmation of friendship, the triumph of lust, the delight of union, the rapture of release, oblivion, timelessness. And, yes, once you've had all that, you can start over and have it again.

"Christ Almighty," Gunner said after maybe two hours (who knows?). "So that's what all the fuss is about. I damn near forgot."

I told him what Jesse had once told me. That life begins at precisely the point words fail.

"Well, then, love," he said. "I reckon we better keep talking."

But when he had said it, he filled his mouth again with my breast.

* * *

That night he talked about his mother, his childhood, his confusion. He spoke easily, without bitterness. His mother came from one of those old southern families that had lost everything but their pretensions. She had been an intelligent, strong-willed, attractive woman, and they had borrowed from a lenient banker to send her to finishing school in Memphis and then to Sophie Newcomb in New Orleans. By then they were willing to accept new money, carpetbagger money, and they hoped she would marry them some. She had her bloodlines for a dowry; surely that would be enough.

"But, Momma, you know, time she was old enough and finished enough for them to send to New Orleans, she was tired of that Old South shit. Man she gave her genteel self to was a thirty-five-year-old merchant marine, name, by God, of U. S. Grant. United States Grant, his momma wanted to get him off to a rousing start. Man of mixed race. Creole Irish. Somebody hiding in ever' woodpile you come to. The melting pot itself. She got pregnant, she took him home—out of spite, I reckon. Them fine-bred old ladies commenced fainting like they just been showed proof Robert E. Lee hisself was a little on the queer side, liked to go down on Stonewall now and again. My granddaddy ran Momma and her man away with a shotgun. And she was free. Been free ever since. That's what's wore her down."

They returned to New Orleans, found a place in Metairie, and Mr., by God, U. S. Grant resigned from the merchant marines and took a job as an automobile mechanic. He stayed with Gunner's mother two years. "Long enough to get me born and see to it I was up and healthy, walking and talking. Didn't want to leave her with a half-wit or a cripple. Man of some honor."

Then he went back to sea.

"That was it, far as I know. Maybe she saw him a time or two after that. But she did, she never talked about it. Ol' U. S. probably figured a woman of her blood wanted money, she could get it. She hired me a baby-sitter and went to work checking at one of them new chain supermarkets that was just beginning to teach the nation to eat flash-froze plastic. She took a new job every six months or so, seemed like, and we moved up and down the river. Hell, I've pissed off every pier between Memphis and New Orleans. And, Jesus I must've gone to twenty different schools. Go awhile and move, go awhile and move. And if I wanted to just hang around the river for the day, or shoot goals with the dropouts, that was fine with Momma. She saw to my education herself. Gave me books to read, saw to it I read them. Gave me problems to solve, saw to it I solved them. Give me maps to study, hoping maybe I'd figure a way out. All the rest was horseshit, she thought. Training school for the suffering class. Camps for killing the soul. I'd go in one morning, say, at Helena High School and sit down in English class and in about a half hour I'd know wasn't anybody ever in that class ever read shit, including the one paid to teach. She was right, it was just a halfway house they'd had to build on account of the child-labor laws. We never passed a church she didn't mock, never heard a politician she didn't laugh at. And, God himself knows she was right. Ever' time. But it wasn't easy being her son. I never knew what she wanted for me. Some kind of freedom she didn't quite understand. It was hard on her too. Like I said, it's wore her down. She goes on, though. There's nobody tougher."

"Were there any men? I mean . . ."

"She needed one, she'd lead him in late and run him home early. A Liberated Woman in the Mississippi Delta in Nineteen Hundred and Fifty-nine. Or Don't Take Your Mind to Town, Girl. A real fucking weeper."

"She was born in the wrong time and the wrong place. It would've been easier for her now."

"Who knows? But she never liked crowds. Maybe just pure rebellion was the whole point of it. Wanting real bad to be one of a kind. Honorable enough ambition. But it made me want to belong to something. I got my draft notice, it seemed like an invitation to a club. 'Aw, hell, Son, you one of us. Always have been. You know that. Come on ahead.' They called, I went. May've been the happiest recruit in America. Could've used me for the poster soldier. Been good duty, too, I reckon."

"And your mother? She tried to talk you out of it?"

"By laughing at me. Mocking. I'd come in the door, and she'd go, 'Hut, two, three, four' or snap to and salute. Her thinking was the world's run by vicious idiots, and the surest proof of that's their armies."

"The truth," I said.

"Sure. And neither one of you know that as clear as I do. A year of watching folks die for nothing'll jerk a man right back 'round. Jerk him 'round so quick it might snap him. Night before I left for boot camp, Momma said, 'When you get back—*if* you get back—don't forget.' 'Don't forget what?' I asked her. 'Don't forget any of it. It happens over and over because the men who survive it forget what it was like. Finger their medals and forget. Or lie. Nobody likes to admit they've been made that big a fool of. So the next generation goes through it all again. So don't forget, and don't lie.' Then she went to bed. I left next morning, she was still there. No call for drama. No last-minute tears. No motherly farewell. I went off on my own."

I didn't know what to say. I touched his cheek, his forehead.

"Well. All she had to believe in was freedom. I wanted to use mine by throwing it right away, trading it for dog tags and fatigues, the chance to be one of the boys, that was my right. Yeah, simple as that. My right."

He lay back on the mattress, hands behind his head, eyes seeming to study the ceiling above him. "She always wanted me to call her Katherine. And here I am, home from the goddamn horrors, still calling her Momma. Both of us wanting something the other can't give. Christ, that may be the oldest story of all."

"Yes."

"Two years later, one doing Nam with Sam, I come back wired, strung out, fucked up. But I ain't forgot nothing, and I ain't lying. She's in Helena, moving up in the world the way she always has, six bits an hour, a grand a year. I come to the door, she opens it, looks me over, and says, 'Think they'll manage to lose it without you?'

" 'Big machine,' I told her. 'Lots of spare parts. None of them work, but there's always a replacement.'

" 'Barnum and Bailey with bombs,' she said. 'Sucker dies every minute, and the show always goes on.'

"And that was that. She didn't want me to forget, she didn't want me to lie, but she didn't want to hear it either. I stayed with her maybe a week. She didn't throw me out. I just didn't belong. She kept herself clear by living to an order of her own. And I didn't believe in order. The war took care of that. I'd start raving on, she'd get up and leave. She knew how it worked, didn't care how it felt. Man with any sense about him at all didn't get caught in that trap. The war, I mean. The army. Chance and causality, the charmed wound, the survival of the weak, the world of whim. She didn't want to hear any of it."

"Like Maledon," I said. "All you need to know about war is, don't go."

"Like Maledon without the laughter," he said. "Without the knowledge of the road out. Momma gets up five days a week and gives them the eight hours they pay for. They don't get her soul, they don't get her conscience, they don't get her mind. They get forty hours a week. Straight-up trade. They want more, she quits. Sometimes she quits anyway. Most of them respect her because she does good work. She's smart, she's tough, she's efficient. Never has trouble getting another job. Maledon, now, he never needs another job. He won't give them even the eight hours, don't seem like it's ever even occurred to him. It's like he was born knowing that as long as you're willing to sleep in the fields when the big boys are watching the house, long as you're willing to eat from the skillet and say grace to the great God Gall, long as you can see the contempt of the rest of the world as nothing more than a help to your slipping past them, well, then, star child, you can be free."

"And being in love?" I said. "Needing somebody? Can you be free and have that too?"

"You on the right island, you can, be my guess," he said. "But, then, god knows I been wrong before."

I kissed his mouth, his neck, his chest, felt him harden against my stomach. "What we need is more data," I said. My mouth worked downward, found his cock, took it.

"Turn yourself around here, love. You ain't the only one needs a friend to work with."

During the days that followed, we sat together beside the river, fished, set out limb lines, explored the island the way lovers do, seeing too much magic, I suppose, in the busyness of squirrels, too human a purpose in the water oaks' ascension toward light, too much intelligence in the convocations of birds, too little threat in the slitherings of moccasins or the power of the river. We were a charmed part of a charmed world. And we feared that to abandon the island would be to abandon the charm. So we stayed on and stayed on. Here we were safe. Like Colonel Washington Hobart, we could declare independence. Unlike him, we could keep it to ourselves. Across the river, either way, was the world of our impotence, frustration, rage. Weeks went by, and we skinned catfish and made love.

Marcus continued to come over in the evenings. He and Gunner nailed a backboard and goal to the trunk of a tree near the shack and, when the heat wasn't too oppressive or they were in the mood to disregard it, they played one-on-one basketball. They had played together one year at Elaine High School, winning a Class B state championship, losing in the finals of the overall tournament to Fort Smith. "They froze the motherfucker on us," Gunner said. "Wasn't basketball, it was keep-away." It had been Gunner's one brief season of belonging, the year that gave him his name. Marcus had seen him shooting baskets on the playground and talked him into coming out for the team. "There was some problem with eligibility," Gunner said. "All the moving, years of truancy, general absence of respect for educators, all that. But then they saw me shoot and the papers got straightened right up. I was a student in good standing, eligible to graduate and run the fast break."

"Man could bring the ball up without dribbling it off his foot, and he could, by God, shoot lights out. Coach sees that light, shows it to the principal, who used to be a coach, who sees it too and shows it to the superintendent, who, course, used to be a coach and sees it too, and a little gymnasium glory comes to Elaine. Me, inside working the blocks and Gunner, my man, out there on the fringe, sending the soft shot home. Jesus, it was pretty."

"Momma didn't like it at first. Didn't come to a game till tournament time. And then one night, I looked up in the stands during a time-out, and there she was, leaning forward, looking at the clock. After that, I made one, came back down-court, looked up, and saw her cheering. And I thought, hell, I should've done this five years ago."

"The man could shoot, lady," Marcus said. "Slow and jumped like a low-ass white boy. But good hands and, Jesus, could he shoot. And he'd take the motherfucker too. Back off an inch, Jack, and it was in the air. Twenty, thirty times a game. Ol' Gunner, firing away. Looked like the easiest thing in the world. Little flick of the wrist."

"They come out on me, I'd feed Marcus, and it's show time underneath. They lay back, it's easy time outside." He shook his head, smiled at Marcus. "Ain't nothing been that sure since."

Later, when we were alone, I asked him why he hadn't kept playing. Surely someone had offered him a scholarship.

"Marcus plays at AM&N," he said. "Couple AIC schools offered me a ride, but I'd've had to live there to play for them, and I'd seen Arkansas. I wanted out, wanted to be part of the big game, and I figured Sam'd fix that for me. He did."

When Marcus came, he usually brought the day's newspaper, the *Commercial Appeal* or the *Arkansas Gazette*, sometimes both. He'd set them on the porch, and we'd read them after he left. One Sunday in early August, after we'd eaten catfish and Marcus'd gone back across the river, I picked up the *Gazette* and saw that beneath it was *The Word*, Adrienne Fielding's underground paper. I unfolded it and saw, surrounded by slightly slanting columns of type, an underexposed photograph of Jesse Cantwell, looking saintly. ARKANSAS DRAFT RESISTERS, the headline said. WHO ARE THEY? There were six of them in the article, including one Jehovah's Witness, whom Adrienne had managed to portray as an idiot by simply encouraging him to talk about his religion, much of which seemed to be based on John's cactus dreams in the book of Relevations. He was the acceptable pacifist, the one granted automatic conscientious objector status, in contrast to the other five, each of whom faced prison or exile and each of whom seemed smarter, braver, more sensitive, more deserving.

One of these, a graduate of Hendrix College, was already in Montreal. He discussed his reasons for going there and his concern for the parents he'd had to abandon. He told how to achieve landed-immigrant status, and he thanked the Southern Student Organizing Committee for being of such enormous help to him. Another was awaiting trial for draft evasion; he was preparing himself for a prison term, considered it his moral duty to go to jail. Two had refused to report for their physicals but had not yet been indicted. One of these planned to get the best lawyers he could, fight the case in court, appeal it as far as he could, hoping that eventually his case, or one like it, would reach the Supreme Court, which would rule the draft unconstitutional or *this* draft, anyway, with its elitist system of deferments. The second man awaiting indictment wasn't sure what he would do. He discussed his options. Stand trial? How? Take it seriously and try to win? Be defiant, disrespectful, mocking? Treat the whole thing as a fascistic farce? Or go into exile? Where? Canada? Sweden? He talked about the advantages and disadvantages of each country. Then, of course, he could go underground. That was the alternative that least appealed to him. "I'd have to change everything," he said, "my whole way of thinking. I'd have to adopt a kind of paranoia I detest. Everybody becomes a potential enemy. Every act would have to be carefully calculated. If it's freedom I want—and it is—that seems the wrong way to go. I'm not a revolutionary. I'm just against the war."

And then there was Jesse, the mystic philosopher, the Zen activist, Mahatma Orwell. He spoke of the mystery and the Way. Clamor and silence. Politics and morality. The false order and the true. He had been arrested, had been released on his own recognizance, was living on the Clear Creek Commune, would be brought to trial, barring further delay, in late October.

The Word. In the meantime, what will you be doing?

CANTWELL. I will *be here.*

The Word. Can you be more specific?

CANTWELL. I will be here completely . . . I say that, but I'm sure I'll fail. I should say, I will be here completely some of the time. You can't both learn to be and be. That's my dilemma. The politics of all this—the draft, the war, civil rights—well, it forces me always to be dealing with paradox. I have to decide how best to resist one world—the one in which rich men in Savile Row suits can, with perfect equanimity, decide that napalming Asian villages or developing ICBMs is a perfectly legitimate expression of national policy, the world where the poor die so the rich can be free—or, at least, *rich.* And I have to do that—resist that world—while learning to accept the world that *is,* has always been. While training myself to be the world that I am.

The Word. But it does clarify things, doesn't it? The contrast being so strong now?

CANTWELL. Yes. *(Laughs.)* But I think I could have seen it without the war.

The Word. I understand you're going to Chicago. For the convention. Why? It seems inconsistent, contradictory even. Zen, the art of being—whatever you want to call it—and the kind of direct, flamboyant, and, I hope, utilitarian protest we're likely to see in Chicago. I mean, it won't be the ideal place to find the ground of being, will it?

CANTWELL. Maybe, maybe not. I'd like to think I can be there, too. But I'm going because I'm curious. I think the paradox may be made manifest there. And I think it may be the end of our innocence.

The Word. Amerika's?

CANTWELL. Yes. Mine. Yours. Hubert Humphrey's. Yes.

The Word. Will that be good?

CANTWELL. I don't know. That's why I'm curious.

The Word. Well, all that brings us to a purely practical question. Will going to Chicago be a violation of the terms of your bail?

CANTWELL. Oh, I don't know that, either. But I do hope you understand that that's perfectly irrelevent.

"Well," Gunner said after he'd read it, too, "looks like we got us a ride."

"You sure you want to go out into it all again?" I said. "I mean, it's been good here. We've found something."

"Got to move by summer's end, love. Come fall down here, the rain makes the fine truck moulder."

A few days later the Republicans gave themselves again to Nixon. And to Agnew. The two most venal looking men in America. The perfect ticket. You had to hand it to Nixon: He'd found the one man in America who, by comparison, made him look good.

"Hard to beat for laughs," Gunner said. "But I reckon ol' Hubert'll give it a run, don't you, island girl?"

We left Confederate Island the Monday after the Miami Beach convention, crossed the river into America, Mother Freedom's spoiled child gone to blood and greed. But we were her children; what hope she had was ours. And I thought I was ready for Chicago, even if it means having to acknowledge that all we could do was fiddle while Johnson and Humphrey and Daley burned it down.

I had found love. I could wait for justice.

4 MALEDON

I should've known better. Christ, me of all people. It still seems odd that all of them saw it clearer than I did. Hell, I was driving a vanload of idealists, people who actually believed that you could do something that would change the course of the world, people convinced they had a personal duty to end the war, feed the hungry, cleanse the air, and lead the masses through the mountain gate to the green kingdom of satori.

Well, that's not quite true. Gunner didn't think that way. I wasn't sure what he believed in, and I don't guess he was either. He may've had the simplest and most sensible motives of all of us. He was going out of curiosity and a need for revenge, wanted to see what the hell would happen and wanted to give Jimmy Song the beating he deserved. Gloria wanted that too, but even though her summer travels had weakened her attraction for gunpowder and the politics of ecstasy, she still believed in the cause, good and true. She was in love with Gunner now, and him with her—that was easy enough to see. But she must've been one of the few people on earth who could become less of a romantic by falling in love. Conrad Villines was older and tougher, of course, and had several layers of crust around the core of his faith. But he was as much a believer as anybody. And now he was going to Chicago because he thought the country was going to hell in a C-141 and every citizen had a duty to try to block the runway. Jesse was Jesse, the apprentice Gandhi. When the cops would commence clubbing him, he'd keep turning his head to make sure they got both cheeks good. Finally, shamed, the cops'd see the truth, repent, and from then on lead the life of the Buddha. Margaret Salter was going because it was something required of good Americans her age. You didn't commit your life to protest. But there were times you had to try. This was one of them. Magdalen was going because she wanted to see America again, and Chicago, she thought, would be where it could be seen most clearly, its contrasts most starkly drawn. And, of course, she thought genuine Christian love might redeem some part of the week. J.D. Hannah had had the good sense to decide, at the last minute, that his commune needed him more than the streets of Chicago did. And I convinced Howdy Hardison that he'd already made his protest. No need for anything more.

So. Chicago, the last week in August, 1968—place and time where good men and women had a chance to make a difference. That's what they all believed. Simple as that. Everybody but me. It had been my idea to go, but I was just stalling, hoping to divert Jesse, thinking maybe something would happen that would get him to see that this road we were riding could carry us on north, that Canada was way better than jail.

As of the twenty-third of August, the Friday we left Clear Creek in the Hangman's van, Mayor Daley had refused to grant parade permits or to revoke the eleven o'clock curfew for Lincoln Park, where the

Yippies planned to hold the Festival of Life. And he was, as all of them pointed out to me, the mayor who had, during the riots after the King killing, ordered his police to shoot to kill arsonists and maim looters. Even Conrad, who understood politicians far better than anyone else in the van did, thought Daley wanted a confrontation with the Yippies. "He'll try to contain it. He'll try to make it look like he and his police and the Democratic party are reasonable men trying to maintain order in spite of the provocations of thousands of drug-crazed, Communist-financed anarchists. He wants to protect his territory, and he wants to win votes by doing it. Even if it comes down to street fights, Daley believes that most of the TV audience will vote for the men from *Dragnet*. You have to remember Daley beat Martin Luther King, and I'm sure he's convinced he can take Abbie Hoffman and Dave Dellinger."

"Maybe so," I said. But it wasn't what I thought. Sure, Daley'd issued the shoot-to-kill order, and if the Yippies torched twenty blocks of his city he might issue it again. But they wouldn't, and he wouldn't need to. I figured he was just keeping the numbers low. There'd been talk of a hundred thousand protesters coming to Chicago. Now, with Daley taking the tough stand, that was way down. There wouldn't be a tenth that many. And, come Sunday night, when the numbers had turned out to suit him, Daley would revoke the Lincoln Park curfew and let the hippies sleep. Maybe do it a day at a time, keep it uncertain. And then on, say, Monday morning he'd grant them a parade permit for Monday afternoon. Do it in the name of democracy, making sure the Yippies and the National Mobilization Committee to End the War in Vietnam had too little time to organize anything impressive.

I mean, Christ, I figured this for the kind of thing Richard Daley could handle without ever having to pay serious attention to it. It seemed made-to-order for him. I thought that by the end of it all the few thousand protesters that stuck it out would leave town knowing they'd been had without knowing quite sure just how. And I was confident that, no matter what happened, I'd be able to keep me and mine clear of real trouble.

I underestimated everybody's tolerance for pain. Including mine.

5 JESSE

It is, as everyone says, the American city.

Which means the aristocratic high-rise steel-and-glass apartment buildings on Lake Shore Drive and the blocks and blocks of firebombed southside ghettos.

Which means a polyglot of neighborhoods and a government that speaks with one harsh tongue.

Which means the metastasis of the suburb and the death of the heart.

Which means raucous speculation in the grain exchange and systematic slaughter in the stockyards.

The lake's water is poisonous, and the air is laden with the residue of money: heavy and yellow with the sulfurous breath of the smoke-stack, rife with the odor of the abattoir, blood, excrement, fear.

And everywhere energy: Greed rushing toward climax; revenge coiling in anticipation.

The city. I am not of it. This or any other. I am most alien here. I fear we have chosen the wrong ground.

Like millions before us we ride in on Lake Shore Drive. We are dwarfed by the great skyline. The works of man mock the soul of man.

Conrad Villines, holding a map of the city, gives directions to my father. We continue north, toward Chicago's International Amphitheatre, where the convention will be held. It is a predawn Sunday morning, and much of the city sleeps. But the police are awake and ready.

Roadblocks surround the Amphitheatre. We are forced to turn back and park several blocks away. Before leaving Arkansas my father had the Hangman's van painted white. It has an Illinois license plate. On each of its front doors is written: OFFICE OF HUMAN CONCERN/ MEALS FOR THE BLIND. He thinks it will prevent either the police or the demonstrators from throwing bricks through his windows. It is the type of thing he always thinks of.

We walk back to the Amphitheatre. The sun is rising. More people are on the streets. The police are still stopping cars, turning most back, allowing the select to pass. We stand outside the ring of security and look at democracy's forbidden temple. Only the corrupt may enter.

Rank after rank of uniformed policemen, the temple guards. Behind them plainclothesmen and barbed wire. Beyond that the massive building. My father begins laughing. I ask him why. He points to a manhole in the street before us. It is sealed with fresh tar. "Don't want the hippies coming up out of the sewer after them," he says.

"Ought to put the motherfuckers in charge of security at Da Nang," Gunner says.

"Or East Berlin," Villines adds.

And I think of the Russians entering Prague just four days ago. The students with their flowers and their poems. The Russians with their tanks and their one idea.

Security. The fearful word.

Evil arms itself systematically. Pragmatism serving power. Its logic a perfect calculus. The abstract in jackboots. The ideal in a tank. Utopia behind barbed wire.

What is a flower, a song, a story, a prayer, the love of one human being for another against that? What is the delight and wonder of the lone man inside the mystery, one and various, against the awful assurance of the tank, the inhuman arrogance of the B-52, the brutal efficiency of the spiked, electrified wire?

I do not know.

But I do believe, must believe, that even in the shadow of the torturer, grace is possible.

Faith restores. Love redeems. Believe that, even if it is not always true. Even if the machine sometimes destroys all before it. For you must go on.

And we do. A few blocks away and there are no policemen. Only lethargic, Sunday morning traffic, free to change direction. This is still America. We have *chosen* to come to Chicago, to the convention, to the Amphitheatre. We could have conceded it to the delegates, the police, the party. To the puppeteer on the Pedernales. We have come because it is too early for despair. They fear us for the same reason.

We return to the van and drive to Lincoln Park. Traffic is heavy—curious tourists, delegates, and locals cruising the bordering streets, looking at the two or three thousand hippies, Yippies, radicals, and plainclothesmen already gathered on the green.

Again we have to park four or five blocks away and walk back. As we near the edge of the meadow in the park's southwestern corner, we hear a folk-rock group singing "Ballad of a Thin Man." At the edges of the crowd are what look to be local youth, Polish and Irish teenagers assuming, a little awkwardly, James Dean poses. They seem uncertain. They have come perhaps to mock, perhaps to fight. But now some of them look as though they might be tempted to join. The girls, the drugs, the freedom. The probability of leaving Chicago. There are a few blacks, showing only a cool mixture of disdain and street-hardened suspicion. Scouts from the Blackstone Rangers? They look as though nothing that could be done here could tempt them.

We make our way through the surprisingly orderly crowd. A Sunday afternoon picnic in the park. Music. Friends. A mild, marijuana high.

The folk-rock group is now singing Country Joe's "I-Feel-Like-I'm-Fixin'-to-Die Rag." There is no stage, no flatbed truck, and poor amplification. The necessary permits have not been issued. But everyone knows the words, and the park reveberates with "1-2-3, What're we fighting for?"

A Yippie hands each of us a flier on which his party's seventeen-point platform is printed.

"Free sex, free drugs, and universal peace," Villines says after he has read it.

"There's been worse platforms," my father says. "But they let all the niggers out of the slam, the streets'll be damn crowded."

He simply cannot resist.

Margaret and I sit in the grass. She removes pad and pen from her shoulder bag and begins to sketch the scene. She works rapidly, in caricature.

Gunner and Gloria make their way through the crowd, looking for Jimmy Song.

My father, Magdalen Abbey, and Conrad Villines stand behind Margaret and me. We listen to "This Land Is Your Land."

"Reckon I better go study the grounds," my father says. "Escape routes, hiding places. Man needs to know where he stands. It's like Jesse's always saying, 'Ain't nothing sacred but the way out.' "

Magdalen goes with him. Villines sits beside Margaret and me and speculates about the convention in a practical, orthodox manner. Will Eugene McCarthy remove his name from consideration, as has been rumored, and nominate Ted Kennedy, who could then have all the peace delegates, a large sympathy vote, and, probably, the Illinois delegation? Villines doubts it will happen but believes it is the only hope of defeating Humphrey.

Margaret sets pad and pen on the grass, looks at Villines, and says, "It'll be Humphrey and Nixon. No peace candidate. It's the way both parties want it. If Ted Kennedy ran, Lyndon Johnson would have him shot. That's what's depressing about it. That's why we're here protesting. After all this, it'll be Humphrey and Nixon. Mafia soldiers."

"You don't look forward to eight years of Richard Nixon?"

"God," she says. "You're worse than I am. Even I don't think it's so bad he'll be elected twice."

"Wallace might beat him next time. But sooner or later all those southern Democrats will realize they're Republicans, and it'll be the dark ages again. All the old liberals like me will have to hole up and wait for another depression.

"At Harrold Smith College?" But she says it without malice, is kidding him.

"As good a hole as any. Makes it hard to have any grand illusions about the American people."

Margaret says, "I think I'd like to keep some of my illusions."

They say nothing more for a few seconds. The band begins to play "Draft Dodger Rag."

"What's really depressing," Villines continues, "is that Hubert Humphrey may be our last hope. And, Christ, not even I can vote for him."

"Then why are you here?" Margaret asks him. Again the voice carries no malice, only curiosity. "I mean, I believe in the counterculture. Or part of it. And I think Daley may make us look good here. Anyway, it's worth a try. Maybe we can make some people see that conventional politics have failed and that there is an alternative. But you don't even believe that, do you?"

"No. I'm curious, but I don't believe. Ten years—at the outside—most of the people here will be saying 'God, it's time I grew up.' And that'll be the end of it. There's some truth in that thing about not trusting anybody over thirty. When you're grown, it's hard not to give up. You look around and see that everyone else has. That's why I like Sam. He's the only middle-aged free man I know. The oldest child in the world. Huckleberry Finn forever. Keeps lighting out for the territories."

I say, "So you came because he did?"

"I came for the wake. Wouldn't want to miss that. But it's strange, feeling like the only one who knows it's a wake."

We listen to more music. I assume the lotus, and time disappears.

It returns with my father. He slaps my back and says, "I got it figured, Son. We're safe. They'll never lay a stick on us."

"Escape is not always the only solution," I tell him.

"No, but it's always one of them. Any good mystic can tell you that."

That afternoon we drive to Midway Airport to witness Eugene McCarthy's arrival. There must be two or three thousand more people here than were in the park. The American left wing, from stoned street freaks to holders of endowed chairs for revisionist history. From middle-aged professionals with the kind of conscience that can be mollified by their doing some canvassing for a respectable peace candidate to student radicals who think they are giving the system one last chance before taking up arms. Lovely young mothers holding babies symbolizing the world's future. Haunted poetesses doomed to years of manufactured suffering after the fierce example set by Sylvia Plath. There are no blacks, except for the few who look like junior faculty members at Harvard and the ones in the band, who are, as Conrad Villines says, high yellows.

"A fearsome bunch," my father says. "Poets, professors, and vegetarians. They going to have to hire help to build the barricades."

"Spoken by a man who would prefer even war to boredom," Villines says.

"Damn near everybody does," Gunner adds, "till they find out they're the same thing. Long time waiting, and then one dead body after another. Life gets tired of you after a while, and you got to woo it back."

"These are good people," Magdalen remarks. "It's just that Sam despises all gentility."

"Life's a raw thing, Meg. A man ought not spurn the underbrush."

From the platform in the section of the airport parking lot reserved for the rally, a young woman in a red dress sings campaign songs, jaunty cabaret melodies with lyrics of predictable liberal wit. Some of the crowd, those who have been to other McCarthy rallies, sing along with her. She is very lively, very pretty in the bright red dress.

Then why do I feel this distance from her, from this crowd? Why this urge to condescend? Perhaps because she, representative of this crowd, has not given up on the American orthodoxy, liberal version: a restored colonial in the historic district furnished with period antiques; the walls hung with prints of the Impressionists; in the library a Ben Shahn *Sacco and Vanzetti*, safe under glass; on the reading table a fat biography of Eugene V. Debs or, these days, a copy of *Soul on Ice*, question marks inked neatly in the margins; from the stereo, softly, a Mozart quartet; the children, a little spoiled, but awfully precocious, enrolled in a school where they can learn Latin; a stock portfolio meticulously purged of any connection with the Dow Chemical Company; consciousness-raising gatherings for the women, who, carefully underdressed for the occasion, talk of sexism in the corporation, plan a sisterhood of the suburb, identify with the American Indian, the ghetto black, the Vietnamese peasant, and, finally, for the session's climax, castigate their husbands, who so rarely help around the house. They are married, but they question the validity of the institution. They are professionals, but sometimes they question the value of their work. They esteem culture and deplore the crass, the transient, the American. Every two or three years they vacation in Europe to admire what half a century of modern warfare has left of civilization. They long for the spiritual, perhaps even the Christian, but their faith is entirely secular, justice being a material thing. Christmas Eve, they may attend an Episcopal mass, a Unitarian candle lighting. Sometimes, over muffins on a Sunday morning, they discuss Jung.

Taste replaces passion; irony replaces anger; urbane tolerance replaces love.

And those here who have not yet gotten such a life for themselves want it—or will want it. Villines is right about that. Barring national cataclysm, they will get it. The system is structured to that end. They are the privileged, the chosen. These doubts, these protests, this commitment, this war will at worst but delay them. But, even after the late start, they will get what they want—the good life comfortably led, the conscience regularly trimmed by propriety.

But why do I think that wrong?

Because truth is not a social thing. Because love cannot be proportionately alloted so as to limit the disruption it causes. Because faith requires passion. Because life is magic.

But there is something else. I am *envious* of their sense of purpose. Here and now. Today. This year. Whatever they do later, however they compromise themselves, they have had this season of purpose. And they have at least partially succeeded in that purpose. They have made a difference. McCarthy will not win. We know that now, all of us. But he and these people have made this election matter. They saw that by winning an election they could end a bad war. It was that simple. They have worked hard to do just that, and they have come very close. Yes, it will be, after all, Humphrey and Nixon and Wallace. But we will know, millions and millions of us, thanks to these people, that those of us who want peace have been denied the right to vote. That much will be clear.

And me? I feel set apart here. A spectator. An outsider. But had there been no war, had I come of age at peace in the Great Society. I would still have been an outsider. I would still have wished to live always in the mystery.

But today I see again that the wish is not pure. For part of me wants to be part of this community of the good, practical cause. Part of me wishes very simply that I had gone door-to-door for Eugene McCarthy, that I had that much faith in politics. I wish I could sing with the woman in the red dress. But I cannot. My voice does not belong in this harmony.

Finally the plane arrives, and while McCarthy, a taller man than I had thought, comes, waving and shaking hands, toward us, the band plays "This Land Is Your Land." He looks like the kind of man who ought to be president: a genial, urban face, the little pouches under the eyes implying thought rather than decadence. The wise uncle. No visible trace of the demagogue. A man of intelligence and restraint.

Placards bob in the air: MAKE MINE MCCARTHY, PEACE NOW, WELCOME TO FORT DALEY, and DUMP THE HUMP. The crowd cheers him, is happy, excited. But not wildly so. This is not a Wallace crowd. These are people who control themselves in public.

McCarthy climbs to the podium and says something into the microphones. But they are dead. And, in this year of paranoia, he laughs at that and, without amplification, makes a joke. "They've cut the power; we're trying to fix it."

There is more singing. The power returns to the microphones. McCarthy introduces Ralph Yarborough of Texas, who then introduces McCarthy. Who makes the speech everyone has come to hear.

The speech is notable for its wit, its reasoned cadences, its speaker's calm certainty that he is right. He assures the crowd that they have proved that democracy can work, tells them that even in these darkest of times, this year of the assassin and the bomb, they have brought dignity back to politics, says that they can build a new society and a new world. Peace can be had. Justice can be had. It requires only a modest use of intelligence.

It is all clear, simple, irrefutable. And he leaves it at that. The whole campaign has been a prolonged experiment in political science. Professor McCarthy's field seminar in the use of the simple truth in the American political campaign. He is a teacher. He will not yield to anger or bitterness. This is a progressive classroom. The final lesson is hard: In a rigged convention they will cheat us of our victory. But if we are to benefit from this course and its last hard lesson, we must not yield to emotionalism. Bear the defeat stoically. Reform the system. Try again. We have come this far on the cold truth. Let us not abandon it now. Let us maintain our dignity.

And then, a smile, a wave, a swelling of music, and he is gone.

As we are driving away, Villines says McCarthy represents the best of white America.

"Ought not be kicking a man that way when he's down," my father says.

"If he'd let himself get really mad," Gloria says. "he might win yet."

"No," Gunner says. "He'd just end up standing there all by hisself, being really mad. You going to beat them at their own game, love, you got to be one cool motherfucker."

Magdalen Abbey says, "Sometimes anger is completely justified."

And my father again, "Well, Meg, temple that poor bastard's heading into'll be fairly swarming with money changers."

"Yes," she says.

I sit quietly in the back of the van, my arm around Margaret. She rests her head on my shoulder. My father turns on the radio. There is news of the McCarthy arrival, a report that Humphrey has just landed at O'Hare, almost in secret, and has been driven immediately to the Sheraton House to meet with Richard Daley and the Illinois delegation. There are arrangements to be made, deals to be consummated. Now and then, ostentatiously, the mayor will shoot his cuff, as if maybe, just maybe, he has Ted Kennedy somewhere up his sleeve. The police commissioner says again that there will be no permits to sleep in the parks, that anyone found there after eleven PM will be arrested.

Then there is a disc jockey: "Whoooeee! Children of light, children of night, it's high summer in the city of Chicago. The mayor and his man're in a room plotting doom, and in all our streets and alleys they can smell the Pedernales. But we got just the song for them, star dancers. You might like it, too. Here's brother Bob."

It is "Masters of War" and I sing with him, pleased with the song and the DJ's demonstration of the gall that freedom sometimes requires. And suddenly I know I am pleased, too, that we have come to where we have to be, to where your stand must be taken, to where we will confront the machine with our flawed hearts. Yes, I am pleased, content, as, slowly we make our way in heavy traffic back toward Lincoln Park.

I have come, for once, to where I belong.

A child bound for the uncertain night, I am content.

Yes.

Just before the pigs came down on us, I saw Jimmy Song.

It was a half hour or so after curfew, and by then there were no more than two or three hundred of us in the park, most of us huddled together in groups of ten or twelve for security or reassurance. Some people were going from group to group, sitting a moment with each, telling who they were and why they'd come and wishing everyone luck and courage through the night. All that evening, as our numbers steadily dwindled, we listened to music and speeches and watched countercultural skits, several of which involved Humphrey Dumpty, the giant egg who was in for a great fall. Pigasus, the Yippie presidential candidate, displayed himself to his delegates before the convention had even officially begun, in violation of convention etiquette. But this was no festival. Fear dominated the night. Later it would be anger, but Sunday it was still only fear.

Paul Krassner, Jerry Rubin, Dave Dellinger, and others advised us to observe the curfew: Don't let the pigs choose the battlefield; live the revolution until eleven o'clock, then retreat until dawn; we had come for a peaceful demonstration, we were not ready for war. Liberal priests and preachers prayed for us, for the city of Chicago, for America, then asked us not to risk our lives in a futile confrontation with the police. Yippie and MOBE organizers gave us a list of the addresses of homes and churches where we could crash.

By eleven the pigs were deployed, surrounding us. A few minutes later one of them spoke into a bullhorn, telling us to clear the park. Any who didn't would be arrested.

"Well, I'll be damned," Maledon said. "It don't happen often, but this time I've overestimated the bastards." He looked at Jesse. "But then, now we know what to expect; we can take the night off, rest up good, and, come tomorrow, we'll be ready for them."

Jesse said, "No."

"All right, then. Conrad, you take the women and get a room somewhere safe. Shit, like Cicero, maybe."

"I've had too much shelter," Magdalen said. "I need to be here."

"I'll run. But I'll decide when," Margaret said.

I said I hadn't come all this way to start obeying rules.

Then Jesse went into full lotus and said, "Om."

"Jesus," was Maledon's remark.

A wind came off the lake. I could smell the stockyards. All of us were looking at Jesse, who seemed to have sunk completely into trance.

Villines concluded, "It's probably the best way, actually. Just sit here. Offer no resistance."

"I thought we agreed," Maledon said. "We'll go to that place I found in the trees."

"Jesse didn't agree, Sam. He's staying."

Maledon stood up. "I'll go talk to the ol' boy with the bullhorn, then. Tell him I got a circle of half-wits down here him and the troops ought not be hitting on."

Magdalen Abbey told him to sit down.

He said, "You know, Meg. Them fucks have beat me a time or two in my life. But I ain't ever just sat and waited for them to do it."

But she reached up, took his hand, and he sat down.

Then she took Gunner's hand and he mine, and I lifted one of Jesse's out of his lap, and Margaret took his other one, and Villines took hers. And Villines looked at Maledon and said, "Aw, hell, Sam. Join up."

Maledon gave him a short laugh, almost a snort, but took the proffered hand. "Why not? Looks like it's going to take all six of us to take care of Helen Keller's baby brother."

Gunner said, "They throw gas, man, don't breathe through your mouth, don't rub your eyes. Just get up and walk slow to the trees. Can't nobody sit through the gas, Jack. Stay together. Don't let them see your fear, it wires them like blood. They come at us hard, let me take them. I done it before. Be a good cause this time."

"If we can't make the trees," Maledon said, "we'll go stand beside a reporter." They stood all around, with cameras and notepads.

And then, their long shadows preceding them, the pigs marched toward us, closing their circle. Some people began singing "We Shall Overcome." We joined them. All of us except Maledon. Even, after a few seconds, Jesse. All around us other groups sang, too, each taking voice and courage from all the others.

Right up until the panic came, I thought it would be that way. The way it should have been. That first night, at least. The simple beauty of the faith's pure song. The dignity of pacifism. The grace of resistance by example. Textbook civil disobedience. They should have had their night.

But then, from not fifteen yards behind me, there came a shout of protest and, an instant later, a scream of pain. Directly beneath the arc lamp between us and the trees, in the place on that meadow where he could be most clearly seen, a cop was clubbing two men. One of them, a photographer, lay curled on the grass, fetuslike, his camera a couple of yards behind him. The second man yelled "Pig," spat on the Plexiglas visor shielding the cop's face, and then, backpedaling away from the nightstick, turned so that I saw his face. It was Jimmy Song. He ran into the trees.

The pig lobbed a canister of tear gas after him and turned back to the photographer, who had rolled over and was reaching for his camera. The pig stomped the man's fingers, picked up the camera, took the film out of it, and, with the butt of his pistol, smashed the lens.

"Jesus," Villines said. "Daley's drawn up new rules."

"There's just the one cop between us and the trees," Maledon said.

All around us, people were running. The pigs came at us, clubbing at those who ran past them, kicking at those who had fallen. The air was suddenly thick and sharp with tear gas.

Gunner told us, "Remember."

He let go of my hand. The arc-lamp pig stood over him. Others jogged heavily past us, chasing frantic, darting hippies. The pigs seemed to have no interest in making arrests. Whomever they caught they clubbed to the ground and kicked. Then they resumed their pursuit. Those who slipped through the law's circle were free to disappear into the night, the trees, the city. A nightmarish playground game designed by the king of bullies.

The arc-lamp pig said, "Curfew time, freedom fighters."

Gunner leaned back, looked up at him, and said, "Fuck you."

As the pig came down with the nightstick, Gunner rocked back, grabbed him by the elbow, and flipped him. Gunner was immediately on him, his knee against the man's throat.

Jesse said, "Don't hurt him, Gunner."

"Up to him," Gunner replied.

Two other pigs converged on us. Maledon took the mace from the arc-lamp thug's gunbelt. Gunner stood, jerked the cop to his feet, and snapped his right wrist up between his shoulder blades. "You be leading us out of here now, queer bait," he said. Then he took the pig's .38 out of its holster. "Over in Nam, J. Edgar, I done way better men than you for way less cause." The two other pigs stopped, looked at one another through their visors.

Gunner pushed the hostage pig forward. "Get us past them trees there, Wyatt, you be a free man again. A fully armed American. Come back tomorrow night, I be here. We'll make it two falls out of three. Three out of five even. Might just keep at it till you win one. Shit, I don't care."

They were walking slowly toward the trees. We followed, coughing and crying now from the gas. Jesse went up to Gunner and asked for the pistol. "Not yet," Gunner said. But he holstered it in the front of his jeans.

The other two pigs followed us, still indecisive. Three more joined them. I was afraid they might draw and shoot. Gunner told us to get up ahead of him. All of us did except for Jesse and Maledon, who stood beside him, facing the other cops. Maledon, poised like a linebacker, held the can of Mace in front of him. Jesse was talking quietly to Gunner, trying to keep him on this side of the edge, I guess.

But Gunner seemed perfectly rational. "Right now, boys, we just wanting out," he told the pigs, his voice clear and calm. "But you boys come at me, I be clubbing you with the captain's arm." He jerked up on the arc-lamp pig's nightstick wrist. The cop groaned, cursed. Gunner said, "Tell them something, Wild Bill."

It took Arc Lamp a few seconds to find his voice. But then he told his troops it wasn't worth it. Then added, "Not tonight," in a voice edged with threat.

"There it is," Gunner said. "Listen to the captain, night stalkers. Bide your time. Wait till the odds ain't near so even."

We were just inside the darkness at the edge of the trees. Gunner and the others backed toward us. The pigs followed but kept their distance.

When he got to us, Gunner turned the cop around and began pushing him fast through the trees. Just before we reached the sidewalk at the edge of the park—North Clark Street, I think it was—Gunner shoved the pig to the ground and told him, "You come, you done, my man."

The sidewalk was crowded with sightseers, newsmen, battered hippies. Three of the pigs came out to the park's verge and stopped. They eyed the crowd for a long moment before making their decision. This night they turned back, but that would be the last time.

A reporter hustled up to Gunner and asked him what had happened in the park. "Jungle drill," he said. "Frenzy time for the Blue Berets."

Silently, still gripped by the combination of fear and excitement, we went south on the sidewalk. Then we turned west on North and followed it to where Maledon had parked the van. After we'd gone a few blocks, I told Gunner it had been Jimmy Song fighting the pig under the arc lamp. "Thought it was," he said. "But we get another shot. He'll be back. Everybody going to be back till it's over."

Maledon drove us to a cemetery a few blocks from Wrigley Field. "I slept here once some years back," he said. "Never had a minute's trouble. May have a dog or a guard now, way times are. But we do, Gunner can just hold them off with that police special he borrowed for us."

"No," Jesse said. "I'll have the gun."

Gunner handed it to him. "Yeah. No point in me tempting myself too far."

I don't know what Jesse did with it that night. Buried it, I guess. But it's a good thing Gunner didn't have it later in the week.

7 MALEDON

So Daley had shown his hand, and it had a club in it. For the next few days swarms of cops and soldiers would have license to live out the lawman's dream—busting heads and shooting off in their pants. And me? Well, first, I resigned myself to it, and then I discovered I was almost happy about it. I mean, if it was suffering Jesse needed, maybe this would take care of it for him quick. A clubbing or two and be done with it. Way more sensible than a stretch in the slam. I was kidding myself, of course, but I had to get through the week some way.

For the hour or so after we got to the graveyard, we sat in a circle at the foot of a monument to a family named Swoboda and talked things over. They all decided to stay on, stick it out, see it through—good citizens marching proper to the drumbeat of duty—but Jesse and Magdalen were worried about what Gunner might bring down on us. Being willing to take a few blows of a nightstick was one thing; taking a cop hostage was something else. Gunner gave them a low laugh and told them that from here on he'd do better. But he wasn't going to sit passively through any police ambush. If we ran, he'd run with us. "We sit there and wait again, though, I'm fighting."

"Sensible enough," I said. "We'll just run."

But Jesse told us he had no intention of running. "Coming here was an act of civil disobedience. Running is just a way of avoiding the consequences of that act."

"Well," I said, "if there's another way of avoiding them, we could try that."

There was no reasoning with him, though. I was right back where I'd been six months earlier, trying to shepherd a boy that had too much sense to fight and too little to run.

"He's not a boy," Magdalen told me later, when we were lying together on a sleeping bag. "And whether you think he's right or wrong doesn't matter now. You've done all you can to change his mind, and you've failed. Admit that. And let him go, let him do it his way. *Help* him do it his way, Sam."

"You mean they beat him senseless, I should roll him over, give them a clear shot at the other cheek."

"No. Just make sure he doesn't have to do it Gunner's way. I like Gunner, Sam, but he makes everything more dangerous. I don't want to do it his way, either."

"They come at you, you run if you can, you fight if you're cornered. Object is to get clear. Makes perfect sense to me. What happened tonight was Gunner saved us all from a beating."

"Then when they come, just walk away with Gunner. And Gloria. And Conrad, if he wants to go with you. Leave the rest of us to the consequences of our nonsensical honor. We have that right."

I was looking at the stars. They seemed clear enough. "Be hard for me to do," I said.

"Yes," she answered. "Because you love him. And because you don't think he has sense enough to take care of himself. But you have to give him the chance. For the same reason. Because you love him."

"It's not just him."

"I know. But I've taken care of myself a long time. I'll be there with him. We'll be fine. They won't shoot us, and we're strong enough to take the rest of it. You have to have that much faith in us."

It was a long time till morning. The ground was soft, the air was as good as you could expect in Chicago, the streets around us were quiet, there weren't any dogs or guards, and the dead kept their peace, as they mostly tend to do. But I couldn't sleep, plagued by thought the way I was.

By dawn, though, I'd decided Magdalen was right. The most practical thing I could do was to leave Jesse to his way, impractical as that might be. I don't mean I could make sense out of civil disobedience. That was beyond me. Letting yourself be punished for the sins of the people who were punishing you—Jesus, you could start a church on that one. But what Magdalen was right about was that I'd had most of a spring and summer to change Jesse's mind, and I'd failed. So maybe the best I could do now was make sure that when the cops came Gunner didn't flip one of them into Jesse's lotus lap.

I had a talk with Gunner and Gloria. They were agreeable enough. Come midnight we'd be leaving my son to his philosophy, poor bastard. Maybe Daley would teach him the lesson I couldn't.

Pigasus: the other parties' candidates ate the people, but the people would eat the Yippie candidate. That was the slogan. And the people had brought hickory chips for the barbecue. Still, I figured the pig was safe. I doubted whether anybody in the park but me and Conrad and maybe Gunner was capable of dressing him out and smoking him.

"The SPCA's going to save him," Conrad said.

It was late afternoon. Gunner and Gloria were walking the grounds looking for Jimmy Song. Magdalen was milling about, asking people where they were from, why they were here, and what they wanted out of life. The wandering angel, scattering blessings over the green. Margaret was sitting across the way, her back to the sun, drawing on her sketch pad. Jesse sat beside her, all folded up in pursuit of bliss. I considered walking down and telling him to just lay his face in her lap, he'd at least be heading in the right direction then. Conrad and me, sensible middle-aged citizens, were sitting in the shade on a rise, taking in the Yippie carnival and making healthy fun of the SPCA. "They couldn't save those mules from the poor people," Conrad said. "But I have to think their chances are good with Pigasus."

"Wasn't nobody planning on eating them mules."

"You never know. Poor folks have done worse things."

"Yeah. And you can't get even the best of them to do volunteer work for animals."

It was like that all that day and through most of the evening. Laughter, mockery. Pranksters out on a lark. The whole meadowful of folks seemed captured by a defiant gaiety. God knows why, but these kids were finally being taken seriously. Like real revolutionaries, like a legitimate threat to the world of Johnson and Humphrey and Daley. Eleven thousand five hundred Chicago cops were on twelve-hour shifts, fifty-five hundred National Guardsmen were on alert, seventy-five hundred U.S. Army troops had been airlifted, on White House orders, from Fort Hood, Texas. Tanks were at the ready. Daley dozers—government jeeps with rectangular grids of barbed wire covering their grills—patrolled the streets. I mean, twenty-four thousand five hundred fully armed, fully supported Christian soldiers, all jacked up to do battle with maybe ten thousand stoned, unarmed Lincoln Park hippies who could've been soundly defeated by being given what they wanted—a few nights in the park, a parade permit, some dope, and the right to barbecue a pig.

And that night we were graced with the presence of the famous. It ain't a revolution without a few TV draws. Allen Ginsberg led us a ways into the Hindu hymnal, while Terry Southern, Jean Genet, and William Burroughs looked on. Abbie and Jerry were there, doing their routines. Rennie was reported to be around, but, more organizer than performer, made no attempt at on-stage stardom. Tom, it was rumored, had been there earlier but had been immediately arrested, on the grounds that if given a chance he might cause trouble. Dave, the pacifist, the link to the old left, a reasonable man, gave reasonable advice.

Of the thousands then on the green, I may've been the only one who didn't recognize any of the Yippie prophets and performers. Even the plainclothes cops knew them—they'd been studying photographs for weeks. Everybody else was on a first-name basis. Abbie, Jerry, Rennie, Tom, and Dave. Huey, Eldridge, Stokely, Rap, and Bobby. The elders, the chroniclers and psalmists of the Church of the New Consciousness, were referred to by surname: Ginsberg, Burroughs, Mailer. "Burroughs," I heard a kid in front of me say of the lean, bored-looking man in the small-town funeral-parlor suit, "is the father of us all." And he did looked fucked out.

We listened to speeches—comic, inflammatory, cautionary—and awaited the next communique from Celebrity Central. Mailer might be back. Dylan was here, having visions of Johanna and suffering from them tombstone blues. Joan Baez sat at his feet, soothing him with madrigals. John Lennon had tried to come but had been busted by the feds at O'Hare. Paul Newman, a McCarthy man, was with us in spirit and might join us in the flesh. Ho—or was it Fidel?—had called Abbie—or was it Tom?—wishing him victory, calling him comrade. And, just as often, the dark rumor, the epidemic whisper of paranoia.

Daley had given the order to shoot. Johnson had called in paratroopers. The names of those arrested and booked were being forwarded to their local draft boards. J. Edgar Hoover was lobbying for Congress to pass a bill like the one sponsored and steered into law by Hubert Humphrey in 1951, which authorized concentration camps for American radicals. Narcs were selling pot laced with a chemical, perfected by the CIA in South Korea, that slowly, systematically destroyed cells specific to the right hemisphere of the brain.

And they took assurance and energy from all this, as much from the bad as from the good. Ho liked them; Hoover hated them; Ginsberg offered them mantras; Johnson, Daley, and Humphrey conspired against them; Mailer would write about them for *Harper's*; Nixon would call them Communist dupes; Dylan, the Dead, the Airplane, and the Stones would play for them; an army surrounded them; and Abbie cracked jokes, hammering home each punch line by blowing his nose into an American-flag handkerchief. So, yes, by God, they mattered. What more proof could you want.

The cops came down on us again at midnight. They gave us the same warning, and most of them came in again from the side opposite the trees we were sitting near. But this time they were better prepared—colder, more systematic, more ruthless. They weren't wearing their badges—no identifying name and number. Many of them wore gas masks, and the rest had their Plexiglas shields pulled down to protect their faces from being hit or clearly seen. And this time some of them drove patrol cars and tear-gas trucks onto the meadow after us. They used more gas this time, and more Mace. This time they didn't deliver a quick blow or two to the fallen and move on; they stood there and clubbed. They were satisfied to punish whoever they caught. It was only the obvious newsmen they sought out in particular. They smashed cameras and tape recorders, ripped up notes. It was strange. If the cops were on you, you could save yourself by throwing a reporter at them. You could hear journalists pleading, offering credentials, shouting the name of the paper or station they worked for. And the cops calmly destroying the equipment and then clubbing the man. It was no police riot. Not this time. That would come later. It had all been coldly planned, and it was executed with the tight-lipped righteousness only a cop is capable of. Daley had ordered them to deal out hurt and destroy all the records. And these were boys that liked their work.

Many of the kids took right off running and made it safe through the trees to Clark Street. Others fought back with rocks and sticks. Some of them wore football or motorcycle helmets. When the cops caught one of those, they jerked the helmet off and clubbed the head. Quite a few kids waited, hoping to hold the ground they sat on long enough to be models of civil disobedience. But after suffering about five minutes of the gas, most of them panicked and ran with no sense of direction. They ran into Mace, went down, got clubbed. The poison air above the green filled with coughs, curses, screams. And they cops came on, slowly, careful not to overlook any of the fallen.

We had sat and watched it all. I'd chosen our spot because right up to the end it would give us a quick way out. And I'd hoped that watching everybody else panic would persuade Jesse to take the short walk through the woods and get clear for the night. So when the police had clubbed their way across three-quarters of the green, I looked the question at him, fearing the answer. He turned to Margaret and said, "Please go with my father. I'll be here tomorrow."

Then he stood and began walking toward the police.

I decided to play it his way, show him I could. I told Conrad to take the women to the van. Magdalen started to say something and I said, "Just go on, Meg. I got to stay. I got a son out there."

And then I walked out after him.

8 JESSE

There are those who say this is a beginning and those who say it is an end, those who say it will hasten peace and those who say it will prolong war, those who say it will enlighten a nation and those who say it will embitter it.

I do not know about that. I do not know about those who say they do. But this I do know: I have chosen a fate I have endeavored to accept. To be whole and to be a part of the whole. I have sought an awareness beyond that of the five senses, but I have sought, too, a practical morality, an ethical way to respond to the world. I have longed like an ignorant lover for the fear and trembling in the hope that they would yield wisdom. I have wanted to be a responsible citizen. I have wanted paradox to embrace me. And I have failed.

Until now.

At this moment, for this moment, beyond which there is nothing, I am alive. Aware. At one with my fate. In this evanescent now I am forever free to do what I must do. To be what I am.

As I walk toward the frenzy, I am at peace.

I turn, and my father walks beside me. Though I can see that he is surprised at himself, I am not. What happens must happen. Because we are free.

I smell the gas, feel it. I hear the cries, the grunts, the curses, my father's heavy footstep. Just before me now a woman falls. A policeman stops beside her, calls her a hippie whore, strikes. I go to her and kneel. I hear my father say, "Aw, fuck, Jesse."

And then the moment is gone.

The sudden silence. Nothing.

Reemergence. A blurred swirling of light. A slow confusion of voices. Pain. The world again.

"You should probably have it x-rayed."

A man is feeling my head, very gently.

"Be a hell of a line," my father says.

I lie at the edge of the green, being tended to by medics from a unit of the Medical Committee for Human Rights. They are busy. Someone is playing a guitar. A woman hums. I do not recognize the tune. Each thing is separate, meaningless. Not even things. Fragments. They will not come together.

I close my eyes, drift away. The pain retreats. I am floating. The pain disappears.

The man from the unit, perhaps a doctor, speaks with a raw voice. He has tasted the gas. "A concussion. I don't think there's a fracture, but he took one hell of a lick. He'll be having headaches for the next few days."

"No shit," my father says.

I recognize the song the man plays, the woman hums. "The Universal Soldier." The pain seizes me. Is song all we have? Doubt, I try to tell the pain, is holy. Is the beginning of faith.

"How about you," the man asks.

"Just my shoulder," my father tells him. "Won't be pitching in the Series this year. But the odds were already getting long on that."

"It's going to get worse," the man says. "You might think about going home."

"Ain't got one," my father tells him.

"Well, then, welcome to Chicago."

The medic moves to the next man. A policeman goes to him. "Been long enough, doc," he says. "They have to leave the park. That's what this is about."

"Then beat them some more," the medic says. "I don't think we can stop you. If we could, we'd have done it earlier."

I sit up, and the pain surprises me. And then I laugh at myself. A fool, I had never considered the pain.

My father laughs, too. "By God, Son," he says, "looks like they beat a sense of humor into you. Always a silver lining, ain't there?"

"Damn, it hurts," I say.

He nods. "Them boys was trained to it," he says. "I did better than you. Had the sense to keep my head down and covered. But I took a good one on the shoulder and another one broadside across the ass. Felt like a goddamn baseball bat. You can see I was down in my fighting posture. Comes clubbing time tomorrow night, I'll have to be waiting for them on one of them doughnuts like they gave Conrad after they cut his hemorrhoids out."

He takes two pills from his shirt pocket, puts one in his mouth, and holds the other out to me. "Man said it was some kind of synthetic morphine," he tells me. "One thing about becoming a hippie, you can always get any kind of medicine you need."

I hesitate, thinking I need to experience the pain.

"Aw, fuck, take it, Jesse. This night's over, 'cept for getting through the rest of it."

I take it, lie back. "What about the others," I ask. "Margaret . . ."

"Don't know," he says. "It got confused. And then I had my head between my legs. Be a good bet, though, they're better off than we are."

I let my eyes close again, yield to the pill. There is nothing I can do now. Rest. Wait. Return.

The guitar plays another song. The woman has quit humming.

* * *

Later they take us to an emergency room, Henrotin Hospital, where we spend the night waiting our turn. All the battered dreamers seeking modern medical treatment. Newspaper editors come in to claim wounded reporters. Cops stand around, looking satisfied, laughing contentedly. Finally, I am x-rayed. They tell me I've suffered a concussion. They'd keep me in the hospital a day if they had the beds. But I'll be fine. Plenty of rest. No sudden movements. Try to avoid blows to the head.

My father has a separated shoulder. They give him a sling. Severe contusions of the buttocks. He asks for the doughnut. They laugh.

"You're too old for this," a doctor tells him. "Leave it to the young."

"Sure as I do, they'll fuck it up."

"So what?" the doctor answers. "It's their turn."

With his left hand my father grasps the doctor's sleeve. "Listen, doc. 'We must love one another or die.' " His face is distorted by an idiot's grin.

The doctor looks at him curiously. "Auden," he said. "He retracted it."

We leave the hospital, enter the reluctant morning, take a cab to Lincoln Park. During the drive my father says, "Just think, Jess, a long morning's ride and a man could be up in Ontario. A cabin by a lake ain't nobody fishes in but him. Big ol' pike. Man wouldn't have to eat them, he didn't want to. Just smarten them up and throw them back. The moose and the elk. The bear and the wolf. The evergreen woods. The peace and solitude of the world gone back to day one. Somebody looking for answers, you know, by God, that might be just the place for him. Keep him a journal. Walk in the wilderness. Meditate. Watch all the cycles come wheeling around slow. He had him a woman, he could bring her. She'd have to be hard minded and love him and be able to fill her days with her own work. Kind of woman that could draw, sing, or paint and was good to look at. Kind that understood silence. Something like Margaret, say. Man and a woman like that, hell, they could make a real start. Get everything clear again. No rules but God's own."

"I suppose they could."

"Need another pill?"

"No."

He takes one. "Might not be a life, Jesse. But it'd sure be a place to go out to it from."

"Might even be a life," I say.

"You want it, Son, you got it. We could go up and scout it out and buy a few acres and then go down and bring Howdy up, and me and you and him and Conrad, we'd build the fucker. Wouldn't have to be Ontario. We could do it in British Columbia. Place up on a cliff above the ocean. One big room, rock and timber, porch all around. You've seen what Conrad can do, and Howdy's better than he is. Probably have to rent a place this winter. Get everything ready for spring. But a year from now, you'd have it."

"The American dream," I say. "A home of my own."

"You don't like ownership, we can make up a name to put on the deed. That's easy. And you get tired of the place, you can always go down to Montreal or Vancouver awhile and watch the people swarm. See if they been training them different while you been gone."

He turns away from me, glances out the window. When he looks back, he asks, "What do you say, Son?"

"I'd like the cabin," I tell him. "For a while anyway. And I think Margaret might, too. Though I'm not sure. But, no. Not yet. I have a sentence to serve."

He nods several times, slowly. "Odd line of reasoning," he says.

The driver stops at a corner two blocks away from the park. "Close enough," he says.

We get out, my father pays him, and we begin walking. "You know, Son," he says, "we don't get too grand about it, we can help each other. Family and friends and maybe a few more. But most folks, they're going to keep right on fucking up bad. And there ain't no sacrifice you can make to keep them from it. They think it's their duty."

"Sometimes it is."

9 GLORIA

America of nightstick and bayonet, of tank and Daley dozer, of tear gas and Mace. My country, 'tis of thee, ward of technology, of thee I sing.

On the streets and in the parks that week it beat us. The America of the machine, of the amoral engineer and the sociopathic chemist, of cyclotron and Styrofoam, of Dow and General Dynamics—land of the standing army and the hireling pig, it beat us. But we exposed it, forced millions of others to look at it, to see the fascist arrogance behind the Norman Vincent Peale bullshit that passes for the American dream. Oh, they may not have really *seen* it, and if they did they may have approved. But they watched because it was great TV: prime-time violence with even the cameramen getting clubbed.

They missed the smells, though—or smell, for by Tuesday night they had all become one. Tear gas, Mace, stockyard blood, and shit, the rank sweat of panic, the few sulfur bombs from our side. Mingling, merging, hanging always in the air, becoming the air, pervading even the relatively quiet daylight hours of peace and recuperation. The smell of repression. The odor of an alien world. The air of the future.

I will never forget it. Years from now, an old woman in another world, I won't be able to smell a bitterness in the air without being called back to that week when we were young and had to either stand up for our dreams or surrender them to the technology of power. And despite the pain and disappointment, despite, finally, the failure of all we did, it would be a memory of the good that was in us when we were innocent enough to dream of a joyous peace and when we were brave enough to commit ourselves, even for a week, to that dream. Because we did at least, stand up. Because we were right, and they were wrong. Because, once and forever, it was just that simple.

Just that simple, yes. And I knew that it might never be that simple again. So I will remember. It will be my assurance. I will remember.

* * *

Jesse and Maledon walked into the Monday-night gas. Gunner started after them, but Margaret caught him, grasped his arm, and said, "Let them go. Both of them want it this way."

We watched Jesse kneel beside the woman and saw the pig step up behind him, take aim, and club him hard. Jesse went limp and fell face down in the grass beside the woman. Margaret was crying silently, but whether from the chemicals or from emotion or from both, I don't know. Gunner took her to Villines, said, "Hold her," and started toward Jesse and Maledon. But by then the woman, whoever she was, was crawling away, ignored by the pig. He was beating Maledon, who had arched himself across Jesse's upper body. The pig's first blow had been aimed at Maledon's head, but Maledon had jerked to one side and caught it on the shoulder. After that, the pig, seeing the chance to get a few laughs back at the precinct locker room, began clubbing Maledon's upraised ass. Then, maybe because he saw Gunner, he quit that and came toward us. And then there were others materializing, one at a time out of the gas, forming a broad V with Jesse's pig at the point. Gunner stopped, and Maledon shouted, "Get them clear. We're all right."

We ran through the trees, forearms in front of our faces to protect us from limbs we couldn't see. In the darkness all around us were the sounds of the pigs doing and loving their work.

Tuesday afternoon we were with three or four thousand others in the Chicago Coliseum, the city's crumbling former convention center, attending the MOBE's anti-birthday party for Lyndon Johnson. The Holocaust No Dance Band played an electric song advising Johnson to commit suicide. Jean Genet and William Burroughs compared the police to mad dogs—the mad dogs patrolling the boundaries of the cold institutions of power were the price of technological order. Allen Ginsberg and Terry Southern sent written statements that were read to us. They were on our side. We represented life and hope. We were resisting the forces of death and despair. Bobby Seale advised us to go barbecue some pork. Phil Ochs sang "I Ain't Marchin' Anymore." And all of us stood and sang with him, our hands held high, making the sign of peace.

Dick Gregory had the last word. "Premier Kosygin has sent a telegram to Mayor Daley," he told us, "asking that two thousand Chicago cops immediately report for duty in Prague."

As we were walking away from the coliseum, I heard Maledon say, "By God, wasn't that something, Conrad. Lot like a good, big brush-arbor revival, I thought. I'm considering maybe getting me up a new road show. The Peace and Freedom Jubilee. I'd have to get off my regular circuit, of course."

"All your bullshit aside," Villines said, "it did feel good. Being at one with truth and justice. Having my righteous indignation more or less accurately focused. I just wish I could keep from thinking the future belongs to George Wallace."

"Too ugly," Maledon said. "Never carry California."

"Well, a George Wallace with plastic surgery and table manners."

"Oh, you talking about that motherfucker," Gunner said. "Shit, nothing new there. Ain't just the future. He's got the past too."

About curfew time Tuesday night we were joined by several hundred local liberal clergymen. Priests, preachers, and disciples wearing white armbands with black crosses. They dragged an enormous wooden cross to the center of the green, where they erected it, and then began to sing the pacifist hymns of the civil rights movement. After they'd done "Oh, Freedom," "Study War No More," "We Shall Not Be Moved" (with extemporized verses that left the unions out), and "We Shall Overcome," they started preaching. We were right, they said, because we were on the side of peace. But we would remain right only so long as we remained nonviolent. If we attacked the police, or even if we just fought back, we would lower ourselves to the level of our oppressors. Our weapons were truth, courage, and morality; if we abandoned them, we would be truly defenseless. Some of the crowd argued with them, told them they were over thirty, the opiate of the masses, irrelevant, and in the way, then ordered them to cut the cross into pieces and build a fire with the wood. Another part of the crowd simply readied its weapons—rocks, bricks, bottles, ashtrays, cherry bombs, firecrackers, baseball bats, golf balls, baseballs, rolling pins, pocketknives, cans of paint, bags of shit, bottles of piss.

"Now I ask you, love," Gunner said to me, "where's ol' Manny Munn when his people need him?"

The bullhorn pig made his announcement, ordering us off the grounds.

"Jesse," Maledon said, "I got a bum shoulder. You got a soft spot on your head. What you say we leave it to the preachers tonight. Them boys, getting a beating ever' so often's part of their calling. Me and you, shit, we got better sense, ain't we?"

Jesse looked at him for a long moment, then said, "I owe you one tonight. But tomorrow night we see it through."

Maledon nodded and grinned. "One night at a time," he said. "I ain't ever asked anybody for more than that."

But Magdalen said, "Sam, I have to stay. I believe in that cross."

Maledon stared at her in disbelief. "Jesus Fucking Christ," he said. "Come on, Meg, don't pull this shit now. Jesse takes another lick on the head, we'll have to put him in a goddamn rest home."

"Take him away, Sam. Take him with you." She looked toward the cross. "I'll be fine. They'll be with me. That's my life." She turned to Jesse. "Will you go with him? And let me do this alone?"

Jesse stared at her a second, then said, "Yes."

She started toward the cross. Maledon took two quick steps, caught her, and jerked her around to face him. I think it was the first time I'd ever seen him really angry. "Sure he understands. He's victim to the same damn thinking. Why don't the two of you take turns beating one another? Save the cops the trouble."

She slapped him.

Maledon let her go, and they stood there staring at one another. Then Jesse was between them. "Some of us want more than freedom, Father."

"I see," Maledon said. "Well, then, Meg. Go on and get you a splinter off that damn cross."

I smelled gas then, thick and new.

"We done fucked around too long with philosophy," Gunner said. "Incoming."

This time they had us completely surrounded. Pigs on foot and in their cars and in the big street-cleaning trucks, now converted to spray tear gas, came at us from every direction, even through the trees. There was nowhere to go but to the panicking cluster at the center of the circle. We followed Magdalen toward the huge cross.

Just before we got there, Gunner veered away, toward the brick throwers, the shit stormers. When I caught up to him, he said, "It's everybody with their own tonight, love. These fucks are as close as I can get."

But most of those fucks had already panicked and were running wildly back and forth looking for an opening in the phalanx of approaching pigs. I picked up a hand-sized piece of what looked like broken pavement and threw. The pigs were maybe forty yards away and slowly, methodically, closing. My shot fell short.

"Wait till they get close," Gunner said. "Aim at the body and back away. You see an opening, run for it."

The Yippie loudspeaker man gave us the nightly tear-gas-and-Mace advice: Don't run, don't breathe through your mouth, don't rub your eyes, spread Vaseline over exposed skin.

Behind us, beneath their cross, the preachers were again singing "We Shall Overcome."

A man burst past us, running, a brick in each hand, toward the gas truck directly in front of us.

"Jesus," I said. "Jimmy." I lunged forward, but Gunner stopped me. "Let's see how they got it planned tonight."

Jimmy yelled. "Fucking pig," and hurled a brick at the big truck's windshield. The brick bounced off, doing no damage. Had they changed the trucks' windshield glass, too? Jimmy leapt onto the bumper, climbed onto the hood, got to his feet, and, legs spread to balance himself, threw the second brick. Again no damage. Then he took a couple of careful steps forward and started kicking at the windshield.

"Helluva act," Gunner said.

They were almost on us by then. The trucks began spraying, and the foot patrol threw canisters at us.

Gunner said, "Throw," and hit Jimmy Song in the back of the head with a baseball. Jimmy fell against the windshield, then slid back down to the hood. The truck swerved slightly to its right, and Jimmy, slipping toward the driver's side, seemed to claw for a purchase on the slick metal surface. Then, seeing that that was hopeless, he pushed himself away from the truck, turned over in the air, and landed on his back. Almost casually, a member of the pig foot patrol paused just long enough to club the forearm Jimmy had covered his face with.

The pig straightened, stepped forward, and Gunner threw again. This time it was half a brick, and when it struck the pig's stomach I could hear the air go out of him. He staggered back and sank to a seat atop Jimmy Song.

The pigs came on, wearing their masks, spraying their poison ahead of them, forcing us in on one another. We backed away from them, throwing whatever rocks or bottles or bricks we could find on the ground as we did. Gunner didn't throw often, but he was always accurate. At first, I threw often and wildly, sometimes a handful of stones at a time. But then I began to choose my targets with more care, aiming at a particular pig and always at the groin.

Behind us all was bedlam—crying, coughing, cursing, people screaming for air and mercy, hundreds of Yippies and preachers corralled into a tight, desperate circle with that enormous, absurd cross at its center. My throat was raw, my eyes burned, my skin felt as though acid were eating it away. We had retreated as far as we could. In my hand, I held only the one rock Gunner had told me to save. The pigs were but a few steps from us.

And I was exhilarated. Maybe I caught it from Gunner, his always-calculating resignation that takes you well beyond fear and seems to set you free. I don't know. But I was fully and consciously at one with the moment. The Zen of violence. Satori in gas. If the pigs had opened fire and shot accurately, I would have died in peace. A consummated life. A natural death.

But we had to go on.

Eight hundred individuals had been compressed into one organism, which suddenly heaved, spewing out first bits of itself and then great chunks. Since we were among the last to be absorbed into the organism, we were among the first to be discharged from it. Gunner and I exploded over the pig in front of us, ran past several more, rushed through an opening between a gas truck and a squad car, and were, abruptly, beyond the law's closing circle.

I wanted to stop there, but the surge of people carried us on. More pigs waited for us in the trees, but our force, the collective panic, overwhelmed them, and we swarmed out of the park and onto the sidewalk and street, where the air was relatively clear.

We stood there a moment, looking back into the park. The ring of trees we'd run through was now lit with small, scattered fires. A great fog seemed to be rising into the sky. Beside us people ripped chunks from the sidewalk and threw them at cruising squad cars. One of the cars stopped and was immediately demolished. On up the street a building was burning.

"There," Gunner said, pointing. Jesse, Maledon, and the others had come through the trees a half-block up Clark Street and were moving toward Division. We stepped out onto the street and ran toward them.

Then, in formation, the pigs came through the woods, the trucks crashing toward us, spraying again, the foot patrol bludgeoning the weak, the slow, the passive, and the wounded. The crowd of protesters filled the street and flowed toward the intersection.

Four squad cars got there just ahead of us. The pigs in them stepped out and fired their pistols into the air. And from every side we threw at them—bottles, rocks, bricks, cans, pieces of tree limbs, hubcaps, shards of pavement. Many overthrew, hitting those throwing from across the street.

Gunner began yelling at Maledon and, finally, when we were a few yards away from him, got his attention. Maledon pointed up the street and shouted "Subway."

But the stairs down to the station were jammed. Reporters, priests, tourists, hippies, and sightseeing locals grimly shoved forward and downward, their faces resigned and tired, as though they'd given up on everything but the one last underground hope.

Maledon said, "Fuck it," and we moved on, with the flow, gaining on the pigs behind us, who, bombarded from all sides, broke ranks and began chasing people helter-skelter. The gas trucks rolled up and down the streets now, constantly spraying. Against the background of coughs, curses, and shattering glass, sirens screamed, pistols fired. Blue lights flashed eerily through the thick cloud of gas. Trash bins roared with flame.

We poured through the intersection, hundreds of us, and, as if guided by some common instinct, headed south, toward the Loop, the Hilton Hotel, headquarters for McCarthy and Humphrey. After a few blocks we were beyond the gas, and the crowd began to spread out, parts of it choosing different streets, moving at different speeds, but all still going in the same general direction, separate platoons of the same maddened company.

Ahead of us someone set another trash bin afire.

"Fucking Zippo raid," Gunner said.

Jesse said, "We're as bad as the police."

"Not yet," Gunner told him. "Ain't got the ordnance for it."

None of us was badly hurt, just burning eyes, stinging skin, bruises. And, now that we were clear, Maledon seemed faintly amused by everything—like a man who assumed the rest of the world was insane and took some small delight from every confirmation of that belief.

"Should've stood back there with us," he said to me. "By God, them preachers were a sight."

Magdalen, her voice coarsened by the gas, said, "They behaved as well as anyone else. And, at least, they tried to do better."

"Ran as fast as anybody," Maledon agreed. "And in just as many directions."

"They were right," Jesse said. "They just haven't yet learned to be brave."

"Ain't something they're apt to pick up passing out communion, either," Maledon said.

"Chaplain don't have to fight," Gunner told them. "Just has to act like he would if God'd let him."

Across the street people were breaking store windows.

"Well," Maledon said, "it all worked out right. When it was over, the cross belonged to the law. May's well be them that's saddled with it."

Villines said, "Let up, Sam."

"It's all right," Magdalen said. "He's just angry with himself. Needs to talk his confidence back."

"Yeah," Maledon agreed. "I keep violating the one commandment."

Jesse tilted his head forward and looked down into Margaret's face. "You know what that is?" he asked her. "That one profound commandment?"

"No."

He took a few quick steps to get ahead of the rest of us, then turned around and, in a voice deep and cocksure, said, out of the side of his mouth, "Ain't nothing sacred but the way out."

Maledon stepped over to Margaret and put his arm around her waist. "Boy's got no respect at all, has he? His poor ol' daddy spends half a lifetime paring it all down to one little nub of truth, and, Jess, there, he keeps pissing on that nub."

She turned her face to him, said, "Move the nub."

Maledon laughed so loudly that the people hurrying around us slowed and stared. "By God, Son," he said, "look what you done hooked onto. A smart woman. Kind that could bring a man proud through them long Canadian winters. And then, come spring . . . Jesus, what she wouldn't look like in the high northern springtime."

"Man's got the answer, love," Gunner said. "There it is."

Maledon told Jesse the whole lot of us could go to British Columbia and build not just a cabin but a community. Villines could be the teacher, Magdalen the preacher, Margaret the artist, Jesse the philosopher, Gunner the sheriff, and me the chairman of the defense committee.

"Can't nobody say we shirked anything here. Took our beatings, good and regular. Sucked in our share of the gas. Shit, paid all our dues. Been good stand-up Americans all the way around. Looks to me like we could leave now with a clear conscience."

"And what would you do in Canada?" Magdalen Abbey asked. "You and your Hangman's show?"

"Hell, I'd be right at home, Meg. I been a foreigner all my life."

He kept it up all the way to Grant Park, half-jokingly elaborating on his Canadian proposal, thinking up new positions for each of us in that absurd utopia, devising a road show particularly appropriate to Canada—he'd call it Fifty-four, Forty or Fight and have all the actors be U.S. draft dodgers ("Work for the needy, Jess. How about that?"). I couldn't tell why he was doing it. He clearly had little hope of persuading Jesse to go to Canada. Maybe he just wanted to divert us, take the edge off our anger and disappointment. Or maybe Magdalen had been right: He was trying to reassure himself that after all this—following Jesse toward the pigs one night, following Magdalen the next—he was still his own man, still free, still able to assume any role, clown to Hangman. And then maybe it was just his way to keep from thinking about what might happen next.

"Well, he said as we walked along the Michigan Avenue edge of Grant Park. "Let's do something useful. How about we wake ol' Hubert up and tell him we don't like him?"

That's about what it amounted to, I suppose, though it did seemed like more at the time.

There must've been five or six times as many of us as there'd been when curfew came to Lincoln Park. We listened to some speeches—God, always some speeches—then went out to the barricades the pigs had set up on Michigan Avenue and started shouting up at the Hilton. The gas trucks sprayed again, but now the wind, coming hard off the lake, blew the gas back toward the hotel. We chanted "Dump the Hump" for what seemed like an hour. High up in the Conrad Hilton, windows opened, lights came on. The National Guard relieved the police. We cheered that. A few people crossed the barricade on our side of the street and tried to dash between the squad cars and Daley dozers to the barricade on the other side, but they were caught and pushed back. But neither the pigs nor the Guard tried to drive us out of the park.

We were now within range of television cameras, standing in front of a hotel full of Democratic delegates and campaign workers. We assumed that as long as we obeyed the new, implicit rules we were safe. So it became the standard, peaceful demonstration. We sang our songs, chanted our slogans, stood on our assigned ground. After we'd been there about an hour, someone shouted, "Flash your lights if you're with us." And then we were all shouting it. Lights began blinking on and off. A window here, a window there, then more and more. And then, as if at a signal, two whole floors. The fifteenth and twenty-third, somebody told us, the McCarthy floors. And they cheered us, and we cheered them and ourselves. Gunner helped me onto his shoulders, and I sat up there, both fists raised, chanting, singing, feeling the power of the crowd, all its rage and hope, concentrate itself in me and then flow outward and upward to the face of that old house of privilege. For whole long moments, I felt as if I could lower an arm and all the great walls of evil would crash down.

And we went on and on with it, jubilant, vindicated, victorious.

The night was ours.

How little, how very little, we settled for.

Late Wednesday afternoon ten or twelve thousand of us gathered around the bandshell in Grant Park, attending a rally sponsored by the MOBE. We had been granted a permit, our only one of the week. But we were denied permission to march on the Amphitheatre after the rally. Still, we would march. It was what we had come to do. And the pigs knew it. They were ready, more eager than ever, determined to punish us for the symbolic victory we had won the night before. Thousands of them surrounded us, waiting for an excuse.

We had listened to what seemed like hours of speeches when three men climbed the flagpole near the shell and tried to cut down Old Gory and replace it with the red flag of rebellion. Forty of fifty pigs charged, scattering canisters of gas ahead of them, but we threw the canisters back, and the pigs started choking, and we drove them back with a barrage of rocks, the thousands and thousands we had gathered for the occasion. And then hundreds more pigs came at us, wild now, licensed street fighters knocking over benches, throwing more canisters of gas, squirting Mace, bashing their way through the crowd, until they got to Rennie Davis, who was on the bullhorn, telling us to sit down, be calm, allow this to pass. The pigs clubbed him, gashing his head open, and he fell, unconscious, blood thickening his hair, covering his face.

Tom Hayden took the horn, told us he was going out into the streets to begin his night's work, urged us to form special units and disperse into the Loop and do what we had to do. A few hundred followed him, but most of us stayed where we were. It was still early. Violence would come again. That was certain. It would have its full time. There was no need to rush into it. The pigs, after making a few arrests, had backed away to plot strategy, to consult headquarters, by means of the radios whose antennae, protruding from their helmets, made them look like the robotic legion of an alien world.

Ginsberg his voice raw from the nights of gas, bid us be at peace, talked of time and the spirit, spoke of the ultimate effectiveness of nonviolence, told us that the best cure for fear, for hysteria, is the chanting of "om."

So we chanted with him. Or most of us did. Even some of the dozens of newsmen. For in those last few minutes before the pigs came at us all out, we wanted to believe, I think, that there was a perfect peace at the heart of things. But maybe most of us were just feeling nostalgic for that old faith, now lost to us. Or maybe we needed that ritual moment of concentration before all hell broke loose—"the prayer," as Gunner said, "before the big game."

"What'll it be, children?" Maledon asked. "We running or standing?"

"I'm marching to the Amphitheatre," Jesse said.

Maledon nodded. "Running, then. Good."

Margaret quickly finished a sketch of Ginsberg, closed the pad, and zipped it into her shoulder bag. Then she took Jesse's hand and said, "I don't know why we keep staying. It's the same simple lesson over and over."

Gunner stood with his back to Ginsberg, watching the pigs. Guardsmen were now behind them, rank on rank of weekend soldiers. Kids our age, mostly. "Draft dodger against draft dodger," Gunner said. And then, "Looks like everybody's agreed. This is the night."

Hippie women began taunting the pigs and the Guardsmen,

offering to fuck any of them who would come over to our side, asking them why they had let their guns replace their cocks, telling them that freedom and ecstasy were just a step away—all you have to do is be a man. The pigs called them whores, and the women laughed and mocked them with shimmying hips.

And then the order came, relayed from the Pedernales to the Amphitheatre to the City Hall to the park. And the pigs were released. The first rank chased the women who had been teasing them. Two or three were caught and brutally clubbed, but the rest managed to run back into the temporary security of the crowd. Ginsberg continued to chant, but many of the rest of us were now standing silently, looking for a break in the closing ranks, a way to the streets.

At first, I didn't think there would be one. The pigs marched forward, keeping formation, backed up by the Guardsmen. And this wasn't Lincoln Park, where there was, if you left in time, room to run and trees to hide in. Grant Park was crisscrossed by streets and walkways. Footbridges joined one rectangle of green to the next. They could come at us shoulder to shoulder. There would be no dashing between them.

If there hadn't been so many of us, if we hadn't been ten thousand, they could have corralled and clubbed us all, arresting a few dozen of us to keep up appearances. But when we began moving, all of us, toward the streets, we overwhelmed enough of them to get through. We pushed our way past the pigs and made it to a footbridge, shrouded by gas and blocked by Guardsmen. We drove the Guardsmen back, trudged through the gas, and ran into the streets.

We wandered through the Loop for a while, letting our eyes and throats clear, avoiding the pigs, biding time until the next battle. And then it happened. Word came that Ralph Abernathy was leading the Poor People's Campaign on a march up Michigan Avenue. They were going to the Amphitheatre. Hundreds, thousands of us ran there and got into avenue-wide rows behind the three wagons of the mule train. We yelled for the people on the sidewalk to join us, and hundreds of them did. Pigs and Guardsmen looked on, confused, in need of further orders. They would have to wait for Daley to decide whether he wanted the nation to watch him gassing the doctor's dream.

I didn't think he would do it. I thought this was where Johnson would stop him. Whatever small hope Johnson had of being redeemed by history lay in his civil rights record. He wouldn't risk being remembered as just another southern politician who set the troops loose on the poor. Daley would have to ask, and Johnson would turn him down. Keep them in line, but don't attack.

Protected by the ghost of the black martyr, we walked confidently down the avenue. More and more people left the sidewalk and joined us until, a block away from the Hilton, it seemed as if everyone was on the street except the thousands and thousands of pigs on either side of us. Their frustration was almost palpable. We sang.

Then, at the intersection of Balbo Avenue, they stopped us. I don't know how long we waited there. It seemed like an hour. Confidence became uncertainty, which became fear. We knew the pigs were requesting permission to proceed with their vengeance. (Why should they be thwarted by one dead nigger?) The longer we waited, the more likely it seemed that their wish would be granted. Almost all the bystanders who had joined us now left the street, some of them merely returning to the sidewalks, others hurrying off into the night. Again Maledon asked Jesse whether he would run or stand. Again Jesse said he was marching to the Amphitheatre. "Well, keep a forearm over that pump knot, son. I'd hate to see blood of mine go down in Chicago."

Then the orders came; they were simple: Let the dead nigger pass, then move. Separate the children from the dream.

They are never wise, those men, but they are sometimes shrewd.

So the pigs at the intersection moved aside, let the mule train go by, then rushed back into position, blocking us again. And then from every side they came at us with gas and Mace and club, working their way back and forth across the street. At first we were so tightly pressed together that many of the clubbed had no room to fall. But then the pigs began to slash into us, forcing us apart, separating us into groups of ten or fifteen, which they surrounded and attacked.

When, finally, we had room, we ran. And because we were so many, some of us escaped. Into the park, into the Loop, behind the barriers in front of the Hilton. But all were pursued, and most were caught. Paddy wagons rolled onto the street, and demonstrators were thrown, bleeding and unconscious, into them. Spectators standing outside the doors of the Hilton—Kennedy and McCarthy people, I guess—started helping some of us into the hotel, so the pigs charged them, drove them through the window of the hotel's Haymarket Inn restaurant, leapt in after them, and kept on clubbing.

Maledon was yelling for us to follow him into the Hilton when he was hit from behind and went down. And then they had us all. I remember flailing at them and screaming "Motherfuckers! Motherfuckers!" and feeling the blows but not the pain until everything went white.

The night came back, and two pigs, one on each arm, were dragging me backward across the pavement. I heard laughter above me and looked up. Gunner was there. Two of them were holding him up and pulling him back while another one used a sap on him. Each time he was hit, Gunner laughed and spat a gob of blood at the pig beating him.

I screamed again, and one of them let go of my arm and clubbed me twice across the face.

And then we were with others in a paddy wagon, riding to jail. Gunner, one eye already swollen shut, his face and hair darkened with blood, his mouth raw, sang "My Country 'Tis of Thee." When he finished the verse, I asked him if he was all right.

"Sure enough, love," he said through a mouth that was now a healing wound. "You looking at a man's done paid off his debt to his country. Private Grant, by God, he's free and clear, Lady Dawn. Done come free and clear."

He started singing the song again. At the beginning of the second line, I was singing with him. And then the others there in the back of the wagon joined in, and we all sang it over and over, same song, same verse—sang it until we were inside the station house, sang it until the pigs had to gag us to keep us quiet, sang it until we were free of it.

10 MALEDON

Well, we got through and went on.

That Wednesday night was the worst of it, the by-God policeman's ball. The other nights there was a way out, if we'd just had the sense to take it soon enough. But not Wednesday. You couldn't run, you couldn't hide, you couldn't surrender. They went mad, Daley's boys did, the way he wanted them to.

Thursday was relatively easy on us. Christ, we were too sore to get in much trouble. I had a throbbing head, a bruised ass, a bum shoulder, and busted ribs. And the others were about as bad off. McCarthy came to Grant Park in the middle of the afternoon and made a speech. He told us not to give up on our country. He told us we'd fought a good fight and won a great victory. He encouraged us to work to reform the nominating process. He called us the government in exile. After that, Dick Gregory led a march from the park to his home, which, he said, happened to be near the stockyards and the Amphitheatre. But there were Democratic delegates and celebrities making this march, and, well, it seemed awful gentlemanly and anticlimactic to such hardasses as ourselves. So, for once, we stayed behind, sat on the Grant Park green listening to music and talking about the future.

Magdalen Abbey was going back to Calvary Key, where she belonged. I promised to go see her a time or two a year and spend a week or so with her. And that'll be good, but it'll never be pure again. There's too many roads between us. Still, in my way, I do love her. And I like the climate down there, and the scenery. And maybe ol' Mason won't be averse to sitting on the end of the pier and sharing a Saturday-night drink with me. A man has to prepare for his old age too. When I get too old to move, Calvary Key might make a nice retirement home.

Conrad Villines wasn't sure what he'd do. Go back to Harrold Smith College, maybe, and teach history to kids who believed its one lesson was that if we didn't keep building the bomb, God'd give us to the Russians. Maybe, Conrad thought, he'd become a dean. A few months earlier, the prospect had amused him, but he'd had some of his sense of humor beat out of him here in Chicago. So now he didn't know. Maybe he'd retire early, live full-time on his place above the Little Red. Or maybe he'd devote himself to politics, pick out good candidates and work for them.

"Hell, Conrad, there ain't no such thing as a good candidate," I said. "A man that wants to rule is a man you want to stay clear of."

"There'll be rulers, Sam," he said. "And some of them will be better than others."

"Damned grim view," I told him.

It turned out to be Gunner and Gloria I talked into going to Canada. Gloria said she'd decided the bumper sticker was right: AMERICA. LOVE IT OR LEAVE IT. She didn't love it enough to go underground and commit herself to a doomed revolution. So she was leaving. She wanted to live with Gunner, at peace in a country content to rule itself. "America belongs to Richard Nixon and Jimmy Song," she said. "I just want out. I just want to start over."

Then she asked me if I'd go down to Wilder Junction in about a month and help them kidnap Aura. "Be my pleasure," I said. "I can be a social worker, a psychiatrist, an officer of the court. Or, hell, I can go down to the Wilder Junction Baptist Church and put on a Puppets for Christ show for the young'uns. Take all the little boys and girls backstage afterward and show them how it works. Mr. Wilder looks up, he won't have nothing left there but the puppets. Lord, it'll be a pure joy, getting back to something I'm good at."

"We want that cabin," Gunner told me. "You serious about it, you can help us build it. Maybe when Jesse gets out, he can come live next door. Anyway, Brother Sam, you ever get tired, there'll always be a good resting place for you there."

And I thought, God, it would be like Jesse to go to Canada *after* he'd served his time. Just the kind of pure-head stunt he might pull. But then I realized that, no, he was a stayer. He'd suffer through. He'd stand his ground and do his time. And they'd probably send him to some minimum-security prison a man with good sense could just walk away from. Not Jesse, though. He wouldn't be walking away. He'd do the two years—or whatever it turned out to be. Do them because that was the penalty they wanted you to pay for not fighting their war for them. It hurt me, finally having to admit there was nothing I could do. It was his way, and he had to go it. I had to let him go, had to understand that he was going to do what he thought he had to do, and he was going to call it freedom. It wouldn't've been my word, but it wasn't my life, either.

So it was already gone, even then, that high summer of my fatherhood. I'd come to understand that the night before. Let me tell you the one last little story, and then we'll be shut of one another.

Out in front of the Hilton that Wednesday night they clubbed me to my knees, kicked me till I fell down flat, and then spent several minutes running me over. Finally some kind soul dragged me into the lobby of the Hilton, where I sat for a good long while, resting my back against the wall, wiping the blood out of my eyes with my one good hand, watching them fill the place with a hundred other poor damned fools, and wondering how the hell a man like me ever got himself into a fix like that. It's a question I still can't answer, except to tell you I underestimated the intelligence of two men—me and Richard J. Daley. So, probably, I deserved a good beating or two. A man ought never make a mistake like that.

After maybe twenty minutes the McCarthy people led us up to the fifteenth floor, where they began binding our wounds with strips of bed sheet and towel. The whole floor was packed with us, the hallway and all the rooms, but I got up there early and had me a good seat on the carpet in front of a TV. I thought I might see kin of mine on the network news. After we'd been there a few hours, looking like Civil War extras from *Gone with the Wind*, McCarthy himself came down and went from room to room, bed to bed, body to body, saying a few quiet words to one or another of us now and then. He looked tired and resigned, but surprised too. I doubt he ever thought it would come to this—his hotel headquarters filled with bleeding hippies, tear gas seeping in through the air-conditioning system.

"It isn't over," he said to the kid next to me. "It's a beginning. You've been brave."

But then when he came to me, he knelt, looked at my face, and said, "And you? Aren't you a little old for this?"

"I fucked up," I told him.

He nodded. "Ah, yes," he said. "But didn't we all?"

I sat there and watched the TV till ol' Hubert had won the vote they'd rigged for him. He kissed his wife's image on his own set and said, "Bless your heart," to Lyndon Johnson. Some of the McCarthy people were crying, and I was wondering again about me being in their midst when Conrad and Magdalen came in, looking like they'd been stringing barbed wire blindfolded.

"My ride," I said to the kid next to me.

"Peace," he said through a broken grin. And I thought it a hard joke for so young a man.

"So how y'all been," I asked Conrad and Magdalen on the way down the stairs we had to take because the elevators weren't working.

"Don't be glib, Sam," Magdalen said. "Not now."

"Shit, I earned the right."

She and Villines had managed to keep their feet and all their blood long enough to see me pulled into the Hilton, Gunner and Gloria arrested, and Jesse and Margaret caught up in a crowd being forced back down Michigan Avenue.

"I fought back with my little academic fists," Villines said. "Magdalen tried passive resistance. It amounted to the same thing. We wound up crawling together back to the park. The medics took care of us." He shook his head. "How was the Hilton?"

"Overbooked," I told him.

There were a few crippled-up stragglers on the street and lots of cops looking awful proud. But nobody stopped us. We walked up and down the avenue, the cross streets, and the alleys, and then we wandered around the park for maybe an hour, but Jesse and Margaret weren't there. We went back over to the eastern side of the park and then a few blocks north and found the Hangman's van. I drove us to the emergency room Jesse and I had been in two nights earlier. They weren't there either. Then we drove to the jail to see if Gunner and Gloria were still there. They were. The place was full up, Gunner and Gloria had been bound and gagged, and a man from the Mobilization Committee told us it'd be hours yet before they could be booked and bailed. So we left, got back in the van, and went looking for Jesse again.

I had one more idea. Two or three times that evening he had told me he intended to march to the Amphitheatre. And he wasn't one to give up easy on an idea.

It must've been somewhere around four in the morning when we got there, but they still had it cordoned off and guarded like party headquarters in Prague. We parked and then walked on up as close to the buildings as we could get. Cops and Guardsmen stood in front of the fence surrounding the place, but they weren't coming out after people now. They'd had their night. And, anyway, there weren't enough of us left to make a real show for them.

We made our way around one side of the building and then another. We turned again, and there he was, standing out in the middle of the street, about ten yards from the soldiers with the bayonets. I went on up to him. His clothes were ripped and begrimed. His hair was matted with blood. He had one arm around Margaret, who leaned against him. In the other hand he held a placard. It said LOVE.

Such a fool. Such a pure, sweet fool.

I said, "Son, let's go home."